Border Dance

Border Dance

a novel

T. L. Toma

Southern Methodist University Press
Dallas

This novel is a work of fiction. Names, characters, places, and incidents are either the product of the author's imagination or are used fictitiously.

Requests for permission to reproduce material from this work should be sent to:
Rights and Permissions
Southern Methodist University Press
PO Box 750415
Dallas, TX 75275-0415

Grateful acknowledgment is made for permission to quote from *The Good Person of Szechwan* by Bertolt Brecht. Copyright © 1955 by Suhrkamp Verlag, Berlin. Translation copyright © 1985 by Stefan S. Brecht. Reprinted from *The Good Person of Szechwan* by Bertolt Brecht, published by Arcade Publishing, Inc., New York, New York.

Library of Congress Cataloging-in-Publication Data
Toma, T. L., 1955–
Border Dance : a novel / T.L. Toma — 1st ed.
p.   cm.
ISBN 0-87074-400-3. — ISBN 0-87074-401-1 (pbk.)
1. Man-woman relationships—Mexico—Fiction.
2. Americans—Travel—Mexico—Fiction.   I. Title.
PS3570.04295B67   1996
813'.54—dc20   96-18371

Cover photo © 1996 Jim Bones "Escondido Agave"
Design by Barbara Whitehead

Printed in the United States of America on acid-free paper
2   4   6   8   10   9   7   5   3   1

To my parents,
John and Carolyn Toma

Acknowledgments

I want to thank
Tim Keppel and J. Jordan Phelps
for their detailed criticisms and enthusiastic
encouragement on earlier drafts of this book.
I want to thank my wife,
Leticia Saucedo,
for her unflagging patience and support.

Border Dance

Part One

One

His wife was in the kitchen, bent over the counter. Slices of cucumber lay like coins. She had scrubbed the mushrooms, shelled the peas. Copper crockery hung from the walls like broad, burnished faces. It was a room in a magazine, a room in a dream. The knife was narrow, the handle of bone. It ticked against the cutting board. Her name was Andrea.

Frank Reed stood in the doorway, breathing the odors of cooking. The scene seemed eternal: a woman preparing food. She was pale, long-nosed. Big with eyes. Her breasts were deep. She made her own sauces, her own bread. She was a woman of talent, a woman of intelligence. Her bridge game was unforgiving. She had read Foucault in the original. Yet her piety was severe. She attended early-morning Mass three times a week. The priests greeted her with smiles, they all knew her name. On Easter, on Christmas Eve, she asked Reed to accompany her. He always refused to kneel. Three hundred people on their knees, his head was like a spire. She worked part-time for a community theater troupe. She didn't have to, she liked to explain, she was paid next to nothing. But there were the young actors, the old woman who sewed costumes, the carpenter who donated his time to build sets. Ionesco, and she had spent a weekend affixing rubber horns to headbands.

"I have to leave at nine."

She looked up, leveling the knife at him. "But you said tomorrow."

He peered down the length of the blade. True, he had said tomorrow. But the rhythms of time, the days of the week weren't his own. He was of that class of workers who move through the skies and arrange the exchange of vast sums they will never realize themselves. "They want me there for a morning meeting."

Her knife clattered to the cutting board. "I wish you had told me. I would have made something simple. Something quick."

"I didn't know until this afternoon," he lied. He had known, he had meant to tell her. He meant to change the oil in the car, to put up the storm windows, to fix the leaky faucet in the bathroom.

"I would have made tuna casserole. I would have made meatloaf."

Reed liked meatloaf. Meatloaf, steak, pork chops. With sides of coleslaw, lima beans. The elaborate meals, his wife's detailed preparations were lost on him. He liked tuna casserole. He liked fried chicken, mashed potatoes. Corn on the cob. The foods of his childhood, the foods of Indiana. Basic foods, essential foods. You knew you had eaten, the blood running thick. "What are we having?"

She reached for a button. The blender blended, harsh machine laughing. "Not meatloaf."

4

Their daughter joined them for dinner. It seemed she seldom did so. It was suddenly an occasion. Laura was almost sixteen and sullen always. Reed had secret hopes for Smith, Bryn Mawr, Mount Holyoke at least. Leonard Halloran's daughter had gone to a school in Vermont housed in a barn. She came back with green hair, zircon piercing a nostril. She came back with ZEKE tattooed on her rump. Every father secretly fears he might have raised a slut. Reed found himself tormented by the idea of Laura's panties gracing a large oak outside a fraternity house. He endured images of his daughter rutting among bales of hay with boys who had been watching farm animals since age three. He worried she might learn Marx from a transvestite. Unfashionable concerns, he knew. But even now, posters of rock stars clutching their crotches, the audience prepubescent and hysterical, lined the walls of her room.

His daughter was long-legged, her breasts promising. Reed had seen the razor in her bathroom, the bra hanging from her doorknob. The boys who occasionally appeared in the foyer were uniformly pallid and slender, their clothes careless in that way which requires much money. Once, while shaking the hand of a boy and weaving with his third gin, Reed had leaned close and muttered, "I know you." The boy was tall, health showed in his face. He would never suffer a toothache, a broken shoelace. Reed had paused to show the boy how much he knew, the boy's hand locked in his.

"Frank," Andrea had complained later, "it's natural." She had talked to Laura already, a tasteful lunch at the best restaurant in town. Andrea relished her role as mother. She cherished instances that gave her the chance to confirm it, to enlarge upon it. Over a meal of sunset melon and Dungeness crabs, Andrea had explained the relative advantages of the pill, the diaphragm, the sponge. The importance of condoms. Then she had come home, told her husband it was time to make the appointment. "It's inevitable."

But he wouldn't hear of it: "It's fucking."

Now the room filled with the tink of silverware. Andrea had

put on a dress. He had given her the earrings for their twentieth anniversary. He was leaving at nine; her dinner was ruined. She should have made meatloaf. Instead she served the lamb chops with sprigs of parsley. She had prepared the mint jelly from scratch. Dinner was the only ceremony left to them. The dishes were delicate compositions of odor and color. Eating was an act of defacement.

"It's not too dry?" Andrea's eyes darted to their plates. She lived her life in unending anticipation. She was ready to reach for the peas, to pass the bread. Reed chewed, his sounds small, testing.

"It's perfect."

"I saw a fight today." It was Laura. She spoke so rarely, they hung on every word. Now she looked to see that they'd heard. "Three blocks east."

Their street was quiet, their neighbors friendly. Weekends, people washed their cars. There was a small cafe at the corner, a rare-book dealer up the street—open only by appointment. The editions were bound in leather. The embossed lettering glittered on the spines. Swedish, German imports lined the curb. The brownstones were well-kept, every doorbell worked. The residents could have afforded the best institutions, but their children attended the public high school. It was a matter of principle.

But three blocks east. You said those words with awe. Drunks sprawled, their cheeks pressed to the sidewalk. Wash hung in alleyways. Dogs showed their ribs. Children ran barefoot amid rotting odors. Packs of teens gathered on corners. They were fearless. Police cars moved like beetles down the narrow streets, their windows black, faceless. Anything was possible: drugs, guns, the murder of another. Disintegration has a feel, a smell; it comes like rain.

Reed listened as his daughter recalled the angry words, the blows. Two men, large and flailing, fists quick with testosterone. Families gathered on their stoops to watch. Everything was understood immediately. The crowd was still, the silence of church—as if witnessing an act of prayer, an act of devotion. It was drugs, a woman; it was the wrong phrase in the wrong bar. Reasons lingered in the air. You breathed them, you took them in. You made them your own.

Reed frowned. The world was condensing. It was closing in. The neighborhood was changing. No one could deny it. Late at night, blasts sounded that they hoped were from cars. Sirens rose in the distance, then swelled toward them. The residents moved quickly through the outlying blocks, past empty store-fronts, public housing. The world intruded too heavily, its sounds were just beyond the door. Existence should be insular, composed of quiet rooms, soft lighting. The sight of his daughter safe in bed. In the previous month, a woman had been raped one street away, in the alley behind the bakery. The great ovens warming early, the odor of bread.

They had talked of moving. To a place in the suburbs, to a place of trees, of long, winding drives. To a place where you could walk. But they could never bring themselves to sell. Though their street was failing, it hinted at a past dignity. Two hundred years ago, farmers, blacksmiths, and cobblers had died at the hands of British mercenaries, defending a hill that was no longer there. Yet there were still the high ceilings, the tall windows. Their days were amber. The fireplace took up one wall of the living room. The stones were large, white as salt. Like pieces to a puzzle they had solved long ago. The hearth was solid, imposing, a monument to their lives.

"Maybe your father will bring you a souvenir," Andrea said now. She did not care about the fight; she didn't want to hear of it. There was an art to talking at dinner. There were rules. "What would you like?" she urged.

Laura considered. Her food was untouched. It was going cold. Cylinders of low-fat cottage cheese, tubs of yogurt lined the shelves of the refrigerator. She always ate little, her bites tentative. Reed worried that in five years, they would learn this had been a bulimic time; her esophagus would have been savaged, a psychiatrist would chart the familial disorders that had destroyed her life.

She leaned toward her mother. "Clothes?"

Their faces expanded with the possibilities. Reed looked on. What does a man think in such moments? His life, his world is the food on the table, the sounds of his house late at night. There are warriors, artists, men of great ambition, their convictions like swords onto which they fall. And then there are men whose families are everything. He worked a month out of the year to pay property taxes.

"A dress?" Andrea offered.

Andrea. He always marveled at the sound of her name. The anticipatory *And,* the tempering dip of the *ree,* the finality of the *ah.* It mirrored the very trajectory of life. Even in recent years, as her waist thickened into a gentle dune, as her breasts crept lower, her nudity astonished him still.

She had been raised in the suburbs. This seemed to explain much. Then, too, there was parochial nursery school, parochial elementary school, parochial high school. "I could've been a nun." But in college she discovered Godard, Lacan, wine, and sex. Her appetites were intense, all-consuming, and French.

They met at a party. Neither knew the host. The friend who had invited him never showed, the woman who had invited her had come down with the flu. He roamed the party, drink in hand, circling back round to a table laden with platters of dark bread, a salmon mousse, a bleeding roast beef. Reed was new to Boston, his voice ringing with midwestern inflections. It made him uneasy. He stood off by himself, he ate, he drank, his thoughts running slow. He looked up to discover a woman leaning against the far wall, her eyes on him. She was comely, her eyes immense. They ruled her face. He stood at the table and ate grandly. Cheeses, pastries, slices of fruit—his eyes sliding to her, then back to the food. The next morning, he would clutch his belly and groan. But now, her eyes were on him.

They did not stray. He responded by stuffing his mouth, as if to demonstrate the enormity of his appetites, to entice her, to warn her. In the end, he set his drink down, crossed the carpet, and planted himself squarely in front of her. Her eyes shifted; they seemed to click into place. He learned later of her vanity. With money from the wedding, she would buy contact lenses. But when she stared at him that evening, he was an ottoman in a room vague with furniture.

They talked. Reed offered to drive her home. She said no. He called the next day, said will you go out with me. No, she said. He was without shame. He called again and again. It was a war of attrition, time his best friend. Maybe, she said finally. Try next week. He tried next week, then again the following week, and the week after that. Then one evening, working late, he found himself talking to a woman from his office. It was she who suggested a drink. Soft, doughy, too much flesh, too much voice. No; it was he. He spent the night at her place, then slipped out at dawn like a thief. At home, his phone was ringing: "But you didn't call."

"Not a dress," Laura decided now.

"A blouse, then," Andrea said. Her daughter looked just like her, everyone remarked on the resemblance. Though Andrea secretly thought her daughter's mouth a bit too small; it hinted at a kind of cruelty. "Or a sweater."

They were married in a cathedral within range of Fenway Park. A ballgame was going. The crowd cheered their union. Her mother wept; Reed wasn't Catholic, her daughter would go to hell. But the priest was young, hip, anxious to demonstrate his tolerance. Right before the ceremony, he offered Reed a hit of marijuana. At the reception, her father stuffed Reed's pockets with money. The man was not wealthy. The bills were greasy; they smelled of aftershave, they smelled of sweat. Again, her mother wept. Reed's parents stood stoically by, quiet and resigned in their Calvinism.

"This is what I want," Andrea told him that night. They had put up in a grand old hotel on Beacon Hill. Obscene chandeliers, a lobby tacky with Persian carpets and eighty-year-old bellboys. At the front desk, they frowned when he couldn't produce a credit card, demanded that he pay in cash. He emptied his pockets of her father's money. They made loud love on a large bed, rain striking the windows. Then she knelt on the sheets, cradled his head to her stomach, and said, "This is what I want."

Reed had waited then, her belly beneath him, her breasts above, drunk with her aroma. He was expecting exorbitant demands, a call for heroic sacrifices. A gabled house, an immense lawn, furs, gems, sixty-dollar theater seats, a beach house, a winter cabin, trips to Europe, to Asia, a gardener. Yet with his head in her lap, her odor still moist on his face, he would have promised her anything: Paris, Hong Kong, sable, emeralds, a second home in the Keys. His prick in a box at the foot of the bed.

She began speaking, her voice soft, solemn, as if entering into profound vows, like a girl at the door of a convent, surrendering her whole life. She wanted nights of steamed crabs, the snow washing past the windows. She wanted a set of mugs the color of chalk, the sturdy sort one finds in cheap diners. She wanted a small house on a quiet street. She wanted to plant tulips in the fall, basil and broccoli in the spring. They would tell the truth always, except at Christmas and birthdays. She would leave him if he ever hit her, was unfaithful to her, or told her she was fat. If she died early, she made him promise he would remarry. If he died early, she promised she wouldn't.

She had the needs of a peasant, a clerical worker, a woman who spends her Saturday mornings at the laundromat. They were simple, tangible; she could have satisfied most inside a week. He understood she had been waiting for him—she had been waiting for someone to sit at a table and help crack the hulls of shellfish, for one who would stand at a window and watch her weed a garden. Life to her had always been within reach; she was only now grasping for it. Slender, kneeling on the bed, her hair the color of scotch in a glass, she wanted

10

nothing more than to sit opposite him and hold his hand above a pair of matching mugs. The future, the truth, the course of his life would never again be so clear, so elemental, so definable. Her sex was small, like a young girl's.

He rushed home from work each day. She was waiting, as if months had gone by. They screwed before dinner, her thighs beating against him, pale and urgent. They ate naked at the table. Her breasts were always bigger than he remembered. The moist, ferny odor they had made together mingled with the smells of cooking. Weekend mornings stretched forever. At work, his energy was inexhaustible. He attacked the day to reach its end. It was one of those firms headed by a dogged gray eminence who is regarded with a peculiar alloy of fear and fondness. The Old Man was watching him, his name was mentioned in the executive suites. Reed was promoted, promoted again. His offices grew larger, his secretaries prettier. He was one of whom all things are expected. His career was a great arc, one could only imagine its end.

They bought the house. Squares of slate marked the path out back. It was anonymous in a block of rowhouses. But there were the high ceilings, there was the fireplace. They refinished the mantel, stripping it to reveal the heavy wood. They retiled the bathroom, the pattern an intricate inlay of blue and gold. They sanded the hardwood floors until they shone. They were laying claim to the house, making it their own. Then, a scalding day in summer, their sweat like a sheen, and Laura was conceived. Andrea was certain; she could feel the very instant. Reed watched in awe as his wife's belly grew, as her breasts rounded impossibly. The odor of milk was like an intoxicant. They made love carefully, as if he were gingerly dipping into the future, surrounding himself with it. Then Laura was born. He remembered it with terror. This was in the days when husbands still huddled in a waiting room, happily ignorant. But Andrea had other ideas. Reed, done up in a green gown and mask, stood off to one side moaning while his wife, knees forked, swollen with belly, gritted her teeth and pushed. Eight hours, twelve hours, fifteen hours. Unending, unendurable. Horrifying images of his wife's pelvic muscles bowing, splintering under the pressure, racked him. At twenty hours, he grabbed the doctor and yelled, "You sumfabitch you, you give her something." The doctor was a slight man, elderly, bored. He had delivered babies on four-poster beds, on an airport tarmac, on a tugboat. That time in the restroom of a gas station. There were things he could give her, yes, potions that would ease the pain. Andrea refused. "I can do it," she hissed, "I can." Twenty-four hours. The longest day in history. "I can't do it, I can't," he pleaded. But she was determined, indomitable. Her hair was a limp rag against the pillow, her odors were fierce. She shook her head, she grunted savagely. Reed was appalled. She seemed another woman entirely. He wanted to explain to the nurses, to the elderly doctor, that his wife was not like this. That there had been a mistake. They had imported a stranger, a wild woman. She stared out at him blankly, her eyes unseeing, the whole of her being concentrated in her crotch.

At thirty-eight hours, Laura was born. She was red-faced, arms waving. She was a boiled lobster wrapped in a blanket. The ease with which they allowed him to take mother and daughter home from the hospital seemed all wrong. The ordeal of the birth demanded some celebration, a summing up. But there were only the nurses impatient to get at Andrea's bed and strip away the sheets. He'd had more trouble getting his car out of the shop.

He rose for feedings at two, at five. He sat with his daughter in the next room and read to her from Bartlett's while Andrea, battered and bloated, sprawled on the bed as if she had been heaved from a high window. Virtue is its own reward. A penny saved is a penny earned. The mass of men lead lives of quiet desperation. He read from the Bible, the Koran, the Tibetan Book of the Dead. The lives of the great composers.

He had been lulled into that sense we sometimes have that nothing untoward can happen, that we are at a place far beyond cancer, earthquake, a failing heart, an unfaithful wife. You have seen such men. They are like nations on the rise; unexplored continents stretch before them, native, untrammeled, waiting. Destiny is projectile, soaring. It strains for the heights. It cannot be doubted. Such men are popular; beautiful women laugh at their jokes. At parties, they pinch the air to indicate the talents of rivals. The larger charities sell their names. They hold season tickets to the Celtics, to the symphony. They know which shops stock the best Iranian roe. They know where to get dim sum at midnight. Tailors recognize them. Life stands known. The moment is pure.

"Not a blouse," Laura was saying now.

"What, then?" Reed asked. His voice had an edge. He groped for his cigarettes.

Andrea scowled. "Can't you wait until we're done?" He smoked, he drank. These facts worried her; they embarrassed her. She stuck articles on cancer, on cirrhosis, on high blood pressure to the door of the refrigerator. He never saw them; he was always intent on the turkey breast sandwich, on last night's roast.

"No clothes," Laura went on. The decision pleased her.

"No clothes," he repeated. His cigarettes, his lighter lay on the table before him. "You'll have to do better than that."

And then, the moment passes. It is a beat of time, nothing more. Suddenly, we have seen too much, we have eaten too much. The belly is generous, the hair is turning. One's breath is bad. Our misery is mute, thick as rich wood. It is not death we fear, nor the tax man, nor the unsanitary practices in the kitchen of our favorite restaurant. It is rotting garbage on a city street at three A.M., the odor of urine in an elevator, an old woman farting on a bus. They bring us to our knees. Our day grows dark; the sky belches rain. A hot dog vendor collapses his broad umbrella. The water swirls in the gutters. The air is heavy, close. A young couple strolls past, the girl crying. There is a fruit stand opposite, graffiti along the wall, peep shows for a dollar at the corner. A rat scurries beneath a rusting green dumpster. A car honks, honks again. There is the distant thunder of the subway, the wail of a siren. The rat, the day is gray. There are instants when life seems to contract, to distill itself into a single hue, a crack in the tile, the tears of a girl.

It began slowly. It began as if nothing. For years, Reed had watched as younger men entered the firm, made their way up the ranks. Early on, he had experienced a sense of kinship. They were like warriors in a great army, comrades on a hallowed quest. As his hair thinned, his attitude turned paternal. Younger workers sought out his advice, his expertise. Reed was obliging; he was generous. But now it seemed they were passing him by. An engineer by training, Reed had risen to a position of management, a position usually occupied by men with backgrounds in finance, in marketing, in advertising. He came to be regarded as an interloper. An impostor. Fresh faces—faces with advanced degrees in economics, in systems management, faces that started with salaries in the sixties—regarded him with contempt. They had gone to Dartmouth, they had gone to Princeton, they had gone to MIT, they had gone to Wharton. They were younger, they were hungrier. They were ruthless. He had gone to Purdue. Reed tossed out a quick inspiration over a drink, and it turned up over another's signature two days later as an interoffice memo. A report was missing from his files. Phone calls were not returned. A man just two years out of college sabotaged a project to which Reed had devoted six months. A small cabal was forming at the highest reaches of the company. Meetings occurred which Reed heard about only later. The firm embarked on a series of risky ventures, the profits only a quarter, two quarters away. The slow, steady accumulation of wealth gave way to precarious investments, to acts of financial daring. No longer an army, but pirates, brigands, cutthroats. The day came when Reed was sitting in a bathroom stall at work and two junior executives slammed into the restroom. He could hear them as they stood at the sinks. "Reed," one of them muttered suddenly, and they both hooted. As if with a single sound, with his name, one condemned him.

14

There followed some ominous trouble with his belly. It seemed the very texture of mortality. Reed went to a doctor, then a second. They referred him to a specialist who tortured him with long tubes and miniature cameras. The nurse was young, a redhead. She snapped on her rubber gloves with the ardor of a fetishist. Reed did not understand how she could watch such procedures day after day and then go home and undress for a man. "Nothing serious," the specialist assured him. But there were moments when his gut seized, the pain bladelike. Reed adopted a slumping posture, his head and shoulders curled forward, as if to shield his stomach. At home, late, scotch seemed to soothe the fire in his belly. Or gin. He would stand at a window, staggered by drink, and look out over the steel gray streets—streets changing before his eyes.

The demographics of a city are subterranean. They move with the leisure of tectonic plates. For the most part, the shifts are incremental, imperceptible. But then an old neighborhood is razed. Condominiums rise abruptly in the midst of a tenement, an office building at the edge of the barrio. The upheavals are seismic. Whole peoples migrate blocks; they bring their pets, their old linen, they bring their language. A restaurant shuts down, a warehouse is abandoned, a florist closes— only to reopen the next week as a video shop. A For Sale sign goes up. Then a fire, an entire block is destroyed. More For Sale signs. An apartment house changes hands. Tenants of twenty, thirty years move out; the rents plummet.

Reed had first noticed the changes on his walks home from the subway. He had traveled the same route for years. There was the supermarket down the street, the bank at the corner, the streetlight illuminating the sign for H & G's Hardware in the middle of the next block. The day came when he realized that the faces he passed had grown darker, he did not understand the sounds that emerged from their mouths. Then the supermarket shut down. The bank was next to go. Vandals broke the streetlight; it was not repaired. In the dim twilight, he discovered that the hardware store had closed, the sign in the window replaced only by a crudely lettered REDEMPTION. He guessed at the series of twelve-step programs—the alcoholics, the addicts, the batterers, the fat, the terminal, the sex-crazed—that must have met where socket wrenches had once hung, next to the caulking guns. A new breed of cars began moving down the street, huge cars, their paint jobs full of hysteria, cars shorn of their mufflers, the music sudden through two-thousand-dollar speakers. Reed arrived home to find his driveway blocked by such vehicles, his own car looking lonely and trapped. More than once he and Andrea missed an evening engagement because of the Trans Am, the '78 Delta, the '69 Mustang obstructing their way. He put up a No Parking sign. A rooming house opened two corners away. Fifty dollars a week, no cooking allowed. The bathroom stood at the end of the hall. Men clutching bottles in paper sacks lounged on the stoop. Summer nights, there was the sound of salsa, of merengue through the open windows. He put up a No Estacionamiento sign. Then a new family moved into the house a block to the north. Their small backyard bordered his own. Their children were many, their cooking spicy. Their dog was a scarred, tail-less creature that ravaged Reed's garbage fifteen minutes before the collection truck showed. Tunafish cans, coffee grounds, empty scotch bottles, eggshells, limp melon rinds lined the curb in front of Reed's house. The father made a habit of rising early and speaking in booming vowels, berating his children, his wife, berating an ear on the other end of the phone. An ear in San Juan, say, or Bogotá. Reed could not be sure. But the man's voice was like a vengeful army that came roaring across Reed's lawn to beleaguer his kitchen, his bedroom, his home.

Reed was no bigot. Cities change, lives change. The country is a melting pot, etc., etc. But property values were falling, the noise was rising. His life had become empty tuna tins, coffee grounds, rotting melon rinds. Three, sometimes four days a week he could not get his car out of the drive. Then, too, his own fortunes were less than happy. An invest-

16

ment he had made years ago, an investment that he had been assured would see him into retirement, carry him safely across that treacherous fiscal land known as old age, unexpectedly went under. He was never clear on the details. There was talk of unscrupulous bankers, of sloppy government regulators, of shady brokers who were now lapping up Reed's money in the form of so many rum punches in a Caribbean port. Reed borrowed money, he borrowed some more. For the first time in his life, Reed was in debt.

They would not starve. They had their home, they had each other. They were luckier than most, Reed knew. Still, it seemed there were ominous tendencies at work. Evenings he found himself at the kitchen window, his belly in full riot, listening to the rantings of his neighbor, the percussion of car engines he was certain had just blocked his drive. Work, his neighborhood, a stubborn rain, a dog squatting in the street, the sound of a child being slapped, the quick din of a jet overhead—it took little to kindle his need for a drink. He entered into heartfelt pacts with himself: no drinks before nine, before eight, before five. Saturday afternoons, he would set out the gin, the tonic, the ice at three-thirty, at four, then pace the kitchen. Four-thirty, and the drink would be poured, the silver liquid washing over shards of ice. Reed would sit before the drink, touch it, memorizing the smooth surface of the glass, the moist beads of condensation. He would smoke furiously. Four-fifty, and the sweat would be flushing from his armpits, his throat dry as wood shavings. The first drink was an act of release. By seven he was red-faced, his mood combative. He would sit and bellow at the evening news; the weekly magazines made him fume. The nation had embarked on a series of toy wars, battles that lasted three days, a week, six weeks—the deeds of a bully. The banks had been looted by men in suits, men who paid fifty dollars for a haircut. Talk of holes in the atmosphere, deadly rays pouring through, made him shiver. Even the commercials angered him; it seemed they were selling back to him, in spare, mutilated portions, dreams they had stolen from him long ago. Reed took it personally. His anger was visceral. He wanted to strangle the men responsible. Meanwhile, weeds were pushing up through the asphalt of his own drive, the gutters needed to be cleaned, the hedges needed to be trimmed. Such demands were crippling. By ten-thirty, eleven, he would be lurching about the living room, his sounds deeper than sense. Evenings passed in which he remembered little, only a fleeting word, a brief gesture, the night falling fast.

"Frank," Andrea would murmur finally, and then he would go three days without a drop. "See?" he would demand. Yet there were always the bottles in the kitchen cupboard, the ice trays in the freezer. They were waiting for him.

But these were the plagues of middle age. Unspectacular, picayune. He was of the city. He understood, he endured. There were still Sunday mornings when he woke early, the warm heft of Andrea next to him in bed, her face puffy with sleep and what he was sure was their love. There was still the composed expression of his daughter bent over a book, not yet sullied by freshmen rubes, by Marx. There was still the sight of a woman stepping down into the sunlight, her shoulders bare. There were still spring days in the park, the sweet odor of honeysuckle. He refused to regard them as accidents; they were essential, definitive, the very scaffolding of his world.

"Or a pair of slacks," Andrea was saying. She turned to her husband. Her look was penetrating. It seemed to reach into places behind places. "Do you know her size?"

"Her size?" It was like an indictment. If he loved his daughter, he would have known her size, her choice of colors, the latest styles. "Well—"

"No slacks," Laura said, saving him.

And then, an evening in winter. An evening when everything is decided. Reed had stopped for a drink after work. The bar was smoky, the faces of the patrons grim. A woman sat alone at a table in the corner, weeping. "Harold, you promised," she said into her beer. "You promised, Harold."

Everyone ignored her. No one wanted to be Harold. Reed had a second drink. At work that day, the Old Man had taken him aside, asked, "How's the wife? The kid?" "Fine," Reed had told him. The Old Man had turned then to look out the window. Reed followed his gaze. The view looked out over the city, you could see ships moving into the harbor. "Eiger is worried about the projections for the third quarter." Eiger was young. Eiger had ideas. Eiger was an innovator. A player, everyone said. "I told Eiger not to worry about it. I told him our man Reed is on top of it." The Old Man glanced back at Reed. Thick brows, jowls of size. "Tell me I told him right. Tell me our man Reed is on top of it." Reed nodded. "I'm all over it. I'm smothering it. I tuck it in at night." The Old Man grinned. "I knew it. Listen: say hi to Sandra for me, will you?" He was leading Reed toward the door, an arm around his shoulder. "I will," Reed told him.

Reed had a third drink. He reluctantly pushed himself away from the bar. In the street, the wind was cutting. Heavy clouds churned across the face of the moon. He descended into the dank mouth of the subway. The crowded train held the pinched odor of sweat. The expressions of those around him were opaque with exhaustion. He could feel the city like a great weight above him. The train plunged through the depths, the rails howling. Cigarette butts, hamburger wrappers, used condoms, broken glass littered the steps to the street. The lights of his block shimmered in the distance. The air promised snow. He paused at the corner to let a car pass. The broken streetlight rose dumbly, a finger of shadow. A man appeared, then a second. Boys, really. Fifteen, maybe sixteen. They wore identical sneakers.

Reed crossed the street. They crossed with him, one at each shoulder. They said nothing; they stared straight ahead, matching him step for step. He looked from one to the other. In the middle of the next block, the boy on his left said, "Five dollars and you can dance with my sister."

"Your sister," Reed repeated. He had not yet understood.

"She's beautiful," the second one urged.

"That's all right," Reed said. His smile was thin.

"Tony," the second one said. "Tony, he don't want to dance with your sister."

Reed walked faster. They walked faster. Sneakers going clop clop. "You think she's ugly." It was Tony. Reed had crapped on his sister.

"I'm sure she's fine," Reed mumbled.

"She's beautiful," the second one insisted.

Reed's street was still two blocks away. He could make out the familiar cars parked along the curb. He could see the Hallorans' freshly painted shutters. He and Andrea had joked about the color that morning. The snow had started in, tight eddies of flakes.

"Five dollars," Tony said again. He had skipped ahead to stand in Reed's path. His face was small, round, his forehead unfortunate with acne. When Reed moved to step around him, the second one was there. His face was featureless, a smear of flesh in the dim light.

"You should pay it," the second boy said. It seemed less a threat than a piece of advice. There was an instant when Reed might have bolted, tearing toward home, flinging himself against the Hallorans' door as the boys closed in. But there were their sneakers, perfect engines of running. His shoes were new, Italian, the leather still stiff.

Reed shrugged. He was of the city. These things happened. Akin to increases in the transit fare, to parking tickets. He shook his head at the inventiveness of the street. He had once given a quarter to a woman who insisted she was seventeen cents shy of the cost of a ticket on the Concorde. She was a duchess, she explained; there were people waiting for her in Paris. Surely he knew it was the evening of the coronation. Fifty cents that time to a man who relayed a long and confusing tale concerning the wrong a certain cousin Clarence had done to him. Clarence had ruined him; fifty cents could save him. A dollar to a hooker who had called him "sugar." She had been homely, she had been short. She had reminded Reed of a girl he had known in high school who never managed a date. See what happens.

So give them a buck. He could afford it. He was Reed, he owned his own house, his stomach was swollen with expensive liquor. Its fumes mystified his brain, gave an odd justice to their demand. Talk of a beautiful sister was not without poetry. Women and money. Things of value. Unenlightened, he knew. But he was thinking as a man among men. He grinned now to let them know he understood.

Reed kept spare bills in his coat pocket. He reached, found one, examined it in the thin light. It took him a moment to recognize Jackson's face. Then Tony snatched Jackson clean in his fingers.

"No change, man." Tony was laughing. The second one made a yukking sound. "Maybe tomorrow I'll have change." His luck showed in his eyes.

Reed stood stunned, his hand still out, watching the boys saunter away. Yet money: it was what he did, what he knew. As familiar to him as the furniture in his living room. It was as if he had awakened to discover two punks sitting on his sofa, watching his TV. Reed's indignation was rushed, searing. It was convincing.

"You forgot something," Reed said when the boys were perhaps five steps away. Tony looked back, his face a question.

"Your sister," it occurred to Reed. "I dance with her, or it's no deal." His tone was low, his words even. They came from the best part of himself. He snapped his fingers. The sound was succinct, deft. Knowing.

"He want to dance. Tony, he want to dance."

Tony sneered. His hands were jammed deep into the pockets of his windbreaker. Along with the twenty, Reed realized. "That ain't funny."

"No," Reed said. "It isn't." This he understood. He wanted

to grab Tony, lean close, say, I close ten-million-dollar contracts. I tuck the quarterly report in at night. I've seen the pit on the stock exchange, men snarling like dogs.

Tony shoved him. The push lacked conviction. But the walk was slick, Reed was three drinks in. He struggled to keep his footing. His hat drifted to the ground. He felt the heat roaring to his brain, the power surging to his arms. Thirteen years old, he decided. No more than fourteen.

Reed shoved back. He saw with satisfaction that the move surprised Tony. No old man he. Tony flailed, arms waving, his hands like claws, making gripping motions. Reed found himself locked in a curious embrace. He clutched back, hugging the boy to him. Reed listened to his own breathing; it sounded far away and animal, like a steer in a stall. He could see the fear in the boy's eyes. He could smell the odor of old clothes, passed down from brother to brother in a family of eight. Say the boy was twelve, eleven even. Say he was still hairless. The thought touched Reed, made him hesitate. Then the second boy stepped forward. Faceless, suddenly big. Hairy. Like anger. Like his fist. The blow dove into Reed's belly, lifting him off his feet. Reed caved to his knees, the pavement cold, shocking against his palms.

Reed heard a moan. He could feel the boys circling. He moaned again.

"Why don't he get up?" It was Tony. His concern sounded genuine. "You hurt him," Tony decided. "You hurt him."

"I didn't hurt him," the second boy said. But he seemed unsure. His uncle had served time; the boy had heard the stories, had heard the things that happened.

"Then why don't he get up?" Tony demanded.

Reed on hands and knees, like Sunday nights in the living room, Sunday nights long ago. Laura wanting to play horsey. Why didn't he get up? A reasonable question, a fair question. An astute question. Tony was not stupid. Why didn't he get up? The sidewalk was cold; home, his family, a roaring hearth were five minutes away. He thought: Get up. Though he was hurt. Even Tony said so. But he wasn't, not really. The punch to his stomach was distant now; his body had forgotten it. He could have launched up from the pavement, his head driving into the belly of one, his hands clawing the air, finding the face of the other. It was what he would remember, it was what he wanted to remember. He thought: Get up. In a minute, in half a minute, he would be revealed. There would be tomorrow to contend with, his face in the mirror, his eyes looking out at him. Convicting him. Tomorrow, the next day, the day after that. Reed was still, unmoving, gathering himself together, preparing himself.

Tomorrow, the next day, the day after that. And after that. As if life had become too far a walk. Reed sighed then, a thin, incongruous sound. A weary sound. Lame, besotted. Like himself. His eyes traveled around the street, saw shadows, distant lights. Saw feet. They needed to tie their shoes. Saw faintly lettered script: REDEMPTION. Trite, fatuous. Maybe cancer victims would emerge, save him.

He thought: Get up.

"He's not hurt," the second boy said. His indecision was ebbing. A new certainty steeled his voice. "He's a pussy."

Pussy. The sound was adolescent, the sound was hissing. Like truth. Purple, intricate, oysterish. Harsh hairs. Architecturally incoherent. Reed lay on the ground, architecturally incoherent.

"He's a pussy," Tony decided. So they were agreed. It was the only jury in sight. The word seemed apt. Twenty years ago, Reed would have shot to his feet. Large, terrifying. But that was twenty years ago. Countless quarts of scotch ago. That was when he still wore thirty-two-inch jockeys, when the hair on his head was thick. When his desk was like the helm of a great ship—money, power, and praise streaming toward him. When his belly was an impregnable fortress, immune to the heat of chili, Szechwan pork, goulash. When he ended every night kneeling between the long thighs of Andrea, like a man saying a prayer. Her palms slapping the sheets. When the atmosphere

23

was not yet rent with great, dangerous holes. When only the incompetent, the unfortunate, the unkempt owed money. A time of Mantle, of Unitas, Arnie charging on the sixteenth hole, three strokes down. It was you who were charging, you ached to see Arnie win. Before foul-mouthed disc jockeys, before seatbelt laws, before coed dorms. When the neighborhood echoed with only the low, discreet voices of parents, with the gentle laughter of children. A time when the country could go to war and believe it necessary, believe it righteous.

The boys sensed his impotence. They could feel their growing power. The fatal instant crested, broke over him. Tony kicked him. Reed grunted, flopped to his side. Then the second one was straddling him, suddenly fearless, fists diving down, fists diving toward Reed's crotch. "Dance dance dance," the boy muttered, his sounds rhythmic, incantatory. Reed writhed, squealing, the blows like things inside his head. Five seconds, seven seconds, no more. But the metaphysics of gin made it eternal. There is a species of buzzard that flings rocks from its beak to crack open the eggs of its prey. "Take my money!" Reed screamed now. He wanted to reach for his wallet, open its leathery fold, delivering up his plastic, his green, his library card, the photos of his wife, his daughter. Delivering up his life. But they were at a place far beyond money. There was only the methodical, pleasing thud of their fists. They were like a wrecking crew, like men demolishing walls.

"I think he done dancing, Tony."

The snow was coming down hard. Like unwanted verities, covering everything. Their sneakers made no sound as they moved off. Reed lay for some minutes, bruised, aching, his breath a whip. He would strangle nothing. The smell of honeysuckle on a spring day was a fluke. A beautiful woman stepping down into the sunlight, her shoulders bare—she removed her teeth at night, her odor was sour in the morning.

Such realizations were more wrenching than blows to the belly, than the fear of blood, of pain. There is a kind of terror that takes hold. It was reinventing his life as he lay there.

24

An unfortunate episode, a minor episode. He should have gone home, had a drink, said to Andrea, "You won't believe what happened." But when he got home, Andrea was stuffing a sea trout. She had invited company for dinner. She looked up, saw only a narrow scrape on his chin. "What happened?" she asked. But her attention was on the crab filling, on the need to warm the rolls. She had yet to polish the dining-room table. If he told her now, her sympathy would be rushed. "I slipped." He would tell her the next day. He would show her the wounds. She would be shocked, her face etched with concern. He would be brave. In the bathroom, he stripped, stood before the mirror, and was disappointed. There was only the scrape on his chin, a thin cut on the inside of his lip, a faint bruise beneath one set of ribs. An invisible ache in his left nut. The sloppy antics of children. He felt betrayed by his body. He frowned at himself, not so brave. Perhaps it would evolve into an anecdote he told at parties.

At dinner that evening, Reed drank too much, he ate too little. His need to dull all was strong. Their guests were a younger couple; they were expecting their first. They had recently moved to a bedroom suburb a half hour out. You could see the hope, the promise in their eyes. The woman ate seconds, then thirds, flaunting her appetite. A mother's hunger. In between bites, she spoke with pride of the cul-de-sac on which they lived, the apple tree in their backyard, the new school going up three streets over. Her husband talked of the shipment of tulip bulbs he had ordered for the front walk, of his plans for a compost heap in the back.

Reed brooded, he drank. He wanted to scream, "I've just been beaten within an inch of my life."

"And garbage pickup twice a week," the woman added.

"You were rude," Andrea said when they were gone.

Reed, rude, went to bed.

In the morning, he woke late. It was snowing still. He had to race to make the train. The street where he had lain was innocent with bundled children on their way to school. That evening, darkness falling, he decided on a different route home from the subway stop, circling five blocks out of the way. A note on the kitchen counter: "Bridge night. Laura's at a friend's. Dinner in the fridge." Reed sat in the living room and rehearsed the episode, how he would tell it. "Boys?" she might say. "Did they have a gun? A knife?" Well, no. "You gave them how much?" And there was the matter of the sister. In the telling, the incident would be tawdry, less a mugging than a botched negotiation with a pimp. He saw the look she would give him. He saw the hint of reproach in the set of her mouth. He heard her ask, "Why didn't you get up?"

In the end, Reed never told Andrea. He never told anyone. He kept waiting for the right moment. But no moment was right. If he had been bloodied, crippled, made lame, any moment—every moment—would have been right. From a hospital bed, his words would have been chilling, choked with indignation. But Reed lived, he walked; nights he sat with the remote control in his hand.

The snow continued for three days. A snow from ancient times, full of portent, a snow the likes of which once moved tribal peoples to fear for the end. The weatherman spoke with uncommon cheer. Reed told himself he was lucky, he told himself it didn't matter. He told himself nothing had been lost. It was a parking ticket, it was spittle on the elevator, pigeon shit on a park bench. He was of the city.

But on the morning of the third day, Andrea warm next to him, he woke toward dawn, the sky pewter. He rose quietly, made his way to the window. The street was encrusted, the moon pale and low. Like a bauble God had forgotten. The city was mute with the peculiar silence of snow, the buildings bulking white. A view from the Pleistocene, life before man. And then, in the distance, a lone figure navigating the drifts, a figure from a failed climbing expedition, an arctic shipwreck. It approached gingerly, the pavement treacherous. The face was dark, the walk of a young woman. Of someone's sister, it occurred to him. The thought brought his head falling into his hands. It had the uncanny logic of the dawn, the mad reason of snow, in which truth is a mood. It was this that had been lost, it was this that mattered. He understood immediately; he understood too much. Her head would have been heavy on his shoulder, his face buried in her hair. Her hands would have been small, there would have been the feel of their warmth across his back. They would have circled slowly, as if in a ballroom, a bedroom. It had all been lost long ago. She would smell of coconut and lime.

That morning, then, it was to begin in earnest. He had learned that he could surprise himself, that he could fail himself. This knowledge gazed out at him from the mirror. It was evident in the taste of an apple, in the feel of his desk beneath his palms. In the moments before he bedded his wife. He was helpless before it. It confirmed all that came before, it insured all that was to follow. The memory rose stubbornly, like a hated statue in a fallen city. The fields have been torched, the men forced to work the mines, the women made concubines. The children receive instruction in the gods of an alien pantheon.

Now Andrea was setting down her fork, her knife. Her plate was empty, but for the single warp of bone. Reed reached again for his lighter.

"But Dad, I'm not finished." Laura had eaten two, maybe three bites.

"Listen." He leaned close, whispering, his tone conspiratorial. "You're not going to rush upstairs and puke it up, are you? Tell me that's not what you do."

"A serape," Andrea said. She was looking at him.

And Andrea. She found herself in the shadow of his brooding. One can ask, "What's wrong?" only so many times before becoming ridiculous. "Nothing," he would insist. "There is too. An idiot could see it, except I'm not an idiot. I'm your wife." "I'll try to remember that." "Please, don't. Don't speak to me like that." "What do you want from me?" "I want you not to speak to me like that." "I'm sorry." "So tell me: what's wrong?" "Nothing. Nothing is wrong." "It's like you've been emptied out. It's like you've been emptied of everything." Silence. "We go to bed, and I can feel you lying there, feel you with your eyes open. It's like I can hear you, I can hear your thinking." Silence, sharp, like a slap. "Then I wake up in the middle of the night, and you're not in bed. I hear you roaming the house. As if you're looking for something." "Look, nothing is wrong. Why do you keep saying something is wrong when I tell you there is nothing wrong?" "Because it's clear to me that you could be equally happy with any of fifty different women." "That's not true." "You could be equally happy with any of fifty different women, working any of fifty different jobs, living in any of fifty different cities." "That's not true." "You could never name my fears. You have no idea. You have no idea at all." "You're right: I have no idea what you're talking about." "I don't ask for much. I never wanted much." "That's good, because we're broke." "Is that it? Is that it?" "We're broke and I'm afraid I'm going to be fired and there's a car blocking our drive." "Listen: I don't care. I don't care that we're broke. I don't care. I don't care if you get fired. I don't care about the goddamn car. Is that what this is all about?" "If you want. If you want, that's what this is all about." "Don't you see? These things don't matter. We can do this. Listen to me: there is nothing, nothing to worry about." "Good. I'm glad. I'm glad. Now shut up. Please, please shut up." "You can't talk to me like that. Please, please don't talk to me like that." "What do you want? What is it you want from me?" "I want you not to speak to me like that . . ."

Meanwhile, lines were coming into her face, into her neck. Fifteen years ago, her beauty had been the kind that you are sure will last forever. Now she believed her ass was too big. Though her legs, she whispered to him late at night, in bed, in the dark, "are still good." There was a sadness, a desperation to her voice that made him tremble. That made him culpable.

He stopped for a drink after work on Tuesday, he stopped for a drink after work on Thursday, he stopped for a drink after work on Friday. He began taking walks through the city, across Boston Common, up past Bunker Hill, down through Back Bay. Past the restaurants, the lights coming on, past the still construction sites, the great orange machinery mute. Past the secretaries emerging late from office buildings, past the gay bars, the movie theaters, the students with their books. He began coming home at nine o'clock, he began coming home at ten o'clock. He came home to burned paella, burned squid. He came home that time at midnight. There followed boiled cabbage on Monday, cold beans and franks on Wednesday, a single raw egg in a teacup on Friday. She began to bring an unkind laugh to bed. Then he forgot to meet her for lunch as scheduled. She sat for an hour and a half, the ice in her water melting, the waiter impatient. The next day, she clipped a telephone pole. The car would never look the same. At a party, she flirted outrageously with the host. Or so it seemed. Reed countered by talking to a young woman, a not entirely unattractive woman. Thick, horselike face, big teeth. Laugh like hahaha. Small eyes set too far apart. But young. She kept punching him playfully in the arm. Her name was Elizabeth Knox. She was a graphic artist for a large company, but she was bored; every day was the same. She rose, brushed big teeth, she ate a bagel, she caught the bus. Did he know what she meant? Reed nodded, he knew. Of course he knew. She crossed her legs, stockings whispering. Small eyes like knives. Was it true what they said about older men? Reed blinked. What did they say? What? But she only blushed, small knives flashing. As the party was breaking up, people collecting their coats, searching out their spouses, she punched his arm: "I'm in the book."

Her voice had been too loud. An awkward silence followed, until a cough set people moving again. Andrea and he drove home in silence. As they turned into the driveway, she announced, "You were a fool."

Spring came, summer came. Hot, muggy streets, sweltering nights. Like their fights. An eager violence entered their voices. There is a kind of contempt peculiar to marriage, it thrives only in the stagnant waters of intimacy. A quick word, a harsh look, a beat of silence poorly placed, and they would stand in the kitchen, their faces inches apart, raging, their mouths large, voices large, words like razors. This would be followed by two, three days of silence, the house tomblike. The house hot. The subway was a furnace, cars overheated on the highways, heat-stroke victims clogged the emergency rooms. Their electric bill was staggering. A garbage strike, and trash rotted on the sidewalks, penetrated the walls of their home, made their dreams fetid. Nights he lay awake, sweating, afraid to turn on the air conditioner, and listened to the sounds of gunshots, of screams, the sounds of breaking glass. The phone book went from Edgar Knox to F. Knox.

"What's a serape?" Laura asked now. She was intrigued.

"It's like a cape," her mother said. "Very colorful. You wear it."

"No clothes," Laura reiterated. Her whims were quick. They demanded attention.

"A surprise, then," Reed said. He fingered his lighter.

"What kind of surprise?"

"Trust me."

But wait. Hope is relentless. It can survive on little. It can survive on almost nothing. Like a weed. A new opportunity presented itself. "Out of the blue," Reed told Andrea. The phrase had meaning for the first time in his life. A friend had a brother-in-law who had this uncle. There was an opening in a strong company. A respected company. It would mean more money, it would mean more prestige. It would mean more power. It would mean more money. Reed's excitement communicated itself to his wife. Andrea was excited. A change, it was what they needed. It seemed a second chance. The last chance. "I'm going to ask for seventy," he told her. They whispered the sum in bed; it was hushed, it was holy. Tiny noises, late at night. Tweet tweet tweet. "We'll be able to turn on the air conditioner," she realized. Reed grinning, Reed bold, Reed saying, "Fuck the electric bill." He had been bludgeoned in the street, but now he would buy ten air conditioners, run them nonstop from April to October. They would buy a new car, say goodbye to the ruined fender. A car none would dare trap in the driveway. They would be able to afford Smith, Bryn Mawr. Holyoke at least. Perhaps they would move after all. To a nice neighborhood, to a place where you could walk.

Reed met with the personnel manager. Reed met with the assistant vice-president. At his own office, he lurked about like a spy selling secrets. Reed met with the executive vice-president. He led Reed into the office of the president, a man named Cruickshank. Cruickshank smiled at Reed, his handshake firm. Cruickshank held a get-together every Fourth of July out at his Cape beach house. A company tradition. Only top management. They all came out, they spent the night. They drank a little, they played touch football, they watched the fireworks from the next village over. They brought their wives. "Bring your wife. Have her make potato salad. It'll be a chance for you to meet the crew, a chance for them to meet you." Reed heard *chance*. He heard *chance* again.

The morning of the Fourth was hot. Soggy air, dense with pollen. Reed watched from his kitchen window as the adjacent backyard roused for a cookout. A cheap charcoal grill, hot dogs, yellow, sweating pieces of chicken. Bowls of rice, bowls of beans. A bag of potato chips. A case of Budweiser next to a stack of tortillas. The food of cultural miscegenation. Barechested, big-bellied men brandishing forks, bawling at their women in a strange tongue. The women bawled back, their upper arms thick, their hair the color of asphalt.

Andrea was behind him, slicing potatoes. Laura was going to spend the weekend at her grandparents. She was not happy about it. Grandpa forgot things. He forgot her name, he forgot they had just eaten, he forgot to flush the toilet. "Why should I have to see that?" He forgot to put on pants when he came down for breakfast.

Reed looked at her. "He forgets his pants?"

They went. Their car moved gingerly along the roads pocked with potholes, past the business district, through a low canopy of smog, then veered onto the expressway, soaring above the neighborhood, above the city. The warehouses, the high-rises fell away. Reed saw birds, he saw trees. He saw blue sky. The beach house was located just outside a village that had once been a center of whaling. There were the white houses with their widow's walks, the roar of the sea. It had been months since he had been outside the city. The odor of brine cheered him. Down through the main square, around a rotary made charming by an old inn, an antique store, a courthouse quaint with age. In the center, a granite sculpture of a tattered colonist, his shoes rags, a bandage wrapping his head, aiming a flintlock yet again at the marauding British.

Cruickshank's beach house was a broad, isolated structure steps from the ocean. The columns were tall, the windows French. Oyster shells lined the walk. It was a place of light, of vivid colors, the air fragrant. A young black woman met them at the door. She led them down a long hallway lined with hunting trophies. An elk head from Montana, a tiger's paw from Asia, a bear skin from Alaska. Past a sitting room, through a parlor, down another hallway (African masks, a medieval tapestry) to a kitchen shot through with sun. Reed at Andrea's shoulder, whispering, "I won't take less than seventy." They arrived at a stone staircase that descended steeply to the ocean. On the beach, Cruickshank stood at a broad propane grill, turning steaks. He moved with authority: a man at ease with himself, a man at ease with meat. "Reed!" Cruickshank screamed when they appeared. He got Reed in a headlock, pretended to break Reed's neck. Reed, lodged in the crook of the man's arm, smiled thinly. Cruickshank kissed Andrea's hand. Cruickshank introduced them to a marketing exec, two vice-presidents, the head of the legal department, an accountant, the director of manufacturing. Cruickshank introduced them to his wife. Carla Cruickshank was thirty years younger than her husband. A slender, agile woman, she had breasts. Cruickshank screamed, "Jenny, goddammit, get your katootie out here." The black woman appeared with a tray of wine coolers.

The din of the ocean, the gulls calling. Faces dwarfed by sunglasses peered up at Reed. They talked. Reed talked, they talked. He ate prize steak, corn on the cob, a green salad. Sun high, fierce, pounding his back, the top of his head. Reed sucked wine coolers—sweet, sickening, a child's drink. No one smoked.

"Where did you say you lived?" one of the vice-presidents asked.

"Boston," Reed said. They waited. He named the neighborhood. It was like an obscenity. Their looks were fast, the silence embarrassed.

"Excuse me," Reed said. He ran back around to the front of the house. Furtive, quick feet. The pale cylinder popping into his hand, he smoked thickly. He primed his drink with the bottle of vodka stored in the glove compartment of his car.

Returning to the beach, Reed saw Andrea talking with the fellow from manufacturing, a man named Evans. She had changed into her bathing suit. Reed watched as Evans patted her knee, laughed, patted her knee again. Reed glanced around, wondered if he was supposed to take offense. Say it was a test. A test he could fail. Perhaps they expected him to throttle the man. Though Evans might throttle back. Big hand, big mitt, covering her knee. Twice Reed made his way back through the heat to huddle in his car and suck at the bottle.

Reed played volleyball. It was the kind of weekend where one puts athletic skills on display and drinks wine coolers. But Reed was something of a lummox; he was drinking vodka. Reed huffed over the sand, his belly hairy and protruding over the lip of his trunks. He whacked the ball with what he hoped was authority. He watched Carla Cruickshank in her bikini, her breasts magnificent, swaying. They made him ache. He aimed shots her way. She played next to the accountant, a short, anemic-looking woman. Reed seemed to know the accountant immediately, to understand everything about her. She was single, what was once called a spinster. A classic. Her dreams were lurid, her life was not. She spent Saturday nights darting her fingers over a keyboard while a spreadsheet hummed onscreen, the lone true love of her life—a cat named Sinbad—in her lap. "Good shot," he kept telling her.

Later, he huddled with Cruickshank. The position involved this and this and that. Much responsibility, awesome responsibility. Cruickshank had plans, big plans; he needed a man of talent, a man of ambition. Reed nodded, a man of ambition.

Evening fell quickly. There was more food, more wine coolers. No one smoked. Their lungs were pink, pure. Reed sneaked back around to his car under cover of darkness. Carla Cruickshank appeared just as he was lighting a cigarette. The bottle was snug beneath his arm. She was a tall woman, her perfume scorching. She reached, her fingernails sharp, and took the cigarette from his fingers.

"Jack doesn't approve of tobacco," she said. She waited, hot ember in her hand. "And Jack doesn't approve of hard alcohol."

Reed stared at her. Jack, Jack, a pinch of fear at the name. Jack had touched those legs, those breasts. A king and his queen. Reed felt like a peasant caught stealing royal liquor. He could cave her head in with the bottle, bury her in a dune. But would he still get the job?

He said, "So maybe Jack doesn't find out."

Her look was withering. Then she took a long, sweet drag from the cigarette. Reed leaned the bottle toward her. He needed to make her equally guilty. She took a sip, then another.

"Maybe," she said. She was Jack's wife. She was never guilty. She tossed the bottle back to him, then strolled off. She was lanky, angular, legs like Finnish nobility. Reed took a studied pull on the liquor, like a man memorizing a phone number, an address.

He made his way back around the house. The light to the kitchen was on; he could see Jenny through the window, pouring custard into ramekins. The woman was compact, her features broad, lips heavy. There were few blacks in the town where Reed had grown up. Jungle films formed him early. Hooting Nubians with painted faces. Between the ages of twelve and fourteen his most effective fantasy had involved a small-breasted negress with surging buttocks. He had rutted among the bedsheets with her, hand stabbing frantically. Reed smiled now, full of the memory. As if in response, Jenny paused over each ramekin and fired a powerful shot of spit dead center. It left him gasping. She moved down the row of custards, cheeks tight, her features narrowing, sucked up into her mouth. Warm, moist oyster leaping.

He considered knocking on the window. He considered telling the Cruickshanks. Perhaps they would thank him. Perhaps Cruickshank would fire Jenny, hire him on the spot. Yet he didn't want to be the maid. And what could he say? "Your mammy is drooling into the flan." Perhaps they would discern a hidden racism at work. He imagined the whole gang surrounding him, blanched, eager faces, contorted with liberal rage. "Katootie," Cruickshank had said. Maybe katootie gave her reason.

Reed arrived at the beach. He would say nothing. Gobs of spittle among the egg whites did not matter. He wanted this job. This mattered. To the west, the light from the seaboard formed a broad corona. An ocean breeze from the east sharpened the air. People were settling back to watch the fireworks. It was a scene from twenty years ago, a hundred years ago. Reed found Andrea wrapped in a blanket against the chill. He slipped into position next to her, brought his arm around her shoulders.

"I'm going to ask for seventy-five," he said.

A rocket went off, then a second, dull popping sounds that exploded high above them, turning the waves red and blue. In the distance, the local high-school band launched into a medley of patriotic anthems scored to a rap beat. There was the staccato of five more rockets, glorious multicolored light that rainbowed over them. The day, the evening, the soothing environs of the Cape—the sight of the red and blue and white lights rising, splintering, then showering to the ground—made his heart turn over. Reed was no dolt; these were banal thoughts, he knew. But the alcohol in his system had dimmed to that thin hum that makes us generous toward the world, open to its gifts. There is a species of good feeling that is content to give life its due. Akin to the sensation you get when you see a young woman bending to prune her roses; there is a scarf around her head, her bare thighs are the color of ginger root, her hands move with care. Or an older couple, walking hand in hand down a mountain trail; they have shared the same bed for fifty years, their love is like a prized antique. Or a gruff, unshaven man—he looks like a biker—peering closely at the variety of cat foods on the supermarket shelves, struggling to decide between tins of beef-liver or ocean whitefish for Kitty.

The sky rained color for almost half an hour. The finale was a grand thundering of light, the piccolos shrill. Reed felt renewed, as if he had forgotten the world, and now it meant to remind him.

"I think he tried to kiss me," Andrea said when it was over.

"Who?"

She pointed. "What's his name. Evans."

"What do you mean, you-think-he-tried-to-kiss-you."

"I'm not sure. I was setting out the potato salad—"

"Nobody touched it."

"—when I looked up and his face was about half an inch from mine."

Reed grimaced. The sea seemed harsher suddenly, the night colder. He could see Evans across the way, talking with Cruickshank. Their voices were low, covert. They were talking about Reed. They were determining his life.

"Frank?"

He turned to look at Andrea. Of course other men found

36

his wife desirable. She was desirable. Who could blame them. Men of talent, men of ambition had pretty wives. Look at Jack. Jack's wife was pretty. He wondered if Evans had ever tried to kiss Jack's wife. He wondered if she had kissed back. Reed kissed Andrea now. She kissed back.

"Listen," he whispered, "don't eat the custard."

Reed woke early. The air was sharp, he could hear the pounding of the ocean. Andrea slept on, oblivious. In the breakfast nook, some of the others had already gathered. Jenny asked how he liked his eggs. She glared down at him, black skin glistening, a spatula in her hand.

Reed said, "Just coffee."

Evans was there, sitting next to his wife. It gave Reed a chance to study her. Mrs. Evans was a large woman, a second, occasionally a third chin. She made puffing sounds as she moved. It would take courage to bed such a woman. Next to her sat one of the vice-presidents. He had visited Egypt the year before. "I ate falafel the whole time," he was saying. "I must've eaten fifty falafels. I didn't shit for a week." Then there was somebody's wife, Reed could not remember whose, then another vice-president. Then Cruickshank. Reed darted looks to the man, waiting for a sign, a signal. A contract waving in his hands. But Cruickshank was intent on his stack of buckwheats. There was Mrs. Cruickshank, her back straight, her hair gathered in a tight bun at the top of her head. She had the lean, gaunt look of models. She wore a pair of cutoffs, a blouse unbuttoned two buttons too many. It would take courage, etc., etc.

Someone suggested a game of touch football. Some firms had bowling teams, others staged golf outings. Cruickshank's crew did touch football. Cruickshank did not play himself. "But my wife, she loves it."

"I love it, I love it," Carla Cruickshank said.

On the beach, she let down her hair. Thick, rolling tides of blonde unfurling. She played quarterback. No one questioned it. Reed eyed those around him. Obsequious, fawning employees. But it turned out she had an arm, she could throw. Reed was impressed. She asked him to play center. Impressed, he agreed. Collegial, corporate, agreeable. The beginning of a new life. Across the line he faced the head of the legal department. Or the director of marketing. Reed couldn't remember.

The sand burned his bare feet. Reed lowered himself over the ball. She crouched directly behind him, her hands snug against his thighs, like in the pros. She was no-nonsense; she aimed to win. Reed centered the ball and was straightaway dumped on his ass by the head of either the legal department or marketing. On the next play, a hand drove Reed's head into the sand. He tasted salt, there was grit up his nose.

His name was Gilbert. Legal department. He had problems of his own. His wife liked expensive weekends at a health spa in Maine. His son was flunking arithmetic. Gilbert had an odd-looking place on his back that he secretly feared was cancer. He had nothing against Reed. But standing on the line, he was standing opposite the Maine masseur to whom he paid good money to play patty-cake with his wife's fanny. He was standing opposite his son's teacher, and her inability to explain the intricacies of long division. He was standing opposite the oncologist who would one day tell him he had six months to live.

Another play, another. Touch football. It had nothing to do with anything. Or say it had everything to do with everything. Cruickshank was watching. Reed tried to remember to keep his chin up, he tried to remember that Gilbert was about to lop off his head. But Reed had to bend deep to reach the ball, there were her hands hard against his nuts. At the snap, Gilbert chopped at Reed's neck with his forearm, made a sloppy bundle of Reed at his feet. On the next play, as Reed hovered over the ball, Gilbert snorting above him, her fingers slid a half-inch along his upper thigh, then went on to graze the elastic band of his jock. Gilbert smashed into him like a runaway truck. In the huddle, Reed tried to catch her eye. She looked at him, she looked through him. Change of possession. Reed was anxious to punish Gilbert, to tear at the man's ears.

38

But it turned out Gilbert was their quarterback; the mousey accountant was their center. Reed shoved her lightly to the ground, he was careful not to touch her breasts. She fell with pathetic, bleating sounds. Reed helped her up. First down, first down, change of possession. Reed was back on the line, the ball at his feet, Carla Cruickshank close behind him. A finger flicked against his scrotum. Gilbert descended, his anger lawyerly, judicial. Again at the line, a long fingernail—unmistakable, sharp—traced the outline of his right testicle. Another play, another. Long counts, teasing counts. Her finger rooting, finding. A strategic pinch. Surely someone saw. But no one saw. Gilbert straightened him up with a swing of his forearm, then felled him as if he were a tree. On the next play, she reached in, all five fingers, cupped his balls. Rolly-rolly. Quick, smart tug. Gilbert slapped him twice, his hand going left, then right, then picked him up and body-slammed him to the ground. In the huddle, Reed again sought out her eyes, stared into them as if they were books. But her eyes were opaque, books in a foreign language. Meanwhile, Cruickshank stood on the sidelines, watching, signaling nothing, not a contract waving. It was clandestine, forbidden. As long as Reed would continue to bend over the ball, Gilbert panting above him, incensed at the world, Gilbert meting out pain, Reed receiving it, a beautiful woman would juggle his prunes. Meanings were everywhere. Work for my husband and he'll bust your balls. Work for my husband and I'll bust your balls. She was instructing him in deep truths. Elusive truths. She was instructing him in life.

The next play, she reached in and squeezed. Hard, viselike. It hurt. Reed whirled, his eyes lashing out at her. He marched off then, big feet making tracks in the sand.

"Where are you going?" Carla Cruickshank called. There was a lilt to her voice. She was grinning, Gilbert was grinning. Even the accountant was grinning.

"I don't want to play," Reed said. "I don't want to play anymore."

Andrea sat next to Evans, his hand on her bathing suit. On her ass. They were talking, immersed in each other. She had seen nothing. As if her eyes were in her ass. Reed, stalking over the sand, boomed, "Andrea, get dressed." But then Reed heard, "Reed."

It was Cruickshank. Cruickshank heavy with signals. The man crooked his finger, then turned and went into the house. Reed hesitated, then followed him back down the long hallways, past the medieval tapestry, the masks, the animal trophies. Up a stairway to a large office on the second floor. Meanings too many. Cruickshank shut the door, then settled behind a broad desk. Cruickshank looked at Reed appraisingly for a minute, two minutes. He had not offered Reed a chair. He was not going to offer Reed a chair. Cruickshank turned finally to stare out the window. Reed stood, sweating. Cruickshank sat, cool. Cruickshank said, "You don't like touch football?" His tone was insinuating.

"Not half as much as your wife does." He had been straining for a touch of levity, a shift in the tenor of the encounter. But Cruickshank's face darkened, swarming with implications. The wrong thing to say. Byzantine corporate intrigue, Reed suddenly understood he would never master it. Yet circumstances extenuated. He wanted to turn on his air conditioner, to send his daughter to college. Maybe move to a neighborhood where you could walk.

In the end, Reed swallowed, said, "Sixty-five?"

But Cruickshank kept staring out the window. The ocean was smooth. Whales fed off this shore. Every summer several managed to beach themselves.

Andrea was waiting in the car. As they drove home, clouds congregated. Ten minutes outside Boston, the sky opened up. The rain plummeted hysterically. It confirmed Reed's mood, deepened it. The gentle hills of the suburbs delivered up the city once again, the air ripe with emissions from traffic and factories, the smell of rotting garbage, the smell of three million people. Down through the crumbling neighborhoods, the streets dark with grime, dark with crime. The subway rumbled beneath them. Overhead, the buildings rose, towered close. The effect was claustrophobic. Despair rose in the back of his throat, tasting of zinc. As they turned onto their street, he saw a large car, Jesus Saves on the bumper, blocking their drive. Of course. And the woman pruning roses was really poised above a stew of toxic chemicals that would kill not only the flowers, but her firstborn. The elderly couple would quarrel that very night, ending only when the old man cleaved the skull of his wife with an ax. He would be led away in chains, prohibited even from attending her funeral. The kind biker in fact had a blind mother; she loved the taste of tuna.

"But why?" Andrea was saying. Her face was racked with disappointment, there seemed a kind of savagery to it.

Reed shrugged. What could he say? Because Jack doesn't approve of tobacco, Jack doesn't approve of liquor. Because nobody ate your potato salad. Because you didn't let Evans kiss you. Because maybe you did. Because maybe I should have said sixty. Because I don't want to play anymore.

Reed was circling the block, looking for a parking space. "He didn't say."

She hammered the dash with her fists, her features a cave. "Let me out," she hissed.

He watched as she ran up the steps, as she clawed at the lock with the key, and then disappeared inside. He circled his block twice more, then drove to the next block, and the block after that. The rain was unending, cataclysmic.

Reed braked the car at the head of the block. The Block. He had avoided it for months. He saw now that the streetlight had been repaired. The light fanned out, severe, electric. There was a space midway down the block. There were two spaces, three. People avoided parking here. Tires were slashed, radios were stolen, windows were smashed. But Reed no longer cared about tires, radios, windows. He eased along the street, edged into a parking spot. He turned off the engine and sat, listening to it tick. The street was deserted, the rain had driven everyone indoors. He stepped from the car and stood, waiting for boys, for men to emerge from alleyways and knock him down, club him senseless, and make off with his money. But there were no men; there would be no men, not on a night like this. Not on a night when you expected it. Not on a night when it would make sense. They came on unthinking nights, unwitting nights, nights when belief still lingered in the air, when conviction was large in a man's face, as prominent as his nose. Reed started slowly down the street, past a fire hydrant, the streetlight, past the sign that hung in the window.

Past the sign that hung in the window: bold, stark, RE-DEMPTION. And then—because he had never been this close, because the city had seen fit to repair the streetlight, because he had always rushed through this street, head down, thoughts already two blocks ahead, thoughts already home, because the light was high, the fine print was unmistakable—GLASS (Tues. & Wed.) / PLASTIC (Mon. & Thurs.).

You have seen such men. You know them. They populate the subways, the eateries, the windows at the bank. They clog the expressways at rush hour. The newspapers are written for them. Their thoughts are found in the voices of strangers. Their victories gather dust. They eat too quickly, make love too rarely, diving toward sleep before the final thrust is done. The last good dream was decades back. They continue to confuse it with life. They were once men of cunning, men of destiny. Matadors of the soul. Now the bulls dwarf the ring. There are nations given over to them, lands in which all the mirrors reflect faces of sheetrock. There are countless nights, there are countless streets. The beatings go unrecorded. In the meantime, there is breakfast, work, dinner, TV, the store, the post office, a movie. They weep at the recitals performed by their children. Only the smaller dramas are left to them. They move through life like somnambulists, intent without reason—placing eggs in the clothes hamper, shoes in the freezer—unaware that there is such a thing as morning.

42

"Nancy Wiley is pregnant," Laura offered now. She had maneuvered her peas to one side of the plate, opposite her lamb chop.

Andrea paled. "Nancy?"

Reed did not recognize the name.

His daughter nodded. "April told me."

Andrea fingered the knife, then laid it at ten o'clock along her plate. "Who's the boy?"

Laura shrugged. She was indifferent now. She chose a roll. Reed watched as she tore it into tiny pieces and arranged them in a neat pile midway between the peas and the lamb. "Tran."

Andrea's look moved to Reed. Her eyes tightened, contracting into hard knots of certainty. "What kind of name is that?"

"He's—just Tran. Can I be excused?"

"Yes," Reed said, the flame leaping alive in his hand.

Andrea drove him to the airport. Their headlights shot out along the wet streets. At the corner, a group of youths slouched, their looks contemptuous. Reed and his wife stared straight ahead, their looks careful, without contempt. Down through the city they swept, their silence familiar, of the sort incubated in marriages of long standing, in which there is nothing more to say.

The airport tower loomed in the distance. Blinking lights moved soundlessly across the sky. In his mind, he was already on the plane, settling back with a drink, stealing glances at the legs of the stewardesses. Earphones, cocktail nuts, the stuffy, recycled air.

"When will you be home?"

"Two days. Three."

"You'll call me?"

"I'll call you." His hand went to his breast pocket.

"Don't," she said.

"What?" He frowned, straining for her meaning. He could not get the lighter to work. It made nicking sounds.

"Please." She indicated his cigarettes with a nod. "You had one not ten minutes ago."

He shook his head grimly. He made a ceremony of rolling down the window. The rain was cool on his face. There was the smell of wet asphalt, the odor of a city at night. He tossed the pack out the window. It glistened white against the black pavement, receding quickly like a dropped letter, a message that would never be delivered.

"Happy?"

She glanced at him, then turned back to the road. "No."

It had been months since they last came together. Even then, they had fucked like factory workers, like those who will punch a clock at shift's end.

Two

It was the Old Man himself who had asked Reed to make the trip. Yates was a large man, imposing. A man hard to deny. Voice dark as shale. He was seventy years old, he was eighty years old. No one knew for sure. The company was his life. Yates Electronics began small—a rundown warehouse stocked with repaired radios, phonographs, electric motors, vacuum tubes, copper wiring. Success came early. A second plant in the western part of the state, another in Providence, still another in Fall River. In recent years, the firm had branched into financial services, securities, investments: intangible wealth, unfettered wealth. The history of capitalism. Yates had associates in Geneva, in London, in Tokyo. He could arrange financing before the day was out. A word in an elevator and zoning ordinances were amended. He pursued the grander projects, mammoth endeavors that changed the face of a city, that altered the landscape—malls, hotels, enormous municipal contracts for convention centers, medical complexes that stretched for blocks. His anger, his appetites were legion. It was said he had fathered children on three continents. He had punched a banker, he had punched a waiter, he had punched a U.S. congressman. It was said he had cancer, a bad heart, failing kidneys. His workers knew better. He was immortal, you could see it in his eyes. At dinner parties he would stand, glass in hand, and recite long passages from Kipling. At board meetings he would pause in the middle of a thorny debate over interest rates, pension funds, three-tiered financing, and say, "Let me tell you about my childhood in New Hampshire."

There were stories about Yates, everyone knew them. His history was like a legend in the making. He had been raised by his mother, she had shucked oysters for eight dollars a week. He never knew his father. As a youth he had boxed, making pocket change and more in the bars and broken-down gyms of Manchester, Concord, Nashua. He had just missed the bronze in single sculls in Berlin. He had fought in North Africa, in Sardinia. Then came a bout with polio. The fear of death was real. At best, the doctors insisted, he would never walk again. Their certainty galled him. For two years he immersed himself in the warm waters of the whirlpool. He swore at nurses, he broke crutches over his bare knees. His determination was mythical, Olympian. The only remnant was a slight limp. It distinguished him, gave him an air of having been here, of having lived. Made him an Ahab in the eyes of his employees. Now he could ruin the lives of a thousand men with a single phone call.

"How's the wife? The kid?" Yates had begun. "Fine," Reed told him. But Yates was already bounding ahead. "It's about the Quincy operation." The Quincy site was the flagship of Yates's empire—the oldest, the first. "I'm closing it down." Reed's look made Yates smile. "It's a dog, Frank." Yet in Mexico, just across the border, the starting pay was fifty-five cents an hour. A dog's pay. "Eighteen hundred miles of promise," Yates whispered, eyes flashing with the possibilities. The Old Man slid reports, charts across his desk. Reed bent, he read, intent, solemn, rabbinical. Yates had made inquiries, he had contacts. If they packed up and moved the entire Quincy operation . . . He wanted Reed to go down for a few days, to make a thorough assessment of the situation. To return with a proposal in hand. "I value your opinion."

The assignment unnerved Reed. Yates had sent Williams to Los Angeles that time. Williams returned to discover that his office had been converted into a stockroom. When Mazzoli stepped out to the bathroom during a meeting, he came back to find his salary had been cut in half. One year, Yates handed down Christmas bonuses equal to three months' salary; the next year, he passed out seven-dollar turkeys. Self-basting. Yates's decisions were capricious; they were law. But: "I value your opinion." Doubtless the Old Man had heard about the business with Cruickshank. Perhaps he meant to punish Reed. Perhaps he meant to reward him. Though Yates's eyes betrayed nothing. They looked out from a cragged face, his features like rock formations fashioned by eons of weather.

Reed had spent his initial years working in Quincy. He had made friends with the men on the loading dock, with the men who stood at the long tables assembling radios, with men who stacked wheels of copper wiring on wooden pallets. Men with names like Moe, Emmett, Seymour—odd names, names from another generation. Men who worked with their hands. Questions concerning the Quincy operation were still frequently referred to Reed. Old fifty years ago, the building now leaned with age. The roof leaked, the floor was buckling. But it was Reed's domain. His turf. The assignment seemed cruel.

"Piedras Negras," Yates went on, pointing to the map. Reed waited. "Black stones," the Old Man translated. The name was ignoble, full of foreboding. A cow town, a hick town. Eiger had flown to Río the month before, to Singapore the month before that. Exotic cities, lavish meals, polite hotel maids, Brazilian beauties on topless beaches. Reed rated black stones. It seemed to signal much. It seemed to signal everything. Yates was emphatic: "This is important," he reminded Reed. "This is crucial." For Reed, Reed understood. Then Yates was up and leading him toward the door. "Be sure and say hi to Angela for me."

Reed stared at the Old Man. He said, "I will."

Air travel always gave Reed a creeping nausea: the air tight, its hints of ozone, the intractable lasagna noodles. A woman of bulk next to him, her perfume cloying. Her children, she informed him, were ungrateful bums; Reed reminded her of her eldest. Then, San Antonio at dawn. The sun was cresting, the heat already murderous. The lack of sleep, the parching air thickened his mood. A town of military bases, of malls, a strip of car dealerships. Off the thoroughfares, there were the adobe buildings, the old missions, the taco houses. At the car-rental booth, the clerk had a wide mouth, a prominent smile. Blonde hair scattered about her shoulders. Her accent was raw Texas, unschooled and meandering. Echoes of vacant Houston condominiums, the fate of the shrimp industry off Galveston, the declining fortunes of football in Odessa. "You be careful over there," she told him.

Reed found the highway and headed south. Billboards promised the Spurs, home cooking, $29.95 a night, the Alamo. The city shrank away, the traffic thinning. Arroyos veered off, scoring the land. Piñon, cacti, mesquite. A grove of pecan trees. A desert flower, surprising and isolated. A two-lane road marked by faded signs: Uvalde, Del Rio, Eagle Pass. Anonymous towns, young girls sit at windows and dream of the ocean. His rented Toyota labored up a hill, revealing a patrol car on the opposite shoulder. The immigration officer was fair-haired, well fed. He stood at the window of a battered Chevy that idled raggedly, the family dark. The father was waiting to explain yet again. Up ahead, buzzards circled. The guano baked on the scorched stones, splattered black from a diet of blood.

Reed stopped at a diner. Pickup trucks in the parking lot, empty gun racks behind the cabs. Inside, booths of ribbed Naugahyde, the linoleum a washed-out turquoise. Men in broad-brimmed hats and dusty boots hunkered at the counter. His suit and tie seemed like lies. Faces turned when he came in, then bent back over their plates. They ate slowly, pausing in mid-movement, as if at a question. Then the clink of forks would start in again. The answer lay in the greasy eggs, the burned potatoes, the smell of frying. The waitress wore a pin: Jolene.

"Coffee," Reed told her. "And change for the cigarette machine."

The coins clanked. He took off his jacket. He settled deep into the booth and smoked two cigarettes. The coffee was bitter, there were grounds on his tongue. The men at the counter were talking: rain was still a week away.

The cracked Formica, the dirty windows. Far from all the meals he had eaten, the places he had been. The calamari at Mi Fong's in San Francisco, the veal sliced thin as Kleenex at Timboretto's. In Montreal, the salmon stuffed with sausage, a snowstorm warring outside. He had been afraid to ski. In Louisville, the bald black waiter who steered him to the catfish. The sounds of riverboats on the Ohio, a bottle of Kentucky bourbon. Charleston that time, and Andrea had come. They took a walk along the Battery, ate fried clams while looking out over a field of Civil War dead. The duck with achiote at a little Peruvian spot in Manhattan. That corporate seminar in Chicago, followed by a sixteen-ounce porterhouse, women dancing on the stage in nothing but red heels.

Reed had joined the firm straight out of college. No one thinks when young: I want to be an engineer. Unless it's the kind that operates a locomotive. He had started school full of only one idea: anything but farming. He had been raised on eighty acres in southern Indiana. Corn, a few cows, pigs, chickens. Dusk meant manure on his shoes. Brutal winters chopping wood, humid, sweltering summers. He once didn't sleep for three nights, lying in wait for the fox raiding the hen house. The crack of a .22 at dawn, the teats of the fox swollen with milk. His mother had cried. As if he had shot her. His life was manure, eggs, fences that needed mending. Then he discovered basketball. Basketball in Indiana is sacred. Whole communities turn out, the farmers pounding their thighs, mothers screaming the names of their sons. The gymnasiums are modest, the uniforms faded. The timekeeper owns the local Feed & Seed. Coach is a drunk. The mayor can be seen berating the referee. The vicar has just punched a man who drove two counties to watch his youngest play. If her team wins, the widow Swanson will permit the center—a gawky, bony boy, his overbite dramatic—a game of stinky finger. Meanwhile, Reed played early in the morning, he played late at night, he dribbled the ball over autumn leaves. He played in the snow. The feel of the ball rocketing into his hands, the implausible roundness, the gentle loft as it arcs toward the basket. The hoop above, nailed to the hen house, the hoop like a hope. One-on-one with his father at twilight, the odors of his father's sweat, his noises, the authority of his father in the bounce of the ball, the big man moving toward the goal, the dull slapping sound of a bank shot, the rattle of the chain net. The intimacy was unspoken, male, perfect. If he had ever told his father he loved him, the man would have been forced to hit him. When his father was not around, Reed played against himself. Two-, three-, four-hour games, scores of 87–82, 146–144, 201–195. Always driving, pivoting, eluding shadows, phantoms, eluding himself. A fifteen-foot hook shot with the clock in his head reading 0:00, like death. But another game, another, another. His life had become the rusted hoop, the rough grainy texture of the ball. He turned into one of those lean, good-looking youths whose shyness off the court is matched only by his energy on court. "A detonator," his coach called him. Game days were electric. He was afraid to eat, afraid to think. He wanted only the immediacy of the court, the lacquered boards beneath his feet. Winning was like salvation, like eternal life. For an hour anyway, for two. The sounds of boys like himself, boys in close, playing for their souls. He and Jimmy Wilkins made up the back court—county champs, regional champs, eliminated finally by tall, humorless blacks from a school in South Bend. That summer he lost his virginity at the base of a grain silo, had his first drink, got his driver's license. It was a time of Vietnam. His teammates, the humorless blacks all went off to war. Reed had flat feet. His freshman year in college, he took a class in drawing to fulfill his humanities requirement. Still lifes, landscapes, flat planes and rounded surfaces. Then nudes at three-thirty, Monday, Wednesday, and Friday. The models were usually older women—faculty wives, secretaries from the English department. Bodies that had made love, birthed babies, suckled infants. Sagging breasts, stretch marks, heavy thighs. This stark evidence of a past to their bodies excited him. They had lain naked in poorly lit rooms with men who were naked too. His instructor said he had talent. Reed took more classes in painting, art history. An idle sketch of his girlfriend, a freckled, towering redhead, on a day they had driven to the beach. Svelte body, fetching smile. She studied it for a full minute. Her silence made him uneasy. But finally, "I want it, I want it." She was trembling. "Here, you can have it." "Not the sketch, you idiot," she hissed, breath hot in his ear. Love maybe, desire probably, narcissism certainly. He had sketched her, made her horny. A tribute to his talent, a tribute to his art. But the truth came early: artists never eat. Architecture, then. He studied color plates of the cathedrals of Europe, German Bauhaus, the soaring skyscrapers that grew in the cities. He traveled to Chicago, stood in the foyer of a Frank Lloyd Wright. He was awestruck, the silence hallowed. His instructor said he had talent. But, "You'll spend your life designing malls," his father insisted. Malls were evil places of fake lighting and false goods. Malls were what was wrong with the country. His father was ill, death appeared close. Reed would spend his life designing malls, his father mocking him from beyond the grave. Reed

switched to engineering. Dams, he decided, hydroelectric projects, bridges spanning torrential rivers. No malls, ever. He
graduated and was offered a job in Indianapolis, a job in
Florida, a job in Boston. Indianapolis was too close, Florida
was rich retirees and swamp heat. Boston was city, chilly
ocean, high-rise promise, sophisticated women clicking down
the avenues in their heels. But Boston: not bridges, not dams,
but phonographs, dishwasher rinse cycles, three-speed air conditioners. Better, maybe, to have starved in a garret, fleeting
romances with crazed and suicidal women, to die ultimately
of tuberculosis, acrylics drying on his hands. Women did not
tremble at a sketch of a stereo circuit board, they never
moaned, "I want it, I want it."

"Anything else?" It was Jolene. She was working a double
shift. Men were always leaving her.

"No, thanks."

The road dipped into a broad valley, the trees few and
spindly. Like ancient, severed hands. Desiccated terrain, roots
straining for meager water. The main square of Eagle Pass held
a bank, a supermarket, two shoe stores. A close-out sale, everything must go. A movie theater—the Aztec—now abandoned,
and hence heroic. Crows nested in the rafters. A town without
a bookstore. People waited patiently on a traffic island for the
light to change. Unhurried, sleepy smiles. Smiles borne of
heat, of starchy foods, of cheap beer. A power failure, and they
would remain stranded in the middle of the street forever.
Small town, quiet town, on the edge of the country, on the
edge of history. Traffic slowed. Like history. The line of cars
wandered south. And then, the Rio Grande, a narrow strip of
brown water. Mundane, disappointing in the end. A cartogra-
pher's joke. It was said Indians lived in the shelter of the
bridge, but he saw only weeds. A parched, incongruous golf
course on the near bank, the sand bunkers bigger than the
greens. Cars moved haltingly up to the lip of the bridge, paid
the toll, then ambled across. In a narrow parking area off to
the side, leashed German shepherds sniffed at the open trunk

52

of a Pontiac. Waves of heat rose off the asphalt, the car exhausts liquid. Pedestrians lined both sides, weary, marching pilgrims. The progress of the river was indiscernible. There was the uneasy odor of chemicals, of raw sewage.

"Business," he told the guard opposite.

The streets south of the river were broken cobblestones, the drivers lunatics. The peeling paint of the tiendas, the farmacias, the dank cantinas. Auto repair shops three to a block. A beggar would wash your window unbidden. Children sold gum, plastic beads. Then a run of shacks following the course of the river, structures of plywood, broken stucco, sheet metal, cardboard. A town under siege, an outpost on a contested frontier. A dump rose up on his right, a white mountain of trash. Birdlike figures picked their way over it, stooping to retrieve an empty bottle, a remnant of carpet. The heat was dry, it scoured his lungs. The children were barefoot and curious.

His contact was a city official named García. Intimates in the business community, intimates in the U.S. consulate. A man who could bestow favors, who could withhold them. García's office was a windowless cubicle. An accountant by training, he was broad, his belly powerful. He smelled of sweat, he smelled of drink. Teeth brown and broken in his face. Earnest, cheerful, the Mexican moved with his head inclined to one side, as if he were expecting a sound. A photo of a plain woman and two expressionless children sat on his desk. On the wall, a map stretched from Matamoros to Tijuana. The sound of typing came from down the hall.

Reed went into his spiel. Talking tough, talking easy, talking talking. How many times had he done this? If he had been a carpenter, a baker, he would have come home with sawdust on his shoes, with flour in his hair. But Reed was Reed. He knew which gestures to make, he knew when to nod, when to laugh, when to appear thoughtful. Given the right property, the right terms, he explained, Yates Electronics was prepared to offer this and this. Though they expected that, of course. And that. And don't forget this. Reed smiling, Reed in a hurry. Reed figured to go home before they turned his office into a broom closet.

Ten minutes in, García held up his hand. To shut Reed up, Reed realized. The Mexican seemed pained by Reed's haste. "Please," he said, "a toast?" He pulled a half-filled bottle of amber tequila and two smudged glasses from a drawer. He paused to turn the photo on his desk face down, then poured. He hoisted his glass.

"Salud," he said. He drank. Reed drank. The alcohol burned. García grinned. He poured a second round—"Amor"—and a third: "Dinero." The Mexican hammered the desk with his fists, went bug-eyed for an instant, then returned the bottle and glasses to the drawer. Reed would have liked another drink. But: health, love, money. It covered everything. Now the Mexican righted the photo, brushing the surface with his forearm.

"About the property—"

García frowned. His frown said wait. Reed smiled congenially. But he wanted to get in, to get out. He imagined Yates at the entrance to his office, personally scratching the gold inlay of Reed's name from the door. Reed's secretary fired, his parking space surrendered. Say they gave it to Eiger. Say they changed the lock on the executive washroom. If he wanted to crap, he would have to go elsewhere.

"You have been to Miami, señor?"

"No," Reed lied.

García had been to Miami. "Meeamee." The sound, the memory pleased him. He knew a woman there. If Reed wished, he knew a woman here. García moved his hands to show the shape of her breasts.

Vulgar offer, friendly offer. Reed was anxious not to offend. No doubt the Mexican's proposal involved some weird amalgam of racial pride. Reed had read of naval explorers who, out of diplomatic exigency, wed the fat daughters of Polynesian potentates. "Your family?" Reed parried, pointing toward the photo, toward thoughts of home, of kin, of fidelity.

54

García nodded. His family. The man's smile was unmistakable. His love of family was obvious, it was effusive. Reed grinned; he had the Mexican's number. Reed had once spent three days haggling with a man in Hartford over the rights to a patent. The man was a crank. Lab in his basement, his wife held two jobs so he could pursue his genius. He was a throwback, "an inventor," he told anyone who asked. Unmindful of the huge corporate laboratories, the teams of research scientists, the multimillion-dollar government contracts. A man living fifty years in the past. Then, one day, he did it. A half-eaten baloney sandwich at his elbow, and truth came to his cellar. But the man was laconic. He was uninterested in Reed, in what Reed had to offer. It was like knocking at the door of an empty room. Then Reed discovered the collection of ceramic tiles in a corner of the man's basement. The inventor's true passion. The next day, Reed made some calls, arranged for a shipment from Germany. A rare find, most had been destroyed in the bombing of Dresden. The inventor was teary with gratitude. He signed over the rights to the patent, called his wife, told her to quit her jobs. Last Reed heard, the couple lived in Portugal, pursuing indigenous clays.

Now García explained that he and his wife had grown up in the same village. They knew from the earliest days they would be married. Her grandmother had foretold it. The woman was a bruja. "A witch." She made magical brews, she cast chicken bones to the ground and revealed a man's character, his fate. Hers was a life of signs, a life of omens, spells. If a black moth appeared, she became hysterical. There were certain days when she refused to venture outdoors. She never sold her wool to strangers; she had promised her sheep. Her granddaughter and García were destined to be married, she had always known it. All the portents demanded it. They would be happy, they would live long. They would have two children.

They had two children. Here García's smile turned sad. There was something wrong with the boy, something to do with his heart. García did not understand entirely. There were

55

trips to the doctors, tests at the hospital. They had been to specialists in Torreón, in San Luis Potosí. Still, the boy was listless. He seemed to sleep always. He would go two, three days and eat nothing. But the girl. García shook his head. It was as if a light had been trained on his face. "The truth: a man worships his daughter. He cannot help it. The daughter means more than a son finally, more than two sons. You see in her face your face. A bit of the nose, your mouth. Your eyes, yes. The eyes especially, I think. But she is a girl. It is this—this miracle. It is the person in your life you would do anything, anything for. The power daughters have. If they knew, they would ruin us. They would ruin us completely."

"I have a daughter," Reed said simply.

"Then you understand. Look at me, and tell me I do not speak the truth." His expression went wide, challenging.

"No. No, you're right." Reed believed it suddenly, fiercely.

García rose, hitched up his pants. Reed had a daughter; he valued her above all else. This was sufficient. "Come."

The roads were bad, the valley appalling. A place of crumbling shacks, groups of people moving like refugees. The air was acrid, biting, the river foamed white and sudsy at spots. They passed a lone man sitting in the scattered shade of a mesquite tree on the near bank, waiting. Nightfall was seven hours away.

García showed Reed an old warehouse stocked with bald tires, a boarded-up school with a cracked foundation, a barn filled with women at sewing machines. They smiled shyly at Reed. The atmosphere was heavy, the odor of mares locked in a stable. The Mexican showed him an abandoned tannery, hides rotting out back. Failing, ramshackle edifices, decay everywhere. Without exception each would have to be razed, a new structure built. Add a quarter, maybe half a million to the start-up costs.

"What gives?" Reed asked. You could hear his irritation.

García shrugged. They had stopped at a tiny comedor for lunch. García was known there, men looked up and called to him. They located a table near a window, a table haunted by large, angry flies; they blackened the flypaper, strips littered the floor. The sun knifed into the room. Reed was sleepy, his torpor thick. García talked on, his stories involved, his stories interminable. A cat wandered among the tables, lapping at scraps. A fat, laughing woman brought rum, she placed steaming dishes before them. She brought a pitcher of water. García took eating seriously. The role of food in his life could not be overestimated. He ate with broad motions, obvious pleasure in his brow, in the working of his jaws. Reed picked listlessly at the food. He feared the water.

"At home," the Mexican asked, "this is how you eat also?"

Reed considered his plate. A greasy tamale swimming in pork fat stared back. "My stomach," he muttered.

"My wife, she makes the best menudo in the state of Coahuila. Excellent for the stomach. Do you know menudo? Tripe."

"About the property—"

García gestured vaguely. Dismissively. He wanted to talk, to tell Reed of his childhood. The Mexican had grown up outside Monterrey, attended the university at Saltillo. "My father, he wanted me to be a priest, me entiendes? I was determined to be an abogado. A lawyer. But my father, he drew me aside one day. 'Nacho, it is shameful, this of the lawyer. They know nothing but how to cheat a man. Then they act as if they have done him the greatest of favors.' My father grew beans, he had a cow. A man of the land. Twice a year he walked the nine miles into town, got drunk, got into a fight, and slept with a whore. He would come home the next day, go to Father Francisco and confess. Twice a year. No more. He would have done it every weekend, 'But Francisco is an idiot. I cannot stand to speak to him more than twice a year. You, Nacho, you are no idiot. You will be a good priest.' He was certain, you understand.

" 'Papa,' I told him. 'There are good lawyers. There are lawyers for the poor, no? I will be that kind of lawyer.' 'Que va,' he would say. 'And the poor, they cannot be cheated? You will still be a lawyer, only a poor one. No, Nacho. No.'

"He would not be swayed. So his son would not be a priest. But neither would he be a lawyer. 'Better a street sweeper, or the man who burns the trash. Anything.' 'OK, Papa,' I said. 'Then I will be an accountant.' He did not know the word. 'What does this accountant do?' 'He counts money, Papa.' 'That is all?' He could not believe it. 'It is more complicated than that, but yes, that is what he does. He is paid very good.' My papa, he went away, he thought about it. Then he came to me and said, 'Nacho, this accountant: everyone knows what he does?' 'Everyone, Papa. It is his job. All understand this.' He shook his head. A man who grew beans and had a cow, he could not understand. 'And he is paid money to count money?' "

García gathered meat, beans, and chiles into the fold of another tortilla. "He has never believed me. To this day, he thinks I am a lawyer who at least has the decency to lie to his father. The last time I visited him, he said, 'It is good that you are discreet, no?' "

García ate. He ate grandly. His joy in life was indomitable, unquenchable. His father thought he was a lawyer, he had made love to a beautiful woman in Miami. If Reed wanted, he knew a beautiful woman here. His wife made the best menudo in the state of Coahuila.

García took a large bite from his tortilla, the juices potent and oozing. As if to demonstrate the power of his belly, its ability to endure all abuses. "Here, we have no bad stomachs." The Mexican tapped the edge of Reed's dish with his finger. Reed was his guest; he wanted him to savor the food, to savor Mexico. García tapped the dish again. His fingernail was cracked, grime was edged deep into the cuticle. He was a man who offended easily.

Reed cut a bite from the corner of the tamale. The fat was seeping, the aroma cleared great hollows in the area behind his nose. Reed chewed carefully, experimentally.

"It's good," he concluded. García's head bobbed. Of course it was good. Reed put down his knife, his fork, made a temple with his hands. "There must be another site you could show me."

García winked. Sí, he had one more property. But now he leaned across the table, put his head close to Reed's. Reed had asked about García's family, he had listened to García's history. He had drunk García's liquor. It gave the Mexican certain rights.

"This of the property—it is a complicated matter," García began. He reached for Reed's pack on the table, withdrew a cigarette. As if the complexities lay with the cigarette; he meant to reduce them to ash. Reed watched as he lit it. The Mexican said, "Understand, we promise companies low wages, low taxes. The companies, they come. Suddenly, there are jobs. The campesino, he says to his esposa, 'Why do I break my back scratching frijoles from the earth, frijoles I will be unable to sell? Why should I live two miles from my nearest neighbor? Why must I continue to coax milk from a cow that has too little to eat, pork from a pig I cannot afford to feed? Why should I have to walk fifty meters to the well every time I want water?' He hears of a new maquiladora, the company is from Los Estados. He has heard all his life about Los Estados. It is said that we Mexicanos are lucky: to go to heaven, a gringo must die first. Here, we need only swim a river." García beamed. "So the campesino comes, he brings his family. It is a new life, you understand. Sometimes entire villages will move north to the border. Poor villages, people have lived there for centuries, and suddenly, the village is empty. It is no more. As if in a war."

Reed shook his head, fatigue overtaking him. Third World homilies, overtaking him. He had not expected a speech. "I don't see what—"

García leveled the cigarette at Reed. Glowing ember in his face. "So he comes, but he does not make so much money. The food, everything is very expensive. Because of the low taxes, the city cannot build sewer lines, hospitals, houses."

"García—"

The Mexican was not finished. "Yet the world is full of towns that have little. It is full of people who will work for almost nothing. So maybe your company comes, the campesino comes. The shacks go up, the water is bad. He cannot afford the food. The campesino, he cannot stay here. But he has left his home. So maybe the unions, they want better wages, enough so a man can live, can feed his family. Maybe the city, it needs more taxes to build the houses, to provide clean water. They appeal to your company. But there is another town, a town farther along the border, a town halfway around the world, where labor is even cheaper, the governments more accommodating.

"And the campesino? There is but one thing left for him." Here García gestured to the north.

"Entiende," he continued, "in a way, we are like a woman." He smiled. The comparison pleased him. "We are like a woman who wants to keep a man. We have met all the other men. They are hopeless, they are without money. They are without. But this man, he is young, he is handsome. He has money. So we allow him to live in our house, we cook for him, we wash his clothes. In bed, we are obedient; we hope to please him. Maybe he beats our children, maybe he shits in our rivers. But we say nothing. We worry he will grow bored. We worry he will find another place to stay, another woman to sleep with." Voice hard, García's words fell like fists. "A woman who is prettier, who will prove even more obedient. He has destroyed our homes, our children hate us. He has taken everything, left us with nothing. Yet we are desperate to keep him. We will do anything. Anything.

"There is a name for such a woman."

"We're prepared to give certain guarantees—"

The Mexican laughed. Destroyed teeth, laughing. He stabbed the cigarette into the ashtray, thin dying tendril of smoke. Eyes bold suddenly. As if he had Reed's number. "And have you never lied to a woman?"

60

Reed sighed. Reed, the detonator. He wanted to scream, Enough of your bullshit nationalism. At this very moment they're converting my office into an employee kitchen. Microwave oven, vending machines, a twenty-cup coffee maker. García continued to peer closely at Reed, eyes boring through to the back of his head, clear on through to the memories huddled there. To the clogged gutters of Reed's home, to the empty liquor bottles lining the kitchen cupboard, to the angry face of Reed's wife. To the bleak, angry streets, Reed on his knees, in fear for his life. García: a man who would understand the rantings of Reed's neighbor, a man who knew how to dance to the music that filtered up from Reed's street, a man who recognized the smells and tastes that wafted through his back yard. García's eyes seemed to be gathering up Reed's memories, stuffing them inside his own head. As if his head were a tortilla.

Reed stared back at the lined face. The silence calculated, saturated with veiled meanings. It was a face heavy with secrets. The lines were clues. As if Reed might decipher them, see on beyond to the workings of some hidden machinery. Craven machinery, an engine of greed. Reed eased back in his seat. The realization came to him all at once.

Reed said, "How much?"

The Mexican hooted, slapped the tabletop. He liked this gringo. "Think of it as an informal finder's fee. A commission—"

"How much?"

"As long as we understand each other, señor. The details— these matters can wait."

"We understand," Reed said. He snapped his fingers, full of understanding. "Now when can I see the other site?"

García considered. "Tomorrow."

"Tomorrow? But—"

"Tomorrow."

Reed napped. He dreamed a deserted beach, he dreamed a voice in the woods. He dreamed an old house on a hill. The shutters are rusty; their hinges complain. Candles flicker in the windows. He woke to a narrow edge of light at the base of the door. The rhythmic squeak of bedsprings came through the wall. A woman's voice, murmuring, "Momentito, momentito." Mournful, unspeakable sadness. As if Momentito were the name of a dead child.

Reed rolled from bed, dim mind, befuddled mind. Dim room. A room from Eastern Europe, a room from the fifties: a bed, a chest of drawers, a cracked mirror, a black-and-white TV bolted to a stand. Cigarette burns scored the carpet. The phone was dark and bulking. Like his mood.

He should call Andrea, he knew. And say what? They would each be waiting for the other to apologize. Neither would. Their words would be grim, sour, accusatory. They would hang up, hating.

Andrea was the better fighter. The escalations of her facial expressions always disarmed him. He would forget why they were fighting, he would forget what had just been said, what he had been going to say. Fragments of their history would come striding toward him, like people rushing down a city sidewalk. One bore the look on her face when she bent to tie her daughter's shoes; another, the way she smiled on a Christmas morning long ago. The look she wore when testing a broth, licking a stamp, polishing the silver. Her face in summer, her face in the rain, her face at the beginning of a snow. Her face the first time they made love.

They had been seeing each other for two, maybe three weeks. Mysteries still. They went out to dinner—Chinese, he remembered; clumsy, clicking chopsticks—and came back to her apartment. Her roommate was in Atlantic City for the weekend with a man named Dirk. Andrea could have gone, she explained, Dirk had a friend; "But . . ." Reed nodded, awash in gratitude. They sat on the sofa and held hands. They were shy in that way which intimates intimacy. They watched a bad sitcom, they watched the evening news. Nixon's troubles were beginning. There had been an auto accident at a downtown intersection; vandals had struck at a high school in a western suburb. A shot of scrawled obscenities along the door of the gym. During a commercial for snowblowers, they kissed. His shoes came off during the weather, her sweater during sports. A test of the Emergency Broadcast System, and she stood in the blue glow of the TV and reached to unhook her bra. Elbows flaring like wings, shoulders hunched, chest hung with promise. Bombs could have fallen, tornadoes could have raged, aliens could have descended and carted off firstborns; nothing could have budged him. A woman unburdening her breasts: there is a luscious vulnerability to the moment, a woman struggling with hooks, a woman lost in the effort, made awkward by it, heedless to the miracle that she is. Then pale, bountiful flesh swinging free. Like parts of his mind. Reed stared, no friend of Dirk's. "Don't move," he whispered. "Please." He was afraid to touch her; a thumb might ruin her. "Can we continue?" she said finally. She was getting cold. A talk show going in the background, and they chafed elbows, knees, they rubbed asses raw on the carpet. Her face in shadows, a single shudder passed through her eyes. "That was sweet," she said afterward, patting his hand. Sweet is a greeting card, sweet is a niece. Sweet is not taking the last slice of pizza. And here he had just sunk himself to the hilt. "Let's turn it off," he suggested, reaching for the TV. He wanted to try again; he wanted to be unsweet. But the late movie was coming on: "I want to watch." A practical woman, lacking in sentiment. They watched. He stole glimpses at her nudity while Charles Laughton lumbered in the bell tower, one eye spilling low over his cheek, the flying buttresses of Notre Dame flung wide like arms. Then a commercial for a local restaurant, big cuts of beef hogging plates, dwarfing potatoes. He had eaten noodles at dinner. "Are you hungry?" "Shhh," she said, not hungry. Reed frowned, bored by Notre Dame. Andrea's roommate was a plump woman, her life one long diet. The refrigerator would hold nothing beyond raw vegetables, expensive, foreign fruit (Asian pear, pomegranate), and boxes of processed food designed to heighten metabolism and combust calories. Reed heard a sniffle. He looked at her perfect face, wondered if it masked a sinus condition, allergies. If she sneezed, her breasts would riot. "Hankie? he asked, looking for hankie. Onscreen, they were pillorying the monster. It was too late for hankie. Lashes ripped the humped back, harsh licks of sound that materialized on her face as quick, unstanchable tears. Quaking shoulders, trembling breasts—trembling for Laughton. Laughton squat, Laughton bellowing in pain. A woman weeping at a movie. A cliché, he knew. But he envied Quasimodo. Reed imagined it was he who was bellowing, it was he who was in pain. It was he that she was crying for; her breasts trembled for him. It would be years before he confessed he had fallen in love that first time he saw her cry. This admission came in the middle of a squalid argument. Obvious, callow bid for tenderness. Her look, her reply had been cold: "I have never in my life seen that movie."

Now Reed staggered to the bathroom, his bowels loose, his belly precarious. Rum warring with tequila, the memory of pork on his tongue. Reed splashed water on his face, took care to avoid the mirror. Out in the hallway, he could still hear the woman, though the refrain had changed: "Ya, ya, ya." Heat to her tone, like a chant.

The hotel bar consisted of a long bank of wood and three tables. The bartender was an ancient man, a dramatic scar linking his nose with an ear. Reed decided his name was Pepe. Pepe did not seem to mind. Reed said, "Scotch," searched for drama in his situation: a man alone in a foreign city. There should be exotic food, compelling scenery, primitive women. But there was only the roar of a truck out in the street, liquor ignorant of tartan, the barren tables, the ravaged face of the bartender. A sharp, cruel instant to his stomach, like teeth passing through. But, "Pepe, I'll have another."

Reed saw the evening as it spread before him, he knew how

it would go: he would numb himself with drink, stumble up-stairs. The walls would weave, the bed would buck. He would miss his wife. In the morning he would rise and lurch to the bathroom, caress the porcelain, retch into the toilet bowl. But what if tomorrow the Mexican said, Tomorrow. Say he spent the rest of his life here—hot land, hot food—waiting for Gar-cía. Laura would grow, she would marry. At the wedding there would be a moment of silence for her long-lost father. He would have grandkids, cute mites with his eyes, his face. Maybe a Frank II or two. They would never meet him, but they would hear stories about him; their memories would have a special place named Grandpa.

But Laura. The thought righted him, gave him purpose. He paid Pepe and stepped into the street. The sun was going, its heat draining off. His feet sounded convincingly over cobble-stones. Vendors crowed to him as he went by. Children came up to him, faces dark, hands out: por favor, por favor. He crossed a tiny square. The shadows of trees fell over it. In the distance, a smokestack puffed black. The lights were coming on in the streets. In the central plaza, cabs waited at the cor-ners, their engines idling, the drivers turning the pages of the newspaper. Cars hurtled through the intersection, horns fre-quent. The city was preparing for night. One could feel its mounting energy. Women were out in floral dresses, faces made up. The restaurants were flinging open their doors. In the bars, groups of men drank. They were gambling at a table in the corner.

Reed passed a leather shop, a jewelry shop. The entrance to an appliance store, TVs on sale for formidable sums of pesos. A shop specializing in sombreros. A cantina, a barber, a bak-ery. His stomach shifted unexpectedly, a violent compression fathoms deep, churning unlikely juices. He paused at the cor-ner to rest against a door. Zapatos, said the window. If death came now, street urchins would descend, make off with his shoes. He gingerly cradled his stomach, mumbled, "Noth-ing serious," echoing medical knowledge. Trying to make his stomach understand. It had taken Reed months to seek out a doctor, to admit that his belly seemed broken. They would find something incurable, he was sure. Virile acids opening new routes through his bowels. Or a suppurating pocket of cells gone amok. But two thousand dollars in tests—four hundred out-of-pocket—and they had found nothing. Now Reed's stomach screamed, Liars.

He continued up the street, patting his belly as if it were an unruly pet. It soils the carpets, eats armrests, it howls late at night. But dispatch it to the pound and the children will never forgive you. Past a fruit stand, a hammock shop, an ice-cream stand. Past a sign: Regalos. He thought regal, regale, regard. Regatta. He searched his pocket dictionary. Old, dog-eared, a quarter at a flea market years ago. Someone had taken the trouble to star entries to choice anatomical parts. But regalos: gifts, presents, delicacies, delights. Either a gift shop or a bordello. Reed, bold, plunged through the doorway, prepared to retreat should he find heavily rouged women rousing from sleep, readying for a long night's work. He smelled—not stale perfume, the piquant odor of spilled seed—but age, the stink of attics. The light was shallow; it was like standing at the mouth of a cavern. His eyes adjusted to reveal a broad tableau: long tables piled with ashtrays fashioned from volcanic rock, wooden masks, colorful piñatas. Hammocks strung along the walls. Papier-mâché burros.

A woman appeared at the rear of the store. Floor-length dress, she waded up the aisle. Her hips were stout, her nose too quick. The air of a matron, air hinting of incense and yeast. An Anglo. A series of gold bracelets ran the paths of her forearms; an immense, gaudy pendant hung at her throat. Long green stones at her ears.

"I'm looking for a souvenir," he said. "For my daughter."

The woman nodded dreamily, green stones kicking, the clank of gold. Thick affectation to her movements, narcotized, maybe drunk. But then so was he. Reed followed the drifting assembly of metal and minerals down one row of tables, up a second aisle. She showed him opal earrings, glass bookends. A pen-and-pencil set sprouting the Mexican flag. An onyx chess set. A wool serape. "No clothes," Reed told her. A leather purse. A Nativity scene fashioned from soapstone. She detailed the items in a high, nasal voice, thin adenoidal compression. She explained how she came to have each article, commented on its materials, its construction, offered novel applications. The bookends could double as paperweights; the piñatas made good planters; she had a friend who used her serape as a doormat. Reed smiled, wagged his head. It's the thought, etc. But his daughter, his wife would assess the gift, see in it ominous indications of character. On past a teak music box, a pair of sandals, dominoes carved from bone. Reed said, "No," said, "No," again.

"Excuse me," she said. She stopped next to a rocking chair fashioned from mesquite. Reed waited for her jewelry to quit. She was looking up at him, her expression rich with hidden pleasures. "You are a man of unusual inclinations, am I right?"

"I'm not sure."

She was sure. "Follow me."

A rear door revealed a large room. Stove, refrigerator, bed. Her home. More knickknacks lined the shelves, spilled from boxes in the corner, hung from the walls. As if the shop had invaded, it was taking over.

"This came in yesterday."

She showed him a small clay figurine, the surface pocked, grainy. The face was broad, negroid, topped by a headpiece of snakes. It held a round plate in its left hand, the right arm stopped at the elbow. A madman's idea of a waiter. She presented it to him proudly, as if she were offering herself.

"Most of what I have is junk." It seemed a heartfelt admission, a treasured communication of professional secrets.

"And this isn't?"

She frowned. He disappointed her. "I suspect it's authentic."

Authentic. Her features gathered around the word, expelled it with force. She examined his eyes for impact. Reed made an impressed face.

"I can let you have it for fifty."

He had thought to get by with five, maybe ten. "What do you mean: 'authentic'?"

She shrugged, earrings popping. "I could be wrong. But I bought it from Carlos. I trust Carlos. If his brother-in-law made it working in his garage, Carlos tells me. But look at the water damage, the azure tint around the crown. The famous Mayan blue." Reed nodded, as though he had once painted his kitchen Famous Mayan Blue. "Then, too, there's a root trace along the base. By authentic I mean old. I mean maybe Pre-Conquest."

Reed said, "Pre-Conquest."

"In which case, it should be in a museum. But I could be wrong, so I only ask for fifty. Money is only a means for me. Money is not the point. The point is, this could be very old."

"Why's it holding a dish?"

She laughed, tight, ecstatic squint. Head tilted back, quick, pink tongue. Jewelry protesting. Reed laughed with her. They put their heads close: hee hee hee. Then she was not laughing. She moved closer still. Her hair was a nest of curls threatening his nose. She whispered, "Time is round."

"Round." He was whispering.

She moved to an end table and lit a candle. It gave off a sharp odor, the pungency of moldy bread. She indicated the dish with a nail painted a neon purple, a color visible from across the street. "It's a calendar. A repeating cycle; you know, like a wheel." Dreamy voice again, dreaming of wheels. "What goes around, comes around." Hands, nails made circles, bracelets tinkled. Some Mayan glyphs revealed to the day—"to the very hour"—the death of a king, the end of a dynasty, "but not the century." She laughed again, eerie sound, knowledge in her white teeth. Then, "This is a gift? This is a perfect gift. It's maybe very old. It has history."

Reed said, "I'll give you twenty."

She looked pained. "I told you, money is only a means. But I couldn't sell it for twenty. I could never forgive myself. It would dishonor the spirit that's behind the figurine."

"The spirit."

"I don't want to dishonor the spirit. If I sell it for twenty, it could bring me bad luck. It could bring you bad luck. Listen, you think I'm crazy, I can tell. But the Mayans took all of this very seriously. I wouldn't want to offend the Mayan gods. Just in case it's real. That's why I have to ask fifty." She handed him the figurine. Light, fragile, he could have crushed it with his hands. "Have you seen the ruins?" She named a town, far to the south. No, he had never been. "If you go, you'll find some striking similarities with your figurine."

"I haven't agreed to buy it."

This irritated her, made her eyes contract. "I saw you, and I thought: the figurine would be perfect. I have this sense. People come in, I know what they want before they know. You want this. You want this. I'm doing you a favor. If I knew it was real, I'd ask a thousand. I'd ask five thousand. It would be in a museum. But I don't know for sure. Oh, I could take it to a specialist. But half of them are crooked, the other half are afraid to commit. Professional pride. So I ask fifty. But less than fifty—it wouldn't be fair. It wouldn't be fair to me, it wouldn't be fair to you. You'd pay twenty, and then say your plane crashes tomorrow. Think how I'd feel."

Reed said, "Thirty."

"No. No, no, no. I'm sorry. It's not a matter of money. We're talking metaphysics." The word swelled her eyes. "We're talking retribution. What goes around, comes around. I know, I know: you think I'm a nut."

Reed thought her a nut, a crank. He thought her crazy. Yet he had read his share of tales in which a man dies penniless, unaware that the print he bought at a yard sale forty years ago—he wanted the frame for one of his execrable watercolors of Mount Rushmore—was a Degas; or a soda machine dispenses a nickel in change to a boy, but the buffalo has somehow grown a fifth leg, one of only thirty-eight minted before the pressman woke; or an old woman, her close friends call her Minnie, discovers the vase she has been using for a chamber pot once adorned the palaces of the Khans. Undeserved riches, as if the universe were really on your side after all. Such lore populates the casinos, the churches. Then, too, the figurine intrigued. Reed tried to guess at the imagination behind it. A potent imagination. Say it was a fraud. Carlos's brother-in-law would still be a man you would chase from your porch with an ax. But its very ugliness awed, suggesting a night long ago: the moon is bold, it illuminates prone cannibals, bones thrust through their septums, quaking with fear; even the priestess—she is naked—prostrates herself before an icon that will travel a millennium for the sole purpose of squatting contentedly on the mantel of Reed's fireplace. He liked the idea of the figurine more than he liked the figurine. In the end, he reached for his wallet.

She smiled, incandescent teeth at the front of her face, quivering jewel at her throat. "Call me Eve."

Though her name was Mabel Slotsky, she explained a moment later. She was a woman who moved in mystery, a woman who counted on it. He had no idea of her life, he would never be able to guess at it. Reed shook his head. He had no idea. She told him. A native of New Jersey, she had been married twice. Both men were named Donald. She thought this significant. She had married Donald-One after her sophomore year in college. The man dealt in pork futures, obsessed with the destiny of bacon. They had a tennis court, a swimming pool, a Guatemalan maid. But Donald-One left her for his dermatologist. "He had moles. A few on his arms, some on his back, a couple up the crack of his ass. Like it mattered. 'Donald,' I'd say. 'It doesn't matter.' But he'd go, she had this zapper. It glowed blue, like one of those outdoor lights that zaps bugs. Can you see it? I could see it all right: white-jacketed woman, this contraption fizzing in her hand, having at my husband.

70

She zapped his moles for months. Listen: nobody has that many moles. Nobody.

"He left me some money, but not enough. For starters, my analyst was charging eighty bucks a session. I worked in a card shop for a while, I worked in a beauty salon. It was humiliating. I'd had two years at Vassar, a maid named Luchita. My backhand was devastating. I haven't played tennis in twenty years. But I still do my own hair, I do my own nails." She fluffed her curls, displayed fierce fingers. "Then I met Donald-Two. A kind man, but he had a bad heart. We'd make love, but he was afraid to get too excited. It oppressed me. It oppressed my sexuality. He was always saying, 'Wait, wait.' We'd have to stop and wait. Then when it was over, he'd jump out of bed. 'That was close. I could feel It coming on bad. It almost got me.' He called it It. Death, I mean. He'd say, 'It hung around me all day. I could feel It lurking outside the door. Driving home, it was like It was in the trunk. It's out there right now. I can feel It. I can feel It.' He was a gentle man—a good man. But it wasn't his heart, it was a roast-beef sandwich in a New York deli. This was years ago. Heimlich could have been a German physicist.

"I was thirty-nine. Twice married, no kids. Donald-Two left me a small insurance policy. I enrolled in school. The program in hotel and restaurant management at City College. I had this dream: a little place on the coast, these cottages painted aquamarine. I even had a name: The Waves Motel. I was going to have the name imprinted on matches, on towels, on ashtrays. A big blue sign, the W like these waves. I could see it. I could see it all." She made wavy motions with her hands. "But while at City College, I studied some other things. I studied history and philosophy. I studied the arts. There was this one professor, she saved my life. She made me understand the patriarchal nature of human existence. Patriarchy is everywhere. You don't believe me, but it is."

Reed said, "I—"

"So I gave up on hotel management. A very patriarchal discipline. I dropped out of school, I went out to the West Coast. I was wandering. I was in search. Then I met Taru Baba Rass. His name used to be Larry Kirchner. He's from Toledo, but he studied in India. He opened my eyes to more things. Herbs, crystals, feeling. Feelings. Things that the patriarchy denies us. He saved my life. Taru Baba—he's casual like that, he doesn't stand on ceremony. 'Call me Taru Baba,' he told us—was the most unpatriarchal person I ever met. And he was a man. I remember one time, we were sitting in the meditation room, meditating. And Taru Baba said, 'Pain is the great teacher. Pain is poignant.' We were all hushed. We were listening. The man had studied in India. 'Pain,' he said, 'is grace.' It was like a realization. It was like he'd opened my eyes. All my pain, all my suffering—Donald-One, Donald-Two; I came from a dysfunctional family, my father never told me I was pretty—it was a teacher. It was poignant. I was in a state of grace, I'd been in a state of grace all along and I'd never known it. I ran out into the street when I realized this. What do you think I saw?" Her eyes glowed with rich hashish heat, the memory baking inside them.

Reed said, "I—"

"I saw a cop beating his horse. This was in San Francisco, where cops sometimes ride horses. But this cop, he was beating his horse. Pain. I threw my arms around the horse's neck." She waited for the meaning of what she was saying to sink in. "Like Nietzsche. Like Nietzsche, just before he collapsed. Just before he went crazy. But I didn't go crazy; I went to Taos.

"In Taos I discovered I was a lesbian. Just for a little while. I was doing mushrooms then, I was doing peyote. I stayed away from cocaine. It's a very patriarchal drug. But Adam— that was my lover, she gave me my name—Adam and I, we would talk. All night long, we would talk. She was a very special woman. She saved my life. Then, toward morning, we'd eat a button of peyote. Five minutes later—I can tell you this, can't I? I mean, I feel this communal space here, this shared sense with you—five minutes later, I was ready to shove my face between her legs. Ten years ago, I couldn't admit that. But ten years ago, I was pre-orgasmic. I'm not now. I'm not now. I orgasm fine. It's like the top of my head comes off. But ten years ago, I was in a serious state of denial. Adam sells real estate in Marin County now, she's married to a guy named Ethan. But that's a whole other story. You don't want to get me started on that. Believe me, you don't want to get me started on that. But it was about this time that I began what I call my researches. My researches into the nature of things. Into the nature of reality. I read. I read everything. I hitchhiked everywhere. I was trying to go back, to go back to the very beginnings. I became fascinated by Native American cultures. They knew all about the beginnings of everything. The Indian way of life is very complicated. Very few people understand it. I understand it. I studied the Apache, the Hopi, the Navajo. I came down here and studied the Maya, the Aztecs. I came to some conclusions. I wrote it all down. No publisher would touch it. Publishing is very patriarchal. I published it with my own money. I'm proud of that. In a patriarchal world, whatever gets published is shit, unless you pay for it yourself. That's how you know you're not part of the patriarchy: you pay for it yourself. Here—" She retrieved a book from a large crate holding several hundred copies, and handed it to Reed. The cover was cheap vellum, the binding of glue; the spine read, *Eve Speaks.* "In this book, I prove matriarchy underlies all civilization. Men don't know it, they try to deny it. Their denial is awesome." She regarded Reed with pity. "But I prove it. I prove it completely. I use the Aztecs as my case study. Take the practice of human sacrifice. Blood everywhere. They once sacrificed eighty thousand people at a public coronation. Eighty thousand. I show how all this blood was really a menstrual thing. Except it was all twisted, the way they did it. What I call the shadow side. It's very complicated, but believe me: it was all about menstruation. It was very female. No publisher would touch it. Publishing is so patriarchal you wouldn't believe it. But I proved my point. I proved it exactly. Look: Cortez arrives with four hundred men and defeats an empire of twenty-five million. How did he do it? Nobody knows. I know. I know."

Reed said, "I—"

"Exactly. Montezuma was a very patriarchal guy. You can keep that. No, I insist. Keep it."

Reed felt winded, as if he had been doing all the talking. He held the book in one hand, the figurine in the other. She edged forward a bit, curls hovering in his face. "I feel a bond developing here," she said. Her voice had grown husky. "Do you feel it? I feel it. I have an idea. I think we should honor these feelings. Why don't you come over tomorrow night, I'll make you dinner. We can talk more about the figurine. We can talk more about me. I'm a vegetarian. I hope you like vegetarian food. Though sometimes I cheat. Just a little."

"I don't know that I'll still be in town."

"Please. Try to make it. I'll be expecting you. I don't want to dishonor what's going on here. Dishonor brings more dishonor."

She saw his hesitation, she seemed to wilt in the gathering silence. She had sold him a possibly authentic statue, given him a copy of her book, offered to break bread with him. She had told him of her life. But he responded with silence, threatening her with dishonor.

"Listen," she whispered, "I'm no simpleton." As if perhaps she were, as if perhaps she knew that she was and yet this knowledge made her not a simpleton, gave her a sudden dignity. "I know I talk too much, I know I have these strange ideas. But I'm no simpleton."

"Of course not." Reed felt bad. Decline dinner, and she would be a simpleton. "What time?"

"Good," she said. "Good." Then she kissed him. The movement was abrupt. She tasted of onions. Reeds lips were confused eels. Liver and onions. Sometimes she cheated. "Oh," she said. The sound was breathless.

Reed stepped back. Her face was open, expectant. Round

74

face, nose too small, lips slight. Hers was a face that transformed itself fully in the second after a kiss, revealing secret needs, dire emotional hungers. Three months with her and your life would be in ruins.

He said, "It's not that way."

She said, "But it's always that way."

He clutched the figurine to his chest as if it were a shield. "I should go."

"I've frightened you." She smiled. Sadly, it seemed. Sad for him.

"I really should go."

She looked up, her eyes swimming. "Tomorrow, then. Are you a vegetarian? Maybe I'll cheat on the vegetarian thing, just a little. Good. Good, good. Don't forget your book."

The bartender rose when Reed appeared in the foyer of the hotel. "Señor," he said. He hobbled forward. He had been waiting. The old man smelled of rum. The scar was like a crack in his face. "My name is Umberto." He wanted Reed to know.

"Umberto," Reed repeated.

The old man was from a tiny village, a village without running water, without electricity. He had moved to the city decades ago to make his fortune. He still had friends in the village, he had family there. He cut pictures from magazines and included them with his letters: this is my house, this is my car, this is my garden. See the size of the mangoes this year.

Up in his room, Reed reached for the phone. The international operator was slow to understand. Yet he longed to talk to Andrea. He needed to talk to her. The encounter with Eve made him yearn for a solid woman, a practical woman. Reed envied his wife these qualities—he secretly coveted them. A man, he had once read, seeks in a spouse one who is stronger; then he spends his life trying to prove her weak.

"It's me." He sagged against the wall, wishing it were she.

"Hi." Her tone was guarded. She still smarted from the fight. She still smarted from the last few years.

"How's Laura?" he tried.

"Fine. I'm fine, too."

And that was how it went. She asked about the flight, about Mexico. He asked about the weather. They were speaking in that code peculiar to trying marriages. All meaning lay in the silences, in the spaces between words.

"I miss you," he ventured toward the end.

"I miss you." It sounded like a benediction.

They hung up. Reed stared at the figurine sitting on the dresser. The mirror doubled it, doubled its crudeness. Made it ridiculous. Not a thing for a daughter, he realized. Authentic. Maybe not. Maybe so. Maybe he no longer cared. The day had gone on too long. He turned on the TV, lay on the bed. A woman with a mustache yammered at him in Spanish. He got up, hefted the figurine in his hand. He examined the rough surface, considered the faint bluish tint, discovered the root trace that Eve had spoken of. The strong, flat features. He leaned close and studied the markings on the calendar. They seemed random, inconsequential. In the end, a waiter. He lay on the bed with the book in his hands. "To Donald." The book began: "The ancient, tragic, proud, deeply suffering, noble empire of the Aztecs, because that was their name . . ." Through the walls he heard, Momentito, momentito. He rose again, changed TV channels. They were playing soccer in Spain.

Andrea had come home from work to discover a van blocking the drive, a mural painted along broad doors: a fried egg, a trident, a scantily clad woman. She searched for meaning, concluded only that her legs were better. She continued on down the street, parking in the next block. Boys at the corner hooted as she walked past, eyes chasing her home. Her heels going clickety-click. Inside, the sound of Laura's stereo thumped through the ceiling. Crashing bass, mayhem, strangled male voice. Andrea turned on the radio, poured herself a glass of wine. A state senator had been sentenced to two years in jail, the firefighters' union had voted to strike, everyone wanted to know what the president knew and when. A shooting in the streets of Boston. A man named Quinto Bernal had been stopped for expired tags. Now he was dead. On the radio, a police officer promised suspensions, an internal investigation. The Patriots had lost again.

And then Reed had phoned. The exchange unsettled her. True, she missed him. Yet she often felt that her marriage lay at the intersection of unpromising pathways, worn trails that no longer took her where she wanted to go.

There is a kind of woman who knows herself, who understands herself entirely. Andrea's idea of herself had been forged early. She had worshipped her grandfather. His photo still sat on her dresser. Short, pale, wiry. She had his chin. As a boy of fourteen, he took part in the Easter Rising. The kitchens of her childhood smelled of corned beef, of boiled cabbage. His voice floated amid these odors, gave them force. "Back in '16" replaced "Once upon a time." When the rebellion was put down, he was sentenced to hang. He spent nine months in a Dublin jail, waiting for death. Over dinner, she heard stories of rats, moldy food, of festering boils; tales of men who were manacled and hung from their wrists until their fingers went blue, then split open, the blood running down their arms, drying on their hands. "And then, a morning in January," her grandfather would continue, voice hushed, eyes narrowed, eyes remembering. A morning in January: a morning when wicked queens die, frogs turn into princes; the wolf falls under the ax. The day still dark, her grandfather had been hustled from jail and tossed into the back of a truck. He recalled the bitter cold, the rough hands of his jailers. His eyes wild, sharp for sight of the gallows. He asked for a priest. The guard shook his head. No priest. Her grandfather begged. Without a priest, he would spend eternity in limbo. But the truck stopped at the wharf. He was going to America instead. They put him in the hold of a ship with a bunch of Poles. They sailed for five weeks. "Jail smelled better." As the boat moved into New York Harbor, he jumped ship. Ellis Island, Statue of Liberty, bring me your tired, your poor, etc. But he had read his Dickens. A minor, he feared the orphanage. Freezing waters, he was swimming for his life. A light shot from the boat, flashed over choppy waves. Voices screaming in Polish. "My name ain't Wesnieski," he screamed back. Her grandfather always smiled at this point in the story, his gums raw, babylike, surrounded by the deep, rucked crevasses of his face. Not Wesnieski. He made his way to Boston where he got a job at the pier. Lobster, crab, the great nets teeming with haddock and scrod. He struck her that Friday he discovered her eating a hot dog.

"Promise me you won't marry a Protestant," he demanded late in life. She had already met Reed; they had been to bed. They had talked of marriage. But her grandfather was old, eyes going. He was dying. She promised. She would never forgive Reed, never. "And always, fish on Fridays," her grandfather added. "Screw the Pope."

Andrea reached for the bottle of wine. Upstairs, the stereo urged promiscuity, cop-killing, drug-induced catatonia. "Laura," she called. "Turn it down. Mother is trying to think."

Mother is trying to think. There are Catholics burdened by a surfeit of guilt, their sense of woe great. Obsessed with stigmata, the Book of Revelation, forty days in the desert only to meet the devil. And then there are those who remember the manger, the star, the lowing animals, the myrrh. One could be sentenced to hang, quartered with unwashed Poles, one could swim the icy waters of New York Harbor—but there would be warm meals to come, spring walks, there would be family, home, steam on the kitchen window. One could be crowned with thorns, pinioned to crossbeams, made to drink vinegar; and three days later the stone would roll away, the ascension would begin. One trusts in the benevolence of all things, it frames the very curvature of space.

Her grandfather died, she married Reed. But even now, Fri-

78

days saw flounder, mackerel, whiting. She still confessed her broken promise weekly: "Forgive me, Father . . ." The priests all knew the tale, she had relayed it countless times. Modern priests, liberal priests. They understood her lie to her grandfather; they understood her marriage to a Protestant; they understood her wish to supply her daughter with contraceptives. They accepted every indiscretion, every confession. She went away cleansed, twenty Hail Marys on her tongue. No sin seemed too big, no deed too black.

She'd had opportunities, of course. A visiting director from a theater company in Upstate New York. He had once been reviewed in the *Times*. It was the highlight of his life. A dress rehearsal for *Streetcar,* and he asked her out for coffee. A tiny cafe, beard and sunglasses strumming a guitar in the corner. The director was unlucky with women, he confided to her. He had been devastated by them, humiliated in cruel ways. He knew she was different; he could tell. No, she assured him, she wasn't. There was that man who sat behind her in Mass every Sunday for two months. She could feel the weight of his presence, she could smell his cologne. Like piney woods. In the parking lot, they stopped to talk of the sermon, of God, of Abraham and Isaac. Harmless talk. Abraham ultimately harmless. A surgeon, he told her. Tall, graying at the temples; he had kind eyes, hands that saved. The following Sunday, the man sat next to her. He smiled, she smiled. During the Eucharist, she saw that he had opened his fly. She began attending the seven o'clock Mass. There was the bridge tournament where she held a winning hand, a grand slam in the making. But then East, a short, intense man—he played at the Master level—ran his hand up her dress. Quick, fleeting, fingers on nylon. "Dummy," she shrieked, heaving the cards in his face. There was Evans, Evans of manufacturing. In the end, an imbecile. When he tried to kiss her, she pushed him away. But women loved him, he explained, they never refused him. She was no different; he could tell. No, she assured him, she was.

Men of standing, educated men; men of some means. Men

like her husband. She could have had any one of them. She could have had them all. But there is one kind of woman, and then there is another. She knew which she was. As if the institution of marriage had first been conceived in order to pacify women like her. It seemed she could no more commit adultery than she could design a jet engine.

Yet there come singular moments when we recognize some new part of ourselves, where we define ourselves even further.

Five months earlier. No, six. She had been searching for goose, not love. A friend had told her about a shop in the North End. The choicest cuts of meat, the Italian sausages were the best on the East coast. The butcher worked in the back, behind a pane of glass. You could watch. She watched. He hoisted a large, gleaming cleaver. It fell like fate. Chicken necks, layers of fat, gristle and bone tossed to the floor. A plain man, a simple man. His shoes were scuffed, he drank cheap wine. Unlit stogie jammed into his mouth. Like a part of his face, as important as his ears. He passed mirrors without a glance. He worked swiftly, there was no hesitation. He did not fear the blade, severed fingers, salmonella, trichinosis. Thought was like a bad habit he had broken long ago.

"A goose," she told the man at the counter. "I'll have to check," he said. She waited a full ten minutes. A line formed behind her. The butcher emerged finally, the counterman close behind him, anger flashing in their eyes.

"The goose is no good today," the butcher told her. He spoke as if her desire for fowl had spoiled the pink meat. Blood glistened wetly on his smock.

"The goose is fine." It was the counterman. His father had opened the store thirty years earlier. Reputation is everything. Businesses thrive, they fail, all because of what Cousin Beatrice thought of the chops. Andrea could hear the other customers behind her, their interest piqued by the unfolding drama.

The butcher shook his head no. He found matches in his pocket, lit a cigar. White, wafting, stinky. The counterman blanched. "I recommend the veal. Or the lamb," the butcher

80

explained. "But the goose is roadkill." He stared at her, eyes unblinking, eyes weighing her.

"The veal, then."

The butcher disappeared. The counterman wore his irritation like a poorly tailored coat. A package wrapped in white paper slid from a slotted door. The counterman stabbed the cash register with arched fingers. "I have the best goose in the city."

She held the packet as if it were a frightened child. The butcher continued working in the back. Lightning arc of cleaver, dull slaps tearing meat.

The counterman said, "I have never, ever gotten complaints about my goose."

She said, "I'm sorry."

She made osso buco. Reed, even Laura complimented her. She nodded, vindicated. "I've discovered a new place."

She went back the following week. The butcher was dressing a rabbit. Skin, head, viscera going glop glop to the floor.

"What's good today?" she asked the counterman.

He remembered her. "Everything," he said. "Everything is good."

The butcher appeared. He wiped his hands on his smock. Massive hands, massive chest. Cold root of tobacco growing in the center of his face. The hair on his arms curled thick and dark. Fingers stained brown, the pores in his nose unmistakable. "The ham," he announced.

"The ham?" She could not decide. "I was thinking of making a roast."

"The ham."

She shopped there on through the spring, all through the summer. Venison, squab, free-range chickens. "We're going to the Cape," she told him at the end of June. "My husband is going to be offered a job. A wonderful opportunity. Though they're going to have to make it worth his while." She stopped. She had talked too much, she had embarrassed herself. The butcher merely grunted, said, "The spareribs are best today." As though he cared only about meat, fat, feathers, intestines. But the next week: "And how was the Cape?" "It rained. Is the foie gras good?" She returned to the store again and again. She had come to depend on his recommendations, to trust him completely. They dictated her menus. He would emerge from the back as soon as she walked through the door, wiping blood from his hands. His teeth were bad, in smiling he took care not to reveal them. His fingers were bare.

She served braised breast of duck, broiled quail in a mustard sauce, pork-loin medallions. She unwrapped a full rack of lamb, discovered ashes dusting the ribs. She closed her eyes, shuddered, licked them off. Cold, cruel meat; bitter, rusty taste of blood. That evening Reed settled back, belly full, and said, "Can't we sometimes have just a hamburger?"

"A hamburger." It felt like a slap.

"You know." He laughed, even her daughter laughed. "Bun here, bun there." He was doing a pantomime.

The next day she drove downtown, blinking through her anger. The butcher emerged from the back, smiling. "Hamburger." She would not meet his eyes.

"Hamburger?"

"My husband."

"Ah." Her husband. This explained everything. Her husband, the Philistine, lover of ground chuck. The butcher winked at her then, made like a co-conspirator.

He reappeared with the package. "No charge," he told the counterman.

"No—" she tried.

"Broil these," he went on. "But first, sear them for a minute in lemon butter."

"Lemon butter."

"Your husband will love it."

Upstairs, Laura had turned off her stereo. Downstairs, her mother now poured the last of the wine. Hints of plum, of walnut; it sheeted beautifully, like a bolt of silk.

It had been a week later, maybe three. She could no longer

remember. Driving down the street, she saw him at the corner. He walked slowly, his head low and weaving. Sloping shoulders, heavy, squat trunk. The gait of Saxon serfs. Overhead, clouds were gathering, full of intimations. She found herself following him from a few blocks back, pausing at stoplights, straining to see which way he had turned. Her mouth was dry. A light autumn rain started in. The windshield wipers ticked. At any moment, she would turn around, head home. He stopped at a newsstand. She watched as he laughed at something the vendor said. He walked the same route every day. He was recognized on the street, he was a fixture of the city. He bought a newspaper, he bought a cigar. The car behind her honked. He was scanning the front page, opening to the inside pages. The vendor gestured, spoke. The car honked again. She put her car into gear, eased forward. At the corner, she turned. She went down the block and turned again. To her left, the road that would take her home. She turned right. She shook her head, laughing at her mistake. Rocking, chortling; silly me. She turned right again. She would circle the block, head home. The sky broke open, heaving great gusts of water. But the vendor was alone, he was covering his newspapers with a plastic tarp. She slowed, braked, head cocked, eyes urgent, eyes ranging up and down the street. The passenger door opened. He slid into the seat.

"I live up on Doyle Street," he announced. "About eight blocks."

They drove in silence. To speak would break the spell. He was enormous. He seemed to fill the car, to displace all the air. She could not breathe. A man accustomed to large spaces, to solid objects. A man who moved unthinkingly through the world, certain questions never occurred to him.

Doyle Street. Ancient building, faded brick, vines groping at its eaves. The home of students, cafeteria workers, undocumented Portuguese eight to a room. She turned to him, a face trying to smile. "Well—"

"You can park right there."

She might have made her apologies, objected politely. She might have fled. Instead she parked right there. He lived on the third floor. Children played on the stairs. The smell of curry in the hallway. A single room, a kitchen nook in one corner, a fold-out sofa, a chair. A radio on the table. Bare walls. Grime crusted black around the burners of the stove. Ashtray the size of a soup tureen, crowded with cold brown thumbs. The refrigerator came to her hip. She stood in the middle of the room, paralyzed by the future. Though she could have been anyone, she reminded herself; she could have been a neighbor borrowing a cup of sugar, a woman collecting for cancer research. He took off his jacket. The cigar slipped from the pocket, dropped to the floor. She stared at it as if it were a finger leveled in accusation. He took off his shirt. She clutched the collar of her coat close. He had the shoulders, the chest of an ironworker. There was blood beneath his fingernails. Cancer research would have fled. He came to her, wrapped her in his arms. The raw, sodden odor of flesh, of inner organs enveloped her. She was limp, she was nuzzling his neck. Then they were kissing. Impossible, she knew. She had a husband, she had a daughter. Her grandfather had taken part in the Easter Rising. There was one kind of woman, and then there was another. But her mouth was open, hungry, feasting. Her tongue in search. She made thin mewing sounds, the sounds heard at a wake. She kicked off her shoes. They clattered in a corner. Big paws spanned her back. He was like a large dog, a leaping animal. There had been dogs that one summer in Rome, snarling packs of them, they stole bread from the tables. A restaurant within sight of the Vatican, the wine as good as any she had ever had. Forty cents a liter. It was what Reed would remember later. That afternoon, they made love on the balcony of their hotel. The pigeons gathered along the railing to watch. North of Naples, their rented car broke down, twenty kilometers from the nearest town. In the distance, a lone farmhouse, the setting sun. They made their way through an olive grove, the hills steep and terraced. The odor like something you only read about. An older couple put them up. They spoke no English. They spoke with their faces, with the food they offered, the bed they gave them. They dined on bread dipped in olive oil, pasta, beans. The old man had known Gramsci, he had visited him in his cell.

"The bathroom," she heard herself say. "Please."

"In there."

Mildew on the tiles, the fixtures brown with rust. She sat on the toilet seat and turned on the tap. She heard the rustle of linen. She wondered if he was undressing, if she should be undressing. Though maybe he wasn't. Then she would have to parade across the room before a clothed man, put on a show. Though if she didn't, he would undress her himself. Big hands moving over her, shucking off her clothes. She would cling to him as her blouse opened, at the rasp of her stockings. There was a run in her left one. Clinging like a woman hanging on, a woman who fears falling. She imagined him above her, crawling over her, moving sideways like a crab, like a mountaineer scaling a cliff. She would be small next to him, she would barely exist. He would be reaching into the very middle of her. Like sex in books. He would break her in half. He would finish with a grunt, a man moving a piano. She would feel bludgeoned, a fighter in the later rounds. Staggering, faltering, the howls of the crowd. How many fingers. She had only wanted a goose.

It seemed a dream. But then so does life. Sitting on the toilet, she found herself rehearsing what she would say to the priest, what she would say to her husband. Or should she wait to be found out. Not by God—God would forgive her, her faith was that strong—but by Reed. Should she wait for him to sit her down in the living room, to position himself next to the fireplace. A pose he would have seen on TV. Should she wait for him to sit up in bed suddenly, to accuse her, to rage at her. He would know, he would know everything. Some subtle shift in the way she screwed, nuances evident to a loving husband. She saw herself admitting everything, her grief scalding. She would wail, collapse at his feet, grope for his legs, scream, "I've debased myself in every way." She felt like a tragic figure, a character in a play—covert, metaphysical themes. Few among the audience truly comprehend.

Fear had arrived then, like a late train. Say Frank never sat her down. Say he never raged. Say he had no idea. But of course he would. He would have to. She would be another kind of woman entirely: her voice, her walk, her face. But say he failed to see it. He was a man who missed much. If asked, she would have explained that it was Hungarian food that they had eaten that first night, not a chopstick in the house. Her roommate was in Chicago with a man named Clark. They had watched a documentary on big-game poaching in Africa. She had wept for the caving elephant. True, her husband could confuse medieval France with modern Namibia, bells with ivory, waddling Laughton with a felled pachyderm. But this was not Namibia. Another had put his mouth on her, was about to make her warble into a pillow. Where she had once been a faithful wife, a dutiful mate, she was about to become a fucker of butchers. Of course he would know. One expects such a husband. One demands it. But say he didn't. Say he said nothing; he understood nothing. Say there was only the deepening air of defeat through which he moved, his moods as he stood at the window, a glass in his hand. A preoccupied stranger, a man you pass on the street, a man you would never think to speak to. This would be the greater betrayal. It was not the consequences she feared, but their absence. As if life might be lawless in the end.

She turned off the tap, stepped from the bathroom. The butcher had opened the sofa. He was lying on the bed, hands behind his head. Tangled shrub of hair. It lolled like an immense vine, shifting with a discrete tropism. She told herself not to look.

"I'm sorry," she whispered. "I have to go."

He sat up in bed. His face held genuine disappointment. "Your husband," he muttered.

"My husband." There are two, maybe three ideas that guide a life. Then, "You wouldn't understand."

He climbed up from the bed, went to the sink, and drew a glass of water. He drank, throat fluttering. It gave her a chance to look. She looked. He had a scar on his thigh, another along his collarbone. His genitals were heavy, like aboriginal carvings. He began talking. Spare details, the facts of his history. He had been in the infantry in Vietnam. He had worked on an oil rig in Louisiana, as a smoke jumper in Montana. She listened politely; she had spoiled his seduction. He talked on. She nodded, looking for her shoes. He had stuttered as a boy. His father had worked as a railroad lineman. He had a wife he did not know where.

She paused, shoe in hand, incredulous. "What do you mean?"

He spoke slowly, without inflection. He had come home one afternoon to find the house spotless. He had lived in a house then, he had a yard, a place for grilling meat in the back. He roamed rooms, calling his wife's name. The stove gleamed, the floors had been waxed, the clothes folded neatly in drawers. He sat, read the newspaper, drank a beer. The sun went down, he watched the evening news. For dinner he ate a peanut butter sandwich. At ten, he called one of her friends, then another. No one had seen her, she had mentioned nothing to them. At midnight, he turned on the porch light and went to bed. He woke, went to work, he came home. The porch light was still burning. She had disappeared. He called the police. The sergeant sounded bored, he heard such stories all the time. "You sure you didn't fight?" But they had not fought. They hardly ever fought. In fact, in recent weeks she had seemed happy, really happy. Happier than he had ever seen her. He said, "I don't know when I've ever seen her happier." There was silence on the other end of the line. He waited, listening to the labored breathing of the cop. She might come bursting through the door at any moment, full of explanations, her apology genuine, credible. His understanding, his relief would be quick. He would hang up the phone, they would embrace. He said it again, as if to seal its truth: "I've never seen her happier."

"Exactly," the sergeant murmured. He had seen certain things, unspeakable things. If the general public only knew.

"I don't think I want to hear this," Andrea decided.

The butcher shrugged. He had begun, he was going to finish. His shrug said, You owe me this.

It was as if his wife had never existed. She had no family; her friends, her co-workers knew nothing. But there was her photograph on the nightstand, there were his dreams filled with her. He hired a private detective. Two hundred dollars a day, plus expenses. But there was not a clue. There was nothing. He became a man who lives alone, a man who eats standing at the kitchen sink.

"Please, stop it," Andrea said.

Eighteen months later, a phone call. He could not believe it at first, he refused to believe it. He was sure she was dead, the victim of an accident, her body long since having decomposed at the side of a highway five minutes from home. But it was she. She told him things only she could know, things about themselves, about their lives together. That waterfall in Newfoundland. The star-shaped birthmark above her left breast. The first meal she ever cooked for him; how she had burned the chicken. What he had said upon learning of the death of his mother. He was reeling now, he was afraid to believe her. He had no choice but to believe her. She told him she was living out West, she would not say where. She told him each day was the same as the one before, the one that followed: mornings she rose, she had a goat that she fed, she was raising spinach and cauliflower in her garden. The snow came early, it left late; the sunsets made her weep.

"There's someone else," he had insisted. His wife swore to him: there was no one else. He called her a liar, a cheat. "Whore," he screamed into the phone. There had to be someone else. There had to be something. One did not just up and disappear; they had been married eight years. What of their life together? "What about us?" There had to be a reason, there had to be twenty reasons, each more compelling than the last. He had begged: "There has to be a reason."

"No. Stop it," Andrea moaned. She was collecting her purse, her car keys. "Stop it, damn you."

His wife had spoken slowly, her patience unending, her voice even. She spoke as if to a child, to a man who has suffered some head injury, to one who would never understand, who was incapable of understanding. She had told him already, she was trying to explain: her days were identical, each the same as the one before, the one that followed. Mornings she rose, she had a goat that she fed, she was raising spinach and cauliflower in her garden.

Andrea had reached for the doorknob then. Naked, he followed her out into the hallway. She fled down the stairs. He was shouting, she could hear him:

"The snow came early, it left late. The sunsets made her weep."

Now Andrea drained the last of her wine. The hour was late. She checked the locks, turned out the lights. She made her way slowly up the stairs, weaving against the banister. In the bedroom, she undressed. Her fingers were clumsy, she stumbled against the bedpost, the walls of her room. Her toothbrush was a weight. The bed seemed too big, a field that stretches on too long, a place in which one could lose oneself, never to be found. She lay, the walls shifting with the wine.

She touched herself gingerly, tentatively in the darkness. Then her fingers were moving quickly, tendons flexing. She rolled onto her stomach, rode the heel of her palm. Her sounds were muffled, restrained; she was like an escapee who fears recapture. She felt old suddenly, a worn-out woman who diddles herself in the solitude of her bedroom, summoning memories with the jerking spasms of her hand. Her hand more real than the memories finally.

Down the hallway, Laura was doing the same. Except she was standing before a mirror, the lights high, her eyes tight, searching; her face pinched as a gargoyle's. She was learning what the boys would see.

Three

Reed adhered stubbornly to the myth of his own insomnia. Such men assail auto mechanics, bank tellers, and the woman at the dry cleaners with tales of fitful nights. Insomniacs struck him as a noble breed, restless, awake with vision; they heard the snores of others. In truth, Reed usually managed a solid nine hours a night. But perception is everything. Then, too, his father had died in his sleep. For Reed, this fact bore moral freight; a good son would never again lay his head on a pillow.

The man had farmed for forty-three years. His father knew each fencepost, every shift in terrain. The ravine to the south, the steep rise to the east, the north pasture. They were like the contours of his mind. In the end, he lost everything, as in those tales of moral woe we use to edify our children. But Reed's father was no Job; he was a large man who, when cows bit, bit back. Collapsing crop prices, spiraling interest rates ambushed him late in life. His father had known the banker for years; he had stabled Chet Morgan's horses, he had helped him dig out during the blizzard of '59. "I'm sorry—" Chet Morgan began, the foreclosure papers in his hand. "Shame," his father muttered. He would not let Chet Morgan finish, he was turning away already. "Shame on you." During the bank auction, his father stood off to one side and watched his friends buy his tractor, his milking machine, his combine. The last time Reed ever saw his father drunk. The man lived another five years, angry at capitalism. Reed had been in a meeting when he received word. He called Andrea ("Pop is sick." "Sick?" "Sick." "Oh, no. Not dying, though." The word was like a punch. "Sick. Dying maybe."), he called the airport. He could not get a flight until the next day. Pop maybe dying. But the following afternoon, a stopover at La Guardia, and the plane was delayed by a hurricane—Dinah—stirring far out over the Atlantic. Reed had once known a Dinah. In bed she was more like a summer breeze. It had ended badly; she mailed him vicious letters for months afterward. But now she had returned to haunt him, a full-blown tsunami, keeping him from Pop. Pop maybe dying. Reed finally arrived late that evening, rainy Indianapolis night. His Pakistani cabby got lost out near the speedway. It took another hour to reach the hospital. As Reed rode the elevator to his father's floor, hospital orderlies descended to the basement morgue with the remains. Reed discovered a stranger resting in his father's deathbed, the man's foot swollen with gout. The affliction of kings and fat men. "Glutton," Reed had screamed. He found his mother weeping in a waiting room that consisted of two plastic chairs, a chipped table covered with old *Newsweeks*, and a plaque on the wall: In Memory Of Martha Dixon Cunningham. A doctor who looked to be sixteen came forward. He needed a haircut. "He didn't suffer," he assured Reed. As if at sixteen one could understand mortality, one could understand suffering. Reed remained unconvinced. He imagined death as a single, omniscient instant, limned deep with inchoate regrets, before blackness closed in.

Good son, then, Reed woke at midnight, he woke at two-thirty, he woke at four. He woke to the sound of a drunk laughing in the street, to the wooden wheels of a cart knocking over cobblestones. He woke to the odor of diesel exhaust. He woke to the noise of helicopter rotors working the air above Texas, searchlight illuminating the weeds and shrubbery of the near bank of the river, intent on routing refugees. He woke to the sight of the figurine—vague, squat lump of shadow.

Thoughts of father, thoughts of death. Never a good idea. But Reed tossed fitfully in bed, all out of good ideas. The sorrows of fathers are everywhere. They pursue us through life. That time his father found those photos under Reed's bed; that time he caught his son torturing a frog; that time Reed stole a dime from the change pocket of his father's wallet. Tiny silver button, it would never be missed. He had wanted an ice cream cone, three licorice sticks. Face tight with a plan, he could imagine the dime in his fingers. His father was always in bed by nine, up at four. Farmer's hours. Ten at night, Reed crept through the dark house, full of stealth. But something had awakened his father, some psychic umbilicus that binds a man to his son. He appeared, face drawn, eyes small with interrupted sleep. He would not hit Reed, he had never hit him. Reed's father had been raised with generous lashes of a razor strop; the sound was burned into the man's memory. Still, Reed's shame was enormous. His father shook his head sadly. His son, the thief. He knelt then, emptied the wallet, counting out the money. "Eight dollars and forty-three cents. Go ahead. Take." Reed took. His father hit him. The time he caught Reed crouched at a neighbor's window, watching Mrs. Woods undress. (Dimpled ass, an appendectomy scar. Surprisingly big feet.) When Mrs. Woods died in a house fire the following summer, his father took him aside, said, "Things happen." (But Reed knew better: God had had to kill Mrs. Woods because Reed had seen her behind.) His father had voted (four times) for Roosevelt, he had voted for Stevenson, for McGovern. His toenails were black, his back was hairy; his love was expansive and silent. He had a laugh Reed remembered as pink. The first time Reed saw his father drunk: 1962, a map on the front page of the newspaper pinpointing the range of Castro's missiles; "We," his father had whispered, finger poised, "are here."

But Reed was there. Possibly an insomniac. He sat at the window now and watched the dawn. Haunting, eerie, like worn metal. It seemed the color of life. Then the sun crested all at once, giving the lie of gold to drab buildings and brown earth. To the north, he could see the bridge, the already-racing traffic of Texas on beyond. As if Mexico were a man who oversleeps.

In the bathroom, Reed brushed his teeth, gagged, then took a shower, the water tepid, smelling of leached chemicals. His bowels were rigid, locked tight. He would bear their weight through the day, like an anvil deep in his stomach. The mirror revealed pasty features, a bloated belly. The look of a stranger. Reed dressed quickly. If things went smoothly, he could drive back to San Antonio and be on the afternoon flight. He could be in Yates's office first thing tomorrow, triumphant, a proposal in hand. Perhaps years from now, he and Andrea would look back on this time with melancholy, shake their heads knowingly, talk within the safety of hindsight of that "difficult period." Possible, yes. Say it cemented their love, insured old-age happiness. The appropriate destiny of all good men. Meanwhile, ample tuition for Smith, Bryn Mawr, etc.

But remember Williams, remember Mazzoli. Now corporate chieftains took care to void their bladders before every meeting. Remember his father. Reed would appear at the Old Man's door more relieved than triumphant. His job intact. But

94

for how long? Another six months, another year. Inevitabilities raged in his head. There was Sid Detweiler; he had lost his job, his wife, he now lived in an apartment complex with a freezer the size of a shoebox. Last time Reed saw him, Sid had developed a harrowing tic, there was a mustard stain on his collar. "Doing good," Sid insisted. There was Dick Taylor, thirty years in sales, a three-state region; his wife now worked double shifts as a nurse to make ends meet while Dick packed his kids' lunches, vacuumed the carpets with the soaps going on TV. There was Newt Ferris (dental equipment, twenty-eight years), Nat Stein (programming, nineteen years), Mike Connell (law, twenty-two years, derailed by malpractice suit; now languishing in the cardiac ICU at Mass General). There were men in the street, handmade signs dangling from their necks like nooses in the moment before the trapdoor is sprung: Will Work For Food. And if García said, Tomorrow . . . The thought was like ice. But he wouldn't. He couldn't. Reed had the Mexican's number. He waited for the thought to cheer him.

Yet small nagging doubt, tight prick of conscience. Eight hundred jobs in the Quincy plant: sons of Moe, sons of Emmett, sons of Seymour. Sturdy men, integrity in the movement of their hands. Men like his father. But failing building, failing factory. Manufacture moving south, a country hemorrhaging at the border. Jobs taken over by sons of Paco, sons of Ricardo, sons of Manuel. Not my problem, Reed assured himself. Yet it was he who would steal jobs from the sons of Emmett, give them to the sons of Paco. "Progress," Reed reminded the mirror. But an obsolete face stared back at him, a face bereft of progress. Still: not his problem. His problem was family, job, home. Home indeed—twenty Pacos in the street.

Then, too, there was Eve. Odd woman, she made one uneasy. She would be expecting him. He could call her later, make his apologies. Though it might devastate her, confirm him as an unrepentant member of the patriarchy. It might drive her to despair, prove that she was indeed a simpleton. It

95

could move her to madness. Nietzsche at last. Suicide is as close as a steak knife, a gas oven, a medicine cabinet. Taru Baba Rass would have lost one of his most faithful disciples. A holy man, he had studied in India. Say a vengeful man. Reed had seen religious fanatics with towels on their heads wielding scimitars on the evening news.

Dense worries, fractious mood. Possible intestinal blockage. But García was waiting. Reed knotted his tie, squared his shoulders. A deal to close, business to see to. Subtle, nuanced negotiations. Reed stood before the mirror, shot his cuffs.

He arrived at García's office in a combative temper. The Mexican, however, appeared pleased to see Reed. He happily took Reed's hand, lightly squeezed his bicep in a show of affection. Yet García: at bottom, an extortionist. Reed glanced at the man as if from a perch. They piled into the Mexican's car, took a road south of town. Reed eased back in his seat and smoked while García talked. The Mexican loved to talk, he needed to talk, as essential as drawing air. Reed learned that García had once played semipro ball (first base); he had secretly named his daughter after an old girlfriend; if you swallowed watermelon seeds you would die an early death. García believed fervidly in the existence of extraterrestrials (strange lights that night in Chihuahua). He had eaten a large breakfast (chorizo). His uncle had three wives.

"You're not serious."

García was serious. Tío Diego had three wives; each worked at a different maquiladora. Three different homes, eight children among them. A heavy man, Diego ate dinner at five-thirty, then again at six-thirty, then again at eight. "He visits his mistress at midnight."

"But the women must suspect."

García shrugged at the gullibility of the species. He knew of another man, the wealthiest man in Piedras, one of the wealthiest in all of Mexico. This man had a large home, four cars, a boat in dry dock five hundred miles away in Tampico. He had a wife. Her beauty was famous. But she had a lover, a teen who

96

worked as their gardener. Everyone in Piedras knew about it. Everyone. People joked about it in the cantinas, they laughed about it over lunch. Everyone knew. Except for the husband. He was rich, he had everything. The man thought his life was perfect. He had no idea. You might think someone would tell him, you might think someone would sit him down and say, "Don Rigoberto, there is something perhaps you should know . . ." But no one ever did. No one ever would. "It makes his wealth tolerable for the rest of us."

The Mexican grinned. The expression seemed eternal, a fixed feature, a landmark on his face. Reed sensed the need to reciprocate with words of his own. He told a joke he had heard long ago, a joke about a man, a monkey, and a woman in a bar, but the punchline depended, he realized too late, on certain linguistic subtleties. García stared at him blankly. Then he told García about the episode with Cruickshank. Only in this version, Reed seduced Cruickshank's wife, he seduced the wife of Evans, Evans from manufacturing. He seduced the black maid. In the end, it was he who declined the job, "though they offered me seventy-five."

García nodded, rich pleasure in his face. It seemed they were making common cause. Men who understood each other, men who had ravished maids and big-breasted Miamians. Life was hard, but they were harder. Men with families, with responsibilities, with jobs. Men with stories to tell.

"About my fee—"

García named a comical sum, a paltry sum. At bottom, a bumpkin. Yates spent more in a month on golf balls. But Reed was smooth: city boy, entrepreneur. He shook his head thoughtfully, hinting at difficulties. Naturally, he would have to discuss it with Yates. Yates had final say on everything. "Naturally," the Mexican said. But he was not convinced. "I should ask for less?" His perplexity was genuine. Yates was a fair man, Reed assured him. A man who understood the complexities. García smiled in the end, satisfied.

They crested a rise to discover a large building. Reed's relief was immense, salvational. The structure appeared sturdy, upright. It would stand for centuries yet. Reed followed García through broad doors fashioned from panels of rosewood. They stood amid clay walls, beneath a roof of curved tiles, a vaulted ceiling latticed with rough-hewn beams. The cornices were ornately carved. Statuary inhabited shallow grottos. There was a resonance to their voices, it reverberated off the heavy timber, the adobe. There was a quick flutter of wings, the cawing of a bird.

"It's a church," Reed realized.

Sí, it was a church. Three decades earlier, the pious had flocked here. Their voices could be heard on Sunday mornings early. But the people drifted away over the years, only the older ones had remained. One by one they died off, the padre ministering to a dwindling congregation of the stooped, the aging. They had to be helped to their knees. The padre finally died. Through some confusion, an error, another was never appointed. There were a few who still remembered him. The rest had moved, or were dead. García's look turned probing: "You are a believer?"

"No," Reed said.

Yet Reed's views on such matters were mixed. No believer he; yet he experienced the absence of the Almighty with an acute melancholy. Raised a Presbyterian, he had attended church as a boy as one bathes, or takes out the garbage. A matter of spiritual hygiene. Fail to brush your teeth, and they turn black. Fail to go to church, and your soul turns black. And now it seemed he was about to turn a temple of God into a warehouse. More unseemly than evil. Like buying nudes that you know are of nuns. Bad manners. Unpropitious.

No believer he. Still, he was a man attuned to the ironies. Reed had come to the secret early: money involves the purest of rituals. By itself, it means nothing. But once set in motion, it transmutes all things. Theology has never been stronger. Those above are always amazed, and grateful, and relieved finally that those below don't storm the boardrooms, lynch the

98

bankers, lash CEOs screaming through the streets. It is only the richest of pieties that enables a man to endure forty years at a job he loathes making money for people he hates raising children he never sees with a woman he has forgotten how to love, only to die with twelve years left on the mortgage, a hospital bill, a funeral bill, and a car that won't start in freezing weather. The process is alchemical, cabalistic.

"No," Reed said again.

García indicated the floor. The foundation was strong. The roof was sound. Naturally, changes would have to be made. But the main sanctuary could be partitioned off. The chapel could be divided into offices. The wall behind the chancel could be knocked out to make room for a loading dock. "I am certain," García went on, "that señor Yates will be satisfied."

They spent another hour inspecting the grounds. They found vestments in a chest of drawers, a Madonna in the basement. The chaplets rose above them. The frocks of altar boys hung in a closet. Sí, the road could be widened. Sí, power lines would be installed. There would be no shortage of workers. The campesinos streamed from the villages, there were never enough jobs. The unions, the unions had little power here. Raw materials could be shipped from the west, a vast underground spring sat a short way east. Reed listened, took notes. Señor Yates would be satisfied.

On the drive back in, they smoked. To the south, the land held an unexpected beauty. A distant run of mountains, verdant slopes, their peaks shrouded by a low cover of clouds. To the north, a cluster of buildings. An abandoned maquiladora. García named a manufacturer out of Chicago; you have worn the name on the soles of your feet. As they neared town, an alkaline breeze rose up. They could see the river on beyond— a strip of brown, foamy water, fleeced in weeds. Down at the bank, dark, corpulent women bent to wash clothes. A long white dress lay on a bare rock, drying in the sun. A dress one might get married in. Farther upstream, a young couple sat in a thistle of reeds, their feet in the river, their shoes in their laps, their belongings bundled in a pack at their side. Their eyes trained north. Nightfall was nine hours away.

Yet in nine hours, Reed would be home. The thought was exculpating. Home for Reed had always been a mythical place, fraught with errant memories. But a myth that endured: it framed his longing. In all those places where ships dock, planes land, trains hesitate before platforms, there was always a moment when home was not Boston, but Indiana; not Andrea, but the girl next door, wearing an apron of gingham—he kissed her that Sunday afternoon; not the clogged gutters, not the cracked pavement of his drive, not the dangerous streets, but a pond bordered by dogwoods, bass napped in the shadows; home was the odors of his mother's cooking, the windows frosted with ice; home was the postman driving the long rural distances, he used to play horseshoes with his father.

Reed grinned now, his face lit with nostalgia. Outside, passing rubble, dilapidated shanties. Passing hotel. Reed pointed, said, "Hey—" García smiled, announced his surprise. He wanted Reed to meet his wife, his children, to see his home. Latin comportment. Reed tried to decline, apologies already forming. But García cocked his head in that way he had, his face earnest, the vulnerability of orphans to his eyes. "My wife, she has been cooking all morning."

Down through the older section of the city, then, García indicating the school attended by his children, the store where his wife shopped, the bar where he drank. And there, over there, is Alejandro, the old man who grinds corn. And that is Miguel, he has only to hear the roar of a car engine from a block away to know what needs repairing. These are the sisters, Adelah and Dora, every Cinco de Mayo they become shamefully drunk. There is Antonio, there is Heroilda; there is the dog Rafael, he barks at the moon. An unsightly dump at the far end of the block: a battered washing machine, pylons of hubcaps, the bare chassis of some vehicle, a soiled mattress with stains like a Pacific archipelago.

García's wife was plump, his son wan. Within two years his

100

daughter would break the hearts of a Roberto, a Jaime, and a Jorge. The family lived in a drab house blistered with peeling paint. There was a jagged hole in the kitchen wall that looked out onto a back yard of weeds and broken cement. Naked wires sprouted from a corner of the ceiling. The two-burner stove leaned left, the refrigerator made a loud whirring sound, the tile on the kitchen floor had separated. The dishes were old and unmatched. Reed's glass said Goofy. A kind of shrine, a replica of the Virgin wearing an odd garland of blinking Christmas lights, against one wall. Next to it stood a shiny TV, the only new thing in the house. On the screen, a woman was laughing in twenty-eight-inch color. The air smelled of soap. Reed understood the children had been scrubbed, been made to don their best clothes. García's wife was one of those women who must touch. Her hands fluttered about, grazing Reed's arm, his back, touching his hair, urging him to sit. He sat. She talked in a chirp. When they were all settled, she lifted the lid from a large steaming bowl with a flourish.

García beamed. "Menudo," he whispered.

Menudo. Spongy, resilient, fibrous stuff, the poached lining of a cow's stomach. It smelled of worn tires. Reed made a determined show of chewing. The García family peppered Spanish back and forth, outshouting the television. García paused every now and then to translate. The daughter had recently won an essay contest ("Don Quixote in America"), the wife had bought lard cheap on the other side of town. The boy wanted to know if Reed had ever killed an Indian. García's wife asked about Andrea, about his home, about his life. Each response made her sigh. A woman whose joys were thoroughly matrimonial. Reed chewed, he answered, he chewed, interminable texture in his mouth. García grinned broadly. He was showing off his family; he was showing off his new friend. His glass said Mickey.

Reed glanced at his watch. He set down his spoon, patted his belly. Acts meant to convey finality. "Please," he begged. "No more." But García's wife rushed to refill his bowl. She respected the appetites of men. She recognized their hollow protestations. Meanwhile, the García family ate like the condemned. Tinking flatware, slurping lips. Gummy texture, latex odor. On TV, the woman was weeping.

The sister saved him in the end. She coughed, went rigid, and upchucked. Half-masticated lumps in a brown stew at Reed's elbow. The act had a grudging integrity. Reed worried he might do the same. The commotion was big, the wife reaching for a towel, García reaching for his daughter. They mopped up the mess, then both parents disappeared into the girl's bedroom, their daughter in García's arms. Reed looked at the boy unsurely. Sickly son, mysterious trouble with his heart. The silence was awkward. Children unnerved him. He could never gauge their ages, guess their interests. They seemed bizarre, unpredictable creatures equally given to unexpected tantrums and surprising bouts of intelligence. Reed offered him a brief smile. The boy's look was stony. Reed suppressed a belch. "Agua," the boy said. High, pleading sound. The water ran rusty from the tap. Standing at the sink, Reed waited for it to clear, but soon understood it never cleared. He filled the glass, motes swirling. The boy drank quickly. When he finished, García's son wheeled around slowly to gaze at Reed. The movement was adult, unsettling, accusatory. As if it were Reed who had queered the water supply. Reed frowned, fiddled with his fork. The boy had García's eyes, García's mouth.

"It's rude to stare."

"Rood."

"Yeah, rude."

"Rood."

García and his wife returned, their faces subdued. Their daughter was ill. Reed rose, said, "I should go." García made half-hearted objections, but Reed was insistent. He took the hand of García's wife. "It was delicious." García smiled now, his disastrous teeth sudden in the room, and spoke long and long, expatiating in rich detail on the quality of the meal. His wife blushed, she hugged herself, she touched Reed's arm, his cheek; she kissed him on the brow.

In front of his hotel, Reed shook the Mexican's hand. Firm, decisive, two pumps of the arm. García seemed touched by the moment. "Nos vemos," he added.

"Nos vemos?"

"It is a thing one says."

Reed stepped from the car. He thrust his head back through the window to stare at the Mexican. An extortionist. No: a backwater rube, a chump. A hole in his kitchen wall, opaque water, his kid pukes up lunch. Reed wanted to say, Yates will pay two, three times as much. Five times, easy. Maybe more. In the end, he didn't. Hard, undaunted, a businessman; his loyalties had been cast twenty years ago. What Reed said was, "The part about the maid—I lied. I never did the maid."

García appeared puzzled. Then a smile surfaced in the middle of his face. He put the car into gear. "And I have never been to Miami."

Up in his room, Reed called the airline. In his mind, he was already making the drive north, boarding the plane, soaring through the sky. But the last flight out of San Antonio left in fifteen minutes. "Tomorrow morning?" the voice suggested. Reed was grudging. "Tomorrow morning." He called the house, anxious to talk to Andrea, to Laura. To hear the sound of home. But there was only the answering machine. Tired voice, dejected voice. His voice. Reed left his flight information, hung up. He called the office. He wanted to talk to the Old Man, to hear a word of praise. A word of encouragement. But Yates couldn't come to the phone. He wouldn't. "This is Reed," Reed insisted. As if his name were a clarion, it would bring the Old Man running. But Yates's secretary was unimpressed. A proprietary woman, she had worked for her boss for thirty years. She had seen men come, she had seen men go. Only she was eternal. "One moment," she said.

"Make it quick," Reed heard then. He winced at the sound of Eiger's voice. Eiger was a man who chuckled continually, a repugnant man. Word was that Eiger had had Elise in accounting, Barbara in advertising, Donna in the mail room. Also wife of Grumbach, Grumbach of the Providence office. Grumbach formerly of the Providence office. Eiger was the kind of man for whom women in bedrooms whoop, "Slay me, slaughter me, kill me," with disturbing brio. But Yates trusted him, depended upon him. Eiger was a tall man, trim; he moved with the unthinking grace of a ballplayer. "Where's the Old Man?" Reed asked. "In a meeting," Eiger replied. "He asked me to take care of it." Reed started to detail the negotiations, the site . . . "You're finished?" Eiger cut in. Well, yes; he was finished. Eiger drew air through his teeth. Reed could sense the man's dismay. Eiger's tone turned dismissive: "Too soon." The Old Man had expected Reed to make a thorough inquiry.

"But I did—"

"You want my advice?" Eiger's voice went chummy. Yet Reed did not want his advice. Eiger's motives at times resembled a gnarled thicket hiding predators. Mrs. Grumbach was an obese woman with tits like pumpkins. It wasn't her charms that had impelled Eiger, but his hate for Mr. Grumbach. "Check out the museums," Eiger suggested now. Take another day, maybe three. Eat hot food. Take in a bullfight. Find a woman.

Reed hung up. His bed had been made, fresh towels hung in the bathroom. The figurine hunkered on the dresser, scowling. Reed scowled back. He had no desire to look at museums, to take in a bullfight. He'd eaten hot food. He wanted to go home. He wanted a good steak, safe water. He wanted two-ply toilet paper. A visit to Mexico was like a visit to an outhouse the size of a country. He would drive north that afternoon, put up in a hotel in San Antonio. A restaurant in the heart of the financial district, the waitress solicitous, her bodice cut low. He would order a thick sirloin, a baked potato, a salad slathered with blue-cheese dressing. American food. Fourteen glasses of American water. Clear, cold. The waitress talking

American. Though a single-malt scotch straight out of Edinburgh. Reed reached again for the phone and called three different hotel chains. Each of the reservationists was polite, female, and adamant: there was a convention of psychiatrists, a convention of football coaches, a convention of Christian mothers angry at rock music. San Antonio, conference town. Not a vacant room in the whole burg. "You must have something." But there was nothing. Try Austin. He tried Austin, but nudists and stock-car devotees were convening. Furious, Reed lay on the bed and smoked a cigarette. Eve's book sat on the nightstand. He flipped to a page: "Menstruation is the tears of the Great Goddess Ur-Mother." He settled back and stared at the ceiling. A drink, then. Reed, a man bearing contracts, he deserved it.

There are beauties to drink. Unfashionable, he knew. But he believed in them firmly. A man remembers his first woman, his first glimpse of a cadaver, his first drink. Three quarts of beer on a Saturday night late, with Chaz Woburn and Keith Gruber, just at the edge of the cemetery. The gray slabs lent dignity to their drinking. They went and stood and pissed on the graves. They meant no disrespect. Keith had read that piss deterred raccoons. They searched for the graves of women who had died young. Those who had died at fifteen or sixteen, those with names like Rose and Catherine and Helen—simple names, the names of their mothers and aunts and sisters. "Damn raccoons," Chaz muttered. Their hate was rich, cleansing. There was the rasp of their zippers, the moonlight making shadows of the tombstones, and then the rush of their urine. It was the thought of a creature pawing above a Rose, a Helen.

Remember the Royal Arms, remember Chaucer's, remember Dirty Frank's. The intimacy of bars is unique, their tranquil brand of darkness. True, the bathrooms reek, the women are suspect, the barstools are precarious. But think of a drinking buddy you may have known. By his mere presence he exudes a kind of power. A buddy who has seen some awful things, say in a war, or in jail, or in a place you have never been. A quiet man, yet he seems to harbor mortal secrets. You buy him a drink from time to time, you ask about the job, the Red Sox, what brand of motor oil he uses. He is always there at the bar, his large hand gathered around a mug of beer. He is the kind of man you see for maybe twenty minutes a week for ten years. You come to depend upon the sight of him hulking, brooding at the bar, to depend on the frosty mug dwarfed in his callused hand, to depend on the sleepy eyes, the slow smile. Then the day comes when you learn his story; he will never tell you himself, but there are others who know. It is always a tale of unfathomable pain: say in Korea he crawled half a mile on his belly to save his squad, and now medals sit in his drawer, there is a steel plate in his head; or his wife suffers from some debilitating disease, they will never find a cure, yet he goes home each night and empties her bedpan, feeds her, shifts her body because the doctors have warned about bedsores; or long ago he killed a man in Montana—a deserved death, he would do it again—but he got ten years in Deer Lodge just the same. And it comes to you one night, a night like all the others, a night when he stands, waves goodbye, makes his way to the door, that here is a man you believe in with your life; here is a man you would die for if you had to. And you don't even know his last name.

Reed sighed. A drink in hand, and his passion for this world—for the taste of steamed mussels dredged in a garlic sauce, for the sight of men on a baseball diamond, for the willful features of women in lingerie ads, for the snores of the dog asleep at your feet—a drink in hand, and his passion for this world was abiding, immeasurable, and vehement.

See Reed, trapped in a foreign land. The air is suspect, the food more so. The knot in his belly is relentless. He goes down to the bar and has a drink. He remembers to call the old man Umberto. Reed goes back upstairs and lies on the bed. He smokes a cigarette. He tries calling home again, gets only his tired voice. Through the wall he hears the woman: "Más suave, suave, por favor." The sound warrants another drink, drives him downstairs. He has one, he has one more. He humps back upstairs. The woman's noises have gone guttural: "Hijo, hijo, hijo." Reed wanders back downstairs, hoists his glass in Umberto's direction. "Salud," he begins, drains his glass, raps the bar with his knuckles. Umberto obliges with another glugging draught from the bottle. "Amor," Reed goes on, but he has forgotten the rest. He troops back upstairs. Dinero, he remembers, nodding at the figurine. The figurine nods back, its face suddenly ennobled, its features crafted by a blunt tool. The look of Homeric helmets. Say it should be in a museum. Not impossible. Reed: entrepreneur, collector. He will have it appraised back in Boston. Though an archivist will probably laugh at him. Maybe not. Imagine a bored scholar, glasses low on his nose, regarding Reed with open scorn as Reed relays the particulars of his find. The scholar takes the figurine in his expert hands, prods it with knowledgeable fingers. He mutters to himself, cocks brow, bends to look more closely. He says, "I'll be right back." He takes it to another scholar down the hallway, a young scholar; ambition steeps in his face. They confer. They continue on down the hall to another office, and another still. A crowd of scholars, Reed lagging behind, trying to keep up, enters a special chamber stocked with sophisticated equipment designed to plumb the secrets of molecules. Reed can see the room, it is dimly lit, it hums with the sounds of scientific efficiency. A beam is trained onto the figurine, every scholar standing on his toes, straining to see. There is the rustle of academic tweed. A gasp rises from the assembly; they begin exclaiming in three different languages. Finally, one middle-aged fellow—Japanese, probably a Nobel laureate—begins a slow, rhythmic clapping, to be picked up by the rest of the group. The sound is crescendoing, ecstatic. "Bravo," someone shouts. Reed is in the background, saying, "What? What is it?" The old scholar he first contacted, his eyes gleaming now with excitement, takes Reed by the arm, says, "This is the missing icon of Lord Popoxocomochomil."

Reed blinks. The scholar shakes him. "Don't you see, man? This is the Rosetta Stone. This is the Trojan Horse. This is the Ark!"

Reed woke with a start. Through the wall, bedsprings barked. Night was coming on. Gray light cast the statue in cold shadow, lent it a forbidding dignity. Reed roused slowly, stepped to the dresser. A thing of great age, witness to barbaric tribal ceremonies. OK, doubtful. But so is the future, so is tomorrow. Reed gently turned the figurine over in his hands.

Eve answered the door wearing a short skirt, a billowing blouse. She had closed up the shop early. The table was set. An event, he understood. He suddenly saw her days, understood her nights: a woman on the downward slope of life, a woman struggling to endure. No publisher would touch her book. He began to explain about his missed flight, about the striking success of the Texas convention bureau. But she touched her finger to his lips to quiet him, purple daggers a quarter-inch from his nose. She said, "It's fate." She took his arm, sat him in a chair. She settled herself on the bed opposite. She aimed green eyes at him, pupils flecked with amber. Their knees touched. He saw that her legs were going. She stared at him now, her yeasty smell filling his face. The silence lengthened, made him uncomfortable. They sat that way for a minute, two minutes. Reed cleared his throat.

She whispered, "Leo?"

Reed looked at her. "Name's Frank."

"Gemini? Taurus? Pisces? Pisces. Of course. I knew it. Pisces. I knew it from the beginning." She loved men in spite of herself. Life would have been simpler if she hadn't. She regarded it as a glorious flaw, a touching inconsistency that made her endearing.

She produced a little baggie now, a narrow sleeve of rolling papers. She worked quickly, her fingers practiced. "Like a taste?" White rod, tapered at the ends, slick with her spittle. Reed declined. He watched as her cheeks collapsed, her face curling tight and knotted around her mouth. Harsh intake of breath, mucus cracking miles deep. Sweet hemp, it made his stomach lurch. She leaned the joint his way. "Are you sure?"

He was sure. She stuck the rolled cigarette between her lips and drew heavily, making the ember at the end flare. She sucked greedily, smoking it down to a tiny nub. A seed popped, showering sparks. She laughed. Dreamy eyes, slits in her head. She laughed again. Then, "Hungry?"

Tripe swimming in a sea of scotch, his bowels as closed as a sealed vault. Not hungry. But the table held a platter of pale slivers—shuddering, tremulous meat. Bowls of anonymous fruit, a dish of gelatinous green things. A feast, it could have fed a family of eight.

She descended on the food like a woman wading into the middle of a fistfight. A fight she meant to win. She ate with intensity. It was like a race he was losing. Quick working of her jaws, jowly effort contorting her face. The pleasure could be seen in her eyes, in her sounds. He could hear her moaning softly. The lack of silverware made the evening primitive. He felt like a man in a tent, a man on a distant mountain top; even the guides are lost.

He ate a bit of fruit, he ate one of the green things. He fingered a slice of the meat. "What is this?"

She grinned. Intriguing grin, intriguing food. Intriguing woman. She thrilled in the role. It was how she saw her life.

"Ceviche." He had her spell it. "Raw fish." He let the morsel drop to the platter. She laughed at his expression. "It's a delicacy."

"My mother always cooked fish to death," Reed tried, straining for minor intimacies. He worried he had offended her. Yet she had made him dinner, offered him potent smoke.

Her features contracted. Her voice swelled with sympathy. "I hear anger. I hear pain."

Reed frowned. "But she did."

She gathered the fish in her hand, her fingers slick with its juices. "Try some."

Reed's brow furrowed. "That's OK."

"Come on. Here. Ask me to feed you." There was a disconcerting lilt to her voice. "Tell me to."

Reed stared at her. Her face was long, wolfish. "Feed me."

The pale meat, purple nails floated toward him. He took a small bite. A delicate bite. The texture was slimy, almost viscous, like something you might find in the street following a thunderstorm. There was the tart hint of lime, queasy suggestions of fish oil. She was watching him, her eyes urging. "Mothers," she whispered. "There's a subject." Her childhood had been difficult, she explained—almost impossible—and vastly complicated by her mother. Eve was a woman who had suffered much. As a girl she had been terrified of clowns, Shetland ponies, and a certain Uncle Roger who used to rock her on his knee, patella against her bum. Her eyes were knowing: "A child understands more than we realize." But her mother recognized none of this, she was unheeding. And as Eve matured, her mother grew threatened. Mothers and daughters, age-old rivalry, bitter enemies. "My breasts were bigger." She had a sister who worked for an Ohio mail-order firm that sold inflatable rubber dolls to perverts, a brother who worked for the Defense Department in a capacity so sensitive she could not go into it here. Her mother had devastated them all. It had driven Eve to wild acts, irresponsible acts. She lost her virginity at fifteen to an employee who worked in the men's (Big and Tall) clothing store owned by her father. "We would do it in one of the changing rooms. These giants on either side of us, trying on suits. It was six months before I learned you could do it lying down."

There were other men, older men, stupid men. Brilliant men. At Vassar, the chairman of the comparative literature department—"He knew Sartre personally"—once begged her to perform an act she had only read about. She declined, claiming it gave her hiccups. "But it doesn't, not at all," she added quickly. Reed listened, he nodded, tried for a show of attention. Though maybe Christians or nudists had made last-minute cancellations. Yet Eve was talking. She was telling him of her life.

"My problem is that I remember so much. I understand so much. I see so much. Fortunately, I'm strong. I survived. I'm a survivor. Years later, I told my mother everything. Everything. I held nothing back. A courageous act. I'd been in therapy for some time. I was opening up to her. I was baring my soul, letting her know the mistakes she had made with me, the damage she had done. How she had ruined my childhood, she had practically ruined my life. And now I had to live with it. She didn't have to live with it, I did. She acted like she didn't understand. She insisted she never knew of my fear of clowns. 'You should have known!' I screamed. But she refused to see my pain. She refused to acknowledge it. Yet it was something I had to go through. It was something I had to relive and then let out into the open, let out into the fresh air of truth. Otherwise, it would remain trapped inside. This is how cancers get started: we keep things trapped deep inside, and they turn into cancers. We earn our pain, we get what we deserve. If we would all just be more honest, more open, there would be no more cancer. There would be no more war, no more disease, no more hunger. It's so simple. It's all so simple. Take this business with your mother. You should work on it. I can give you the name of a therapist if you want. Work on yourself, get your head right. Get your heart right, and the world will take care of itself. Can you imagine what a wonderful place the world would be if everyone did that? Can you imagine what a wonderful place the world would be if everyone were just like me?

"I know: Aquarius? Pisces? I knew it: Pisces. I could tell you were a Pisces from a mile away. Want me to do your chart?"

Reed gaped at her. He felt exhausted, stunned with strange food. Stunned with her talk. The flurry of details was like a heavy wood in which he had lost his way. "Maybe later." To his dismay, she was rolling a second joint. Reed came up with his cigarettes.

She shook her head. "I'm sorry, but that is a disgusting habit. That is one disgusting habit. It's a trap. It expresses a hidden need. A repressed need." She shook her head, lit the joint. "You know why you do that?" She spoke with an abrupt animation. "You know why? I know why."

Reed sighed. Women were always objecting to his smoking. "Why?"

"It's so phallic." The word was like a gunshot; it gave her a kind of joy. Her voice was loud, a voice anxious to be heard. She said, "It's a control thing, you know. Your need to control fire." Another seed exploded, showering her blouse with sparks. She slapped at her breasts with frantic hands. Reed tried to help, hands batting in the vicinity of her chest. Reed with his need to control fire. They both went still then, his hands holding her breasts through her blouse. Soft, considerable, unkempt heft. The cloth was flecked with burn holes. Reed released her. "Sorry," he murmured.

She smiled. Unsorry. Passion pinched her eyes, made her nostrils flare. She leaned toward him, breasts heaving beneath scorched cloth, and whispered, "Tell me to kiss you." "What?" "Tell me. Do." "Kiss me." She kissed him. Large tongue, moist tongue, her breath smelling of fish. Postdiluvian. The truth: he had never been unfaithful to Andrea. Statistics said otherwise, he knew. Every second guy humps his secretary. Friends, colleagues frequently leered about their affairs. Though they never called them affairs, they never used words like *adultery* or *betrayal* or *infidelity*. Big words, officious words—words that burden transgressions with too much meaning. They talked about "running around." Even the phrase put him off; it evoked images of men in shorts and specially crafted shoes entering marathons, pounding great distances through far-flung neighborhoods, stopping occasionally to fornicate on front lawns while children and dogs watched.

Eve rose now, eyes shimmering, and crossed the room. Dramatic action, dramatic woman. Color to her face. A survivor.

She threw open the windows. The sounds of the street came pouring through, a breeze carried the odors of car exhaust, of gasoline. The streetlights had come on. They made a silhouette of her body, outlined the density of her hips, her stout thighs. Reed thought: her legs are definitely going. "Would you have anything to drink?"

"I have something better." She indicated the dish of green things. Reed understood immediately: gleaned from cacti, psychedelic potency. She launched on a brief history of the peyote plant, its mystical legacy. Ancients big on the substance. Said to induce visions, religious states of being; said to explode the parameters of chauvinistic thought. "Experiment. Life is experimentation." She slipped another button between her lips. Like eating life.

Reed waited, keen for the sound of sundering parameters, perhaps an overpowering urge to shove his face between her legs, make the top of her head come off. He tried to remember how many of the green things he had eaten. Mathematical cretinism a possible side effect. "You should have told me."

She rolled her eyes. He was being silly. "The ancients considered it a sacrament. Victims of sacrifice were drugged, you know. It was considered a great honor. You should feel honored. It's all in chapter three of my book. Did you read it? Thank you, thank you. That's very kind of you to say so." She proceeded to recapitulate the themes of chapter three, like a woman displaying photos of her children. A seminal chapter, a path-breaking chapter. Mesoamerican studies would never be the same. "Those sacrificed went willingly. They went lovingly." Thirsty gods, she explained; had to keep them happy or the sun wouldn't rise. It seemed the ancients' fear of the end was all-consuming. "An obsession." They were always coming across omens that signaled Armageddon: volcanoes, eclipses, plagues, a comet. "That's who they thought Cortez was, they thought Cortez was this ticked-off god, bent on retribution. There's such a thing as repercussions." She repeated the business about time being round, her index finger looping through the air, purple nails harsh. "It's all right there in your figurine. I know, I know: you probably think this is so much nonsense. I can't say that that surprises me. I have this special insight into people, into their natures, and I can't say that surprises me at all. No doubt part of this great need you have to control. Anyway, they worried constantly about the end of the world. I mean, they fixated on it. The smallest screw-up, and the sky could fall." Moral decay, cosmic decay, "it was all the same thing to them. See, the Aztecs were open to the Oneness of all things. That's 'Oneness' with a capital O. I insist upon it. Then the Spaniards arrive, and it seems to confirm everything. There's such a thing as consequences. Imagine: a society that envisions its own demise. An incredible insight, when you think about it. Like the discovery of fire, the invention of the wheel. The invention of zero. Tell me to crawl across the floor on all fours."

"I don't want to."

"Come on. I want you to."

"But I don't want you to do that."

"Come on."

"Crawl across the floor on all fours."

"No." She laughed, mouth wide, carnal. Reed stared at the lines in her neck, a bit of jowl, thought vacantly how their coupling would be clumsy, cetacean. Their bellies loose and slapping. Skin making sucking noises. An ancient fuck. Unseemly, sordid. Though Andrea would know. She would know as soon as he stepped onto the airport concourse. No: she would know by the sound of the jet engine as it approached, she would know by the color of the sky, by the arrangement of the clouds. She would know the moment it happened; she would awaken from a deep sleep, her eyes wide with uncanny knowledge.

"I would have loved to have lived then," Eve went on. "These times are so boring. It bores me." She clenched her fists, threw back her head. "I deserve better! I have these dreams—" She paused now, her voice hushed, amber distance in her eyes, intimacies in the offing. "I knew this hypnotist, he took me back. Regressive analysis. Very sophisticated stuff. I know, I know, you think I'm babbling. But they laughed at Archimedes. They laughed at Galileo. They laughed at Werner Erhard. But this hypnotist, he said I might have possibly lived then. Inconclusive, but he said it was a definite possibility. I would not be surprised. I would not be surprised at all. It must have been such an exciting time. Can you see it? I can see it. I see it in my dreams." She closed her eyes, seeing it. She opened them, a woman frightened by clowns. "Let me tie you to the bed."

Reed stood. "It's late."

"You're afraid you'll like it, is all. Listen: fear is a trap."

Reed eased toward the door. He was an animal gnawing off its leg. "It's late."

"I don't believe this." She moved to intercept him. "You kissed me. You touched my breasts. Or did I just imagine that?"

He had kissed her. He had touched her breasts. It seemed he had been implicated in some arcane feminine calculus unknown to men. Touch a woman's breasts and you enter into certain obligations. A better man would have kept his hands in check, or else touched her breasts with rich heat, squeezed and pulled their pucker, then gone on to shove his face, etc. But not Reed: he touched, then ran. As though it were his recipe for life.

"Sorry," he groaned.

"You used me. You can't just fondle and run. It's not that kind of a deal. I have needs. I have my needs. I'm a survivor. I've survived. And who are you?"

Reed edged along the wall. The world was happening too quickly. To his alarm, she followed him, need large in her eyes. He made his way down through the shop, past carved masks, papier-mâché figures, soapstone Nativity scenes. Past the pen-and-pencil set, the Mexican crest—eagle devouring a serpent—looking particularly alarming. His pace was unsteady, weaving. She pursued him, fists waving. "You need help. You need serious help. It's people like you that is wrong with the world. Just who do you think you are? I could recommend a therapist. I could, I could; but you know what? I won't." Reed grazed something, there was a shattering crash, souvenir exploding to the floor, onyx shards rocketing. The sound of Armageddon. Then he was in the street, an iconoclast, a masher.

She braced herself against the door, her face contorted, her voice Wagnerian. "There's such a thing as repercussions, buster."

A crazed woman, perhaps, but it's said that madness neighbors truth. Her words came at his back, hounded him down the street. Past the drunks outside a cantina, a harlot at the corner. A man lay beneath an old Ford, changing the water pump. A young girl sat in a window, earnestly picking her nose. A blind vendor across the way pushed a cart, selling lottery tickets. Reed hurtled on past, feet drumming, belly churning with bad liquor, unlikely chemicals, icthyological resonances, his head dense with implications.

He had danced on his share of tables, he had slept under others. He knew well the continent of drink. He had explored its rivers and valleys, its deserts, its mountain ranges, its tropics. He had stood at its poles, planted numerous flags. But this was psychedelic topography, alien, forbidding, the interior of some unmapped region.

Reed had never experimented with recreational narcotics. Hardly ever. His bent ran to drink. Liquor was card games, cocktail parties, after-dinner highballs; it was fraternal, sophisticated, relaxing. Drugs were long hair, stained clothes, questionable politics. In his youth, the state of Indiana had mandated classes in Health & Hygiene. His teacher, a brusque war veteran with a crewcut and a glass eye, had made it his mission to expose the drug culture and redeem all that was good and true about America. It was the man's personal odyssey, his vendetta against life. His glass eye frightfully askew, the teacher read from convincing studies that spoke of irreversible chromosome damage. He relayed tales of stoned youths who leaped through thirty-story windows, or shuffled down the middle of busy interstates late at night wearing dark clothing. He preached about licentious women who preyed on boys with impaired brain functions, infecting them with nihilism and crabs. Even at that early age, Reed already suspected that his was a questionable constitution; he emerged from Health & Hygiene convinced he was a promising candidate for genetic corruption and moral anarchy. He refused the mildest of painkillers, the most innocuous of sleeping aids. A tablespoon of cough medicine might lead to an evening in which he would don a black suit and fling himself through a sliding glass door to land unconscious in his neighbor's drive, but only after impregnating various promiscuous hippie women with his tainted seed. His lone lapse in college appeared to confirm his worst fears. One evening he allowed a coed from the wilds of New York City to talk him into taking a yellow pill. She seemed worldly, hip, wanton. Little of that night remained in his memory: she recited Mao's poetry, they ate sandwiches of cucumber and sprouts, her pubic hair was abrasive. Walking back to his dorm early the next morning, he stopped to pet a dog lounging on the campus green. He and the dog were getting along famously until Reed realized he was scratching the ears of an animal that had been dead for some hours.

Back at his hotel, Reed took the stairs two at a time. His thoughts were feverish, unfamiliar, his stomach undone. In the bathroom he collected his shaving gear, his toothbrush. A glance in the mirror revealed ashen features, eyes rimmed in red. A face in a police line-up, all the witnesses point to him; the victims are shrieking: they want his head. He set his bag on the bed and tossed in dirty shirts, dirty underwear. Eve's book. A fleeting fantasy of himself hog-tied, Eve circling the bed, making voodoo sounds. He shook his head, as if to hurl the thought against the far wall. Though there was the figurine to consider. Incorrigible features, fate in his hands. It seemed burdened with too many meanings, smug with rugged secrets.

He could leave it for the cleaning woman. But he had promised his daughter. Dutiful father, he wedged the figurine next to a pair of socks.

He wrestled the bag downstairs, settled the bill, anonymous Spanish profiles staring out from the stack of pesos in his hand. Outside, the night was charged with an unhappy electricity. The roar of the car was shocking, the sound too big. Reed drove carefully through town, the moon reflecting off the river ahead. He would cross the bridge, drive straight on through, fill himself with coffee in a San Antonio diner while waiting for his flight. A turn, a second. A long line of cars, bound for Texas. Fifteen minutes, twenty, and he would be at the border. It seemed a magic line; it would return him to himself, render the world familiar again. Once across, he would be kind to his wife, understanding toward his daughter. He would mend the broken shutter, change the leaky washer in the upstairs bathroom. He would weed the cracks in the drive. He would contribute generously to public TV.

But traffic slowed. Another corner, and he saw the workers out in their green vests, bathed in the harsh glow of a portable light, sitting atop orange machinery. It took him a moment to understand. The road was being widened, gas lines were being repaired, electric cable was being laid. One of those endless municipal projects by which we mark the progress of civilization. There was a detour, a second. Darting cars cut him off, horns shrieking. He was like a frightened child on a carnival ride. Signs for dentists, for doctors, for pharmacies. Then the long stretch of shantytown, the haggard faces, the pantless children. The full moon lit their buttocks. All the roads ran the wrong way. He doubled back, then turned again. The moon appeared to his left, where it had no business being. The river had vanished. A Ford materialized in his path, the eyes of a frightened Mexican coming at him through the windshield. Reed's Toyota swerved, Reed wondering about the DUI laws in Mexico. He had been stopped two years earlier, a rainy night in May. He had been made to walk toe-to-toe, touch his nose, stand on one foot. The cop was angry that Reed had made him miss his doughnut run. Stomach growling, the man took Reed downtown, made him blow into a tube. Then they took Reed's belt, his shoelaces, and stuck him in a cell with a young black who kept saying, "What is de secret? Dat is not de secret." Reed could not understand why the black got to keep his shoelaces. Andrea arrived an hour later, grim with fury. Yet Mexico was not Boston. Reed's foot grew lighter on the gas pedal. There was a quick tickle of juices deep in his bowels, it seemed a kind of warning. The road eased down into a narrow valley. The river reappeared in the distance, Texas behind it. Reed drove on, praying for a turnoff. His stomach seized then, fierce inner compression promising insight: he was lost. His mind went to ancient maps, the parchment cracked and yellowing: Here Ye Finde Serpents.

A dirt stretch appeared, narrow, unassuming. Little more than a broad footpath. Reed hesitated only a moment, then followed it. The limbs of trees whipped at the car, lashed the hood, the roof. A blade cleaved his belly. Reed clung to the steering wheel. Once across the border, both his mood and his belly would relent. He was certain. The road was not. It dipped sharply, the wheels sliding over the dirt. His headlights rocked jarringly over a rut. The night sky said Cassiopeia, it said Orion, it said the Bear. A dizzying decline, then the unmistakable odor of water. He took a final turn, ready for sight of a tollbooth, a line of cars, immigration guards. Instead his headlights flashed on the end of the path as it slipped straight into the water. There was the glint of the river, and on beyond the rise of the bank opposite, high beams playing among the weeds of Texas.

Frowning, Reed killed the engine, turned off the lights, and stepped into the moonlight. The night was still. At the edge of the bank, he could hear the low chuckling of water. He looked around, prayed for clarity. What he got was roiling belly, noxious fart. Hot release of gases. Pincers clenched his colon. Inopportune, yet inevitable. Pork tamales, menudo, raw fish, rum, tequila—cholera was raging in southern portions of the country—the truth arrived all at once: he was going to crap his pants. His mounting sense of urgency had confused gastric torment with homesickness. Reed ran in brief circles, making yipping sounds; a man in search of a place to shit. The most primordial of homes. But the desert was a blank slate, sloping down to the bank of the river, ending in sparse weeds. A modest man, he finally flung himself toward a tiny outcropping, fingers ripping at his belt. He squatted in the here and now, the lulling of the river on beyond, the beep of Texas traffic. He dropped his pants and gingerly spread his feet. The wind was up, shocking desert cold fanning his ass, shrinking testicles. His sounds were loud, booming, oracular.

Thirty seconds, thirty minutes. The exigencies of his belly warped time. He would remember only the breeze as it rustled the brush, the gurgling of the water, the percussive force of his bowels. The fusillade slowed, concluding in a final, awful rending noise. He smelled sage, river bilge, surprising hints of rosemary.

He reached into the darkness now, reached as one who has lived a lifetime with indoor plumbing, his hand coming up against nothing. A desert, after all, the trees few. He kept the realization at bay for a few moments more, casting about for an old newspaper, a palm frond, for anything. He considered his hand. He had heard Arabs made a practice of it. But he was no Arab.

His dictionary was packed deep in his suitcase. He could waddle over, soil himself in the process, desert creatures laughing. Dignity strikes at the oddest moments. There was his underwear, his socks. Expensive material, Andrea paid fifteen bucks for a pair of jockeys. He looked about again, but there was nothing. He beat back the notion that he had somehow earned this. Even the most venal of men deserves an honest crap.

He hit upon the idea of his wallet. Reed smiled, a man outwitting the elements. He fished out the leathery fold, rifled through the sleeve, hunting for promising candidates. It held tattered bits of paper, wrinkled fragments. There were his credit cards, his library card—when had he last been?—four of his business cards. A two-for-one pizza coupon. A receipt from a gourmet food shop: prosciutto, Gouda, lox. If Mexico was an outhouse, the U.S. was a deli. A Xeroxed take-out menu from a Greek place in Brookline, famous for its moussaka. A receipt from a liquor store (quart of Cutty, half-gallon of Stoli). A note from Andrea, reminding him to pick up a pound of shrimp.

Reed kept pulling one piece after another from his wallet. Like summoning up bits of his history. The process was mesmerizing, revelatory. As if he had come across himself for the very first time. Scatology recapitulating autobiography. Reed spread the shreds of paper at his feet. They seemed unworthy, abject. A better man, it occurred to him, would have a far different wallet—a wallet filled with minor trophies attesting to his business acumen, to his sexual proclivity, to the love of good friends. Yet Reed's wallet continued to disgorge meaningless tidbits: a perforated card certified that he carried ample auto insurance; two theater stubs (*Phantom*); a tag from the dry cleaners; a note from his dentist. His appointment had been two days ago. A plastic facsimile of his birth certificate (weight: 7 lbs., 8 oz.; hair: brown; eyes: brown; The State of Indiana. Reed, Benjamin Franklin. His father's idea, amateur student of colonial history.) There was a scrap covered with what appeared to be his own craggy scrawl.

He paused now. The whole of his life seemed to lie before him. The scattered papers stared up at him in the cold truth of the moon. The montage was disheartening. His life was shrimp, missed dental appointments, auto insurance. His life was a message to himself—a message he could no longer read.

It might have ended there. A man in a fit of self-pity, he would shake his head, rise, head home. Home. There was that at least, there had always been that. One grand thought is enough to sustain us, to see us through everything. But home was now the fragments at his feet. It was this to which he was returning, it was this that awaited him. Chilling realization. When had the ponds of his childhood gone scummy, the dogwoods diseased? When had the girl next door traded her apron for the tools of a dominatrix? The postman was dead. It seemed a scandal of national proportions, a massive failure of tribal character. The betrayal felt profound, generational. It was his age that had lost a war, despoiled the rivers, looted the world. An abdication of life's rightful claims. He regretted suddenly all the women he had never loved, all the friends he had lost track of. He regretted all the times he should have placed his hands at Yates's neck, shouted, "Andrea. Her name is Andrea." He regretted the artist he never became, the drink he never turned down. He regretted his failure to recycle plastics. A thousand memories wheeled toward him now, memories of half-hearted acts, night after night slumped before the TV, besotted, his terrors early in the morning, counting the hours toward another drink. He was a man who would draw a glass of dirty water and give it to a sickly boy, a man who buys churches, who touches a madwoman's breasts. A man who lies moaning in the street. Acquiescent, dissipated, a man conquered. Cowardly acts, they spoke his name exactly. Forty-six years: what had he been thinking? What had he been doing? He stared off into the darkness, the night hushed. It was the hush of the Colosseum.

He had been eating moussaka.

It might have ended there. But take a man far from home, a stranger to recent successes. Bloat his stomach with suspect food, fill his head with bad liquor, psychic elixir. Savage him with self-doubt. Give a quick stir to his colon, then plunk him down on a riverbank made dramatic by the moon.

Then put sounds in the bushes.

Put sounds in the bushes. Distant, thin, he could not be sure. He heard it again. Quick whisper of underbrush. He licked his lips. Sough of weeds answered. Reed froze, his heart racheting in his ears. Common sense told him it was the wind, it was nothing. Common sense told him to pull up his pants, to zip himself up. But he was far from the tranquil valleys of common sense. It was night, the land was silver, a chorus of sounds rose up about him. His thoughts were rabid. Commands flowed from his brain: run, hide, flee. But they got fouled in the vicinity of his thighs, they died in his knees. The wind climbed with renewed force, no mere desert breeze, but an encroaching gale. It ravaged the weeds, whipped the water. It tore through his life, scattering the scraps at his feet. Reed, uncomprehending, groped for them. But pants at his ankles, he managed only a heavy belly flop, sand up his nose, grit in his ears. The night hissed, lament in the wind. Reed hugged the soil, refusing to believe, yet sensitive to the possibility of epiphany. As if on cue, the sky obliged with a shock of light. The world roared. Reed covered his face with his hands, peered through slits in his fingers. The light was shattering, apocalyptic. Immense, booming voice then, it shook the earth. Like God. Except God was speaking Spanish. Spanish with a Texas accent. The light found him, voice found him, electrical, megaphoned. Reed writhed, a man trying to burrow into the ground.

Spooks appeared then. They did. Like creatures vaulting from the walls of his brain. Shimmering figures, milky white in the harsh light. They descended on him. Rebukeful spirits, angered at life's misdemeanors. An army of consequences, an army of repercussions. Reed's thoughts were scorching, theological. And Moe begat Paco, Emmett begat Roberto, Seymour begat Jorge. Perhaps son of Jorge would one day appear on the streets of Boston, finish the job once and for all. The justice of it would be precise, exacting. Reed heard a low keening noise. He keened again. But the wind wrenched his sounds clear, carried them off. Deaf spooks, fortunately, they ran on past. At the bank, they all stopped to remove their shoes. They gained the river with metallic eruptions of water, robust splashes. Perhaps a dozen—tall spooks, short spooks, old, hobbling spooks. A spook wearing a hat. Another with a mustache.

Spooks carrying their footwear. Reed stared as they made the opposite bank, scrambled up the ridge, mounted it, and disappeared. God turned then, gave chase. God was huge, illuminate, big rotors working.

The night went quiet. Reed lay for an hour, maybe more. We will never know. He finally rolled to his knees, considered the possibility of prayer, then rejected it. He was twenty years too late for prayer. He duck-walked to the car, his pants flapping about his ankles. He felt unclean, unmanly, unprincipled. Searching his bag for a change of shorts, his hand fixed on the figurine. In the moonlight, the countenance appeared dire, ghoulish. It looked pissed-off. It seemed the face of cosmic redress. Reed wanted to dash it to the ground. He wanted to clutch it to his heart. Instead he pulled up his pants, mindless of shit stains. In the car, the engine started with an embarrassed cough. He managed a fourteen-point turn, found the road again. Behind him, home. Yet home now seemed another name for the ills of the world. Its powers of consolation had been rescinded. He was mocked at the office, despised by his wife, ignored by his daughter, threatened on his own street. It was a world full of Chet Morgans. Reed's thinking was fractured, kaleidoscopic. Return now, and it seemed the very worst of his fears would come to pass. Return now, and he would be fired, cast out into the street. Return now, and his wife would leave him, take his daughter. Return now, and he would require expensive, invasive dental procedures. Return now, and dun-colored foreigners, recently employed, would murder him on his own block. Dread threatened to overwhelm him. He craved mitigation. He looked up, saw Mexico before him. An outhouse, perhaps, but he was sitting in a pair of clammy, rank jockeys. A befitting land suddenly. His reasoning coursed along unfamiliar routes. Recumbent vista, it now seemed to beckon. A land of heat, a land of dust. The climate of the prophets. The realization washed over him like sweet waters. Potentially, a land of assuagement. For a day, anyway. Maybe three.

He would always remember the night indistinctly, like a smudged word on the page of his life. Straight on through, stopping only for gas, the proprietor's children watching him guardedly. He drove for miles without seeing another car. There was only the reach of desert, a spire of cactus, a hawk circling above. Dawn, and mountains surged into clear view, precipitous shocks of earth, straining, like the fingers of a hand. He skirted wide around Mexico City, plummeting due south. The road atlas, courtesy of the rental agency, lay open on his lap like a prayer book. He drove big-eyed, intent, man hunkered at the wheel.

The sound of the rain forest at dusk. The rich overhang of the jungle canopy, the birds mere shadows moving through the trees. The streets of the village were narrow and of mud. Past a gas station, a cantina, a cobbler, a comedor. A drive through a strange town is like a drive through a hidden part of your brain. It is yourself you explore; you wait to see what you will do, how you will react, what you will say. You've never been here before.

Andrea was always early. She was early for lunches, meetings of the civic association, doctor appointments, parent-teacher conferences, Mass, teas, the hairdresser. That time she refused to enter the theater because Reed had made her late. He was insistent. It was a film he wanted to see. "Go see," she told him. "I'll take a cab." "Andrea—" But she was already standing at the curb, legs forming the bottom of a K, hand up in a hailing gesture. He had gone into the theater, mumbling to himself. She followed a moment later, sat three rows back. The movie was terrible, blood and sex where the plot should have been. The couple to her left were young, their necking rowdy. Reed kept rising, stealing down the aisle. Popcorn, chocolate mints, a soda. Popcorn. Reed's third trip and the girl whispered, "He's disgusting." Andrea left before the final credits, arrived home before Reed. "It was a great movie," he gloated. "A brilliant movie." She woke him late that night, her mouth to his ear: "You ate enough popcorn to choke."

She was early. She wandered through an airport gift shop, mugs bearing a spare likeness of the Old North Church, Boston Celtic pendants, a sweatshirt announcing Lobsters Are For Lovers. Men stood at the magazine rack, flipping through famous nudity.

In spite of everything, his absences always left her empty. If the trip had been a success, Reed would emerge from the plane, red-faced from drink, his mood boisterous, his humor high. That time at the baggage area after a trip to Chicago, he had lifted her off her feet, spun her around. Admiring, envious glances came their way. A couple in love. She had clung to him, whispered into his shoulder, "Take me home." If the trip had been a success, he would be full of talk of the venture, the meetings, the food. He would make himself the hero. She would smile, she would laugh; she would wake in the middle of the night, relieved to find the bed sagging with his weight. If the trip had been a failure, he would be dour, complaining. Red-faced from drink, he would make himself the victim. She would frown, shake her head, the picture of understanding. She would wake in the middle of the night. She would be relieved to find the bed sagging with his weight.

She checked the monitor. A half hour yet. She took a table in one of those tiny lounges peculiar to airports, the tables pushed close together, the prices extreme. A decor of fake wood and plastic plants. At the bar, two sailors sat, their hands clutching icy mugs of beer. Three men in expensive suits drank coffee at an adjacent table. The waitress was young, mid-twenties, her hair an unflattering red. She wore fishnet stockings, a short dress that showed her breasts.

"A glass of dry white wine," Andrea told her.

She had come straight from the theater. They were in the middle of rehearsals for *The Good Woman of Szechwan*. It was a

126

play she loved, a play she had fought to produce. There was Brecht's moral heat, his acid prose. The troupe had almost broken even on the Pirandello. Andrea enjoyed the gradual progression from initial auditions to the first reading, the evolution of the bare stage to floodlit scaffolding, the sound of hammers, the props rising in the darkened theater, dress rehearsal, opening night—there was a sense of mission to the process, a sense of inevitability that excited her. She sometimes painted a backdrop, or helped sew the costumes, or worked at the ticket office. Once she sat up in the mezzanine and helped a heavy, sweating college student named George work the lights.

It was a small troupe, an eager troupe. To her mind, a heroic troupe. Performances were attended by relatives of the cast, friends, roommates, parents who had come to town especially for the event. The theater company managed to survive from year to year on local arts council grants, a private foundation or two, last-minute fund drives. Their precarious fiscal future heightened the sense of mission, the air of camaraderie. At any moment the doors might be padlocked. They regarded themselves as voices of culture in the capitalist wilds. At cast parties, their jokes were erudite, their laughter knowing. The liquor was watered.

The waitress returned with her wine. "Miss?" Andrea called.

"Waitress," one of the men at the next table said. "Hey, waitress." He was looking at Andrea.

The waitress halted. Andrea said, "I asked for dry."

"Dry?" The girl appeared confused.

"She did," the man said. Soft, southern tones. An unfortunate tie. His friends peered over at Andrea. "I heard her. She said 'dry.' "

The waitress picked up the glass and sniffed at it delicately. Andrea looked away.

The waitress said, "But this is our house Chablis."

"The lady doesn't think so," the man said.

"It's all right," Andrea said. "This is fine."

"I was just trying to help." The man had risen, moved toward her table, helped himself to a seat. His two companions smiled now—discreet smiles, eyes shifting above them.

"It wasn't necessary," she said.

He smiled, unnecessary. His name was Darryl, he explained. A Baptist minister out of Dallas. They had been to a conference in Boston. The Baptist church was in a state of turmoil, hard-line fundamentalists taking over. Himself? He stood with the more moderate wing. "The farsighted wing." He sighed, the conservative threat everywhere. His past showed in his face. Late thirties, a drinker of milk. He had played football when young, he bought a new car every other year. Meaty, well fed, he was a man who spent his evenings at home, his evenings with his family. Though there was the occasional conference, God's work in a strange town. There had been that woman in Atlanta, there had been that woman in St. Louis, there had been that woman in Knoxville. Shy women, they had never done anything like this before, they assured him. Then they shed their clothes, screwed with undisguised zeal. Women far from home, he was careful about that, women who never threatened his idea of himself. Afterward he insisted the women kneel with him; they prayed together, elbows on the bed. The women listened to his words, to his rich voice. They felt ashamed, they felt uplifted. Now he gestured toward the wine. "At least let me pay for it. You can't trust these places to give you a decent glass of Chablis." She cocked an eye. He rocked his head. "I know, I know, you're thinking how would a minister know. The world has changed. Times have changed." He looked at his friends. Moderates, they nodded.

"Where are you headed?" he asked.

"I'm waiting for my husband. His plane is late."

"Your husband." He grinned. As if she had played her trump prematurely, now he held the winning card. He eased back in his seat, crossed his arms over his chest. "My plane is late, too." He said it softly, like a man laying down a wager.

128

Her response could make them both winners. When she said nothing, he employed that voice of his. Half the women in his congregation were secretly in love with him.

"Perhaps there's a place nearby that has good wine. Dry wine." He put his hand on hers. The gold band was thick, three large diamonds embedded in the amber.

She inclined her head, said nothing. He took it for assent. His eyes went triumphant. He slid his chair closer. She could see the hairs he had missed in shaving. His friends exchanged glances. With a casual flick of her wrist, she upended the wine glass. He jumped up, knocking over his chair. His shirt, the bad tie were soaked.

"Christ—"

She rose slowly, deliberately, a comely bird taking wing above some remote savanna. "Exactly."

She passed through the metal detector, found the gate. Jumbo jets formed a long line, each waiting for word from the tower. The lights of an approaching plane grew, then eased down onto the runway. The distance made the landing appear seamless, untroubled. She touched her hair, smoothed her skirt. There was a garbled announcement. Those waiting to depart on the final leg of the plane's itinerary—Bangor, the sign said—began to collect their bags, their children. An attendant threw open the door to the ramp. The travelers spilled out onto the concourse. The flight was long; it had been delayed. They looked irritable, impatient, their eyes seeking out those who would meet them.

She patted her hair again. One look and she would know everything. He would be smiling, he would be frowning. She was a cautious woman, a prudent woman. She had anticipated already how it would be should he lose his job. She would find employment as a secretary, a receptionist. Her age would make personnel managers pause, but there were her looks, her intelligence. A woman supporting her husband, her daughter, while he searched for a job. She would be silent, uncomplaining, dutiful. Like a nurse in a combat zone. The line thinned.

There was a break in the trail of passengers. A young girl, flying by herself for the first time. Then an attendant pushing an old man in a wheelchair.

She waited as the call for Bangor was announced. She waited as the first passengers boarded—the young, the old, the infirm. The wealthy in first class. She waited as the rest of the passengers boarded. She watched as an attendant closed the door to the ramp. She could see the lights of the plane as it taxied out of the way, making room for the next.

She waited another ten minutes, as if the plane might return, might disgorge one final passenger, a passenger locked in the bathroom, a passenger who had fallen asleep and was missed by the stewardesses. But the plane was rising now. She could see its nose lift, she heard its roar. The night would be clear and starry. A clerk was changing the sign at the gate: Denver.

"Excuse me."

"Yes?" The clerk was young, his cheeks heavily pitted.

"My husband—" she began. Then, "I'm sorry." She turned to go. "I was mistaken."

She drove through rush-hour traffic, arrived home at dusk. Laura was in the living room, watching TV. The autopsy report on the death of Quinto Bernal had been made public. A .38 fired from five paces, a hole the size of a nickel at the back of his head. The round tore away the lower half of his face when it exited. Lacerations along his wrists from the manacles. Hundreds marched through the raw autumn day, fists clenched, shouting. The mayor had appeared, the investigation was proceeding. On TV, the crowd booed, a few people scuffled with the police. Some arrests were made. The suspended officer's name was McCormick. He had received death threats, he had sent his family away. In the kitchen, Andrea began preparing dinner. She took down a bowl, some pans. Flour, eggs, butter. She worked quickly, thought like an unwelcome visitor. She barred its way with the clang of crockery, the breaking of eggs.

Laura appeared at the door. "Where's Dad?"

Her mother was sifting flour, measuring off three table-spoons of butter. She would not look at her daughter. "There was a delay. Business. He called, of course." She looked at her daughter. "I didn't entirely understand."

Laura took a stool at the counter. "So when's he coming home?"

"Soon. Hungry?"

The girl watched her mother work. She said nothing as her mother poured the batter into the tins. She said nothing at the bleep of the microwave. She watched as her mother combined the coconut, the chocolate, the sugar. She listened to the whir of the beater. Finally she said, "Mom." She made a face. "That's dinner?"

The cake was almost done. Andrea was laying down the frosting with generous sweeps of a knife. She stopped now, tossed the knife into the sink. Her laugh was weak, unconvincing. "Let's go out to dinner." An Ethiopian place had opened over in West Roxbury.

"I'm meeting some people. At the mall."

"I thought, with your father gone—"

"I'm meeting some people."

Laura had two, maybe three close friends. April, Karen. Eileen. They were quiet girls like herself, the bright ones who sat in the rear of the class. You could see already the beauty they would come into in two, three years. Boys were drawn to them without understanding why, taunted by their own hormones. Despite her father's fears, Laura had allowed only one boy to kiss her, and that had ended badly when the boy thrust his tongue into her mouth. She had pushed him away, saying, "Stop it." But he pressed against her, his body boring down onto hers. His fingers went to the buttons of her blouse. They were sitting in the front seat of his father's Oldsmobile. The boy had just spent forty dollars for a dinner of bad pasta, another fourteen for the movie. His father always checked the odometer the morning after, charging him twenty-eight cents a mile. But Laura Reed. She was in his geometry class. He had been watching her for two semesters. Algebra I, algebra II. She had a long face, a long nose. An intelligent face. Curves were coming into her body. He had followed their progress through polynomials, through the elusive x on the blackboard. With Euclid, her breasts had ripened. And so he had kissed her. The previous summer a girl had lifted her skirt, allowed him to look. Though the girl was his cousin; it did not count. This would count. But, "Stop it." Yet he was heated, breathing hard; his hands straining to touch. So she bit him. He had recoiled then, holding his hand in the other as if it were a block of wood.

"You'll give me cancer," he had whispered then.

"Don't be an idiot."

"I wish you'd stay home," Andrea said now. "Your mother is lonely." She tried to make it a joke. Yet it was true: her mother was lonely. Her mother had been lonely for years.

But friends, they were waiting. Laura went to the closet, put on her coat. "I'll get something to eat at the mall."

Her mother followed her into the hallway, her face drawn, hurt. "Do you need a ride?"

"Subway."

"Who are you going—"

"April. April and Karen."

Life to her had always seemed some vast experiment, death like a shutting off of funds before the hypothesis can be confirmed. She was willing to try most anything once. She prided herself on it. She could take a memory, store it up, and savor its meaning slowly, like a snake ingesting a small mammal. A cigarette in the restroom at school, half a bottle of brandy in a friend's basement, a joint at a party. One evening when her parents were out, she had taken the car keys and gone for a drive. Down Mass Avenue, across the Charles, up through Cambridge, Somerville, over to Concord. Walden Pond in the snow. She had once skipped school, taking the train south to New York City. A salted pretzel in Central Park, then a walk

132

through the Village. She had been to a synagogue in Dedham, to a Black Baptist church in Dorchester. One Saturday, she stole a book from the city's largest bookstore. A volume by Galeano, in Spanish, which she could not read. She smuggled it out between her knees, cold, broad binding against her thighs. It sat on her bookshelf still.

She had grown up in the city, she knew its streets. There was the hardness that comes from them. It showed in her eyes. She had seen drunks sprawled in alleyways. She had seen men beaten, cats tortured. Her purse had been rifled on the bus. An old, toothless woman once spat on her in the subway. One of her father's best friends—they went back years, they had gone to school together—had fondled her in the kitchen. Next to the cutting board. There is a kind of pride that comes from having endured.

He was waiting for her next to the escalators.

His name was Xavier. He remembered little of Port-au-Prince. It was the faded photos on his father's dresser, the names of family members he had never seen. Tales of Papa Doc, the tonton macoutes. An occasional, dim recollection of fires and gunshots appeared in his dreams. They had made the crossing when he was four years old. He remembered the boat, a leaking craft smelling of shit, the odors of fifty refugees crowded together. He remembered the hunger, the pirates. Two men were killed, a woman was raped. The pirates took jewelry, suitcases, clothing. He remembered the Coast Guard craft—white, sleek on the horizon. In the end, scarier than the pirates. Xavier was dark, his face the color of dirty motor oil. His mother had died two years earlier. A suicide. His father worked as a busboy in a downtown restaurant famous for steaks. His father always arrived home at two, three in the morning, smelling of animal fat, dishwashing detergent, smelling of rum. His father settled in the big wicker chair before the picture window and continued drinking until dawn. His thoughts were five thousand miles away, twelve years ago. Old songs, old memories came slurring from his mouth. His

English was haphazard, broken. His son dealt with the utility companies, the bank, he did his father's tax returns. He answered the phone. There is a loyalty so fierce that to speak of it is to demean it. They saw each other in the hour before the boy went to school. The boy cooked his father's breakfast—an egg, a hard roll, black scalding tea—then helped his father stagger to bed. The rest of the day was his. He was popular among some at school, feared by others. It was said he carried a knife. It was said he carried a gun. His arms were like bunched strands of thin cable, the sinews prominent.

That morning in school, she had found him waiting for her at her locker. He casually named a shopping mall in Back Bay. He mentioned a time. She opened her locker, deposited a few books, retrieved some others. She had occasionally seen him in the hallway, she had noticed him at some of the school assemblies. But they had never spoken before.

She said, "I don't understand."

"Sure you do. I'm saying let's get together."

"Oh, I understand. But I don't understand. You know?"

He grinned. He liked that. There was an odd cadence to his inflection, surprising, headlong shifts of emphasis. Lean, shiny features like the black death masks of the ancient Egyptians.

"South entrance," he had added.

He smiled when he saw her now, then motioned for her to follow. They went into a record store. Laura watched as he flipped through cassettes of Schumann, Mussorgsky. Scott Joplin. His talent was native. His mother had studied piano with the masters in the fifties. Paris, Salzburg, Vienna. He was one of those who, with a single hearing . . .

"Do you know this?" The question was like a reproach. She looked up quickly. He held a tape.

No, she had never heard of him.

He continued to pick through the cassettes. She wandered a short way, then returned, a CD in her hand. "He's good, too," she said, holding it up for him to see. The cover displayed a rap artist out of White Plains; he sang about the ghetto. Xavier

134

pursed his lips, said nothing. Her color deepened. Then he gently gathered her elbow in his hand as if it were an egg. Dark fingers against her skin. She could feel his heat.

"Stand there."

He shifted a cassette into the pocket of his jacket. He stole two more, each time positioning her to block the view of the cashier. She was fearful, silent, compliant. He moved in measured rhythms, his actions unhurried. His jacket bulged. Her armpits were damp.

Without warning, he veered toward the door. She raced after him. Out on the concourse, her heart beat like a fish caught in the nets.

He was hungry. They strolled to a deli at the far end of the mall. Inside, sandwiches wrapped in cellophane sat on the counter. She worried he might sneak one into his pocket.

"My treat," she said.

She watched as he ate a turkey on white bread, potato chips. They shared a soda. His cheekbones were high, then drove fast to his chin. He ate quickly, his eyes intent on the food.

"Here." He tore the sandwich in half. His fingers left deep impressions in the bread.

"No. Thanks." She could not decide what to do with her hands. They fluttered about her, flew from her lap, they went to her face, to her hair.

He glanced up. A girl who refused food. He gestured vaguely. Long fingers, bluish palms. His bites were large, he ripped at the sandwich with white teeth that seemed shocking in the black hole that was his face. She felt as if it were her flesh: he was tearing out her eyes, ripping at her throat. There was something unharnessed, almost reckless about the way he ate, the way his eyes shot about. The way he pocketed the tapes. An animal that fears another creature will come along and make off with its dinner, with its young. He was looking into the distance now, he was searching the mall.

"Why don't you get CD's?"

"I like tapes."

"But the sound—"

"I like tapes." Then, "There's a store downtown. The selection's better. I go there two, three times a week. They've seen me, they see what I do. They don't say anything."

"Why? Why don't they say anything?"

He said nothing. It was as if he had not heard her, as if she had never spoken. Without warning, he reached. A murmur of surprise escaped from her. She was wearing a small gold watch at her neck, a gift from her father. Eighteen carats, the mechanism was German.

"I want to check the time."

She closed her eyes, she opened them. His fingers grazed her flesh. The moment was raw, unadorned. She thought he was lingering; she could not be sure. "I've got to leave soon," he said. "You know." He released the watch. The chain trembled against her skin. He reached for more chips. He was oblivious to her, his eyes off again, roaming the shop. She was sure he had forgotten she was there.

"Where are you going?" She hated the words, the way they sounded. But he would rise, he would leave. In the hallway at school, he would avert his eyes. She would cease to exist.

He shrugged again. These shrugs, they seemed his permanent state, they told the story of his existence. She felt him drifting away, he was gone already. She felt herself shrinking, her back pressing into the ribs of her seat. His eyes were dark, the pupils tight.

He stood. She understood he was dismissing her. The scrape of his chair across the floor was like a rebuke. She stared at the plate. The remains of the sandwich were like some broken animal, a mess by the side of the road. She thought she might be sick.

"Why did you come?" He spoke gingerly, like a man baiting a trap.

"Why did you ask me to come?" A calm had entered her voice.

He smiled then, teeth erupting in his face. "The place

downtown," he said. "Maybe you'd like to go with me sometime."

She looked up. She shrugged. An exaggerated roll of her shoulders. He understood she was making fun of him. His smile broadened. She said, "Maybe."

His hands were deep in his pockets. A cassette poked from one corner. He seemed to be considering something, weighing things. He looked away. As if he had heard a sound, someone calling his name. Then his head came around, his eyes claiming her, gathering her up.

"See you," he said.

She watched him leave. She swallowed, rested her elbows on the table. The plate was before her. She picked up the remains of the sandwich. She took a bite. The action was absent-minded, unthinking. Turkey, bread, mustard, lettuce. She could taste nothing. She took another.

The village was renowned for rain and malaria. Ten months out of the year, the sky boiled. Drinking water came from the steel barrels that caught the runoff from tin roofs. The inhabitants lived long days indoors, talk impossible, the rain like hammers. The streets were unpaved. The mud was rich; it swallowed shoes, boots, a dog that time. The local tienda had always just sold the last of the mosquito netting. Mold was a way of life. Men drank a brew of corn liquor in the local cantina. Out in the plaza, two teenage boys wandered past. Their heads were bare, their hair lay flat against their foreheads. Their footing was sure. One carried a machete, the other a long pole honed to a point. In the storehouses, the corn rotted. Parasites swelled the bellies of children. Cattle stood in the shelter of trees. For twenty thousand pesos, a pair of yoked oxen would pull your car from the mud. It took the conquistadors thirty years following the fall of Montezuma to discover the village. Resistance had been great, the armor caked in mud and blood. Then the priests had come. The church was the only stone structure in town. Sunday and the faithful moved to their knees, the wine was passed.

Reed had arrived the previous evening, the windshield wipers beating. A storm thrashed all about him. He crossed a narrow wooden bridge, it spanned dark mists. The ancient struts creaked. He emerged into a dense shroud of undergrowth, the trees joining to form a canopy overhead. The jungle at night. It triggered worries. A flat tire, a broken fan belt, and by dawn jaguars might be feeding. But he had been crazed by exhaustion, by hallucinogens, by loopy, twisted ruminations on fate. Complicated stew, his brain simmered in its juices. Death by jungle cat would prove more noble than cancer, than being hit by a laundry truck. When at last the lights of the village appeared in the distance, they were few and isolated. Like lines in a poem that make you look up. An occasional figure in a poncho moved through their glare. The buildings were crude. The tires of the Toyota waxed dangerously over the mud. Reed drove slowly through the main square, his heart beating like tribal drums. On past an open-air market, its ceiling of corrugated metal, the stalls closed down for the night. In the distance, a hand-lettered shingle lit by a single bare bulb: Hospedaje.

An old man met Reed's knock. A bent, toothless man, he had lived long, he had seen much. Little surprised him. But his head rose at the figure before him, his eyes seeking out the face. Tall gringo, trembling hands. A gringo smelling of shit. Reed said, "A room. A bed." Reed said, "Sleep." The words were like pleas. The old man led him inside. He spoke through phlegm, pausing frequently to bark, to spit. His skin had the texture of an old boot about to crack. "Five dolla'," he said. "How much in pesos?" "Five dolla'." Reed could see the destroyed gums. "I don't have anything smaller than a twenty." They were shouting over the rain. "Four day?" Reed nodded. Four days, forty days, he didn't care. He was a holy man lost in the wilderness. The old man guided Reed to a tiny room in the

138

rear. The walls were unfinished boards. A single window allowed a breeze, a frequent spray of rain when the wind turned. There was a low cot shrouded in white netting, a chair, a table that held a pitcher of water and a shallow basin. A candle cast shadows along the walls. A mosquito flailed at it. The air had a fungoid odor, the smell of plowed earth. Reed tumbled into bed like a body pitched from a moving vehicle. Twelve solid hours, not even dreams could reach him.

Now Reed woke to the drip of rain, the odor of damp wool. He waited for his sense of self to congeal. He could have been a Russian peasant, a sleeping animal, a creature at the bottom of the sea. He lay with his eyes closed, willing himself together, straining to fix himself once again on the map of his mind.

He filled the basin with water and splashed his face, his neck, his hair. The roof rattled as if the sky were spilling gravel. He dressed in a cotton shirt, cotton slacks, a pair of deck shoes. His Lord & Taylor raincoat. Ridiculous garments, he knew. His thinking was rueful. The young blonde at the car-rental booth in San Antonio would click her tongue at the numbers on the odometer. Perhaps he would one day joke about that time he went a little crazy down in Mexico. He worried he had embarrassed himself mightily. He would make his way north, call Andrea, say, Car trouble, terrible. Yes, I know. Cheep cheep cheep. Small sounds, domestic sounds. Hubby coming home, Daddy coming home. Tell Laura I got her a souvenir . . .

Yet there was a reluctant thrill to the smell of old wool, to the sight of the rough boards, to the feel of chilled rainwater on his face. His was a life of synthetic fabrics, enamel paint, umbrellas. Suddenly, he was a man who had traveled far, say a man who had lost his mind, if only for a night and a day. Every man secretly believes that he has something of the psychopath about him, that he is capable of outrageous acts, profane acts, unconscionable acts. It is only this belief that keeps him from performing outrageous acts, profane acts, acts without conscience.

Reed found the old man sitting on the front stoop, spouts of rain falling from depressions in the eave. When Reed asked for directions back to the highway, the old man rose in alarm. He had been cheated before. "Four day. You pay for four day. No refund." He moved his hands as if shooing insects. Besides, the bridge was out. The bridge was often out. The river was so swollen not even boats could cross.

"A phone, then."

The phone lines were down. The phones were often down. It would be a day, maybe two. Depending upon the rains.

"There must be another road."

"No road. No refund."

"You're kidding."

"No." The old man shook his head vigorously. Where money was involved, he was not a man who joked. "No refund."

Reed scowled. "I don't suppose there's any food."

Sí, there was food. Of course there was food. They were a civilized people. The old man grinned, indicated the mercado. Reed had emptied his belly on the banks of the Rio Grande, driven straight on through. His dread from the day before had reappeared as a scalding hunger. As if angst were ultimately an intestinal condition, a product of poor diet.

Reed's shoes, the cuffs of his pants were coated with mud by the time he arrived at the central square. The roof over the mercado dinged with rain. Women labored over fires, working broad wooden spoons through iron pots of black beans and rice. Their faces held aboriginal breadth. There was the hiss of frying food, the smell of grease. There were tables covered with soap, clothes, baskets of fruit, exposed cuts of gristly meat. Vendors whispered to him as he walked past. He was taller by a head, it was impossible to ignore him. Children stared. Men peered out from under broad hats.

In a corner of the mercado, a long table sat empty. A girl stood to one side, slapping tortillas into shape. Reed took a seat at the opposite end. She was young, a curious distance between her eyes, her face flawed in the end by its brusque features, the dark stain of her cheekbones. Her hair was the color of fresh tar. In the States she would have been a clerk in a wholesale clothing store, a receptionist at a failing business, a girl who falls for well-educated men, men with money, men who treat her shamefully only to marry women from Barnard. Her nails were unpainted, her face blunt. It lacked all makeup. Her face, her presence were uncomplicated. An unintelligent face, Reed decided, a face for whom life is simple; it confronts only the most basic of obstacles and spends itself in overcoming them—a face for whom happiness, like God and justice, is an abstraction.

She finished with the tortilla, adding the smooth disk to a pile. She gathered a clump of moist cornmeal in her hands and began fashioning another. Behind her, a low flame crackled. Bits of scorched meat were arrayed along a spit. A dented pot held boiling water. The girl eventually appeared at his side, drying her hands on a rag. "Comida?" she asked over the din.

Reed told her he wanted a steak. Rare. Two eggs over easy, a side of fried potatoes. Tomato juice. And a bagel. Did she have a bagel?

She waited patiently until he was done. "Comida?"

Food. Drink. Weather. Life. Simple, solitary words, fundamental. Impossible to confuse. Language like a dart. All the times he had sat in a restaurant and debated whether the chicken or the pork, the scallops or the shrimp. Which model car, which color the walls. Summer, and there was the problem of the mountains or the shore. Which school to attend, which woman to marry, which day of the week. His love of complexity, his immersion in it. As if his life were a desert he sought to populate.

He turned his palms to the ceiling. "Comida."

At the hearth, she reached into a bag for a handful of grounds. The coffee foamed in the pot of boiling water. She laid two tortillas, still sizzling, on a tin plate. She halved an avocado, then freed the pit with a single stroke of her knife. Large, nut-colored, it thudded into the mud. She cut a slice from a wedge of pale cheese. She slipped three pieces of meat from the skewer. Her acts were deliberate, ceremonial, almost Oriental. She poured coffee straight from the pot into a chipped mug. The sugar was coarse, like aquarium rocks.

She brought him the mug, the plate filled with food. Grill marks scored the meat. The coffee was steaming, achingly sweet. He drank half a cup quickly. She returned with a fork. He could see the backs of her knees, the sturdy calves.

Meat, rice, beans, cheese. A feast. Given his mood, more desirable than riches, than women, than power. A jar of chiles floating in vinegar occupied the center of the table. He took his time, relishing the food. It seared his mouth. The cheese had a salty aftertaste. His tongue was the most conscious organ in his body. As if eating were epistemology. The whole of his existence seemed to reside in the power of his jaws, in the pressure in his brow as he chewed, swallowed, forked more food to his mouth. He ate like a young beast, like an infant; he was unthinking, engrossed. A man eating. It seemed great poetry. Each moment rose slowly, then burst upon him, shocking and palpable. There was only the food, the cup, the movement of his hand. The way his fork tinked against the tin plate. The feel of the clay mug against his lips. He was far beyond thoughts of phones, thoughts of bridges. His head seemed clear, his head seemed empty. The same, when you think about it. But don't think about it. Eat. He ate.

"Más?

He jumped at the sound. She faced him, hands on her hips. "Más comida?"

"No. No, thanks."

He smoked as she cleared the dishes. The next stall over, a woman was nursing. The infant made sucking noises, greedy sounds. The nipple was large, puckered, the pink mouth in search. The sight touched him. A woman giving succor; her destiny was succinct, direct, it was borne out every day. In the distance, the thunder crashed. Lightning turned the land silver, trees the color of cold steel. The world was no longer a place of demands, a series of questions he had to answer.

142

Reed slid back from the table, threw down a bill, hesitated, then added a second. He looked to see if it was enough. Intent on her tortillas, she would not meet his glance. "What was it?" he asked. "The meat, I mean."

"Comida."

The two boys returned from the jungle, struggling with a trussed animal. It hung limply from the pole. Reed watched as its head lolled at the end of its body, mouth loose, bleating raggedly. Blood pumped from a wound at its neck, washed by rain into the mud. A boar, Reed guessed. The land seemed savage suddenly. The bristles, the meat, its hoofs, its snout. None of it would be wasted. The dogs in the village would fight over the remains.

Reed turned to go. Then she was at his side, touching his wrist lightly. He gazed down at her. A dark face, a faint barbarism to her eyes. He had yet to see her smile. She indicated the table with a jutting action of her chin, her lips shaped in the moment before a kiss.

He had forgotten his cigarettes.

"Thanks," he murmured. He reached for the pack as a shard of lightning cracked, made her face white. He could not imagine her life, her worries, her future. Her mind, her hopes were an implacable terrain. He could never cross it, he would have died in the effort. She reached to brush a strand of hair from her forehead. The act was elemental, unthinking, singular. She was a woman at a washtub, a mare in a paddock, a child listening to a story. Her face bore tribal lore, men sitting around a fire would remember it. As if history is the teeth, the whorl of an ear, the burnished cheekbones. It spends itself in the line of her nose, the light of her eyes, her lips as she smiles. A facelift would obliterate the evidence of forty generations.

"Listen," he heard himself now. The girl looked up. The moment was naked. It seemed as if the tin ceiling, the crackling fire, the dirt floor—the rain itself—were waiting. He had nothing to say; he wanted only to prolong the moment, to extend her look. He seemed on the border of something, on the very cusp. "Listen," he said again. She was examining his face, searching for what might come next. It was the look of an animal at some unexpected noise. Not yet fearful, but curious, watchful. The animal, the girl would wait forever. In the States, a woman would have been frowning, leaning forward, impatient. She would have been saying, "What? What?" There were times when he was talking to Andrea that she would rise, as if at some signal only she could hear, and leave the room. He would sit, waiting, holding the story inside, refining it until she returned.

"I don't know if you understand." He was casting about for words. He felt like a figure in a bourgeois novel. The intrigues are delicious, the suspense thick. There are wanton women, dejected men—even a mysterious talisman. A novel of flight. The land, the weather are moments of portent. Coincidences abound, they assume meaning through their accretion. Novels that we hope will go on for a while yet. "I was told there were ruins nearby."

She listened closely, her head cocked. Then she turned and pointed toward the far end of the plaza. To the east, he realized.

He turned to go. She touched his arm a second time. She smiled. Her teeth were small and even in the space of her mouth, her eyes playful. It was like a prize one has not earned. "The region," she said, her voice lower, a bit heavier than he had first thought, "is famed for its iguana."

Reed blinked at her, shocked by her English, shocked by his breakfast. He turned quickly out into the heavy downpour. The girl went back to shaping cornmeal. Up in Reed's room, the clay figurine waited, defiant. At a clearing at the far end of town, one of the boys hefted the machete. He knew where to thrust. He had done this before.

Plato said the face is the window of the soul. Reed's soul was lined, aging, the nose veiny with drink. It was a face in decline, a face one turns away from in an elevator, a face at which one cautions children not to stare. Sickly pallor, flesh flaccid, the look of a beachcomber, an itinerant, a peddler. A man whose life adds up finally to nothing. No one can mistake it.

But the closest mirror was down the street, past the livery, south of the church. An old woman—her name was Migdalia—plucked her chin hairs twice a week. Reed saw only the food on his plate, the woman in the mercado, the rough timber of the buildings, the unending curtain of rain. His life was three thousand miles away. Sitting on the edge of the bed in his room, he felt like a man lost to history, a man who appears full-blown on the surface of the earth. A man thrown down into the middle of existence. For a day, anyway. Maybe three. Delicious conceit. The vertigo that comes with having nothing to do. He ought to have been at home, he told himself; he ought to have been huddling with Yates. But in the pitch of the land, in the sound of the rain, in the warm mesh of the mosquito netting, there was no ought. Reed recalled now the dizzy freedom that came with a day of hooky. Sitting with a cane pole in your hand, waiting for bass to strike—the sensation heightened by the fact that others sat in stuffy classrooms, studying the history of Persia. In the end, the bass were more real than Persia. Reed grinned at the clay face. As if it were a comrade, a buddy, a partner in hooky. But the figurine glared back, a partner in nothing. A jealous cipher, it guarded secrets. Reed studied it as if the secrets were his own.

Word had spread that there was a stranger in town, a brooding man who spoke no Spanish. A man, it was said, who carried a bundle of pesos the size of a human skull. That afternoon, Reed went back down to the market. The girl was there. "Comida," he said. She smiled, she remembered him. She wore the same dress; she had only two others, they were drying in her room. The slices of avocado were larger. She placed four chunks of meat on his plate. A young boy approached, hand out. The girl chased him away. When Reed finished eating, he went to the tables arrayed with goods. A heavy woman, rolls of flesh at her upper arms, gestured broadly, her Spanish like an assault. She urged one pair of boots on him, then another. They pinched the knuckles of his toes. He settled on a black pair. He selected a poncho. The hood dwarfed his head. Reed hesitated, his deck shoes, his Lord & Taylor raincoat in a bundle under his arm. A man of the city. The thought was mocking. The boy sat a little way off. Reed motioned him over. "Here."

The villagers gathered at their windows to watch as Reed, boots strapped high along his calves, the hood of the poncho shrouding his head as if he were a lost monk, made his way along the central square, through the perpetual downpour, to disappear inside the jungle fringe. Reed in his poncho, Reed in his boots. He was like a man on the threshold of an unexplored region, a man whose destiny swings between extremes, one about whom schoolchildren will one day read, or who will die alone and unknown, devoured by beasts. Not even his bones will survive.

The owner of the hospedaje had given him detailed directions. Reed's interest amused him. Now Reed followed a muddy path that wound beneath the palm fronds. The day was gray. There was the moist odor of fungi, of rotting vegetation, mingled with the sweet and unexpected fragrance of an occasional jungle flower. Mystifying smells, liberating odors. The footing was soft. He groped for vines, for low branches. He walked some thirty minutes, then paused for a smoke. He could see coconuts in the highest reaches of the trees, banana and guava growing wild. Luxuriant purple flowers, the petals open to receive the rain. He worked his way along a ravine, slipping deeper into the jungle, wending farther from home.

He circled wide around a large tree, its trunk the width of a car, to find an outcropping of low walls. They formed a vague triangle. He knelt next to one and ran his hand over the wet rock. The outlines were faint, impossible to make out. Still, they were clearly fashioned by human hands. He went to the second wall—it was as low and ignoble as a park bench—and then to the third. Patches of moss grew here and there, bird droppings graced its top. A broken bottle lay splintered at one

146

end. Tecate, read the label. Twenty yards on, he found the path blocked by an abrupt, towering rise of rock.

He tried to make his way around the obstacle. The undergrowth was dense; he found himself brushing past broad palm leaves, straining to separate gnarled knots of vines, mosquitoes feeding. He found himself worrying about snakes—fat, slimy hoses, their skins braided in a kind of Navajo weave. Or spiders the size of his palm, hairy-legged creatures that would fall from the trees and easily strike at his brain through the thin rubber membrane of his poncho. He wondered if there were apes, or pink-assed baboons, or raging gorillas. Or guerrillas. He envisioned angry men, done up in jungle green, hefting AK-47s, eager to kidnap wealthy landowners, government officials, and wayward gringos.

He had come full circle now and was back at the path. It was as if God had fumbled an errant boulder. He leaned against the stone and smoked another cigarette. What had he expected? He had expected maybe revelation, illumination. He had expected maybe Lord Popoxocomochomil. He had expected maybe Delphi. He expected to be able to say to his daughter, "This is maybe very old." He expected forgiveness, he expected absolution. He expected redemption. Unworthy thoughts, he knew. He was a man of the twentieth century, a man in an age of penicillin, high-speed trains, junk bonds. Admittedly, a man on a lark, impelled by murky whims. Yet he was unprepared for the intensity of his disappointment.

But the bridge was out. The phones were down. He needed to piss. Being a man of the twentieth century, he made a quick check to insure that no one was around. He unzipped, took himself out, and pissed long and hard, splashing along the base of the boulder. He sighed then, a thin, bittersweet sound. Man pissing in the woods. His life had come down to the most basic of functions: eating, pissing, breathing. There was only the boulder before him, rough, cragged, structurally confused. Higher up, there was a severe indentation sheltered beneath a sharp ridge.

There was a parallel indentation, an identical ridge, far to the left.

He backed slowly up the path now, member in hand, his eyes selecting the details, picking them out, arranging them in his mind. The face leapt out at him as if someone had flipped a switch. Some ten meters high, the same hooded brow, the same broad nose, the same flat eyes.

He had mounted the Spanish steps in Rome. He had stood in the shadow of the Sears Tower in Chicago. He knew the World Trade Center in New York, the TransAmerica Building in San Francisco. The Astrodome. The Eiffel Tower, Saint Peter's Basilica. Hadrian's Wall. The soaring surfaces, the great domed interiors, the classical lines, the gables, the vaults straining with ancestral dignity. He had studied the paintings of the masters, he had stood in museums and leaned close to follow the line of the brush stroke. He could discuss the merits of pointillism, the evils of minimalism, the challenges of cubism.

But this. His figurine all right, though the vast scale brought out unanticipated depths, hidden intricacies. Dense, abrupt, crude; call it "beautiful" and you would choke on the word. The mind behind it could never be breached, you would lose yourself completely in the effort. It seemed less a work of the imagination than an act of will.

The sky cracked thunder, threw harsh light over the stone. Reed stared, thoughts swarming in his face. He was not a superstitious man. He avoided neither black cats, full moons, nor the number thirteen. He did not believe in UFOs, the afterlife, or a realm apart. Yet he experienced occasional bouts of uncanniness. If he was not superstitious, neither was he oblivious. The world is attended by certain inexplicables. A star-filled night, a woman's laugh behind a closed door, an animal's spoor in the snow—each could render him mute. It was all he knew of reverence. Now the face rose before him, brute, awesome, opaque. Like life. As easily ask after the meaning of a city, a woman's cries, the course of a river. Reed found him-

148

self remote from questions of authenticity, monetary value, the opinions of an aging archivist. The sheer dimension of the stone, the chiseled features—its nose was like the prow of a ship—filled the jungle with intimations, hinting darkly that fate might be far different than we first imagined, or may ever know finally; that the real business of life occurs where our thinking is too afraid to go. That our days might well be ruled by hidden logics, by occulted cycles of recompense and retribution. It was as if he had seen, not the face of God, but the face of the earth itself.

Reed made his way slowly back through the jungle. He crossed the central square, where people paused. The men gawked, the women blushed. Children laughed. The old man was waiting for him at the door of the hospedaje. He sat Reed down, placed a glass of mango wine before him. "Señor." He indicated Reed's pants. "Close yourself, please."

A day passed, a second. The bridge was repaired. The phone lines were up. Each morning, he would rouse, tell himself it was time to depart. Time to go home. But he could not quite bring himself to leave. Not yet. It seemed he was in the throes of a kind of enchantment. It thrived on the imposing visage of the ruins, the chaos of the rain. On the dense, ubiquitous odor of humus. Leave, and he would break the spell. Then, too, there was the mercado every morning, and again in the evening. The rough boards of the table, the simplicity of the food, the noises he made as he ate—he had never listened to himself so closely, there had always been conversation, the TV going in the background, the fanfare of other diners in a restaurant; he sounded like an animal—gave him a curious pleasure. The girl was always there, her face blank, her hands busy chopping plantains, patting tortillas into shape. Her question was always the same: "Comida?"

"Comida."

Meanwhile, he was becoming known around town. He bemused the locals. Children begged nickels from him. The vendors waved to him. Nights he drank in the local cantina. He was like an amnesiac, a man who has forgotten everything, everything. A man who never existed. He returned to the ruins again, and then again. As if sufficient scrutiny might reveal their secrets. The giant face was like a hole in his understanding, a citadel against which the weapons of meaning were useless. Evenings he played chess with the owner of the hospedaje. Reed played slowly, guardedly; the owner always went for the mad sacrifice, the dashing combination. He beat Reed unfailingly. Reed would laugh then, his laugh clear, untroubled. One morning, the runoff from the mountains broke through a ridge, threatening a cornfield, a mango grove. He worked alongside the others, filling bags with sand, hefting them onto his back like a pack animal, placing them on the lee. Men joined in a tribal effort, men saving their village, their homes. Men doing what needed to be done. He smelled their odors as they worked; they smelled his. Later, he sat in the cantina with the others and drank from a bottle of mescal, understanding nothing that was said, ignorant, content in the way that dogs are content, mute with the happiness of monkeys, of oxen, of the rain.

Primitive land, noble savagery all about. Plans began to brew—wild plans, outrageous plans. In spite of himself. Unthinkable scheming, it revealed impossible futures, made them possible. He would contact the rental agency, offer to buy the car outright. He would purchase a plot of land outside town, perhaps set up an export outlet. Yates would be enraged, of course. He would be apoplectic. Andrea would be crushed, an abandoned woman, a bitter woman. Her greatest fear would have been fulfilled. His daughter would smoke pot, flunk out of school, work as a cashier in a supermarket. She would slash her wrists, she would marry badly. She would run off with bikers. He would miss his wife's thighs, his daughter's virtue. His home would fall into disrepair: the paint would fade, the shutters would slip from their hinges, the storm windows would never leave the basement.

But he was deep in the reverie, he was too far gone. Perhaps he would farm. Yes, farm. Work with the soil. Integrity in the ache of his back at day's end. Yucca, coffee, cane. He was his father's son; his genes contained the secrets. He smiled through the welts made by the mosquitoes—large, unsightly wens. He did not care; it seemed a kind of consecration. Quasimodo at last. He washed his clothes in the cement basin on the grounds of the hospedaje, he bathed every morning while standing before a steel drum. He had seen his first macaw, his first toucan, an ibis with the broad bill.

On the third morning, the rain let up. He stood at the window of his room and watched as a cloud of butterflies skirted the jungle rim, Carolina blue and each the size of a fist. The mud baked in the sudden heat. The odor of cocoa was in the air. At breakfast, the girl blushed. She could barely look at him. She had a surprise. She had been saving it. And now, amid the rice, the beans, the green tomatoes, the cheese, the curving hulls of avocado, there was a single egg, anemic, pale yolk. In that rainy land, it seemed a piece of the sun itself. He ate it solemnly, gravity in the action of his jaw.

He had become a man intent on fleeing himself, on reinventing himself. The dream is riveting; it is inscribed in his face. Happiness flowed through his mind like floodwaters rushing through the streets of a valley hamlet, sweeping away everything in its path. Joy is the rain, the mud, a glass of mescal. Rapture is a lone egg served by a peasant girl.

"¿Más?" she asked. Her face was open, expectant. She waited for his answer. The instant was like a space that had opened up before him, revealing a yawning stretch in which one could live a life. One could live twenty lives.

"No," he whispered. A satiated man, contentment is spoken in the movement of his hands, in the way he walks, in unworried sleep. "No más."

That evening, he broke. He could be seen weeping in the central plaza, unshaven, a bottle of tequila in his hands. The owner of the hospedaje was summoned. Children stood off to one side, staring. Crows gathered along the eaves and peered down. Men looked away. Women crossed themselves. The owner came running. A crowd lined the street as he gently led Reed away. "Señor, what is it?"

It was the most banal of things, the most ordinary. It was a hot dog on Boston Common. It was the smell of a woman's perfume as she stepped from an elevator. It was a lone bloom piercing six inches of snow. It was the way the Charles River looks early in the morning, the soft cadence of the coxswain's voice, an old man—he must be eighty—jogging with a Labrador at his side. The peanut vendors are already out. It was a bar full of fans, screaming for Bird one last time, that final time. It was the national anthem at hockey games, baseball games, football games, basketball games—trite tune, impossible tune; yet it drove his heart into his throat. It was ice outside the window of a room in which you have just made love. It was the mottled, warped ashtray Laura had fashioned for a Father's Day ten years ago. It was an old woman on the subway, reading a cheap historical romance and crying. It was why returning prisoners of war, astronauts, and sailors thought lost at sea dropped to their knees and kissed the ground. Fatuous, mawkish, he knew. But then so was he. Confused, impure fragments of life. Hence crucial, ineliminable. Inescapable, in the end. History is a jealous woman; she pulls at your coattails, she pleads, she rages. She complains to the neighbors, the minister, your boss. When all else fails, she flings herself against the door, bars the way, her face drawn, wild, a pair of scissors in her hands. It is not your love for her, but the obvious depth of her feeling that ultimately brings you home.

The following morning, the final morning, he sat at the window of the room, felt the rain on his face. The figurine hunkered on the table, glaring out at him. After the ruins, the face seemed odd, incongruous in the closed space of the room. Like seeing a photo of a linebacker with his family. Reed began packing. Dreams are only as necessary as they are impossible. He experienced a morbid sense of relief. His course was inevitable, inexorable, like the path of a storm, like the workings of a machine. It seemed the suspense had ended, the final heroics had been played out. He was like a man who suddenly understands. His despair was complete, he could no longer recognize it; it had soaked into the landscape of his mind.

She appeared as he was placing his things in the back seat of the car. She wore a simple white dress. She had washed it the evening before. It was still damp. Her arms were bare, her hair was up. Spare strands lingered at her neck. It took him a moment to place her. She was carrying a cloth bag.

"Señor . . ."

"Mmm?" He was adjusting the position of the suitcase. The figurine formed a lump against the leather.

"You are leaving."

Reed blinked at her. Then, "Of course. You've been very kind." He reached for his wallet, pulled some pesos from the fold. "Here."

She frowned. She did not want his money. "My father. He lives to the north."

"Your father." He understood nothing.

"It is not far."

"Ah." He shook his head. His smile was narrow, apologies were already collecting. "I'm afraid I'm leaving right now."

"I am ready," she said. She had little. Everything was in her bag, on her back.

"But there must be buses."

Her disappointment was sharp. She turned to take in the village. No, there were no buses. Sometimes she caught a ride with Eusebio when he drove north with a load of coffee beans. Sometimes she rode in the back of Adolfo's truck when he needed supplies. She had ridden with doctors, with priests when they came through. But the coffee harvest was over. Adolfo had purchased supplies just last week. The priest was not expected until Sunday. Yet her papa. He was old, she had just received word that he was sick. She must go today. "Today." Her eyes were imploring. "My name," she added, as if the mere sound might decide the issue, "is Socorro." Her face was crude, planed, a face of the soil. There are faces destined to captivate, fated to rule.

Reed sighed. His weariness was like a board pressing down onto his back. "It's not far?"

It was the kind of moment biographers emphasize, to which they devote entire chapters.

Part Two

Four

Quinto Bernal was born in the town of Mayaguez, on Puerto Rico's western shore. As a boy, he could stand in the kitchen and see the beach through one window, the mountains through another. His father tried farming, he tried fishing, he tried making hammocks. But the man's passion was politics, not money. A Puerto Rican nationalist, he had chained himself to the gates of a military base, he had lain in the middle of highways, he knew of secret caches of rifles. Files in Washington bore his name. He entered jail when Quinto was two, again when the boy was seven, again when he was eleven. When Quinto turned thirteen, his father disappeared. It was said he was in Havana, others said he was in Managua; a few suggested Moscow. Some said he was dead.

Quinto dropped out of school to work on his uncle's boat. His uncle was hardheaded. He cared nothing for politics. Ten dollars would buy a two-hour tour. A shark sighting was guaranteed. "There, there," his uncle was always saying, pointing at nothing. "Don't you see?" The boat was small. It held eight passengers, twelve when the coastal authorities weren't looking. The men were always pallid and heavy. They stood at the bow and rocked on their heels like commodores. Their wives sunned themselves in the deck chairs Quinto set out before every trip. There was that one who removed her top. His uncle had to let him go the day he caught Quinto with his hand in the till.

There was rum in the evenings, fishing during the days, the occasional odd job working as a waiter, as a yard man at the hotels. For banquets he was issued a white jacket and a platter of hors d'oeuvres. There was a golf course in town; it was said Nicklaus had played there, Trevino, Snead. He could always caddy. Nights he went diving in the pond on the fourth hole. A dogleg par five, too many golfers tried to clear the water with their second shots. He worked for a while for a man who fashioned birdhouses from coconuts. Damp weather and the birdhouses rotted, but by then the buyers were a thousand miles away. The man had to let Quinto go the day he caught him with his hand in the till. There was María Elena, there was Leticia, there was Guadalupe. Brown bodies, willing bodies; the sun glistened off their skin. There was that middle-aged gringa, she parted her flabby thighs and made chuffing sounds in his ear. Her husband had gone snorkeling. She did not miss her emerald earrings until she was back in Omaha. In the end, Quinto married the girl Lupe. She had a gap between her front teeth, a laugh that made men exchange sly glances. They had a daughter, they had another. Twenty years old with two children, a wife to support; there was that week he made eighty-five dollars.

But Lupe had a sister in Boston. Her sister had an apartment, a car, she had a job. The letters Lupe received made her weak with envy. Lupe threatened to leave him if they didn't move, she would leave and take the children. She would take her laugh. They found a three-room apartment in East Boston, rats and cable TV. Quinto bought an ancient Chevy. The tires were bald. It burned a quart of oil a week. His brother-in-law knew where to get the tags, the inspection decal, the required stickers—"Puerto Rican insurance," he laughed. Quinto worked at a carwash, he worked on a loading dock, he worked at a gas station. They had another daughter. She slept in a crib in the corner of their bedroom. Winters they turned on the oven, made love in their clothes. The blue glow from the TV could be seen through their windows. Evenings he drank with Fernando, with Pato, with Rico in a little bar down the street. Merengue and cumbia played on the radio. Lupe was getting fat, Quinto told his friends, Lupe did not always bathe. Fernando knew a woman. Ten dollars. Twenty if he wanted the other. Her name was Rosa, Fernando explained, she would undo your zipper with her teeth. A few weeks later, Quinto was pissing razor blades.

A winter, two winters, three. They moved, then moved again. He played Lotto every day, the Lucky Seven once a week. Rico paid him thirty dollars to ride the T to Braintree with a paper bag in his hand. Quinto had the good sense not to look. He sold pretzels from a cart that summer on Newbury Street. He was mugged in broad daylight; the first punk straightened him up with a blind punch, the second had his wallet before Quinto hit the ground. Quinto owed Boston Edison three hundred dollars. Then the owner of the gas station caught him with his hand in the till. He worked one month at a bakery, the next month painting houses. He was two, then three months behind in the rent. Christmas and that Jew who paid him twenty bucks to babysit three hundred Douglas firs on a vacant lot. Rico gave him forty dollars to take a paper bag to Cambridge. The Sunday he took Lupe and the kids to the zoo, they returned to find the TV gone, her jewelry, the refrigerator. Somebody had stripped the bed, crapped in the center of the mattress. What kind of place was this, he wanted to know, where people did such a thing? They moved again. Quinto was arrested for shoplifting—a two-hundred-dollar leather jacket, a pair of boots. He got off with a fine, six months' probation. He owed Boston Gas ninety dollars. Rico gave him seventy-five bucks to take a suitcase to Chelsea. Lupe went into the hospital, mysterious female trouble. The details made him queasy. The gas was shut off, the electricity was shut off. He gave blood. He sold his car to a black kid with a hair-cut that said X. The gas came back on, the electricity would be on the next day. Three o'clock in the morning, he took a bus to Dorchester and stole his own car.

They had another baby—a boy. They named him Sexto. Quinto's pride was choking. The nurse held the baby up as Quinto pressed his face to the nursery window. Then he and Fernando went to a bar, they went to another, then another. No one would let him buy a drink. Rum and Cokes appeared in front of him three at a time. Outside, a gentle rain fell. It seemed to be the song of his son. Sitting at the bar, Quinto talked about how he would teach the boy to play baseball, to change the oil, to catch a girl's eye. How to catch a fish. How to saw a board, hammer a nail, drink a beer when the time came. "Kicker on a football team," Rico told him. Fifteen minutes a week. It was the best job in the world.

Driving home, Quinto was stopped by two cops. White cops. Quinto lurched from the car, said, "I have a son today." But the police didn't care. His tags said August. The police-men spoke with clipped Irish vowels, one muttering something about bean-eaters. "I ain't no Mexican, you fucking Mick." The cop set the flat of his baton smartly along Quinto's skull. But Quinto had been drinking; his head was dense with fumes, impenetrable. He had a son today. Quinto got up. The baton again, he fell again. "Stay down." Quinto got back up, laugh-ing, sneering, spitting. "Come on, Roy," the second cop said. Roy McCormick swung one last time. A glancing blow, but it found Quinto's nose, planting a red rose in the middle of his

160

face. Quinto's fist began from down low, a fierce uppercut, the whole of his weight concentrated in three knuckles of his right hand. McCormick fell heavily. He rose, hitched up his pants. "Roy," the other one said. He had already cuffed Quinto, slammed him against the car. Blood flecked the hood ornament Quinto had stolen off a Mercedes. "Roy, now." The next day, neighbors would say it sounded like a car backfiring.

Three thousand people turned out for the funeral of Quinto Bernal. They had to block off Green Street, Forest Hills Avenue. The gangs stood in their colors, keeping a cautious distance from one another: the Muchachos Rojos, the Latin Princes, the Amigos. The church overflowed; mourners spilled into adjacent yards, onto the grounds of a school. A city councilman spoke, a state senator. Regrets came from the office of a U.S. congressman. Sexto Bernal was four days old.

The cop who had been with McCormick—his name was Leary—was in an office, explaining for the seventeenth time: "The man was drunk. It looked like he was going for a weapon. A knife, maybe." "But there was no knife." "It was dark, it was hard to tell." "There was no knife, the guy didn't have a gun. He didn't have so much as a tire iron in his car. All he had were the cuffs around his wrists." "It was dark. The man was drunk. It looked like—" "You're saying it was righteous?" "I'm saying it was dark." Leary's father had been a cop, his grandfather had been a cop. It is a fraternity, the fiercest kind of loyalty.

The casket was lowered into the damp earth, borne by six men who had never met Quinto Bernal. Lupe hurled herself into the grave, she lay weeping. The footage would headline the evening news programs. Two million people heard her cries. Afterward there was a rally. The sound system crackled, communicating fury in three languages. A police lieutenant from internal affairs was on the phone with the mayor:

"I can't give you any guarantees."

Socorro had learned English from the nuns. "Sister Miriam, Sister Bernadette, Sister Alice." They came to open a medical clinic, then stayed to start a school, a worker's cooperative, a water-purification program. "Everything." She still had her confirmation dress. Now Miriam was dead, Bernadette had gone on to an abbey in Tehuantepec, Alice had left the order to marry. "An ex-priest," she said, her voice leaking scandal. Her mother had died seven years earlier during childbirth. Socorro had five brothers, she had her father. Reed saw her then, a woman in a house full of men; there was the cooking, the wash, the water from the well. The mounds of soiled clothing, the sounds of male eating as she served them. She was the oldest. She had left home two years earlier. She returned once every month or so with a shirt for her father, with sugar, salt, a toy for a brother. With money.

She asked if he was going home, too. He nodded. She smiled. It seemed they were alike. He wanted to shake his head, to tell her that she did not understand. She would never understand. That there is a kind of longing which no home can cure. Yet he said nothing. He had become a man of infinite patience. He tolerated her talk as one tolerates an old woman on the bus; she wants to tell you about her husband's bunions, about her grandchildren, about how she was two numbers away from winning the lottery the previous week.

But she was looking at him, waiting.

"I'm from Boston," he said.

"Boston."

"In Massachusetts."

She looked troubled, lost. It was the face of a student working a math problem, figuring the velocity of falling bodies. Then her eyes brightened. "I am familiar with it. A land of mountains and wild game. Near North Carolina, no? I have a friend who picked yams in North Carolina."

There followed a confusing tale concerning her exboyfriend, a certain Epifanio of yam-picking fame. His passion was horses. He knew them better than anyone. He knew them

162

better than he knew people. Sitting astride a horse, he was happy. "He could make a horse do anything. Anything." Her face broadened with the memory. This Epifanio wanted to marry her. She could not bring herself to agree. Her life would have been a life in the village, a life sweeping dirt floors, a life making tortillas. She wanted more. She had read the magazines, she had listened to the radio. There was life beyond the village. The world was a huge place, an unimaginable place. Epifanio could not understand. He would not understand. They would build a small house; she would wash his clothes, cook his food. At night she would open her legs. What more was there to understand? "I said to him: 'Epifanio, there are people in the world who eat meat every day.'"

But then, "A puta." Her name was Mireya. She was a tall girl, light-skinned. Her family claimed descent from Spanish viceroys. A beautiful girl. A girl with a painted face, rings on the fingers of both hands. Her clothes were expensive, revealing. Her father owned a stable of horses. She lacked nothing. Meanwhile, Epifanio wanted a family, he wanted a house of his own. He wanted a wife. "Go," Socorro told him. "I do not care." He married Mireya in the end, now he spent his days riding, his nights trying to make babies.

"A puta."

Socorro nodded. "A war."

Reed looked at her. "A whore," he realized.

"Sí. A war." Then, "A plane waits for you in Mexico City?"

"San Antonio."

"In Los Estados?" The name excited her. Something new entered her tone. Her face appeared open, expectant. If she had been born two thousand miles to the north, she would have been a devotee of rock stars, a girl on the swim team, a girl whose complexion has been ruined by chocolate. She would go out with a Joshua, she would go out with a Kurt. She would favor lame movies of love, her gum popping. She would eat meat every day. She would eat hamburgers, French fries, pizza.

"In the States, yes."

They crossed the old bridge. He could see the new boards where it had been repaired. On either side the drop was steep; the river wound its way far below. They were emerging from the rain forest. There were breaks in the canopy of trees, the sun poking through. They were climbing. The day was warming. A broad mesa appeared in the distance, a dim suggestion of mountain peaks on the horizon. When he turned on the air conditioner, she made a show of shivering. Her shoulders were naked, her legs bare. Her hair was up. He reluctantly turned it off. His shirt clung to him, his temples were moist. "At least roll down your window," he said. A breeze rustled the loose strands of hair at the nape of her neck.

"I am nineteen," she announced.

At nineteen, men still dream of greatness, women still believe in love. Death is an unreachable star. The number was like a train bearing memories. At nineteen, Reed had taken a year off from college to earn tuition money. Times were failing; the farm was already in trouble. He worked at the GE plant in Louisville, the graveyard shift, bending to insert a screw here, a screw there, and then the rubber gasket. He was the one who put the spring in the door of your dishwasher so it sprang shut.

The regimen was strict, the assembly line unremitting. The noises were immense, conflicting: the rasp of drills, the roar of the generators, the clanging of the great sheets of metal. They were the sounds of medieval battle. He stepped into the light of early morning at the end of the shift with his ears ringing. He found the work appalling. He found it oddly gratifying. On days off, he sometimes wandered through department stores, stopping to examine the appliances.

"Doors," the foreman had told him his first evening. The man's name was Billings. His head seemed like an afterthought next to his enormous body. His flesh chafed the insides of his thighs. He carried the odor of talc with him everywhere. "You do doors. You don't do dish racks, you don't do motors, you don't do fans. We have a streamlined operation here, we turn out ninety thousand dishwashers a year. That's a lot of doors. It's what you do. Now say it."

"What?" Reed had donned gloves, goggles.

"Say 'doors.' "

"Doors."

The women worked side by side with the men on the line. Reed was surprised at the range of female scents. Most of them were young. They had husbands, several bawling kids at home, damaged skin. Their names figured prominently in the fantasies detailed on the walls of the men's bathroom. The women envied Reed, they resented him; he would eventually return to school. They all lived to be elsewhere. Yvonne hoped to go full-time as a cosmetician. Karen took classes in data entry. June's husband was based at Fort Knox and would be out in another year. It was as if life were some distant port. They were only waiting until they could arrive.

Reed liked the men better. They had arrived at life long ago; they had already overshot it. Their histories were tragic, often comic, like characters in a farce. Stints in jail, ex-wives who hated them, bad checks written in southern states. They stood at their posts on the assembly line, half-crazed, hung over, waiting for break, for lunch, for the end of shift. They lived in trailers, they knew how to set the timing on a car. Their capacity for drink, for weed, for pills was staggering. They owed enormous sums of money, they cheated on the women they were with. Their hopelessness was genuine. To get up every morning and make the drive on in, then stand for eight hours on the line amounted to a kind of heroism. When young, they had laughed at Popeye cartoons, they had sung Christmas carols, they had dressed as pirates and ghosts on Halloween. Now they sneaked hand tools out the factory gate, they drank beer in the spray room, they occasionally worked off quick fucks in the storeroom. They were unbelievers, saboteurs.

Billings disappeared every morning around one and did not return until four. "If his wife ever shows up," James told Reed, "he's off doing inventory. You can't miss her; she looks just like Billings, only bigger. No ma'am, impossible to get in touch with him. All these warehouses full of parts. Yes ma'am, he could be anywhere. Anywhere." When Billings disappeared, James rolled a joint, then smoked it standing under the exhaust fan, his eyes knit with pleasure. The women took the pins out of their hair, let it cascade down their backs. Carmine ran to the restroom to cart off papers towels, liquid soap, rolls of toilet paper. "I got three daughters. I got a wife. Her mother lives with us. Her aunt keeps talking about moving in." The radios would come out, the volumes all the way up to compete with the din of the factory. "Billings never comes back?" Reed asked James one night. James leered. "Her name is Rowena. In shipping." Reed started packing a pint of scotch in his lunchbox.

It was during this time that Reed let his hair curl over the edge of his collar. He would go two, three days without shaving. He was drinking every day. He would drive over to Boyd's or James's at shift's end and spend the morning playing poker. Their women would set out plates of bacon and eggs, white toast. The coffee was spiked with bourbon. A child in soiled diapers always played in the corner. It seemed Reed had some native skill. He would win fifty, seventy-five dollars, then take them all out for a steak dinner, drinks that evening. They would arrive just in time to punch in, running a red light or two, slamming into the parking lot, the tires screaming, then barrel through the large factory doors, drunk, exhausted, bleary-eyed. During breaks they lined up at the garbage cans and heaved up their steak dinners, the bourbon. Weekends they went bowling, they drove to Lexington to watch basketball games, they went waterskiing on the Ohio. Reed had become their friend. They invited him over for large Sunday dinners, to Labor Day picnics, to family outings. That time Carmine's wife took Reed's hand and pressed it to her breast. Two, three years in a factory, he came to understand, and he would be a different person entirely. He would be unrecognizable. He had it in him. It was as if he were merely a fragile community of moods, and now they were being altered, different impulses surfacing for the first time. Possibly truer impulses.

Five stations down the assembly line, her name was Elaine. She bolted runners for the dish racks into place. He noticed her that first day. She was small, compact, her hair platinum, stiff with chemicals, years of dyes. Her eyes seemed the site of great distances. She was forty, she was thirty-eight, she was forty-two; it varied with her temper, with the day of the week, with whether they were going into town for dinner or sitting in her trailer listening to the radio. With whether they had just made love or were about to make love or were going to make love yet again. He worried she did not take him seriously. "But I don't," she kept insisting. In bed her eyes went big and her sounds grew harsh. She enjoyed sex, its sweat and juices. At the highest pitch of the moment, she boxed his ears, slapped at his balls, yanked his hair. She bit. She was like an animal straining at the end of a tether, snarling, hungry, her movements quick, desperate. "You, now, yes you now," she whispered as he rode out the last of the ride, at a place far beyond where they had begun. She broke wind in bed and laughed about it later. But the sight of her nude, straining for a bottle at the top of the cupboard, made him weak. She had a passion for peanut brittle, Sinatra, and cheap gin. She had been married twice, divorced twice; she had a child in St. Louis, two children in Memphis. At Christmas she sent them bizarre, inappropriate gifts: tins of expensive chocolates, large wheels of Camembert, eighty-dollar music boxes. She had no idea how to be a mother. It was like some natural skill that she had lost along the way. One night he pulled off her pants only to discover she had shaved her cunt hairs. "But I thought you'd get a kick out of it." Bald vulva, stark, startling labia; he got a kick out of it. When drunk, when angry, she hurled dishes, they crashed against the walls of her trailer. She would wield shoes, the spike heels thrusting. Later, he would go out and buy her plastic dishware from drugstores, from discount shops, the sets fixed in slotted cardboard. She had mice. She refused to let him set traps. In the morning pellets lined the counter next to her sink. He picked up smoking from her, a genuine passion for detective novels—Hammett, Chandler, Jim Thompson—she taught him how to make a Rob Roy. There were entire days spent indoors, days of liquor and backgammon, days of fucking. He loved her meatloaf; she used mustard. He loved the way she swore at policemen, he loved the odor of gin on her breath, he loved the way her hair glistened in the rain. That fall, he returned to school. She knew he would; she had known all along. "I don't have to," he told her their last night. He meant it—he was certain of it. One word from her and he would drop out of school, live a life in a factory, pursue a different history, become a different man. Outside, the winds were high, tornado warnings came over the radio. She stood at the window with a drink in her hand. "I don't have to," she mimicked. The trailer bucked, the wind was shattering. Toward morning, she wept. "It's the weather, you idiot." Reed felt the loss suddenly now, he felt it all over again. A deep, scalding sensation in his groin, as if he had only just learned of a death that had happened years ago.

Reed glanced at Socorro. She was hunched forward in her seat, peering anxiously out at the road. Questions crowded her face. She set them out as if she were laying down a trail. She wanted to know about his family; she wanted to know the name of his wife, the age of his daughter. She wanted to know what he did for a living. He had difficulty making her understand. The idea of investments, financial services, market speculations struck her as odd—not the sort of thing a grown man would do. She wanted to know the size of his house. She wanted to know what he liked to eat. She wanted to know about Boston. She asked if he had ever been to Los Angeles, if he had ever been to New York, if he had ever been to Houston. She listened closely to his answers, she watched his mouth as he talked. There was a creeping hardness to her voice as the questions flowed out of her, to her face as she heard his responses. She was a woman who had endured certain privations unthinkingly, she could never have explained them; yet they were evident in the way she tilted her head, in the directness of her speech, in her looks. She asked about snow.

"Snow?"

She had never seen it.

Was it true that everyone owned two cars. Were the stores really stocked with food to the ceilings. Did people really travel beneath the ground. Were there really procedures where women could get their faces changed, their breasts made bigger, their bellies made smaller. Was it true there were machines that dispensed money. She had heard so much, she had read so much. She had lived too little, she was sure of it. The tallest building she had ever seen was three stories. She had never eaten lobster, she had never ridden a plane, a train. She had never eaten a bagel. She had never taken a shower.

The radiator boiled over, rich plume of steam. Reed swore, jerked from the car. She got out, watched closely as he kicked a tire. She hesitated, then kicked the tire opposite. She lingered at his shoulder as he bent under the hood. The failed car mystifed her. She looked to him for the answers. She wanted to know what that was called, and that. "Don't touch," he cautioned her. They had to wait, he explained, until the motor cooled. He leaned against the car and smoked a cigarette. The sun was directly overhead, the heat dry and searing. His head ached.

"Now?" she kept asking.

"I'll tell you when."

She settled against the fender. She looked bored. Reed felt oddly responsible, as if her boredom reflected badly on his companionship. He found himself telling her about how his father, on frigid winter mornings, would have to build a fire beneath the tractor to warm the engine. Timing was everything. The fire had to be hot enough so the engine would turn over, but not so hot that the gas tank exploded.

169

She appeared to be fascinated. She listened as if he were describing Martian mating rites. Then she squinted against the sun and countered with a story of her own. "My mother used to say, 'Socorro, there are three things you must remember above all else.'"

"Three," he said.

"'First, go to confession once a week. Less than that, and you will forget all that you have done. More, and you will have nothing to say. God is busy; you must not waste his time.' These were serious matters, you see. 'Second, never kiss a boy before he marries you. But if you must kiss a boy, kiss him only once you have a ring on your finger. And it is best if it is his ring.' Understand, my mother did not often talk of God. She never talked of men. She hoped to pass on to her daughter the wisdom that her mother had passed on to her, and the mother of her mother before that."

"And third?"

"'Always soak beans overnight.'"

"Beans."

"Sí. Beans." She smiled at the memory. Reed watched now as she reached with both arms to undo the knot in her hair. Her underarms were unshaven, like the first strokes in a charcoal drawing. She froze when she noticed Reed's gaze. He looked away. The hair fell about her shoulders.

Reed coaxed the car north, stopping twice more to let the engine cool. In the next town, they filled the radiator with water, topped it off with antifreeze. "I thought you said it wasn't far," he scolded her. He was anxious to drop her off, to have the privacy of the car. He needed time alone, time to think. Time to fit the last few days comfortably into his mind. Into his life. He was unsure what they meant. He was unsure whether they had any meaning at all.

Yet she was hungry. "Please." They found a quiet comedor. Shop owners, city workers, payroll clerks all looked up as he and Socorro came in. The Mexican middle class. Their stares made him uneasy. They looked at him as if he were a man abducting a young woman—she could have been the babysitter of his children—a man who forces her to undress in cramped hotel rooms so he can take photographs he will one day sell to his friends. But Socorro ignored their glances. She ate two tacos and one of his. She filled her belly unthinkingly, as one ties a shoe, buttons a shirt. She ate without talking, her elbows on the table, her head low. She ate like a day laborer. He drank two beers and the rest of hers.

"Do me a favor," he said as they stepped back into the street. A phone booth stood at the corner. She followed his instructions, explaining everything to the operator. Reed mopped his brow with his handkerchief. He took the time to refine his story. Car trouble. True, suddenly, but lame in the end. Implausible. Car trouble and one is two hours late, not four days. He could tell Andrea about involved negotiations, the numbing intricacies of international finance. He could say some other business had come up, a new assignment from Yates. Or should he simply say, "I needed to get away. A fishing trip. Museums." Maybe he should tell the truth. But he was unclear as to what that might be. A little clay statue, a wrong turn, a crap in the desert? Far less plausible than a host of lies. It sounded like the tale of an unstable man. The kind of man you did not want to be married to. Or should he meet the issue head on, should he say, "I ran. I bolted. Out of my mind." Make his voice light, lilting, a lilt to let her know that she was to smile, that it was nothing to be taken seriously. That he was a man who played jokes on himself. Though Andrea would not be smiling. She would think it was something to be taken seriously. One trusts a man who is home for dinner.

But when Socorro handed him the phone, he heard only the chime of the answering machine, trailed by the sound of his own voice. He shook his head. "Andrea? Andrea." There was an instant where he could have gone on, where he could have talked about García, about the figurine, about the long drive south. He could have talked about the rain, the ruins, iguana

171

breakfasts: "I could have been a farmer." The machine would cut him off, he could have called back again, and then again, filling the tape. But Socorro was watching him. His words would have been pleading, full of apology. He hung up.

"She is not home?" She looked at him. She was trying to figure him out. A strange man, a curious man. He appeared in town one day, she served him food. Then the final afternoon, there had been the scene in the square. His tears had embarrassed her. Now he was giving her a ride north. He seemed a man preoccupied, a man who lived deep in himself, fitful energies far below the surface. They appeared only fleetingly as a brief frown, an edge to his voice.

"She is not home."

Back on the road, she asked if his wife was pretty. "Andrea," she remembered. Reed nodded. She was pretty. "And she misses her husband," Socorro added, as if to herself. The idea of Reed with a wife, a home, the idea of Reed's life cheered her, filled her with images of domestic bliss. A family that ate lobster, she was sure, they took showers, lived in a tall building. Two cars occupied their drive.

"How much farther?"

"It is very close."

He wanted to know what was wrong with her father. Oh, he was ill. He was very ill. He was old, you see. There were problems with his back, problems with his lungs. Problems with his heart. Death was attacking on several fronts. He had worked hard all his life; he was a man who never rested, who never took a day off. And now life was catching up to him. Her arrival would make her father happy.

"Look in that bag, will you?" He was out of cigarettes.

She found the pack, she discovered Eve's book. She bent over it like a monk over a scroll, her lips moving. She heard the words in her mind.

He lit a cigarette. "Can you read it?"

She cocked an eyebrow. Of course she could read it. She was anxious to demonstrate her ability. She read haltingly, stum-

172

bling through Eve's twisted prose, her bizarre jargon. She read like a schoolgirl, her voice small, testing, anxious to do well. She stumbled over "phallocentric," looked to him for an explanation.

"Skip to another section."

She came to a long fragment from a conquistador's journal. It seemed Eve had included numerous excerpts, extended passages from first- and secondhand accounts. They filled pages, they gave the book heft. There was much about the King of Spain, about God, about cacao, about the search for gold. Aztecs were forever falling down in ambush, their tortures creative. The Spaniards were forever surviving. They understood themselves to be men of destiny. Both God and history had a role for them.

" 'And they took some of our ablest men prisoner, and we heard their screams until far into the night. In the morning, we learned that they had flayed our comrades, and their holy men now moved about in their skins. We wept then in anguish, and fear. There were many among us who demanded we return to Cuba that very evening, as we had surely come to the land of the Devil, a place that our Lord Savior never intended Christians to be.

" 'Cortez listened closely to their complaints. He agreed that it was a terrible fate that had befallen our comrades, and that this did indeed seem to be the land of the Devil. "And yet where better to spread the Word of our Lord?" he demanded.

" 'Next Cortez ordered that four of the savages be brought to him. These he had tortured in order to learn of the men responsible for this terrible act against our brothers. As the savages lay weeping and in great pain, and when they had told all that they knew, Cortez ordered that they be put to death and their bodies set in plain sight so that their kind would see what we had done, and that of which we were capable. One of the priests came to each of the savages as he lay dying, and softly explained the ways of God and His Kingdom, and asked each to repent on his deathbed, so that he might enter into the

Kingdom of the morrow. All but one of the savages agreed, and these were given the Last Rites by the good father, who assured them that they would soon know a glory greater than they had ever conceived. This last, an older man who carried himself with great dignity, and who refused to cry out as even the most ignoble—' " She faltered, her face a question.

"Something without honor."

She stored the information, determined to remember. " '—even the most ignoble punishments were inflicted upon him, asked if all Christians entered the Kingdom upon their deaths. When the priest assured him that this was so, the savage made it known that he would rather reside in Hell, as he did not want to spend eternity in our company.

" 'And so the savages were laid low with the sword. This done, Cortez then commanded that each of our boats be put to the torch, so that we would have no choice but to continue on our journey. A great lamentation went up from our number then, but the commander's orders were carried out. Many among us fell to their knees, tore at the earth, gnashed their teeth: our sails were burning, our boats were in flame.

" 'In the morning the waters ran black, and the sky was gray, and it rained ash.' "

She closed the book, set it on the dash. "That is very sad."

"They probably built new boats."

"I meant the old man."

She slipped into a light sleep. The beer, the travel, the heat. He considered waking her, demanding again to know how far. But her presence was rich beside him, dark. She lay huddled against the door, her knees tucked up into her stomach, her arms crossed over her breasts. She sighed thinly. Her sandals were worn leather, frayed rope. Her ankles were fragile twists of bone. He reached across to lock her door. She smelled of citrus.

Dusk. The line of volcanoes was clearly visible now, startling humps of earth that looked as if a scythe had cleared their summits. The lights of a village appeared like fireflies on the horizon. They lent a greenish corona to the twilight. Reed drove past a row of adobe buildings, the dull glimmer of kerosene lanterns showing through the windows. Past a wandering goat, a rooster, three cows that looked bored in their chewing.

"Socorro."

She yawned, stretched, minor hairs beneath her arms. She massaged her eyes with her fists. She looked like a child on the frontier between dreams and wakefulness, at that point where they appear equally compelling.

Sí, sí; they were close.

He balked when she directed him off the highway onto a broad dirt road. "How much farther?" But they were almost there, she insisted. The shocks groaned as he took the path. Mexico City was still some six hours away.

Ten minutes, twenty. A turn, another turn. Three-quarters of an hour. "How am I supposed to find my way back?"

But, "Here," she said. Reed braked the car. He saw nothing. "Here," she repeated. She rapped the dash with her knuckles. The act was definitive, demanding. A woman returning home. He squinted through the windshield, saw finally a small building of troweled stucco sitting in the middle of scrub brush and cacti. There was a warm breeze, hints of cilantro in the air. Socorro opened the door and stepped out. She reached into the back for her bag.

"Well—"

"Come meet Papa."

"I should go."

"He will want to thank you."

Reed hesitated. Papa was very old, Papa was dying. But old to a nineteen-year-old might well be forty, fifty. A boy had once appeared at the door, asking for Laura. A man. He had a deep voice, a thick beard. He was twenty-four. "No," Reed had insisted. He and Andrea had retreated to the kitchen while Laura sat with the man in the living room. "You're being arbitrary," Andrea told him. She wanted her daughter to be popular. The joys of mothers are largely vicarious. But Reed imagined the man placing hairy lips on his daughter's mouth, coaxing her with his bass voice into sexual acrobatics unknown to Reed. Reed was resolute, determined. The ice floated in his scotch like teeth. He and Andrea fought for another ten minutes, their voices low, strangled. In the end, Andrea swept back into the living room. As if it were her mouth the man would kiss, her sexual acrobatics, etc. Reed rushed after her, the ice tinkling in his empty glass. He would make a scene if he had to, embarrass his wife, humiliate his daughter. A man defending the integrity of his home from hirsute marauders with fully developed genitals. He found Andrea standing off to one side, looking distressed. Laura sat alone on the sofa, watching TV. "Where is he?" Reed demanded. "I didn't like him much," Laura said. She had met him in the library; he had been making a pest of himself for three days. On TV, the laugh track was shrieking, hysterical. "I made him leave."

Reed reluctantly got out of the car. Socorro grinned when he locked the doors. He followed her up a narrow path. The roof was flat, wood beams showed here and there through the walls. A boy appeared at the door, followed by two more. They ran to her. They cast uncertain looks his way. Socorro spoke then, reassuring them. They looked unconvinced. He was not Eusebio, he was not Adolfo. He was neither priest nor doctor. He was a tall, heavy gringo. Two brothers took her hands in theirs, the third knotted a piece of her skirt in his fist.

"Papa," he heard. Reed stepped inside, where Socorro introduced him to the oldest man alive. His face was heavily lined, the nose flat, the brow prominent. A man who moved in great silences, who used his hands, his back. He never looked in a mirror. His walk was ponderous. A hearty man, health showed in the size of his arms, in the breadth of his forehead. He would outlive Reed. He gathered his daughter in his arms, kissed her. She always reminded him of his wife—the alert eyes, the quick laugh. He asked nothing from her, nothing; he had given her everything.

His name was Onésimo. Reed met her brothers: Daniel,

Manuel, Sencillo, Alberto, Pablito. The same eyes, the same mouth, the same deep expanse of face, a face honed with an adz.

Reed shook their hands. Their expressions appeared empty, closed to all interpretation. Socorro went to stand before the hearth set into a wall. The fire popped. She began preparing dinner. As if she had never left, as if her father and brothers had been waiting for her to return so they could dine once again. Reed said, "I should go."

She said, "Eat first."

Her father and brothers looked up at her words. The sounds of English coming from her mouth always surprised them. Unassuming folk, they had eighteen hectares of corn out back, a burro, a pig that they would butcher in another two weeks. Their days were cold mornings, scorched afternoons, evenings around the hearth. They inhabited a stony quiet.

Rice, beans, green chiles seared black. Thick tortillas. They sat at a long table, the largest piece of furniture in the room. Reed watched as Socorro ladled food onto his plate, and then onto her father's plate. The brothers waited. Their anticipation was like another person seated at the table. But her actions were austere, unhurried. She moved with deliberate dignity. As if feeding her father rice and beans were her crowning achievement, her reason for being. They all paused, dipped their heads, crossed themselves. Belatedly, Reed did the same, a finger moving vaguely, touching one shoulder, the other, the gesture fading when he could not remember whether forehead or chest came next. Then the old man reached with a tortilla, working it like a shovel. The moment was instantaneous, filled with commotion. All began eating as if at some signal. They ate quickly, with a kind of furor. They ate like the truly hungry. Food was serious business. The silence was rich, masculine, the silence of men eating. Reed took a tortilla, tried to ape the man's actions. He was too embarrassed to ask for a fork. Perhaps they had none. The thought made him acutely aware of his surroundings, of the strangeness of the coarse walls, the

177

blackened stones of the hearth. A life without forks would be a far different life. A life without forks, without electricity, without running water. One would become adept at eating with his hands, at ferrying buckets of water, at building fires, at butchering pigs. Watching the others eat, Reed had the sensation of witnessing a scene through the window of a house he could never enter.

After dinner, Reed said, "I should go." But the old man had produced a jug, he now filled two tin cups. Socorro was clearing the dishes.

"You will offend him."

Reed had a drink. It tasted like fiery licorice. He had a second. He asked how to get back to the highway. It became a family effort, fingers darting along the table, all talking at once, Socorro trying to translate. You took a right at the old well, continued on past a shallow ravine. At the piñon tree you turned, then turned again. If you reached the fence, you knew you had gone too far. If you reached the house of Claudio Vallejo, you had gone much too far. "Beyond that," Onésimo laughed, Socorro translating, "you fall off the edge of the world." Reed listened, looking from face to face, struggling to remember. Outside, the wind was up; it whistled through cracks in the walls. The hearth was warm, the chair he sat in comfortable. He had another drink.

Onésimo pulled a box off a shelf. The dominoes clattered to the table. Reed said, "I should go." But the brothers gathered around, their eyes glinting with excitement. Onésimo played with disconcerting enthusiasm, dashing slabs of bone to the grainy surface. There were shouts of encouragement, muttered warnings, shrieks when a good play was made. Onésimo beat him, then Daniel beat him. Manuel beat him, Sencillo beat him, Alberto beat him. Reed was their guest; it was understood he played every round. Reed had another drink and finally beat Pablito, the youngest. "My turn," Socorro announced. She played in earnest, ticking the ivory-colored rectangles against her eyetooth in heavy concentration. Small hands, skinny arms, but she was her father's daughter. She played with an alarming intensity. There was the knock of dominoes on wood. Reed let her win. So maybe he didn't. "Again?" she asked. She loved to play. He understood she loved to win. "No more," Reed replied. The brothers all lined up then and shook his hand solemnly. They rarely had company. The closest house was two miles away.

Outside, the wind moaned. Reed could feel the chill. He offered the old man a cigarette. Onésimo took it with a nod. Men sharing a smoke. They smoked in silence. There were the sounds of the boys preparing for bed, the sounds of Socorro's voice as she talked to them. Her words were caressing, affectionate. When her mother died, it was Socorro who had held them together; it was Socorro who had been the strong one. Her father had been hysterical with grief, her brothers too young for understanding. It was Socorro who saw that they bathed at night, that they ate every morning, that the crops were brought in, the burro was fed. They all remembered this. They looked to her still for guidance, for strength. There was something unique about her. Every village, every generation sends forth unusual individuals, those of effortless grace. Life comes naturally to them, philosophy does not. You could see it in her face, in the way she moved. A kind of fearlessness. Now she was tucking in the youngest. Reed had another drink. "I should go," he said again. But he did not go. Onésimo gazed at him, the old man's eyes like nuggets of obsidian embedded deep in his face. Reed felt himself drifting. His head snapped up with a start. He could see Socorro kneeling at her father's side, talking, explaining. Their sounds were muted, their heads close together. The intimacies of a father and daughter, joined in a tangle of emotions, shared memories resurrected in an instant by the tilt of his chin, the way she touched the old man's shoulder.

The unvoiced truth: Reed had wanted a son. The sentiment was fabricated from stale, unoriginal images, he knew—images borrowed from posters in sports bars, color illustrations in history books, Norman Rockwell paintings. A man and his son playing catch, tracking game, eating ice cream sundaes at a soda fountain. It offered a second chance at innocence. His son would have been a duplicate of himself, though one in which the mistakes had yet to be renewed.

In the end, he welcomed the birth of his daughter. He reveled in it. If they could not toss a ball, he would drive her to dance lessons. If they could not hunt together—admittedly, it had been thirty years since Reed last held a firearm—he would teach her to draw. They would still eat ice cream sundaes.

But Laura had come of age toward the close of the millennium: she threw a nifty curve ball, summer camp had made her proficient with bow and arrow, she claimed to hate ice cream. One sight of a tutu and she rejected ballet out of hand. The poverty of Reed's grasp of the situation was made clear the Saturday he watched her play left wing in a field hockey game. Two goals that day, two assists. Reed's pride was geysering. "That's my daughter," he kept telling those seated around him. Laura's play was controlled, circumspect, her passing astute. This despite the fact that an opposing back—a heavy, bull-like girl—hacked at his daughter's legs with a stick in ways not only illegal, but dangerous, he was certain. Toward the end of the game, the girl took a vicious swipe at Laura, knocking her to her knees. Reed was on his feet and roaring. He felt helpless, miserable. On the very next play, however, as the girl bore down on Reed's daughter, Laura executed what he remembered now as a kind of pirouette, coupled with a discreetly placed stick that sent the girl crashing into the goal. The whole structure collapsed, posts and crossbeam swatting the girl during the tumble. The girl emerged unhurt but crying, her dignity stung.

Driving home from the game, Reed had pulled the car over to the curb, turned off the engine, and faced his daughter. He wanted to convey to her the reach of his feelings. Sentimental, he knew. Her look told him so. He settled for, "You're really good."

180

Her look lost for a second the mask of teenage disdain she always wore. Her expression was guileless, innocent. Loving, he realized. He had been strangely touched by the fact he could still touch her so. He thought: I will cry at your wedding.

"I really should go," Reed said now. But Socorro and her father talked on, ignoring him. Reed's head lolled at the end of his neck. Sleep came then, like the fall of a blade.

He woke in a narrow bed in a strange room. A table stood in one corner, draped with tinsel one bought at the five-and-dime. It held three candles, rosary beads. A gray photo in a gilt frame. Socorro had the woman's mouth, her cheekbones. Reed went to the window and opened the latch. The sun was just cresting. Two of the boys were already out in the field, working hoes. He could see a third fetching water from the well. Onésimo was off to one side, his arms crossed, taking in the scene. His land, his boys. His pig. Farmers, they had been up for hours.

Reed's mouth was woolly, his bladder pinched and urgent. He ventured into the narrow hallway, heard splashing sounds. He turned the corner of the central room, the room where they had eaten. He started to call for Socorro, but the sight shut him up. She stood with her back to him. The edge of the table rose to just that point where her hips began to flare, obscuring everything below. Her spine straddled tight ridges of muscle as she leaned. Her skin was even darker than he had guessed. She dipped a rag into the washbasin, ran it under her arm, around her neck. The cake of soap was a broken, yellowish chunk. Her hair was wet.

A woman's nudity. They stand like horses in a field, wild orchids in a forest. Unwitting, unthinking. You want to ride the horse, you want to pluck the orchid. You want to eat the petals. He stared at the thin shoulders, the slender arms. It was the back of a boy, a lean farmhand. But the high break of her hips promised much more. He found himself wishing the table were shorter.

A knock at the front door, and panic gripped Reed. Like that time Sheila Dalrymple's father caught the two of them in the dark as they sprawled on his living room sofa, Reed's hands entangled in the puzzle of her bra. The man ran around flicking light switches, madness in his eyes. It was not Mr. Dalrymple, but Pablito who appeared just outside the door. "Choco?"

"Momentito," she replied.

Yet Pablito was not listening. He gaped at Reed, then reddened horribly. Seven years old. His understanding was still raw. No, no: the boy understood perfectly. Aging, bloated gringo, gawking at his bare-assed sister. Reed withdrew quickly back down the hallway, tiptoeing like a voyeur, calling himself geek, smuthead. He sat in the room where he had slept and smoked a cigarette, feeling swinish, loathsome. Feeling a raging need to piss. The boy would tell her everything, a brother worried about the honor of his sister. There was no doubt a machete or two on the grounds. Reed waited for Onésimo to appear and exact brutal but appropriate Latin justice. But after a time, Socorro knocked, said, "Breakfast is almost ready, yes?" She craned her head around the door. She was freshly scrubbed, mercifully clothed, smiling. Pablito, discreet boy.

"Your father seems well," Reed said now.

She nodded. "We are very lucky." She turned to go.

"I was looking for the bathroom," he remembered.

Her head reappeared. "Outside."

"What?"

"It is outside."

In the outhouse, he fretted about lizards, spiders, snakes. The night had been cool, but now the sun was a fat bubble climbing the sky. He could feel the air warming as he sat. He knocked before reentering the house. She stood at the hearth, her hair still damp about her shoulders, enveloped in the smell of wood smoke. Back in the room, Reed found his toilet kit. He shaved bent over a broad bowl, wishing for a mirror. He took a long drink from a clay pitcher. It was like a museum piece. His thirst was enormous. The water was tinny—a taste of unearthed metals, of sand, of iron.

The men had returned from the field. They ate a modest breakfast of goat cheese and beans. Reed helped wash up afterward, carrying a bucket from the well. As Reed packed, Onésimo appeared at the door. Reed understood now that it was the old man's bed he had slept in. Onésimo came and placed a hand on Reed's shoulder, gave it a fraternal squeeze. His gaze went to the figurine nestled amid Reed's clothes. The old man spoke, he spoke again, cragged voice, the sounds like involuntary spasms, mere shuddering sounds. Then he adjusted Reed's socks, fashioning a tidy nest for the figurine. Satisfied, he retreated back into the central room. Reed heard the creak of the chair as Onésimo settled in; he heard the old man's sigh. Onésimo sat as he had been sitting the evening before, when they first arrived. It was as if he had never moved, as if no time had passed. An hour, a day was nothing. He lived centuries in that chair, he knew the speed of vast ages.

Reed, his bag in his hand, thanked the old man, then offered him another cigarette. Onésimo took it with a nod, stuck it behind his ear. There was an awkward moment where Reed stood shifting his weight from foot to foot.

"Socorro?" Reed asked. He wanted to say goodbye.

The old man blinked at Reed, his eyes welling. "Choco," he whispered.

Reed found her leaning against the car, her bag at her feet. Her brothers circled the vehicle, inspecting it, exclaiming over its many features. Pablito was crying. Now each came forward and shook Reed's hand. "Nos vemos," Reed recalled. Delighted, they bobbed their heads: "Nos vemos." Pablito refused to meet his eye.

Reed turned to Socorro. She smiled sweetly. He frowned. But her brothers watched; he worried about creating a scene. He finally unlocked the door. She set her bag in the back, then slid into the passenger seat. When Reed got in, she stared straight ahead, her eyes prominent, her lips full. Reed cleared his throat. Her brothers stood waving.

She said, "The first time he tried to cross over, he was sixteen. There was work in Houston. A coyote had promised to get them across if they could find the money. He and Carlos Ruiz used a scorpion to rob a cantina. They did, truly. Papa used to talk of the way the eyes of the clerk went wide at the sight of the curling stinger. They came away with a six-pack of beer and a pouch full of corn tortillas. For that they spent six weeks in a Matamoros jail."

Reed shook his head. He said, "No."

"When they got out, they heard of a shallow route across the river. The river looks small. Here we call it the Río Bravo. Do you know the word? Men drown in the river all the time. Women and children. But there was work in Houston. That night, they tried to cross. The water was freezing. There were snakes, a swift current. There was la migra waiting on the opposite side. My father and Carlos Ruiz were taken into custody. They were beaten. My father received a black eye, a split lip. He was the lucky one. Carlos Ruiz lost four of his teeth. But there was work in Houston. This was everything. They heard word of a boat that would move through the waters of the Gulf. It would arrive on the beach south of Corpus Christi. Ten minutes out, the boat sank. People swam back to the shore, their possessions gone, the women crying. Then he and Carlos Ruiz learned of a tunnel. 'Ratones,' my papa used to explain to me. 'Ratones del tamaño de un perro.' As big as dogs. They ran back through the tunnel, chased by rats."

She stopped now, her eyes lingering on the small house. Reed took the moment to study her features, trying to picture what her father must have looked like at sixteen. He said, "No."

"He and Carlos Ruiz finally got across. They crossed for twelve seasons. Oranges in Florida, peaches in Georgia, apples in Washington State." Her eyes shimmered. She had heard the stories her entire life, she had grown up on them. They were like fairy tales, they had the air of legend about them, of some tremendous dream. Her father had seen snow. "They would do anything, they would do any kind of work. Whatever there was. He broke his arm falling from an apple tree one season. He came down with pneumonia in Pennsylvania. He was threatened at knifepoint by a foreman who refused to pay him. But it was work, you see? There was this. There was always this. He might return in September, he might return in October, he might return in November. We never knew. He would appear one day, unannounced, with no warning, a man on foot, a man walking slowly. He had hitched rides in cars, ridden freight trains, he had sneaked onto buses when the drivers turned their heads. Beginning in August, my mother left a candle burning every night, all night long. Once he did not arrive until the New Year. And always, he returned with a roll of money hidden in the heel of his boot. He would go out, buy clothes, shoes, things that we needed. He would buy a goat to roast. Suddenly, it was everyone's birthday. It was all the holidays of the year, yes? Other children think it is the Three Wise Men who bring them gifts on the sixth of January; they are disappointed when they learn that it is only their father. I was not like other children. I knew all along that it was my father. Not that there were no Wise Men, do you understand? But that he *was* one of the Wise Men. I relied on this. Yes."

She turned to Reed now, her eyes large, beseeching. She had been different from other children. "Do this. Please."

Reed groaned. The old man had known, he had known all along. She had known. Even her brothers had known. She had only been waiting for the right moment. Only Reed had been ignorant. She was introducing complexities he did not want, he refused to tolerate. She was confusing the issue—she was confusing his life—at a time when it seemed everything had been decided. Yet he was one of those who eats meat every day. "Only as far as Mexico City," he said grudgingly. He tried to

185

make his voice firm, unyielding. "You can catch the bus there, a train. I don't care. But no farther." He wagged a finger in her face.

She grinned. She had never been to Mexico City.

Andrea woke early. She dressed quickly in the cold room. A woman who did not want to sit at home. The rooms of the house were filled with Frank. His suits hung in the closet, his bottles lined the pantry. His hemorrhoid salve was in the medicine cabinet. She kept expecting him to walk casually through the door, to make for the kitchen, to return with a glass in hand, a kiss that tasted of gin. She had been going to Mass every morning. As though her husband's absence were at bottom a spiritual gnaw. She meant to feed it with God.

The day before, Andrea had phoned Frank's secretary. She was a young woman who changed hair color the way others change sheets. There were always four hoops in her left ear, none in her right. She could not type, Frank often complained. No, the girl told her; she had heard nothing from Mr. Reed. Andrea had called the airline, the Eagle Pass police department, the hospital there. She had called the Mexican consulate in Boston. Nothing. She had played the tape over and over again, her ear close to the speaker, trying to divine the hidden nuances in the sound of her name, the slightest modulation in its repetition: "Andrea? Andrea." Doleful, tired, the sounds on the tape would tell her everything if only she listened closely enough. But it was the voice of an enigma, the voice of a stranger.

She feared the worst. She was being premature, she knew. Yet there was Danielle, there was Elizabeth, there was Marsha. Andrea had known them for years; she had played bridge with them, talked to them over the phone. She knew their most sheltered secrets. Women whose husbands had left them. They came to parties alone, wandering rooms with vodka gimlets in

186

their hands, their laughter strained, their talk shrill, demanding to be heard, to be acknowledged, looking for someone, for anyone to listen to them, to compliment them on their dresses, their jewelry, their wit. They ended such evenings drunk and sometimes weeping. They went home alone. Though there were the occasional dates with men who mumbled to themselves, someone's brother, someone's uncle, men who fumbled absently with their flies, they had lost most of their teeth, men whose voices trailed off into nothing; men who insisted on splitting the check, then argued for a reduced tip. Such women had children in college, there were the tuition payments, the insurance, the heating bill, there was the mortgage. They owed money to plumbers, the grocer, the auto mechanic. Alimony checks were a month late, three months, eight. They had never worked, not really. Now they struggled to get by on the charity of relatives, or working part-time jobs in the library of the local country day school, or evenings as a hostess at a third-rate restaurant. The owner occasionally cupped them through their dresses, whispered unrepeatable invitations in their ears. Such women were always visiting their lawyers, they needed to renegotiate the settlement. But there were more motions to file, delayed hearing dates. Their husbands always found good attorneys, smart men—"piranhas," everyone said. "But I need the money now." Our hearts go out to them; we cannot stand them. They wear their rejection like the clothes on their backs. You can see it in their makeup, almost kabuki-like, in the coiffure they had gotten just that morning. They live out their days obsessed with worries about incontinence, hair loss, menopause. They are women for whom life no longer has any patience. They are women who have lived too long.

Harsh judgment, Andrea knew. Yet it reeked of the truth. Now it seemed she might join their ranks. Though she had moments of morbid, twisted hope, moments thinking car accident, kidnapping, heart attack. A widow rather than a divorcee, she could bear betrayal by the universe far easier than

187

betrayal by her husband. It was like discovering that a man you have known for years, a man you trust, a man you have bedded, you have cooked for, a man you were prepared to do anything for, was in fact an ax-murderer, a pederast, a fifth-story man.

She left church in a strange calm. There are athletes who feel it in the very moment before. It seemed she was being tested. Whatever does not kill us, etc. She mined the notion for consolation. A wayward husband, the dangerous streets; the mortgage payment was due on the eighth.

She had turned forty-two the previous month. She had her figure, she had her brains. Her legs were still good. She had herself. She believed in herself completely. There are certain ideas you adhere to no matter what. Meanwhile, there was the mortgage, there was the car payment on the twentieth. They needed to order heating oil. They would cut back. There would be a jar on the mail table in the front hallway for change; she would roll coins once a month and carry them in a heavy bag to the bank. Laura would attend the University of Massachusetts, the University of Rhode Island. A public school, yet they would still have each other. Andrea was a woman confronting the realities. She would throw herself into her theater work. *The Good Woman of Szechwan* was to open soon. The gods in search of that lone, good soul. It suddenly seemed Brecht was addressing her directly. She would play bridge. She would give dinner parties, intimate affairs, dinners from a different epoch—parties of the sort common two, three generations ago. There were books she had not read, there were plays she wanted to see. There was still the symphony, there were still the museums; there were cooking classes she could take. There would be nights before a flickering fire, a cup of Earl Grey at her side. She would reread her Balzac, her Flaubert, her Stendhal. Her French was rusty, she would pore over the dictionary. The mere declension of a verb would give her a kind of joy. There would always be the broad, pale stones of the fireplace, the deep wood of the mantel. Her

188

daughter asleep upstairs. Her life would be full. She would be deepening her understanding of who she was; she would be completing it.

"Stop it," she whispered.

Premature, she kept telling herself. But Frank always called, he always called until he reached her, he always left his number. A worrisome father, a dutiful husband. It was his way. She could not shake a haunting presentiment. Her grandfather used to joke that they came from good Druid stock. The mysticism of trees. And here she had cooked his meals, she had washed his clothes. She had cleaned his shit stains from the toilet. She felt like a woman duped by poems.

Laura arrived home from school to find her mother sitting at the kitchen table. The days were growing shorter; dusk had set in. The room was dim, the silence ghostlike. There was the distant ticking of a clock. She took a moment to study her mother. Andrea was a striking woman, Laura understood. When her parents had friends over for drinks, when they gave parties, Laura saw the way the men looked at her mother; she saw the way their eyes followed her around the room. Boys from school, whenever they spied her mother, always dug their elbows into the ribs of their friends. She was a woman who dressed simply. She wore little jewelry: a single gold bracelet, tiny diamond studs at her ears. They were like the most basic of punctuation marks. Her mother knew that a naked wrist, a bare nape, the back of a woman's knee could be far more alluring than rubies, sapphires. Now Laura reached for the light.

"Mom?"

Her mother's head came around slowly. She looked as if she were awakening from a long dream.

"Mom, are you OK?"

Andrea stepped to the stove. "I was just making some tea."

"You hear from Dad?"

Andrea was filling the kettle. She turned on the burner. "He's fine. He says hello."

"Is he bringing me something?"

189

"What?"

"He said he was going to bring me a souvenir."

"I'm sure he is."

"When's he coming—"

"How was school?"

She had gotten a C– on her geometry test. Andrea grimaced at the news. Was it the teacher?

"It's not the teacher."

The kettle whistled, spewed steam. Andrea set out lemon and honey. Beyond the windows, the day had gone dark. They sat in the soft glow of the kitchen light. Erin Moran's boy Toby was going to be in town for Thanksgiving, Andrea said. He was a freshman at Brown. Perhaps he and Laura could—

"Don't you think he's a little old for me?'

Andrea was taken aback. "You're almost sixteen."

"That's nothing," Laura said.

"Two generations ago, you might have been married."

"How old were you?"

"When I got married?"

Laura's gaze was frank. "No; that's not what I meant."

The sight of Andrea in a bathing suit always embarrassed her daughter. The woman looked too good. Though the suits were of the finest material, the cut classic, the effect seemed brazen. It was like having a mother who frequented piano bars, a mother who told off-color jokes.

"Older than you," Andrea said. Then, "You don't want me to call Toby's mother?"

"I don't want you to call Toby's mother."

Laura was going out for the evening. She had some study-ing to do at the library, she said. Andrea would have liked to prepare an elaborate meal, to cook for someone. Instead, she made herself a grilled cheese sandwich. A simple meal, it seemed to hit just the right note. She sliced the cheese, she chopped some green onion, a tomato. The butter sizzled in the pan, there was the hiss as she placed the bread. She turned it with a spatula, part of her set of twenty-eight kitchen utensils from an Italian export shop in New York; they shipped everything in from Genoa. She placed the finished sandwich on a small plate. It was good china, a beautiful pattern. She seemed to see everything, to take in the smallest details. She garnished the plate with a sprig of parsley, a fluted radish.

She ate standing at the kitchen sink.

She took a long bath, settling back in the steaming water, Segovia going on the radio. True, she had been older than Laura. His name was Ethan Biddle. She had met him during her first year of college. He was a grad student in Russian history. He wore a beret. He nurtured a scant beard, it looked like broken foliage. He was short, skinny, with small hands. A small prick. He believed in the peaceful transition to socialism. Andrea had thought him scholarly, insightful, an original thinker. His semen had a coppery, caustic taste. He came with a barking sound that put her off. When she ended it, he was inconsolable. He dropped out of school, went to work for a radio station, selling advertising. She met Frank three years later. The memories drifted up to her now, like fish rising to feed on the surface of a pond. She wanted to scatter them, to chase them away. But the more stubborn ones kept returning. There was the hotel room off Central Park, there was that bed-and-breakfast in Virginia, there was that cottage on Nantucket. There was that time early in their marriage when they pulled off the highway at a rest stop and made love in the back seat. The cop was not amused. There was the string of pearls he had given her on her birthday, there was the crotchless teddy that Valentine's Day, there was the Mother's Day he insisted on making breakfast. There was a blackened patch in the ceiling still. When one of the cast members in a production of Ibsen came down sick, and she had stepped in—it was only two lines, a single scene—he had risen at the curtain call, his clapping prolonged and embarrassing, thundering, "Encore!" He had come backstage with three dozen roses, his pride towering, foolish in the end. She had never been more in love with him than she'd been at that moment. There was that video he rented. Two couples on a yacht. The women were stupid, sloppy-breasted creatures; the men were enormous. After five minutes, she rose in a huff and left the room. She watched it the next morning after he went to work. She dreamed ax handles for a week. That time Laura—she could not have been more than four—walked in on them and saw everything. Everything. Reed had been mortified. For days, the girl's questions were persistent, relentless. Reed finally explained that it was a small pet parents often kept in the bedroom. No, she could not see it; it had run away that very morning. But Laura demanded to know its name. "Buck," he told her. "Buck?" Andrea teased him. That New Year's Eve party where stunning women moved about in two-thousand-dollar gowns; at midnight, he kissed her, said, "You're the prettiest one here." He had believed it, that was the thing. There was the evening he ate three dozen oysters on a bet. He threw up in the car, he threw up in the living room, he threw up in bed. A cruise to Martha's Vineyard when that woman fell overboard and Frank jumped in to save her. An octogenarian from Great Neck had pulled them both from the water. The time they made love in the laundry room atop the washing machine; the time they made love in a hammock on Long Island; the time he buried his face between her legs and she proceeded to cut his hair. He promised not to stop until she was done. "I look like a goddamn marine," he told her afterward. When Laura once asked why he didn't go to church, he said, "Because your mother is good enough for two people." He used to cup her face in his fingers and kiss her nose. He used to hold her hand on the subway. He used to hold her hand in the park. He used to hold her hand at the dinner table.

Andrea went to bed. She lay with her feet crossed at the ankles, her arms flung out to her sides, like one waiting for hammer blows, spikes piercing flesh, the spear in the side.

She was awakened by a sound. The sound came again, a light metallic clang beyond the window. The sound of a car door. She waited to hear the scratching of Laura's key, her daughter's footsteps on the stairway. But there was no scratch of a key, there were no steps on the stairs. There was another sound, it came from just outside.

Andrea went to the window. The floor was cold against her feet. The car was there, the streetlight lit the roof. The car door was open. She stared, not understanding, muddled with sleep. But the car door was open. She should have called the police, she knew. Yet say it was Frank. She could see the police report, it rose up before her eyes: Domestic Disturbance. There would be shouts, recriminations, she would whip him into the street, her anger magisterial. The lights would come on in the surrounding houses, more police cars would arrive. Neighbors would appear at their windows, step out onto their front porches.

She put on her robe, clutched the folds tightly at her neck. She crept downstairs, moved through the kitchen, toward the back door. It was late; say he had taken a cab back from the airport, he had lost his house key. Or else he was out of cigarettes. He had flown for four hours, mad for a butt. There were always some in the ashtray of the car.

At the last instant, she reached for the cleaver hanging from the pegboard in the kitchen.

She stepped gingerly out the back door, then circled around the side of the house, her feet making crunching noises. Her bare soles ached with the cold. She peered around the corner, saw a leg protruding from the open car door. A body stretching along the front seat, perhaps a body rooting in the glove compartment, in the ashtray. "Frank?" she said. "Frank." A figure leaped at the sound, too small to be Frank. A boy. He tore toward the street, disappeared. She ran to the car, waving the cleaver as if it were a lantern, a standard. It was only when she turned that she saw the second boy. He was even younger. She stood between him and the street. He stared unsurely, his eyes hard on the cleaver. It gleamed brilliantly in the glare of the streetlight. He held the car radio; cables hung from it like viscera. She took in the scene slowly, trying to understand.

There was a single raw moment then, she thought she might scream. Instead she said, "Put it down."

She spoke softly, almost tenderly. She was not sure he had heard. But he nodded, carefully placing the radio on the hood of the car.

"Lady," he said. He shook his head. "Lady, now." As if that were all, as if the issue were finished. He sidled along the house, heading toward the street. She moved left, cutting him off. She held the cleaver with both hands, as if it were a broadsword.

"Lady."

He wanted only to flee. But she refused to let it end like this. There were things that had to be said. The matter had to be put right. He must be made to understand. She wanted to be sure he did not return in an hour, or in a day, or in a month. She wanted him to know that she was a woman who had been through much. She was a woman who could take care of herself. She wanted him to go out and tell his friends, to tell everyone, to avoid this house; the woman would come at you with sharp implements in her hands. She would stand barefoot on a freezing night if she had to. That this was her car, this was her drive, this was her house. That she was not the kind of woman such things happened to. There had been some sort of mistake. That she was another kind of woman entirely.

She took three steps toward him, clipped, rapid movements. She waved the cleaver in his face. She was maybe six feet away.

He said, "Lady." His eyes were big. He pressed against the side of the house, his palms, his back flat to it.

"Listen," she whispered. The sound was scratching, it seemed to rattle in her throat. "Listen to me. I want to be sure you understand."

"Sure, lady. Sure." He watched the cleaver guardedly. She waggled it for effect. Her robe had fallen open; there were her breasts, there was the flaxen plume of hair below. There was the cleaver. All seemed equally terrifying suddenly. His pants were wet, he had soiled himself.

194

She said, "I have done nothing wrong."

His eyes followed the cleaver; if he looked anywhere else, it would crease his skull. She said, "Do you hear me?" He was her witness, her sole judge.

"Please, lady." He was crying. Then he was staggering, fumbling toward the curb, blubbering. She ran after him. He was already far down the block. She stood in the middle of the street, gripping the cleaver high above her head, the robe flapping about her. Her voice was shrill, irrefutable:

"I have done nothing wrong."

Five

Socorro talked. She was full of stories; she told each with a sharp immediacy, as if it were unfolding at the very moment and she, too, wanted to see how it would end. She talked, she gestured, she shifted in her seat. Twice she slapped the dashboard for emphasis, once she touched his arm to make sure he had understood. Reed smiled, said, "Really?" said, "You're kidding," said, "He did?" She grinned. He did. Her grin was effusive, infectious. Her legs were pretty. He told himself not to stare.

But Reed was a watcher of women, champ of the lingering look. It was not thoughts of seduction that turned his gaze, but a vague yearning, almost helplessness. At a pool party once a man had come up to him and said, "Buddy, you're scaring my wife." The wife in question was a bundle of flesh testing the seams of a light blue bikini. Reed had made heartfelt apologies, spent the rest of the afternoon doing a study of his toes. Yet a tawny swell of haunch, a shock of red hair, breasts rolling beneath a silk blouse could bring him to a standstill in the middle of a crosswalk. At the beach he was a man agog. Juvenile, he knew. Still, a faithful husband, it gave him certain privileges. Andrea even teased him about it. In a restaurant, say, or in the lobby of a movie theater, she would place a hand on his arm and say, "How about her?" It was invariably a tall woman, a lean woman, her hair fair. A woman not unlike herself. "Yes," he would admit. "And her? Or her?" "Yes. Yes." She would laugh then, slip her arm through his. "Well, you can't." Her humor, the feel of her pressing against his side, seemed proofs of his innocence. Though he once followed a woman for sixteen blocks through downtown Boston, beguiled by the working of her hips beneath a brief skirt, her endless legs. A woman in a calendar, a woman in a dream. Lagging half a block behind, he invented a whole life for her, imagined wealthy Republican lovers, a bathtub resting on porcelain paws. She would have a mole there, another there. Meanwhile, he had a meeting to get to, he was expecting an important phone call from Philadelphia. But there were those legs, long heels striking down. Reed followed her into a little gallery. While the woman paused before a silk-screen, Reed took up position in front of a large mural depicting a well-known author—his first book was a smash, now he combs the drawers of his study for half-finished manuscripts that the men's magazines breathlessly publish in miserly portions—being carried off in a winged chariot. The painting was puerile. It was shit. The woman materialized beside him suddenly. Reed stared straight ahead, though his peripheral vision was keen, straining. "Brilliant, isn't it?" he muttered. She said, "Go away." Her accent was irksome, Cranston, unfinished. Her legs deserved better, her legs warranted refined Yankee inflections, Boston Brahmin. "Go away before I call the guard."

198

Up from the rain forest, then, across the vast plain of central Mexico, a woman next to him. He was quick with glances. She had removed her sandals, tucked her feet under her, put up her hair. Her thighs were dark, like stretches of buffed wood. They echoed the glimpse he had had of her naked back. An unanticipated intelligence had slipped into her face. She was a woman he would have noticed on the subway, he would have paused to watch as she stepped from a taxi.

But her mood was ingenuous, disarming. She told him about the time Gabriel Arcadio fell down a well, she told him how a snapping turtle had bitten off the finger of Ursula Portocarrero, she went on about the rabbit—its name was Mucho—she had raised as a child. In the end, they were the memories, the concerns of a young girl. His inclinations turned paternal. He had met her father after all, they had shared a drink, a smoke. He found himself talking about Laura. His daughter had his eyes, he explained, the resemblance was stark. He worried about his daughter, he worried when she did not eat, he was concerned about the boys she ran around with. He was unsure how he was going to pay for college. That year she gave up television during Lent—"It has to be a sacrifice," Andrea had insisted—Reed watched cartoons with her whenever her mother went out. Clandestine Saturday mornings, both of them in their pajamas. They were like thieves, spies; was that the sound of the car turning into the drive? "We won't tell Mom," Laura kept whispering. "No," he said, "we won't."

When the twin peaks of Popocatépetl and Ixtacihuatl appeared in the distance, Socorro made sounds of awe. The Mountain that Smokes and the White Woman. Fabled volcanoes, she had heard about them her whole life. It seemed the conquistadors had negotiated the snowy passes on their approach to Tenochtitlán. Though now, the sun was punishing. The car overheated, it overheated again. They were limping toward the capital. The day lengthened, made Reed clammy, crabby; sweat dripped into his eyes. His cigarettes tasted bitter.

But Socorro's excitement was ripe, flowing; nothing could threaten it. She talked incessantly. North, north, the journey had begun. The dream lay before her. She loved even the heat. A woman from a wet land, she had never experienced such sun.

"Tell me: what will you do?"

She had a distant cousin in San Diego. A woman from her village worked in El Paso. Her father had given her a list of names, addresses. Half were probably dead, the other half may have returned home years ago, may well have moved on. But there would be others. There were always others.

"My people, you see—my people are everywhere."

They stopped just south of Mexico City for gas, for something to eat. A large restaurant with fake matador gear on the wall, bulls glaring out from fields of velvet. The waiters all wore cardboard sombreros. Spanish arrangements of rock tunes played in the background. Latin kitsch. The Mexican equivalent of a fern bar frequented by optometrists and realtors. Yet the place delighted her. She ordered something called the Plato de Oro: tacos, enchiladas, burritos, all beached in the sludge of refried beans. "Scotch," he told the waiter.

He smoked while she ate. She held the fork near the tines, as if it were a pencil. Her bites were broad, undisciplined. Her cheeks puffed with food. The scotch was foul. Reed drained his glass, signaled for another.

"You drink very much, I think." It seemed less a reprimand than an idle observation, the report of a fact. She kept peering at him, scrutinizing his words, registering his moods. As if she expected to find the States populated with nothing but tall, aging, chain-smoking scotch drinkers.

Reed frowned. "Do I?"

"Yes." There was no doubt.

"And you eat very much."

She blushed. Another story: her parents had met during a time of famine, a time of immense rains, legendary rains. The sky came unleashed, heaved great gouts of water, washed the crops away. People were living on straw, roots, lizards. Her father had come north to the village in search of work. One afternoon, Onésimo noticed a girl digging for grubworms. When fried, they were a tasty source of protein. She was on her knees, her back to him, digging with her hands. A girl in the rain; it plastered her hair to her head, her dress against her body. Onésimo studied the outline of her hips, her breasts. A woman kneeling in the mud. In town, he learned her name was Blanca. That night, he slept on the floor of a stable— Blanca, Blanca, on his lips. Onésimo returned the next day. The girl was there, digging again. Blanca's father was ill with the dengue, her mother spent all her time caring for him. It was left to Blanca to find food. On the third day, she dug up a bag of dried frijoles, a small bunch of plantains, a thin sliver of bittersweet chocolate. Staggering bounty, impossible luck; all from a hole in the ground. She ran home, but of course no one believed her. One finds worms, not chocolate, beneath the soil. But they ate the frijoles, the plantains, they broke the chocolate into tiny fragments and scattered it like dust onto their tongues. Blanca went back the next day, and the next, always digging at the same spot. Tortillas wrapped in waxed paper, jicama, a half-cup of rice, a cactus pear. Onésimo hid in the underbrush and watched her unearth her treasure. Blanca, Blanca. He scoured the tiendas each day, buying what he could; he sneaked into the homes of the rich, stealing what he could not buy. Meanwhile, her family marveled; no one could explain it. It was a miracle. Blanca's parents knelt and crossed themselves. Nothing like it had happened since the time Salazar the viejo claimed to have seen the face of the Virgin in the knot of a tree.

It ended when Blanca unearthed a ring of hammered gold, wrapped in the softest of cloths. It was a thin ring. An inexpensive ring. But they were campesinos. They were peasants. The gift was extravagant. Blanca was still on her knees, the ring on her finger, when Onésimo stepped forward. He had been waiting for the right time, the perfect time to show himself. They stared at each other for a long while, neither speaking. A singular moment—it seemed love was happening, their futures were being forged. Then she said, "Can you never find cheese?"

These tales of family, the minor histories. The unwritten narratives we keep trying to read. Reed's memories of his own mother tended toward the dim. No, that wasn't right; he remembered her clearly. It was only that she always moved through a dimly lit world. She had grown up in Michigan, the daughter of a shoe salesman. A man always on the road. He died of electrocution in a Grand Rapids boardinghouse while trying to change a light bulb. Reed's mother was forever turning off lights in a bizarre kind of homage. A taciturn woman, she loved blueberry cobbler, the fiction in the *Saturday Evening Post*, and his father. She was a composer of lists: lists of chores, lists of purchases, lists of matters she wanted to discuss with her husband, lists of people she should call, lists of bills that had to be paid. Lists of the lists she needed to make. At Christmas she prepared rich platters of cookies, pastries, and divinity. She made her own eggnog, her own wreaths. She could pluck a chicken, clean a fish; she ground her own sausage. She was one of the last of the canners: canned beets, canned turnips, canned okra. When Reed, having overdosed on Camus in a high school literature class, loudly proclaimed his atheism, she placed her hands on his shoulders and faced him squarely: "Kneel, say the words, and you will believe." At her son's wedding, she drew Andrea aside, urged the bride toward the cloakroom of the church. A man's mother and his wife. Onlookers smiled at one another. It seemed a precious moment, a profound exchange of female confidences. The photographer had even memorialized the scene, it lived on in their wedding album. "She said, 'Pasta gives him gas,'" Andrea reported later.

They entered the city along a central artery, cars racing about them like frightened fowl. Careening cabs swerved across five, six lanes. Klaxons sounded. The thronging boulevards, the avenues teeming with people. Buildings rose up, modern high-rises, office complexes, all shrouded in smog. Off the thoroughfares, there were the older neighborhoods, the broken streets. Socorro pressed her face to the window. Her eyes were large, filled with the sights, drinking them in. It seemed the world was rising to greet her. She asked which was more expensive: a bus or a train. Reed considered: "Train."

"The bus station, then."

Reed nodded ruefully. A girl alone, a girl on her own. Say it was his daughter. "Let me buy your ticket."

She refused. She had the money; she had been saving for years. And he had been too kind already.

"It's nothing."

"No. No." A woman who knew the value of things. "It is everything."

It took them over an hour to find the station. The parking lot milled with people. Like all bus stations, it was overrun by lunatics, pimps, thugs, the poor, those on the run. A dwarf with a film clouding his left eye. Stay out of the bathrooms, put your wallet in your front pocket. Socorro held her bag to her breasts, hovered close to his shoulder. "Thank you. You have been very kind," she whispered.

But Reed felt less than kind. He felt wretched. That time they sent Laura off to summer camp in Vermont, she had sat at the window of the bus and cried. She was eight years old. It was a wonderful camp, Andrea assured him. An expensive camp. They had everything: horseback riding, computer programming, underwater acrobatics. The staff were all skilled professionals with advanced degrees. The daughters of judges, the sons of doctors went there. Laura was gone for three weeks. Tears stained her letters home. She cried over the phone. The following summer she went to a day camp down at the neighborhood Y. Finger painting, macaroni glued to construction paper, cookies and milk at ten o'clock. She played with the children of cabdrivers, schoolteachers, plumbers. She cried when the summer ended.

Standing in the parking lot, Mexico City loud all about them, Reed strained for a conclusive utterance. An appropriate send-off. Yet Good Luck seemed lame, Have A Good Life cruel. But she eclipsed his thoughts with a brief, tentative hug—the feel of her arms appropriate. Reed stood confused, his hands hanging useless at his sides. He was of the city, after all. She was not. He imagined con men lurked inside, waiting to steal her money, lechers who would be drawn to her innocence. To her legs. "I'll come inside, make sure you're set," he said.

He waited while she stood in a long line filled with old men hefting canvas sacks, teens in scuffed boots, heavy women holding crying children. He waved away a beggar, then a second. The noise of the hall was deafening, a continual uproar. Socorro returned with a third-class ticket. She would change buses in San Luis Potosí, continue on to Matamoros. A day and a half, maybe two days. It depended on whether there was a flat tire, it depended on the driver. They faced each other, the moment awkward. Reed was still casting about for some coda, a word, a gesture equal to the moment. She hugged him, said, "Thank you."

These hugs. Reed swallowed, peered down at her. Her face was open, vulnerable. She would board the bus, he would drive north. He would never see her again. The past few days would stand disconnected from all the rest, inexplicable, incomplete. An episode that would never fit his memory. Like trying to step into a pair of poorly tailored pants. They hang in your closet, unworn. Yet they are pants you like; it never occurs to you to throw them away.

He said, "I'll wait until you board."

They sat on a wooden bench along the wall. He asked if she wanted a sandwich, a soda. No, she wanted nothing. Her eyes roamed the place, darting at sounds, rapid movements. She was like livestock awaiting shipment. Once she placed her hands over her ears, squeezed her eyes shut. Reed fumbled for his wallet. "Take this." "No," she said. No. The color of the bills turned gaudy in his hand. An announcement over the speaker system: her bus. She whispered, "Thank you. Thank you very much." She hugged him again. Reed hugged back.

He took her bag. "I'll help you board."

Out on the tarmac, people were amassed about the bus. The doors were shut. He and Socorro joined the edge of the crowd. The odors were close, dense, the smells of sweat, of cooking. Of travel. Clothes that had not been changed for days. More people congregated behind them now, the crowd was growing, people shifted with impatience. Finally the driver, a swaggering fat man assured of his own importance, pushed his way through. The crowd closed in behind him, they rushed forward. Someone stepped on Reed's foot, he got an elbow in his kidney, a knee in his crotch. When the driver opened the doors to the bus, the rush became manic. Socorro disappeared into a sea of arms, eager heads.

Reed experienced a burning sense of loss, of fomenting regrets. Here he had closed a business deal, purchased a possibly authentic statue. He had crapped on the banks of the Rio Grande. She had served him an egg. There had been that one crystalline instant, that pure instant, when he had dreamed hugely, impossibly. When his life had made a kind of sense. He would raise yucca, etc. So now he wouldn't. But there had been that moment, one is only allowed so many. To have it end like this—a terrified girl, abandoned to a mob—it was this that would seal the memory, poison it. A piece of him would always be looking for her in supermarkets, along crowded streets, on subway platforms. A small, dark girl in line at the bank, and his throat would tighten, his legs would grow weak. From guilt, from longing, from a misplaced nostalgia for what never was. "Socorro?" He was shouting. "Choco!" He glimpsed her then, her eyes large, bewildered, lamblike. A big man, he reached, gathered her arm in his hand. Her bones were slight, her flesh warm. He hung on. At the steps to the bus, someone leaned into him, forced him inside. He pulled her up after him.

It was a scene of madness, a scene of mayhem. Third class.

Like Third World. Appalling. All the seats had been taken in the first few seconds. People were packed into the aisle, men with sacks of rice over their shoulders, bags of dried beans. Compact, sweating women. A squawking rooster, spurs bound. A baby had puked on a seat back. The space was sweltering, crushing, the heat of eighty bodies. There was no air conditioning, no bathroom. Footsteps sounded over the roof, people would cling to it as the bus ambled over the roads. Reed struggled to turn in the tight logjam, Socorro pressed against him. Faces stared up at them, the faces of peasants, the illiterate, the poor. Faces going to Nuevo Laredo, to Ciudad Juárez, to Matamoros. Faces like her own.

The crowd surged closer, forcing them against each other. As if the crowd were urging them toward unexpected truths. A little boy was wedged between them, butting Reed's belly with his head in the fight for space. Like knocking at the door of his bladder. It occurred to Reed that at any moment the bus might start up, go rocking down the highway, moving on dusty roads. A day and a half, two days. Yet he would need to piss soon. He had given her a ride north, offered her money, put her on a bus. He had done what he could. A helpful man, there was that time he went a little crazy down in Mexico, drove all night . . . The girl? Put her on the bus myself.

"I should go," he told her. She nodded, murmured, "Thank you." He understood it was the last time, the final time. She placed a hand on the boy's forehead, edged him clear. She leaned then, her lips grazing Reed's cheek. Moist heat to her breath. He wanted to shrink-wrap the memory. He wanted to shrink-wrap her face. The lone, fading witness of the way he might have been. In the crush, he could feel her breasts against his chest, her thin arms in his. Reed closed his eyes, breathed in the biting, herbal scent of her hair. The odors of a woman, they are like warnings, they are like cries for help. Her look was wide, shocked, the eyes of a hare stunned by light. A woman going north, a woman in flight. She would find a way to get across, some way or another, she would hire a coyote, search for a shallow place in the river, hide in someone's trunk. All while Reed was cruising along in his broad auto, like a barge on calm seas. He would arrive home, mount his wife, kiss his daughter. He would eat meat. She would work as a seamstress in a sweatshop—piecework, twelve, fifteen hours a day. She would stand high up a ladder, straining for oranges, pesticides burning sores into her fingers. She would work as someone's maid; rich whites in Houston, they would give her a tiny walk-in closet in the rear of the house, every other Sunday off. The threat of deportation always a phone call away. The father would be a plastic surgeon, or a real estate magnate, or a broker for one of the larger firms. One of those occupations you have always despised; its ranks are filled with the haughty, the condescending. A comfortable man, a long driveway, a time-share at the shore. He would appear at the door of her room one night, wearing only his boxers and a leer, saying, "I thought we'd have a little chat."

"Come on." Reed grabbed her hand now, turned, bulled his way back down the aisle. A creature of the moment. Tall gringo, large gringo. A gringo going in the wrong direction. He elbowed people aside, his legs were big in the aisle, unstoppable. "Out of the way," he bellowed. Socorro in tow, she lurched after him. Down the steps, then, the driver heavy, blocking the door. He had a schedule to keep. Reed lowered his shoulder, aimed it into the driver's chest. The man grunted, staggered clear. Reed plunged on, inevitable, a force of nature, as inexorable as history, stopping only when they were back on the tarmac. Forty faces stared down at them from the windows of the bus. It seemed a drama was unfolding.

The driver swore, then closed the doors. The engine raced. They could see the man's arms through the windshield, winding as he wheeled the bus out of the parking spot. They watched as the bus rumbled across the lot, eased into traffic. It backfired, the sound already fading.

She peered up at Reed, her look confused. Her ticket in her hand. He avoided her eyes. Even his silences seemed significant. That morning in the mercado when she had served him the egg, he had sat motionless for a long while, his eyes locked on the yolk.

"You won't like it." He made his voice flat, decisive.

Awareness seeped into her face. "I will like it." Everything she had heard, everything she had read. Her father, Epifanio, the nuns. She would like it. She knew she would.

Reed shook his head. It seemed the head of experience itself. Older, wiser. "It's not as good as it sounds."

But she was wiser still. Her gaze was appraising. "Life," she said thinly, "is like that."

Reed stared. Life is like that. Hard truth, elemental truth. Its simplicity convinces, makes it ineluctable. Her mother had dined on grubworms; eat such a meal and life can never again disappoint. A light breeze now, it waved through her hair. She reached, brushed a strand back from her face.

He said, "I thought I'd lost you."

She knew. "Yes."

"On the bus," he went on. As if she had not yet understood. "I thought I'd lost you." Then, "Let me buy you a drink."

"I am not—"

"Let me buy *me* a drink."

Down the Avenida Juárez then, through the Calle de la Revolución. Past the gardens, the blossoms large, along the monuments to martyrs of the revolution, on up to the Zócalo. A drink in a cantina, then a second. Back out on the street, the sunlight was waning. "Perhaps there is another bus," she ventured. He nodded. Of course there was. Of course. There were always buses. But the drinks had lubricated his mood. He did not want to be alone. He did not want to let go of the last few days. Not yet. He said, "The States will still be there tomorrow." Her smile was watchful, uncertain. But then a toothless woman sold them ice cream; a monkey sat on a man's shoulder and juggled balls. Her face brightened. There were the museums, the fountains, the broad murals. A large market, the long tables filled with leather goods, gold and silver, terra-

208

cotta vases and jugs. A cab ride out to the ruins. She had never ridden in one. She was like a queen suddenly, like one of the elect.

A man and a woman. It is impossible to say the moment they both know, the instant they share a common, fierce understanding. But the signs were gathering; even the most casual observer would not have mistaken them. Reed placed his hand at her elbow to help her up the steps to the pyramid. At its summit, they stood close together, leaning into the wind. The city lay at their feet. They spoke with their heads close together, intimacies, whispers swarming in the air above them. She seemed an adventurer, a bold explorer. There are intrepid women, undefeated women. Fate is not yet done with them. She took his arm as they were standing in the shadow of Chapultepec Castle. One hundred and fifty years earlier, Juan Escutia, an army cadet faced with imminent capture, had hurled himself from the ramparts, the Mexican flag in his hands.

The lights of the city were rising, the crowds were spilling into the streets. The noise was like a low grumbling, a creature rousing. The waiters were already standing by the bars, waiting for the first customers. A fire-eater performed on a street corner, the flame blue and lunging. Coins lay scattered at his feet. On stage, a woman was shedding her clothes, her breasts lifting. A table of Japanese roared. The pickpockets were working the buses, the subway. The museums were closing down; a guard walked the long hallways, his heels echoed among the priceless treasures, the antiquities.

They ate dinner in a tiny restaurant. The lighting was low, there were only six tables. There was her laughter, the energy with which she ate. There were stretches of silence, they no long hurried to fill them. Though a small insistent voice reverberated inside him, a voice going, phone your boss, phone your wife. Phone your life. And say what? His story had not yet congealed. He was a man in the middle of a torrential river, ignorant of what lay on the far shore. Meanwhile, there were her narrow shoulders. There was the telltale distance between her eyes. There was the gentle sweep of her neck. His wife, his life would still be there tomorrow. Reed drowned the voice with drink, smothered it with food. Mexico City, cosmopolitan town. One could get anything, anything. He ordered a bottle of scotch that had spent twenty-eight years in the barrels; he could taste the smoky wood. He ordered a steak, then sent it back, demanding another. "I said rare." An evening of expansive acts, the grand gesture. She basked in his bluster, in these minor displays of authority. A gringo out on the town. Reed's mood came unhinged, ran broad, celebratory. He hammered the table, screaming, "Más, más. Más comida." He tipped handsomely, exorbitantly. Back out in the streets then. The city was a flower, it was opening for them. The crowds were emerging from the opera, the symphony. She grabbed his arm, pointed: "Here." A loud place, mariachis stood at the head of the room. She taught him how to say scotch, how to say bourbon, how to say gin. "Bebidas," he thundered in the end. She was drinking wine; Reed had switched to tequila. Scalding shots, salt, lemon. He drank them like a frat boy, like a man debauched. The band played, couples drifted onto the dance floor. Socorro watched them closely, eyes eager, her sandals tapping in time to the music. It was a life she had read about, it was music she had heard. The tune was quick, raucous. She writhed with the beat. Her hair was up, her neck, her ears were bare. Young bucks lined the wall. Reed saw the looks they gave her.

He touched her shoulder lightly. "Go ahead and dance if you want." Avuncular, accommodating. He gestured toward the floor, toward the line of youths. "I don't mind."

She grinned. "Thank you. Yes." She stood, waited. Reed understood she had misunderstood. Bumbling moment. Reed never danced. Never, never. His body was not built for such maneuvers. But the music boomed. Pretty, young, she wanted to dance. He could make out the rise of her breasts beneath her dress.

Reed danced. Young bucks, rife with envious glances. In

210

spite of himself, he basked in their looks. She rocked with short, swaying movements—precise, birdlike gestures. Reed felt like an overbearing mammal loose in an aviary. He threw out his arms, he shuffled his feet. He moved like the black teens he had seen on the Saturday morning dance shows. The music was dinning, they could feel it through the soles of their feet.

They danced another tune, then another. Reed's clothes were drenched. "Let's rest—" "No. No, please." A woman begging to dance. As if the world might end tomorrow. The mariachis howled, thick animal noises. Reed spun around, clapped his hands. His hips went cha-cha-cha. A fool, maybe, but a fool who was enjoying himself. She laughed; he laughed. The back of her dress was dark with sweat. He could smell her dusky odor. Still another song, frenzied, rabid beat. She was moving wildly now, an unbroken horse. The night was like a fever. Reed raised his hands above his head, snapped his fingers, made doo-wah doo-wah sounds.

Then a slow tune, languid. Her smile was unsure. Unsure, she stepped toward him. Reed, arms tentative, like unwieldy cranes, encircled her. Her head heavy on his shoulder, his face buried in her hair. Her hands were small, he could feel their warmth across his back. They circled slowly. It could have been a ballroom; it could have been a bedroom. It was a tune she used to sing to her brothers, she explained, her mouth at his ear. They fell asleep listening to it.

> Allá en el rancho grande
> Allá donde vivía
> Había una rancherita
> Que alegre me decía
> Que alegre me decía
> Te voy hacer tus calzones
> Como los usa el ranchero
> Te los comienzo de lana
> Te los acabo de cuero

Socorro translated, her voice hushed. Some business about a farmgirl on a ranch where you used to live. Reed heard only fragments, a word, an occasional phrase. She would make you a pair of pants like the cowboy used to wear. She would begin with wool, she would end with leather. Socorro's sounds trilled lightly in his ear. Reed could hear her happiness. But it was brothers she was thinking of. Still, it made his toes scrunch up in his shoes. Hard knots of knuckle. Uncowboylike. Then she was laughing, he laughed. Ha ha ha. Lights flashing, mariachis sweating. They clung to each other, circled smoothly. Reed grinning, head rocking. Like a man impersonating a man laughing. She sought out his eyes, her lips full, earnest, lips aching to convince—lips whispering, "I will like it."

He kissed. The lips, not her. Like kissing hope itself. Not her. Crucial distinction, he would have slain innocents to sustain it. An idle urge, innocuous. Like kissing aunts, babies, Russian generals. A bare moment, then it was over. He wasn't even sure it had happened. But her look told him it had happened. Her expression came undone, rearranged itself. A face between emotions; it was trying to light on one. They had stopped circling. The band played on, oblivious, woeful mariachis. The same song she used to, etc. But farmgirl lips, now they kissed back. No Russian general she. Lingering, darting tongue, surprisingly cool. It reached clear to his heart.

The set ended. They stood as if stunned, like men who have been shot, it is the instant before they fall. The silence was hollow, unbalanced. They walked woodenly back to the table, sat. He looked at her, looked away, looked again. She said. He said. He dared to touch her hand. She gripped his thumb. Their fingers became intertwined. Their voices were faint, reassuring. Like voices in a storm. He said, he said again. She nodded, he was nodding. They kissed.

He whispered, "Look: you don't have to."

The foyer of a hotel within sight of the National Museum, Reed saying, "You don't have to." But she was not listening. Her eyes were taking in the broad entryway, the walls, the carpets. They followed a bellboy onto the elevator, Reed behind her, Reed murmuring, "You don't have to." The boy threw open the doors to reveal a large room, the ceiling high. It thrilled her. She ran the tap in the bathroom, she rushed to peer out the window. She opened drawers, she bounced on the bed. She turned on the TV, flicked quickly through the channels. A soccer match, a clown, the news. The weather. Reed stood in the middle of the room, big map of Mexico on the screen. Clear skies in Michoacán, high winds in Oaxaca. Tropical storm brewing off the Yucatán. He said, "Listen, you don't have to."

She was undoing her hair; it avalanched down her shoulders. There was the hiss of her dress, the long sheaf coming off. She was braless, her nudity shocking. Andrea would know, etc. But guilt was suddenly a lonely man on a deserted island. We'll save him next week. Her breasts were smaller than he had expected, they canted away from each other as she moved. He stared, groaned, "You don't have to." Not having to, she placed a hand on his shoulder for balance, bent to snare the waistband of her underwear. Her breasts floated into the middle of the room, tight, swaying. Cotton fell to her feet. She stepped clear, a doe picking its way across a stream. You could have counted the hairs. He felt oafish, leering. As if her nudity were the pure thing, it was his clothes that were obscene. Her waist bore a slight, inviting swell of tummy, her backside was broad; full thighs telescoped quickly to firm calves, little feet. A body built for childbearing. He gawked, felt guilty only about not feeling guilty. Then he was taking off his clothes. Fumbling fingers, they plucked at his belt, tore at shoelaces. Man in a hurry. She stood off to one side, watching him—her look, he was sure, assessing. Fat man climbing out of his clothes. His jockeys got knotted at his ankles. He was rigid, looming, waggling helplessly. Like wielding a two-by-four in a tiny room. She felt too small beside him. He was like a man standing next to a tricycle. He stared, she stared. He said, "You don't have to."

She said, "Shut up."

Reed had known five women in his life, maybe six; there was that one he was not sure counted. On the lower end of the scale, he suspected. But enough to appreciate the differences. His lovemaking was stodgy, he knew, mundane; his demeanor arid. His prick always seemed like some distant acquaintance he had met once, long ago, under awkward circumstances. You keep seeing him—across the street, in a crowded theater, buying wood polish at the grocery—but you never manage to speak; you are not sure he will remember you.

But women. Their fucking was richly textured, heated, lush. He was the lone dandelion, they were the arboretum. The intensity that ripped through their faces, that fired their limbs awed him. His ardor always seemed too meager. It seemed beside the point. Adrift on a woman, Reed found himself marveling at her movements, her noises. A woman smiles, she parts her legs; for that single moment, she is his lamb chop, his pumpkin, his girl from Ipanema, his dearest, his gumdrop, his gal Sal, his liebchen. She is his. All is well. Then she moans. The sound is boding. Some men mistake such sounds for cheers. All their efforts go toward making a woman whinny, moo. But for Reed, the noises of a woman belonged to the acoustics of injury. She moans, she groans, she snuffles. She screeches in his ear. The sounds are orchestral. She is a bellowing Valkyrie, a chanting monk. She is Tchaikovsky's cannons. It seems a piece of dark theater. Meanwhile, there would be Reed, merely Reed, tossing out the occasional grunt, his fucking workmanlike—a man hanging sheetrock, a man rowing a boat. A man who does not get it. It was as if he were always waiting for the usher to tap him on the shoulder, rudely show him to the door. All meaning lay with the woman. It lived in her cunt.

And then there was Andrea. Of course. One exhausts another's sexual repertoire in six months. Cruel hoax of nature, matrimony is the butt of the joke. Their fucking was practiced, their movements rote. Her sounds were liturgical—though a liturgy far removed from the mysteries. Like a people that continues to perform a ritual the meaning of which it has long since forgotten. A digital clock sat on their nightstand. Despite himself, he had begun paying attention: 11:03 to 11:18; 10:47 to 11:05; 10:08 to 10:51 (including the half-hour phone call from her mother); 12:07 to 12:19 (New Year's Eve).

But the hotel room had no clock. In bed, Socorro's movements were abridged, inchoate. Unformed. Her noises were sheared, lopped off, syllables bitten in half. They punctuated the silence. The sounds of what might one day, in some distant future, become words. The acoustics of discovery. Fire, the wheel, zero. There is nothing yet to get. The usher is unborn. Reed flung himself at her again and again, a man trying to break down a door. She responded with heaving buttocks. Her odors were heavy, pungent. Like strong salts. She was a lone drum on a distant mountaintop. They fucked like Luddites.

They lay like the massacred afterward, limp, sprawling. Reed roused slowly, an amphibian dragging up from the muck, and went to hunt down his cigarettes. She lay on her back, her arms thrown out to her sides. As if he had indeed murdered her, he was her executioner. Reed's hands were shaking; the lighter was a torch carried by a bungling arsonist. It kept going out. He gave up, tossed the cigarette to the floor. From across the room, Reed said, "I'll drive you."

She rose on one elbow. Her clavicle was sharp, jutting, an escarpment at night. She said, "I know."

The dawn brought an instant of amnesia, the morning groggy, distended. Reed woke gradually to the feel of a hand wrapped around his stiff member. Benumbed, unaware, he grinned at the ceiling; he worked to remember whether it was his birthday, Christmas, whether he had recently bought her a new dress. Andrea preferred nights; she thought mornings were for moving your bowels, brushing your teeth. Sex early in the day was a rare reward. The morning following his first promotion he had awakened to the touch of a feather boa, Marlene Dietrich on the stereo. The sex had been vigorous, Teutonic. But today was not his birthday, it was not Christmas, it had been years since he had presented her with a dress. It was not his ceiling. He prayed the hand was his own. Reed inclined his head, peered down the shelf of his paunch. The fingers were short, dark, outrageous against the backdrop of his sallow flesh. She sighed in her sleep then, made light smacking noises into the crook of his arm. His own hand cupped her left buttock.

A man cheats on his wife. He is a man divided suddenly, a man of two minds, or three, or twenty-four. On the one hand, there is the church, there is the state, there is civilization as we know it. The sanctity of the family is the fundament upon which it is built. Infidelity is an act of civil terrorism; it is the death of statecraft. It is assassins at night. On the other hand, there is the committee of males, winking, nudge nudge, guffawing, TV fooball, nudie mags, the snap of a towel in the locker room. They are the hunters, all gatherers beware. It is Bedouins ripping off the veil, the alpha male thumping its chest. A man feels mortified, a man feels good. He is on the high wire strung taut from one emotion to the other; sooner or later he will fall. But for a moment, there is the tantalizing sense of death-defying, the world below a place of thimbles and ants.

Reed felt mortified. He had taken unfair advantage. But her grip was firm, proprietary. No Madonna she. Reed felt good. The tips of his fingers grazed tiny hairs, perineum. A man who ran around. But consider the trophy, the cheers in your head. Porcine thought, he understood. Yet the clandestine coupling, the smells of unearned intimacy, the stolen pleasure—they shade the fucking in delicious ways. In crime, the money is greener; the coins jingle more loudly. He raised his head again, wanting to contemplate what he thought of now as his brutish stump in her fingers. But they were the fingers of a child—a child clinging to a walking stick, to the banister along a steep staircase. One slip and she would fall off the mountain, break bones on the steps.

"Socorro?"

Her eyes fluttered open. She sat up, stretched, her ribs shallow, lean arms in the air. Her breasts vanished. A girl imitating a woman. She relaxed then, breasts, woman reappearing. She smelled of sleep, the odor of turned earth. Inept moment, they blinked unsurely at each other. Eyes sought curtains, the dresser. The foot of the bed. Eyes averted. But he needed to piss. He carefully gathered the sheet around him, crossed the floor like a Roman senator. He closed the bathroom door, took aim at the side of the bowl. Minor splashing sound—it seemed important that she not hear. He finished, flushed, confronted himself in the mirror. Bulging belly, broad ears, his nose bulbous, red spider webs from drink. Rump the color of the inside of an apple. Mealy fruit. Mealy mood. He stepped back through the door, sheet in place. He paused at the foot of the bed. She rose now, trotted across the room. Her turn; she would show him how it was done. Bare back, prominent scapulae framing dark hair. Buttocks firm, the color of teak. She did not bother to close the door. He lay and listened to the rush of her urine. Thin fart. Oboe noise. "Discúlpame," he heard her mutter.

A woman unashamed. She pisses, she farts. She screws. Yet a parking meter would have confused her. The distance between them could not be measured in years. It was tribal, epochal. It was ontological. She knew how to grind corn; he knew how to program a VCR. This said everything. He could not decide whether he had been a lecher or a chump. No doubt the truth lay midway in between. But Andrea would know, etc. Shame, he tried now. Shame on you. It was like hearing a bad actor reading bad lines. He had been indiscreet, he decided. Feeble, mincing word. Also tempered, unhysterical. A word he liked. He hung all meaning from it. She reappeared in the doorway. Her hips broke sharply. Hair small between her legs, dark dust at her armpits. She strolled back across the carpet, arches firm, heel to toe. Thin knots of muscle bunching and releasing at her calves. Surging ass, lilting breasts. He had stroked those breasts, kissed that ass. He felt like rising, doing cartwheels through the room, shredding phone books between his teeth, tossing furniture out the window.

She hesitated at the side of the bed. Her proximity made him stir. He secured the sheet more firmly around him. She said, "Do we go, or—"

"We can go."

"You wish to go?"

"We can go."

"You wish to go."

"No."

She grinned, climbed onto the bed like a woman easing onto a raft. A morning adrift. A boat appears on the horizon, sails broad, the crew capable. But you let it float past. You have ample food, ample water. The skies are blue. You don't want to be saved just yet.

How to explain the thoughts of a man as he nuzzles the armpit of a woman? Her feet, her calves, the backs of her knees. He counts her hairs with his tongue. He was a man crossing a continent. The rain forest, the central plain, volcanoes up ahead. He could not remember their names. He was a man pitching from the ramparts. Her breath was bitter, it tasted like turned wine. Then he was moving above her, moving slowly, like the door to a vault, teasing sounds from her. Afterward they lay in a heap, unmoving. Her hair covered her face, spread across the pillow like spilled ink. Her hair spoke: "I am hungry."

He picked up the phone, made room service understand. Odd concept, she had never heard of it. They lay beneath the sheets while the waiter rolled the cart into the room. The waiter carefully kept his eyes trained on the tray before him. Reed signed the bill with a flourish, the tip too much. He had ordered eggs, coffee, meat. Two filet mignons, thick as law books. He had ordered champagne, pears in their own liquor. She fingered the knife, the fork, then pushed them away. She took the steak in her hands. She was ravenous; she had no patience for utensils. Her eating was indelicate, barbaric. Her breasts trembled as she tore at the meat. Reed wanted to stop right there and come lunging across the table, laying his lips at a point behind her ear. Instead he gripped the knife and fork in his fists, waved them like clubs. A man attacking a steak. She chewed noisily, licked her fingers, drank heavy draughts from the champagne. A section of glistening pear disappeared between her lips. He experienced a vast pandemonium of the spirit.

"Tell me: if I weren't going north—" He stopped. Her look was sharp. Disingenuous question, he knew. She knew. Feckless, pathetic. Yet he wanted to hear her protests; he wanted to hear her say no, no, it is not like that. As if she longed for his beaten nose, she lusted for his broad paunch, she could not get enough of his large ears. "If I weren't—"

"No," she said levelly. "No, I would not." Her tone was matter-of-fact. Reed was scarlet. "And you tell me: if I were not—" and then she touched herself. Openly. Obscenely. The gesture was deft. It spoke the truth.

Reed scooted out of his chair, lit a cigarette. He felt chastened. "I guess we should be going."

She sighed. True, she was a woman who wanted a ride north. But he moved her in unexpected ways. He had shown up in her village one day, a man alone, his vulnerability as plain as the lines in his face. There had been his tears in the square; there had been the tenderness with which he had treated her father, the tenderness with which he treated her; there had been the way he had wrenched her off the bus, burly gringo in a dark sea. A gringo with money, a gringo with a car. A gringo going north. It was all she knew of the States. Yet he weeps, laughs, blushes. In bed he is solemn, gentle; he is earnest. As if behind the fact of his money, his car, the direction in which he travels, there survived a hidden sensibility—one that does not get talked about. It is meager; it seems almost nothing. Yet it secretly informs the countryside, the cities, it informs its people. She liked to think that this was maybe true.

He said it again. He said, "I guess we should be going."

From behind him, she said, "If you wish to."

"Don't you want to go?"

She was at his shoulder. "If you wish to."

"You want to go."

She reached, found him. "It is tired?"

"What?" His chest tightened. "Maybe." Then, "I don't know."

A moment, another. Her movements were measured. His breathing was not. His cigarette dropped to the carpet. She picked it up without stopping, managed to set it on a plate. The ash grew long, a gray rod, the wisps of smoke thin. It fell without warning.

She had been seduced at fifteen by a carpenter in her village. He had a wife, four children. She had lain amid the sawdust, tools hanging along the walls of his workshop. Her cries were lost in the knocking of the rain against the roof. They always finished quickly. Someone could walk in at any moment. A neighbor might see her emerging from the shop, straightening her dress. She went early in the morning, late at night. The Day of the Dead. She imagined that she loved him. But there was talk in the village. There is always talk in such villages. They are too small, one knows with a look, a mere glance; sins stand out like eyes in the face. Her mother had died several years earlier, it was left to her father. He sat her down one morning, he had certain things he wanted to say. She denied everything, she laughed it off. The old man turned to gaze out the window. Papa, can I go? No, she could not go. Not yet. A few minutes passed. But Papa, I have work to do. There is the wash, the hearth is cold. The boys will want breakfast. But no. They would wait. An hour, two hours. There was only the silence of her father, the sound of the rain. Papa, what are we waiting for? He turned to her slowly, then looked away. It seemed it hurt him even to look at her. The truth, he said. We are waiting for the truth to arrive. Then he went quiet. His silence, his very presence was like an indictment, a writ of wrongdoings. A man sits with his daughter. They wait, they wait. He will wait as long as it takes. Only she can free him. She told him in the end, she broke down, she told him everything. Her shame was choking. Papa, she begged, oh Papa, please. He said nothing. He said nothing to her for a full month. He refused to allow her brothers to speak to her during that time. She would rather have been beaten, whipped in public. She still cooked, she still washed their clothes, but she was not permitted to sit at the dinner table. In the meantime, her father had gone to the carpenter, confronted him. The carpenter denied everything. He had a wife, he had a family. The very accusation, the carpenter cried, was insulting. Socorro felt abandoned; she lived for a month like a hermit. There were the walls of her home, there was the familiarity of the walk to the well. But her family refused to speak to her, the carpenter would have nothing to do with her. The villagers drew their children indoors when she appeared on the street. At the end of the month, her father cradled her face in his hands. He touched her cheeks, her chin, her eyes, like a blind man remembering. "I missed you," he whispered. It had been far harder on him, she understood then, it had been unbearable. That night he went over to the carpenter's, and under cover of darkness, filed all the man's tools—the saws, the drills, the sander—to blunt edges. He tossed the man's nails into the river. He scored the lengths of timber with lime. The carpenter knew who had done it, of course. Everyone knew: "That was the point." The world had suffered an imbalance; it had to be set right.

She lay across his chest now, her head in the hollow of his throat. Reed said, "This carpenter—" She was listening, the words came through his rib cage. "I think I know this carpenter."

She laughed, then asked how he had gotten the scar on his

shoulder; she wanted to know what that place was on his back; did he know there was a bump on his right buttock; she wanted to know what was wrong with his left foot. The contours of his flesh fascinated her—his hair, the shape of his ears. Reed said barbed-wire fence at age fourteen; Reed said burn from a wood stove at six. The memory floated toward him, harsh winter day, fire popping beneath the black iron. Reed said wart; he said corn. He was cataloguing the wages of age.

Her nose wrinkled. "Corn?"

A day of humping, a day of rutting. A day of soft words, warm looks. A day of alcohol, of food, a day sliced free from all the rest. But, but—"I love my wife," he blurted at one point. It came from nowhere, it was without context. The sound of his voice startled her. It startled him. It was disproportionate, intemperate. As if the need to say it, to confirm it, had been stayed too long; it had been welling up within him, it had bypassed his brain finally, charged straight to his tongue. He reddened. Yet—his wife. He loved her, he said again. He did. He did. He sat up, pounded the mattress with his fist. He did. His wife and his daughter formed the foci of the ellipsis he called his life. He had always counted on it. He always would. Though it was not exactly the life he had planned; it had not turned out quite as he had expected. But—

"It is your life," she finished for him.

Midday. A broad mirror hung from the east wall. She had never seen one of such size. She stood naked before it, eyes roaming over the smooth surface, seeking out the details. She would never return, she began now. Her voice was hushed; it seemed she was talking to herself. She had already decided— she had decided long ago. "But your father. Your brothers." She shook her head, addressed the mirror. Some are born in the wrong place, just as others are born at the wrong time. It was important to recognize this possibility, to embrace it. She was not so much headed toward a new future, but finally claiming the proper one. She could see it all; she had been seeing it for years. She would one day live in a modest house with indoor plumbing. She would have two children (Onésimo and Blanca), she would have a little garden. She would have a dog, she would have a car. There would be a shower in the bathroom, a closet full of clothes. She could see herself in the kitchen, peeling fruit for breakfast. The windows are long, the sunlight floods into the room. She dresses the children for school. She kisses her husband as he leaves for work. Every evening, they sit down to a meal of meat. And then, once everything is in place, once every detail of her life has assumed its proper proportion, she sends for her father, for her brothers. She has rehearsed the moment a hundred times. A thousand. They emerge from a bus, they file down the steps, their eyes unfocused, made weary by the great distances. And there is a daughter. A sister. She is waiting for them. She has been waiting for months, for years. They are astonished by the size of her car, by the beauty of her home. Her father has his own room; there is another for her brothers. That first night, the table groans under the weight of the food. The air fills with their laughter. The walls resound with an unbelieving joy. Her father embraces her. He is weeping; she is weeping. She whispers, "I missed you." She has accomplished the impossible. Her brothers will find jobs, the youngest will go to school. They will go to ballgames. She will show them how to open a bank account, how to shop at the store. How to speak English. They will do everything, they will learn everything. They will have everything. Destiny is a seed. She is the blossom. Her father will drink the nectar.

Reed lay on the bed, stunned by her words. A home, a family, her father stepping from a bus. This was what she wanted; it was all she had ever wanted. Modest wants, yet improbable wants. But there is a kind of woman who is indomitable. She is always braver than we. Set her down in a wilderness, and she would know how to trap game, find water, build a shelter. He would lie in a bed of poison ivy, be plagued by insects, eat toxic berries, only to die from hypothermia. Reed had worked himself into a frenzy the last time his cable went out, berating some innocent clerk over the phone.

Socorro, standing naked before the mirror. Faintly muscled back, sturdy hips, firm legs. Her body excited him. As did the breadth of her vision. She found magic in an open tap. Seeing his country through her eyes, he could not recognize it. Where he saw ruin, she saw promise. For the first time, it came to him that the myopia might be his. He no longer had the stomach for marshaling hopes. And so he no longer deserved them. As if he and his ilk had dropped the baton, squandered a bequest. Abdicated a kingdom. She was reclaiming it. She was like an athlete, a warrior. He had relegated himself to the sidelines; he would be the first to evacuate the village when the army approached. She would be at its head.

"Do you want to leave?"

"Do you?"

She wanted to take a shower. "What do I do?" Reed showed her how to work the controls, how to adjust the temperature. But: "We are wasting much water?" Reed started to say, No, no. There's plenty of water. There's all you want. Instead he made his face severe. Shouldn't waste the water. He climbed in. Suds on her belly, along the two dimples at the base of her back. "Hotter," she insisted. "Make it hotter." She wanted to sample the extremes, to eat from every dish, to try everything. She would be denied nothing. The steam wound around her. She was an apparition in a dream. He knelt in the tub, scrubbed the grime from her ankles, from in between her toes. He found a tube of hotel shampoo. She stood with her eyes tight as he worked her hair into a lather. He reached for a towel when they were done. She raised one leg, the other; she lifted her arms to bunch the mane of hair at the back of her head.

He stood the figurine on the dresser as he pulled a clean pair of underwear from his suitcase. "A gift for my daughter," he explained.

224

She caressed the headpiece, the pocked torso. She cupped it in her hands. It appeared large, substantial in her fingers. As if it were his prick.

They dressed, went out. The sun beat down on their heads. A girl from the sticks, a girl from a land of rain and mud. They strolled down the avenues, hovering close to each other. They held hands. They stopped to kiss. They were like teens in love, like newlyweds. "I want to buy you a gift." She wanted nothing, she said. She needed nothing. But, "I want to." Inside a large department store, her eyes shone with the false lighting. Racks of clothing, long glass banks crowded with jewelry, perfume, scarves, leather. She spun around; she was a woman assailed on all sides. "Clothes?" she asked. She chose a dark blouse, a pair of slacks. Pedestrian fare. "Pick out a dress," he insisted. Reed stood outside the dressing room as she changed. He could hear the rustle of her clothing. "Frank?" She wanted his advice. He parted the curtain. She wore only her panties. They were faded, threadbare. The hole at the side made his heart pitch. She held a dress to her breasts. A simple pattern of cream-colored silk. "This is nice, yes?"

His throat was filling. "This is nice."

Out in the street, the light was waning. He carried the dress in a box under one arm, a bag containing women's underwear in his opposite hand. She stopped to speak to a street vendor.

"Barbacoa," she explained. A favorite dish, she added, a treat reserved for Sunday mornings.

"There's money in my—"

"No." She was resolute. He watched as she came up with a tiny pouch fashioned from rawhide. The coins looked large in her fingers. She counted them out slowly, then counted them again.

"Socorro, you don't need—"

"I want to." The vendor handed her a bulging tortilla, the smells heady. Reed's hands were full; she rose up on tiptoe to reach his mouth. Standing in the street of an ancient city while a woman crammed food into his mouth felt pagan, illicit.

"Barbecue?"

"Barbacoa." She patted her cheek, touched her forehead. Flesh from the face of a cow, the brain, the tongue. "The eyeballs are valued highly."

"You finish it."

Up in their room, they undressed quickly. Their clothes lay scattered about the floor. The figurine crouched on the dresser.

"He watches us."

"I'll put him in the drawer."

"No," she said. "I want him to see."

They could hear the sounds that came from the restaurant downstairs. A restaurant favored by tourists. The tink of silverware, the shouts of the cook. Bits of conversation drifted up to them. A woman was discussing her son; a husband and wife quarreled. Two Texans were debating the plummeting price of real estate in Amarillo. The figurine was hawklike. It made their coupling blasphemous, forbidden. She was on her hands and knees, he knelt between her legs, stared down the length of her back. He was like a man sitting down to a feast. In the restaurant, the woman was worried her son might not get into Yale. One of the Texan's said, "I told him six percent floating, or eight-and-a-half fixed." There were the sounds of eating, of water being poured, a patron scolding a waiter. But Reed was touching her, he touched her again. "Do you like it?" he whispered. Silence. She was like an Arab in prayer, her forehead lay flat against the bed. She was stockpiling the power to speak; the effort was almost too much. "Do you?"

She clenched the sheets in her hands, between her teeth. "Sí," she cried out. "Sí." Towering affirmation, he felt a great wash of happiness, unbearable, uncontainable. Then he was diving into her, plunging. His sails were burning. His boats were in flame.

Morning. He eased gently from bed while she slept. The cord to the phone was merciful, long. He sat on the toilet, closed the door. The international operator spoke a broken English. Reed strained to make her comprehend. There was the scratch of static, what he imagined was the hiss of ions ricocheting off distant satellites. He felt alert, nervous. He prepared his explanations, his excuses. He was ready to counter scalding indictments, heated accusations of professional incompetence, of irresponsibility. Of betrayal. "This is Reed," he said, his voice low, a man who fears being overheard, a man plotting a heinous crime. Then, "Out of town?" "Out of town," Yates's secretary reiterated. "A meeting in Washington." She was an old woman, this Miss Corrigan, a doughty woman. Rumor was she had no first name. She was always and forever Miss Corrigan. Among company associates, she functioned as part den mother, part wicked witch. She had never married, she had no children. She liked ocean cruises: the perpetual buffets, shuffleboard, Mardi Gras Night on the upper deck. Reed had once overheard her scolding her boss because he had forgotten his hat. Her power, it was said, was surpassed only by that of the Old Man himself. She terrified the younger associates. She could summon up facts, figures, the texts of entire letters the way others recall phone numbers.

"Would you like to talk to Mr. Eiger?" she asked. No, he came back. No.

"Miss Corrigan . . ."

He wanted to sound offhanded, hardheaded.

"Mr. Reed."

"Miss Corrigan: am I in trouble?"

It came out dispirited, plaintive.

This attempt at forced intimacy, his affrontery, unsettled her. She was about to upbraid him for it. As if she had no clue to his meaning. But she did. Of course she did. Frank Reed had been in trouble for some years now. She thought him weak, ineffectual. The man's wife, however—his wife she liked. Miss Corrigan had once found herself seated next to Andrea at a company dinner. The younger woman had been amiable, witty, and sincere. They had talked of Ireland.

Unaccountably, Miss Corrigan's tone now thawed; he was talking to the den mother. She turned confidential, almost chatty. Trouble? No, not really. Not yet. Though Yates would be back in two days. "If I were you . . ."

"Thank you, Miss Corrigan."

"You're welcome, Mr. Reed."

Reed hung up, took a deep breath, thought, That went well. He felt like a man who just might get away with a crime. He is inside the bank, the customers lie prone on the floor, the guard has been subdued. But he still has to get the combination to the safe. Reed dialed again. A different international operator, her English was scrambled. The phone rang once, twice. He waited, thinking, Car trouble, protracted negotiations. He waited, a man prepared to lie, to confess if he had to. A man prepared to beg.

"Hello?"

The sound of his daughter's voice was like a punch in the head. "Dad?" Then: Mom wasn't home; she had already left for work. Reed said, Car trouble, etc. He rambled on, ridiculous bantering about fuel injection systems, Mexican import laws, the complexities of international finance. The lie was fantastic, detailed. But Laura sounded preoccupied, in a hurry. "Your mother's not angry?" Laura did not understand. Why should her mother be angry. Andrea had said nothing; she had told her daughter nothing. "You're sure she's not angry?" "Dad—" "Tell her I called, I'll be home in a day or two." Then, "I got you a souvenir." "Dad, I've got to go." "Tell your mother I called—"

The door opened. His heart caught. A man who had been found out after all. Socorro filled the doorway, her nudity oppressive. There were her veering breasts. There was her sparse divot of hair, funneling out of sight. There was Laura in his ear, saying, "Dad? Dad, I've got to go." As if her voice had entered the room, it now beheld a naked father on the john, his mistress at the door. Reed bleated, "What?" unsure whether he was talking to Socorro or to his daughter. The instant was scorching, incestuous. The power of daughters: they would ruin us if they only knew. Yet, "Dad, I've really, really got to go." Reed clung to the phone, gaped up at Socorro. She frowned, shifting her weight from foot to foot. An impatient woman, a woman who wanted much; she had once had a rabbit named Mucho. Reed's mood was spiraling suddenly, vertiginous. He had seen the movies; he had read tales of wronged women, vengeful women. Say she sent him unseemly letters, suggestive postcards months from now. Extortionary postcards. Five thousand dollars in select denominations in a wastebasket at the corner of Exeter and Commonwealth. Say she appeared at the door of his office. At the door of his house. He would come home from work, find Andrea and Socorro at the kitchen table, poised over cups of cooling coffee. Andrea proper, smoldering. Socorro weeping: a woman spurned, a woman used. A woman victorious. He understood that with a word, a look, she could alter his life. He made his voice cross. "What do you want?"

She shifted her weight again, breasts quivering. "I want to pee."

Reed blinked, then spoke into the phone. "Honey, I've got to go."

"Tell me about it," Laura said, her tone sneering, impatient with all things.

He hung up. Socorro peed. He lay on the bed. His boss was out of town, his daughter had to go. Why should his wife be angry. He had worried that Yates's temper would be punitive, that Andrea would scream barbed recriminations. But it was as if nothing had happened. Here he had crossed a subcontinent. He had played dominoes with Methuselah. He had betrayed his wife. And yet it seemed nothing, nothing had changed. Reed knotted his fingers behind his head. A man in repose, an untroubled man. The toilet flushed. Reed glanced at the mirror, saw his grin. Rogue, ne'er-do-well. Seducer of dark aboriginal women. They pee in adjacent rooms.

He thought, That went very well.

A day of driving. They had both known it was time to leave; some unspoken accord had been reached. She insisted on setting the figurine in the nook between their seats. "He should not be made to ride with socks." Reed, a woman, an ugly nub of clay. He told her every joke he could remember. She wanted to see which she got, which eluded her. "So the man says, 'I can't hear you, I have a banana in my ear.'" She shrieked, her eyes teary with laughter. But, "The rabbi says, 'No thanks. I just ate,'" drew a mystified look. The mountains lagged behind them, the day warmed quickly. When the radiator boiled over, they made a joke of it: life is like that.

They stopped in San Luis Potosí late in the afternoon, some eight hours from the border. They could have gone on, pushed through the night. But they were like a couple on holiday, like retirees with time. It was a town of refineries, a town of warehouses. They managed to find a hotel with a lobby done up in marble. A mynah bird sat in a cage on the bar. The staff wore dark suits with yellow piping. The courtyard held a large pool centered amid lush greenery. The water was blue and untroubled.

"Can I?"

The front desk arranged for a suit. Reed sat in a deck chair, a drink in his hand, and watched her swim. The sun was sinking into the horizon, but the heat was still thick. "Come in, come in," she kept saying. He wagged his head no, beaming. Her strokes were graceless, but functional. She was used to river currents, boulders to be avoided. She emerged dripping from the cold water, her hair sleeked black. She tugged at her suit, adjusting it. "It is too small?" It was the kind of swimwear worn by elderly German tourists. Any bigger, and it would have fallen off. At dinner she drank Kahlua over ice; he ordered a martini and was surprised by its quality. "I'll have another."

Midnight. She sat on the bed, the figurine in her hands. Reed lay sated, watching her. A man with a full belly, a weary prick. She studied the statue as if it were a window through which she could not quite see, a cloudy mirror. The instant seemed solemn, touching, full of crafted dignity. And yet, "Why does he hold a plate?"

230

Reed started to explain that it was a calendar, to say, Time is a wheel, time is round; to talk about repercussions, about consequences, etc. But it seemed irrelevant. No: it seemed false. As if they were at a place where nothing could reach them, a place torn out of time. History had fissured, splintered apart. A unique moment, an anointed moment. He was in the thrall of a soaring gratitude. He leaned now, kissed her shoulder lightly. He said, "Maybe he's a waiter."

She woke first. "Frank," she whispered. Emerging sun, and he eased on top of her. A farewell fuck, then. He wanted to memorize her face, her sounds, the way her hair splashed across the pillow, the shuddering of her breasts beneath him. He wanted to inscribe his name on the inside of her thigh. But, "Sorry," he said finally. He rolled off her. They both stared at it. Her nudity was everywhere, it filled the room. But he was like a blind man in a museum. So he would inscribe his name on nothing. She started to reach for him, but he waved her off, found his cigarettes. He felt ancient, withered. Embarrassed. She sat up, looked at him with concern. He shrugged. He was tired. It was tired. For the first time in days, his stomach had come unsettled. "I don't know what to say," he muttered.

"Say you will miss me."

North then. North at last. Monterrey, Saltillo, Monclova. As they approached Nueva Rosita, she told him how it was done. Best if he dropped her at an inexpensive hotel. It would take a day or two to locate a coyote, to arrange to be smuggled across. Her father had explained it all to her. Coyotes could be found at the bus station, in cantinas, in comedors. They could be found anywhere. Never pay more than half of what a coyote first demands. Lie when asked how much money you have. It is best to travel with a group, though a small group; alone, you might find yourself abandoned by a coyote in the middle of the desert. He would take your money, your boots. "Everything."

Too large a group, and la migra would discover you. Travel at night. Wear dark clothing. Always carry your shoes.

"Your shoes?"

"When crossing the river, always carry your shoes."

Speak to no one, stop nowhere until you are well beyond the interior checkpoints—at least twenty, thirty miles. Within that perimeter, la migra stopped cars, they searched buses.

"And then what?"

You arrive in a large town, look for some little business run by Mexicans. A restaurant, a laundromat; for some reason, "video shops are good." Not Chicanos, not Mexican Americans, but Mexicans. They understood. Ask to use the bathroom, ask for a glass of water. A meal. Say, "My name is Socorro, from the state of Chiapas." Then wait. Say nothing more. Sooner or later, someone will say, "Isn't Tomás González from Chiapas?" or, "My primo knows a man from Chiapas," and it will turn out that Tomás González has a friend in San Diego, or the primo has a sister who now lives in Los Angeles. And you say, "González? I believe I know the family, sí," or, "A sister in Los Angeles, verdad? Why, I have an uncle in Los Angeles." This was how it was done.

Now the town of Piedras Negras wheeled toward them, the river like a winding brown ribbon on beyond. Texas was a thin strip at the edge of the horizon. A searing afternoon on the border, the heat dry, angry, unrelenting. She rested her arms on the dashboard, pressed her nose to the windshield. She wanted to know in what direction San Diego lay, Houston, New York, Chicago. She wanted to know how far. She was like one standing at the edge of a vast frontier. These names, these cities were the stuff of fable.

"And Boston is that way," Reed added, in spite of himself. "About twenty-five hundred miles."

They were moving through the long run of shantytown now, past the crumbling shacks, alongside a maquiladora overflowing with workers. The squalor crashed down about their ears. It was grander than he remembered, more pronounced.

232

As if the past week had sharpened his vision, made his thinking acute. There were the harsh odors, the begging children. She shrank back when one of the bolder ones ran forward, rapped at the window. Reed leaned on the horn, drove quickly on through. She glanced back over her shoulder, then peered at Reed. She wanted to know where the beggars came from, all the workers. She wanted to know why their homes were made of cardboard. Her father had last made the crossing years ago; he had talked about the border, told her what to expect. But this—he had not talked about this.

Her face clouded over as she listened to his explanation. She cut him off with a wave of her hand, taking in the panorama.

"This," she said, "is what you do?"

No, no, he said quickly. No. She did not understand. Admittedly, his company had some minor dealings down here . . . but he was involved in high finance, mercurial deals; he worked with ledgers, spreadsheets. He had an office on the ninth floor, there was a coffee maker out in the hallway, there were the conference rooms; a computer sat on his desk, 16 megabyte RAM, 750 megabyte hard drive, CD-ROM, 24,000 baud fax modem. It was all far away; it had nothing to do with this. It—

"Yeah. Yeah, this is what I do."

She looked at her hands. "The bus station. A video shop. Anywhere."

He said, "Let's get something to eat."

They stopped at a taco house. The tink of coffee cups on saucers, the scrape of a fork across a plate. Their talk was subdued. He ordered a beer for himself, a sandwich for her. Their table looked out over a narrow alley; they could see a dump at the far end. An old woman picked her way through it, a young man was unearthing a plastic tarp. A girl sat in the seat of a junked car, pretending to drive. Socorro pushed her plate away after a few bites.

He had driven her through a gauntlet of the poor, the hungry. He had managed to ruin the appetite of a girl who ate like

233

a football team seated at a training table. He found himself reaching for his wallet. "I want you to have this. I insist." He tried to sound magnanimous, but his tone was pleading, penitent. He counted out fifty dollars. On the broad surface of the table, the bills looked meager. Yet he had begun to worry about his money. The hotels, the meals. He had spent lavishly, he had spent too much. Yates's accountants would send him a nasty memo, a detailed itemization of what they would, and would not, pay. Champagne breakfasts, lingerie, a woman's bathing suit. He would have to hide the credit slips from Andrea when they came in the mail. A month, six weeks from now, she would look up from the checkbook and demand, "Frank?"

Socorro regarded the money with open distaste. "You owe me nothing. We owe each other nothing."

Reed added another fifty dollars. It was like adding fuel to a fire that has already gone out. "Take it."

She refused to meet his gaze. "I am not your war."

"What?"

"I am not your war."

"It's 'whore.'"

Her head came up, she looked at him full. Her eyes glinted with rich color. In anger, her face contracted, narrowed like a blade. He saw it then, he knew it in an instant. She would one day learn to hate him, to detest the memory. He was an old man who honks at begging children. Reed stared at her now, as if he might detect the first inkling of hatred in her features, as if it were already forming. But looking at her, Reed saw her on the banks of the river, hanging on to the hem of her dress as the water rushed higher. He saw her crawling through a dark tunnel, burrowing like an animal. He saw her picking her way through the scrub brush late at night; he heard the barking of pursuit dogs close behind. He saw all the places she would sleep: a bunkhouse on the grounds of a vineyard, a fallen-down concrete structure within sight of the peach groves, a bedroll in the shelter of an apple tree. He saw her slapping down plates of bacon and eggs at some hash bin. A layer of grease over everything, the truckers cursing softly under their breaths. He saw her bent over a sewing machine, a naked bulb above, the air sweltering, a large fan whirring at one end of the room—a fan that does no good. He saw another like her, twenty others like her, a hundred, a thousand, the tens of thousands. All while other men, paler men, men with homes, with families—men like himself—bought that new car, paid for the wife's tennis lessons, went to Key West next year, the Bahamas, maybe even Paris, held the club memberships, paid green fees, went to the occasional play, bought the occasional bottle of liquor, the occasional hooker, managed to send their offspring to Smith, Bryn Mawr. To Holyoke at least.

But in the end, he came back to the gentle heft of her breasts, to her thighs, to her lean arms in the moment she stretched, first thing in the morning. To the shocking contrast of her skin against his. His flesh was weathered birch, felled ash; hers was rosewood, mahogany.

He said, "Let me drive you across."

His words surprised him. They baffled her. Yet the idea exercised an unflinching appeal. Let me, he repeated. There were other ways, she began slowly. Better ways. Perhaps if her skin were lighter, if her features were less severe, less indio, if her clothes were finer . . . but no. She would be caught. She had heard the things la migra did. There were some immigration officers, there were some . . . Her face tightened. "And you could get into trouble as well."

"Let me drive you across." He would drive her all the way to San Antonio, put her on a bus to wherever she wanted to go. He wanted to suddenly, he was desperate to. He felt fearless, assured. When he had crossed over from the States, the guards had seemed listless, perfunctory. And this would be the consummate resolution, the bow to fit the package of these last days. It would complete the memory. A story with a happy ending. He waved his arms; his voice turned adamant.

"I'll tell them you're my housekeeper."

She laughed. The sound was unexpected, redemptive. "Your housekeeper?"

" 'It's important she get across, officer. There are bugs in the cupboards, mold in the bathroom, mice in the basement.' "

She cocked her head. "Bugs in the cupboard."

"Mold in the bathroom, mice in the basement."

She smiled. She was enjoying the game. "The dishes, they are dirty in the sink."

"The windows need washing."

"You do not know how to cook. 'Officer, he will go hungry.' "

Reed blinked. "He will starve."

There had come a moment the evening before—he lay with his face between her legs, his head moving in a lazy figure-eight, she had a faint, oniony taste, he could not get enough of it, her hands playing a soft timpani on his head, her gasps were like the urgings of a crowd, the sounds of a mob in the instant before it explodes, ransacks the train station, burns the court-house—when he had entered into a brief fantasy: they would move to a city in the Midwest, he would get a job at a little fixit shop. A ruddy health would steal into his face; the sun would work his skin. He would be a man renewed, a man with a sec-ond chance. He would come home to Socorro, to two kids—dark children, bilingual from the very beginning. Their meals would be celebrations of meat. Nights there would be the shock of her hair fanning across the pillow, there would be her sounds. The bitter taste of her breath on waking.

But it was only a moment. Beginnings grow harder. They grow impossible. There are those who must make the great journeys, those who must take the impossible risks. But he had a home, he had a wife, etc. He would return, live out his life. There would be backyard barbecues, there would be the ride on the T, there would be his office. He would watch his daughter graduate, send her off to school. He would age, the gray would deepen. There would be the howling fights in the kitchen, his wife's tears in the bedroom. There would be the bedlam of the streets, his failing fortunes at work. But there had been this. The memory was already ossifying, like a memento, an amulet—an insect visible through the amber.

Reed laid his hand over hers. He said, "I don't want to say goodbye here."

"But—"

"I want to say goodbye over there." He gripped her thumb in his fingers. It was the bone of a bird. "You owe me this."

She hesitated. "This is unwise." Yet her hesitation was like a passage through which he had already jumped. He got up from his chair.

"Come on."

She gestured with that disarming, jutting motion of her chin. "Your money," she reminded him.

Past the farmacias, the cantinas, the dentists' offices. Texas neared. Socorro's face was tight with anticipation. A striking face, he had decided; one came to learn the extent of her beauty only gradually, like an appreciation for fine wines, for escargot. Yet doubts hovered in her eyes, her features brimmed with second thoughts.

"This is unwise," she said again.

The traffic was heavy, people streaming north to work, to shop, to visit relatives. The line to the border was several blocks long. He edged the car forward. He glanced at her. A bead of perspiration appeared on her upper lip. He wanted to lick it off.

"What if—" she began.

"We won't. They won't. Nothing, nothing," he went on, as if he made sense. "We'll pull up to the guard gate. Some bored man who's worried because his kid is sick and his wife can't cook will lean in, say, 'U.S. citizens?' and I'll say yes. And he'll say, 'Anything to declare?' And I'll say, 'No.' And he'll say, 'Have a nice day.' "

She was unconvinced. "Please. This is dangerous—"

"Shut up."

The weeds along the bank, the golf course, the traffic of Texas running in backdrop. Like a memory you had always mistaken for a dream. A red light flashed next to a sign that told him to wait for the green. Up ahead, an elderly couple in a new Cadillac; the driver was talking to the guard. Reed watched as the driver gestured, gestured again. The guard laughed. A pleasant man, this guard; a man who refrained from complications. The light changed. Reed eased the Toyota forward, a smile plastered to his face. Socorro stared straight ahead. She gripped her bag as if it were a life preserver. He could hear her breathing.

"Socorro—"

But the guard. He tipped his hat, said U.S. citizens, said, alcohol, food, anything to declare. Reed said, Yes, no, nothing. Reed darted a knowing look toward her, I-told-you-so in his eyes.

The guard was about to wave them on. Reed could feel it. He could see the man's head already lifting, his eyes going to the car behind them, then the car after that, and the one after that. Eight hours worth of cars, the mind glazes over. Reed had put the car into gear when the guard said, "Ugly sucker." His tone was convivial, warm.

"Pardon?"

The guard indicated the figurine squatting between them, snug in the change tray. He had placed his hands on the roof of the car. His face filled the window.

Reed laughed. "A gift for my daughter."

The guard looked up now, peered at the line of cars backed up to the tollbooth. As if he were weighing things, easing into a decision. Eight hours. He was a man who had time.

"Bought that in Mexico?"

Yes, he had bought it in Mexico. Reed detected a subtle shift in the guard's voice, the warmth cooling. It was a trinket, Reed explained quickly. He glanced at the figurine. Squat, hooded brow. Suddenly scary, a thing of consequence. But no:

238

junk. He had paid—he had paid ten dollars for it. The guard drummed the roof of the car with his fingers. His child had been fully immunized; his wife wrote cookbooks. If he could see the receipt, he said. But there was no receipt, Reed told him; why should there be a receipt? He had never thought to ask. The guard shrugged. Maybe you should have thought. "But why?" Reed asked. "Why? Why?" Like a man shouting at God. Recent agreements with Mexico, the guard went on; illegal to take certain artifacts out. Reed stared at the figurine with a mixture of horror and fascination. "Officer, I don't understand." Socorro's face was stoic, unblinking. The guard sighed. An unpleasant man in the end, a man opting for complications. He pointed. "Park it there."

"But—"

"Park it there."

A second guard appeared, asked them to get out of the car. He hefted the figurine in his hands, prodded it with his fingers. The figurine appeared unkempt, faintly comical in the guard's large hands. "It's junk," Reed insisted. Couldn't they see that. A third guard began to search through their luggage. Reed's shaving kit, his shirts. The underwear he had bought Socorro. It smelled of her. She hung close to Reed's side. She seemed insubstantial, swaying. A German shepherd was brought in. It sniffed at the tires, along the doors. It nudged Reed smartly in the crotch. The guard holding the figurine said, "How much?" "Ten dollars." The guard cocked a skeptical eye. Reed licked his lips, sweating furiously. Bitched by eight ounces of terra-cotta. Eerie, fiendish countenance, the figurine looked as if it might wink, give him away. "Fifty," Reed admitted, regretting it immediately. A mistake. He was now a man who would lie. No, no, he had no receipt. He had no bill of sale. He had nothing. The guard clicked his tongue, small knock of admonition. He disappeared through a door, bearing the figurine. Another guard looked through the trunk, the glove compartment. As if he expected to find a cache of pre-Columbian pieces in the tire well. The situation seemed unreal, all out of proportion. They asked for his driver's license. "My driver's license?" Routine, they assured him. They asked for the car-rental papers. They asked for her driver's license. She was like a child kept after class. No, she had no driver's license. She had no passport. Several more guards gathered around. Reed could see the faces through the windows of passing cars, cars that rocked up to the booth, hesitated momentarily, then eased on through. He envied them. He hated them. But: a Social Security card, any proof of U.S. citizenship? You must have something. No; she had nothing.

The guards exchanged glances. Their eyes were rich with meaning. Reed experienced a sickening lurch, as if the world had tilted off its axis, it was flying unmoored through dark space.

"Miss, are you a U.S. citizen?"

There was an air of finality to the question. As if everything had already been decided. They were only playing out the inevitable, moving in ways they had to move, saying the things they had to say. Adhering to a script with which they had grown bored long ago. The officers were big, broad, heavy-necked cowboys. She was mute. Her lower lip quivered. Reed's nausea was complete.

"Miss . . ."

"She's my housekeeper."

One of the guards snorted; another rolled his eyes. The heat swept into Reed's face. Officer, he said, officer. Keep the statue. "I don't care." Reed opened the fold of his wallet. The edges of green bills were visible. The guards stiffened; the air went taut.

"Put that away." The guard wagged a finger in Reed's face. Reed wanted to chew it off. Instead, he slapped shut his wallet. He was like a chastened dog.

Then Socorro spoke. It surprised them all. She said, "He does not know me."

Reed puffed with disbelief. "Socorro—"

She appeared calm now, resigned. "He does not. I knocked

240

on the door of his car in Piedras. I said, Please señor, may I have a ride."

"Is this true?"

"It is true. He does not know me."

"I'm talking to him." The guard jerked his thumb at Reed.

Reed said, "Officer—" The moment was disintegrating. "Officer."

The guard crossed his arms over his chest, assumed the posture of a man at a lectern, a man explaining. He spoke to the air above Reed's head. There were penalties for transporting undocumented persons across the border. Fines, possible jail sentences. In fact, they had arrested a guy just last week . . .

"Do this," she whispered out of the corner of her mouth.

"Choco—"

"Please."

Reed brought his hand to his forehead. He kept it there. They all waited. "It's true."

The guards all smiled, as if they had been rooting for him. A uniformed matron led Socorro to a large cinder-block structure off the line of customs booths. Socorro glanced back at Reed. Her eyes were moist pools. He searched them for condemnation, for hate, for a sense of betrayal. But there was nothing, only a raw yearning. It seemed the very hue of forgiveness.

Reed was directed into a tiny room, told to sit in a chair. He made a saddle with his hands and rested his chin there. A sign opposite said No Smoking. The rationalizations were already jostling for position in his mind, leapfrogging one over the other. He had a home, after all, a life to worry about. He had responsibilities. He had offered to do her a favor; it had not worked out. He was sorry. But life is like that. He was a simple man, an uncomplicated man. He was a man who did what he could. Now he would go home, there would be days in the park; winter and he would shovel the front steps; nights he would sit with the remote control in one hand, a drink in the other, an overflowing ashtray at his side. In the fall he would rake leaves. Spring, he would carry an umbrella, bring down the storm windows. Summer and he would stand out in back, grilling meat.

And this had nothing, nothing to do with any of it.

But you touched her and parted her legs and put your mouth there and there and there. She fed you, she bedded you. She watched you weep. The thin slide of her neck, breasts floating beneath you, thighs rising to meet you. Pelvis rushing against pelvis. Abrupt, scalding sounds, sheared noises, bitten off at their cores. Yet as sacred as oaths, promises, vows of trust. He stared at his hands. They were the hands of a carnivore. His shame was the largest piece of furniture in the room.

A guard appeared with a clipboard. He asked for Reed's full name, his address, his place of employment. He asked if he had ever been to Mexico before. He asked about his job. He wanted to know if Reed had a criminal record. He asked where he had bought the figurine; how much he had paid. He asked how he had met the girl. How much he had paid.

The color flew from Reed's face. "I don't have to take this." "Yeah," the guard said, not a hint of irony in his tone. "I'm afraid that you do." He made Reed sign one form, then another. The guard disappeared through a door. Reed sat, clenching and unclenching his fists. He moved his head back and forth. Half an hour, forty-five minutes. Reed left alone with his thoughts. They were like bars on the windows, locks on the door of a prison. A place he would never escape. A thin man in a business suit eventually showed. He sat on the edge of the desk. A name tag identified him as Investigator Ross. He took his time studying Reed's face, sizing him up. "Sorry for the inconvenience. Understand, it's a tricky matter. We have to be careful. But you're right: fake."

Reed did not understand. "The girl?"

Ross gave him an odd look. "I was talking about the figurine," he said slowly. "We've got a guy here who knows his stuff. When it's genuine, we've got to return it to Mexico, then decide whether to prosecute," he continued. A man who liked his job, he found it fascinating. "Frankly, you don't seem like the smuggler type. We got profiles, you know; you don't match what we call the smuggler profile. Usually some long-hair, maybe got booted out of grad school. It's a booming business now. Collectors stateside will pay a bundle for this stuff. So we've got to be sure—"

"What happens to the girl?"

Ross stared at Reed. He lit a cigarette, circled the desk, leaned against the wall opposite, No Smoking above his head. Reed ached for a taste. Ross said, "You know, I see it ten times a week. Some guy alone, guy on a business trip. He's bored. Say he can't stand the food, the heat. Say he misses his wife. He decides to sample the local color. Some wetback mutters a little of the español in his ear, and next thing you know he's dressing her in silk underwear." Reed went plum. "He's a decent guy, never broken the law in his life, but he's out of his head. Stick it in the guacamole—"

"What happens to her?"

Ross's eyes grew closer together. Reed could almost see the thoughts spinning behind them. "We'll make out a report," he said evenly. "Maybe hold her for a day or two. We'll question her. Try to scare her a little. We don't want her doing it again. Then she'll be returned to Mexico." An unkind smile formed. "In a few days, I'll probably be sitting here with another guy, some new guy she's met."

Reed licked his lips, rubbed his hands back and forth along his thighs. He shook his head, started to speak, then decided against it. Ross drew heavily on the cigarette, dense smoke streaming from his nose. "Understand," he went on, "we keep a record of this. It's cross-referenced to Brownsville, Laredo, to Mexicali." He leaned close. "Wouldn't make a habit of it."

He patted Reed lightly on the shoulder. A friendly gesture, Reed understood. A gesture of assurance. "This kind of thing, it looks bad for the home team." Ross repeated the business about fines, possible jail sentences. He mentioned public scandal, stories in the local newspaper. Say his wife found out, maybe his boss, his friends all reading about how Frank Reed tried to sneak a beautiful greaser across. "I bet you got you an important job back home." He was warming to the subject. "I bet you got you a wife, a family. A nice house." Ross had a family, he had a nice house. He was proud of it. He went to church on Sundays, got drunk on the Fourth of July, fucked his wife with the shades drawn. Reed felt as if he knew this man, he knew him intimately. He had seen him watering his lawn in the summer, burning leaves in the fall. He had seen him on the subway, in line at the grocery. He had known him all his life.

Ross took a last puff of his cigarette, tossed it to the floor, stepped on it. It left a black scar in the linoleum. His smile turned pensive. One gringo helping another. "If your boss is anything like my boss, he wouldn't understand. If your wife is anything like my wife, she sure wouldn't understand."

Reed said, "My wife is nothing like your wife."

Ross's smile froze, then shrank bit by bit, the muscles in his face twitching, condensing. The process slowed, then reversed. The grin was grim now, predatory. He did a pistol-thing with his hand, pointed it at Reed. "I'll remember you."

Reed drove north, the figurine in the nook next to him. He wanted to hurl it out the window, smash it against the asphalt. But she had liked it; it had seen the things they had done. "He should not be made to ride with socks." Past a field of alfalfa, past tortured mesquite. A sign said, San Antonio 137. Vultures circled in the distance, steady, arcing, ugly.

He pulled into a truckstop. He thought, gas, he thought, coffee. He thought, steady, steady, steady now. Bleary-eyed patrons, the air choked with tobacco smoke. A condom dispenser in the bathroom, aging waitress at the counter, waitress calling him, "Honey." Coffee sloshed into his saucer. His cigarette tasted acidic, all wrong. Small knives in his stomach seemed to be slashing their way from the inside out. Two truckers sat at the far end of the counter, one explaining to the other: "She gets one look at me, she says, 'Sweety, I won't let you put that thing in me for any kind of money.' " Truckers chortling, slapping thighs, wonking sounds. Going hardee-har. Fraternal noises, male. Squawking voice of a radio in the corner. Civil war in Europe, starvation in Africa. The Maverick County School Board would meet that evening. Ida Mae Rubens left yesterday for a two-week vacation, visiting her sister in Tulsa.

Reed's head dropped into his hands. As if he were trying to hold in his brain. From the north, cars continued to shuffle up to the customs booths. A honeymooning couple out of Cincinnati—they'd been to Six Flags, the Alamo—in search of colorful native tapestries. A petroleum executive driving a Lincoln with Oklahoma plates, on his way to a meeting with Pemex officials. College students down from Austin, in search of cheap Mexican liquor, cheap Mexican whores. To the south, black smoke billowed into the air. Chemicals gushed from broad pipes into the river. Big-bellied children begged in the streets. A man would wash your windshield for a quarter. Socorro stood in a windowless room of the cinder-block building, shivering. A guard hovered just outside the door; she could hear his snickering. Her clothing lay in a pile on a table. She had been made to open her mouth, to raise her arms. "Bend over," the matron was saying.

On the bank opposite, a family waited. Nightfall was three hours away.

"Dad, I really have to go."

When she got off the phone with her father, Laura raced to gather her books. She had been late to school twice that week. The morning before she had missed her stop on the T, daydreaming all the way to Alewife Station, the end of the line. In her room, goldfish floated at the top of the tank. Overdue notices from the library sat on her desk. She lost her gloves, a pair of earrings. She missed the deadline for a book report. Her socks did not match. She forgot, she lost, she put off, she could not remember.

She was a girl in a hurry. A girl confused by her own chemicals. Yet she had the hips, the breasts of a woman. Her body was speaking in tongues. There is a species of pigeon that must set eyes on a member of the opposite gender before it can mature.

They met before class, after class, they ate lunch together in the school cafeteria. They took walks together, wandered through Copley Square, Chinatown, the zoo in Franklin Park. They went to a matinee. But when the heroine took off her clothes, Xavier muttered, "Let's get out of here." They spent the rest of the day riding the T south to Quincy, north to Revere Beach. The afternoon was windy, there was a chill in the air. The waves smashed against the shore, plumes showering over them. There was the odor of brine, the endless gray expanse of the sea. At a rocky stretch he took her hand. On Saturday morning they went to that record store downtown. The clerks saw everything, but they said nothing. White, well-scrubbed clerks, they wore ties; she understood they had been afraid. One day he presented her with a single carnation; the next day she gave him a satchel filled with sheet music. He gave her a tape of piano sonatas; she gave him her CD player. There was that day on the Common when a squirrel ate from his hand.

They told each other everything; it seemed there was nothing they could not say. He talked about his mother. In her last year, arthritis had stiffened her fingers, made it impossible for her to tie her shoes. She played like a drunk, like a child who refuses to learn scales. Laura told him about the time Nick Dawson and Dave Abelson said they would show her their things if she would show them hers. She was seven years old. They were playing in Nick's back yard. "You first," she insisted. Nick pulled down his pants, then Dave pulled down his pants. Like acorns, is how she remembered it. But when she lifted her dress, Nick screamed and Dave screamed and they

246

both ran. Xavier talked about the time those two Italians jumped him when he got off the subway in the North End. A policeman found him, bruised and bleeding, next to a dumpster. The cop shook him by the collar, yelled, "What did you do?" The summer he turned thirteen he participated in one of those programs developed for inner-city youths. Weekends, he and three other boys were bused to a neighborhood in Newton, to a home with a tennis court, a putting green, a fenced-in pool. Opportunities for fresh air, exercise, interracial understanding. The lady of the house insisted swimming trunks were unhealthy, then invited friends over to watch. Rich white women sitting on the deck, sipping drinks, eyeing him as he did dark backflips off the diving board. One Lent Laura's mother pointedly informed her husband that he was foregoing drink for forty days, her daughter was giving up TV. Andrea was giving up bridge. The following Saturday, while her mother was out, Laura found her father cowering in the walk-in cupboard, sucking at a bottle of vodka. He looked like a man caught peeping through a keyhole. Without a word he took her hand, sat her down, and they watched three hours of cartoons together. "My father kept saying, 'We won't tell your mother.'" Following graduation, Xavier planned on joining one of the services, then making his way on the GI Bill. "The conservatory," he explained.

"My mom thinks I look just like her," Laura told him. "My dad thinks I look just like him. They fight about it, act like they're joking. Except they're not joking."

They talked with urgency. It was like a race that might end before they could win. She found herself dreaming about him—half-formed dreams, the narrative clipped, a series of jump-cuts that never added up.

Laura was again late for school. Third time in a week. She was ordered down to the office of the girls' dean, a plump woman in her late twenties, a doctorate in education. She hoped one day to be named principal of a large school in the suburbs: Chestnut Hill, Arlington. A school with a generous budget, a gleaming cafeteria, the latest in laboratory equipment. A school with unbroken windows, a school free of obscene graffiti in three languages. A school where the doors were still on the bathroom stalls. As girls' dean, she dealt with pregnant Puerto Ricans, foul-mouthed blacks, that Vietnamese girl who had threatened her with a knife. An ambitious woman, this was only a way station.

"I don't understand," she said. Laura's file lay open on her desk. Honors classes, the math club, field hockey: a model student. Laura hadn't missed a day of school in two years. But now . . . The dean made a show of closing Laura's file. As if it were the book of the girl's life. "Problems at home? With other students? A teacher, then."

"I don't know what you're talking about."

The dean placed her elbows on the desk. A kind of pleasure entered her eyes. She whispered, "A boy?" Then, "A boy." She imagined there were signs, that she had seen them. She had had years of training; these matters required a specialist such as herself. "I have one word of advice." She eased back in her chair, crossed her arms over broad, untidy breasts, shapeless as water. "Don't." The word was hushed; she offered it as if it were a gem. "Trust me on this." With her record, Laura could go to a good school. To any school she wanted. The dean knew someone on the admissions committee at Smith, if Laura was interested. She would meet someone there. A boy from Amherst, a boy from Williams. "You remind me of me at your age. You do. I know what you're going through. You're brighter than the others, you see more. You don't fit in. Not really. But you will. It's hard, I know. It was hard for me." There was a certain kind of woman, the dean went on, the kind of woman that certain kinds of men wanted. Men from Amherst, etc. It lay in the intangibles, in the way a woman spoke, in the way she carried herself. In her past. With one look, men know. "You want to be that kind of woman. You want that kind of man. This may sound unfair, it may even sound cruel—but we're alike, we understand each other—

248

don't waste your time on the boys here. You'll regret it." The dean knew what she was talking about. She had lost her virginity years ago during homecoming weekend at Holy Cross. She had called the boy every day for three weeks afterward, wanting to see him again. She filled the margins of her notebook with his name. He ultimately refused to come to the phone. It was only recently that her counseling group had gotten her to see that she had in fact been raped.

"He'll ruin your life," the dean added now.

She loved the sound of her voice at such moments. She loved being able to help. It was what she had been trained to do. Her calling. Few could do it properly. At parties, slightly drunk, she told anyone who would listen, "My girls need me. They rely upon me. Without me, they're lost. I save lives every day. Every day."

Laura said, "Are we finished?"

Xavier met her outside her last class. They were going, he told her, to his house for dinner. "My father wants to meet you."

"He does?"

The subway was crowded. Uniformed police patrolled the platforms during the hour when school let out. It was a neighborhood she had never been to, one of three-family homes, dirt lawns, dour women looking out second-story windows. Chien Bizarre, said the plaque on a door.

Two rooms, a kitchen, a bathroom. A crack that traversed one wall. The furniture was old, unmatched. But a baby grand, it filled the main room. His father was a thin man, stooped, high forehead. Intelligence written all over his face. He took her hand shyly. He spoke slowly, the rhythms of his speech hesitant, faltering, as he prepared the words in his mind: "Xavier . . . has spoken of you . . . many times."

They sat down to dinner. A chicken in a thick broth, the meat falling from the bones. Rich, peppery taste. Coarse bread, a bowl of fava beans, rice. A dessert of tropical fruits. Stretches of silence while his father mulled over the right phrase. "Please . . . you will . . . have more."

"Thank you. But I'm full."

". . . Please."

Toward the end of the meal, the man got up, bowed deeply. He had to go to work. Forgive his rudeness. He was honored, he told her. Laura started to stand. He motioned for her to sit. He turned to Xavier, spoke in a singsong voice, quick vowels erupting in a strange language. Xavier replied; it sounded like an ancient and venerable anthem.

"What was he saying?" she asked when he was gone.

Xavier didn't respond. He began to clear the dishes. She pitched in to help. They carried the plates down the hall to the kitchen. Shriveled, blood-colored peppers suspended from a string, a jar of instant coffee on the counter. A bottle of dark rum above the stove. In the hallway, there were photos, posters, a pegboard on the wall. A large print showing the broken streets of a Caribbean city, women carrying bundles on their heads, baskets of produce tilted for display. His father's diplomas hung next to it. He had been a teacher of classics back in Haiti. Books had lined the shelves of their home. Cicero, Aristophanes, Seneca. Now, his father bowed to men half his age, he removed their dirty plates. A bitter edged entered the boy's voice. Men with a third of his understanding, yet they commanded him to bring meat, fowl, dainty desserts. He brought. Years ago, his father never drank. But his father had tried, he had failed. Now his life was over.

"My father drinks," Laura offered. "A whole lot."

Xavier pointed to himself: he would never work as a waiter. Never. He would rather steal. He would rather starve. But no: military service, then the conservatory. Then greatness. He was certain of it. In his dreams he heard the shouts of the crowd, he saw them rising to their feet, their applause sustained, an outpouring of acclaim. His music was like a lifeboat. It would save him. There would be pirates, bandits who would try to sink him, to rape his kin. Italians who would beat him. But there was his music; this was everything. It could not be destroyed. "It is here," he whispered, tapping his skull. "And here." He displayed his hands. Fine, tapered fingers, full pads of flesh at the base of his thumbs.

Laura stopped to look at a lone photo of a woman. She was tall, straight-backed. A round face, stern features. The face of a huntress. Her hair cut close to the skull. She wore a long gown that bared one shoulder, a shoulder the color of a moonless night.

In the living room, Xavier set out a bottle of wine, glasses. Good wine, she knew. Expensive wine. Her mother always waited until it was on sale.

"You stole this," she realized.

He continued to work the corkscrew. Her accusation left him unfazed. Of course he stole it. If she couldn't understand that, she understood nothing. Besides, "It improves the taste."

They sat on the sofa, sipping the wine. He asked if she had ever had a boyfriend before. The *before* was like a coronation. The wine streamed to her face. "Not really." Then, "Not at all."

"Would you like to hear something?" Unabashed question. He was good, he knew. People liked to hear him play.

The legs of the piano bench scraped across the floor. He sat for a moment, unmoving, his fingers poised. It was like the instant before a bolt of lightning. His arms violent suddenly, they jarred the air. The piano emitted quick notes, as if caught by surprise. A fast riff, climbing the scale, then descending. Minute variations on the same, themes repeated, then repeated again, the variations broadening, about to push through to something entirely new—only to return to the original notes, a few simple measures, pristine, unadulterated. He did this again and again, venturing out, always coming back to the same bars, the same but now no longer the same. Their deferral had changed them. He was beating the piano into submission, taming it. It was like watching a horse being broken. Twenty minutes, thirty. It seemed he could have played forever. He stopped unexpectedly, stretched, circled the room quickly. His energies were incomparable. He slept three, no more than four hours a night. There was so much he wanted to do, there was still everything to accomplish. He was breathless now, an eager excitement crept into his voice. Did she know what he meant? Did she have any idea?

"I know," she whispered.

"He said you are pretty."

"Who?"

"My father."

She reddened, stood. She should be going, she said. He kissed her. She let herself be kissed. Her lips were tentative, wary. His tongue was like a fervent invitation. Her hands came up, she clasped them at the back of his neck. A kind of heat came over her. His finger traced the line of her throat. He was unbuttoning her blouse. The beating of her heart reached her ears. Her breathing quickened. She felt the nick as he undid her bra.

"I won't like it."

"You'll like it."

Her breasts came free and shocking into the room. Overwhelming, almost clinical whiteness—their size was blatant. They surprised even her. She started to cover them, but in the end let her arms drop to her sides. He stepped back, as if in the moment of a vision. Her gaze fell: she wanted to see what he was seeing. Her pendant, the watch, gift from her father, hung between her breasts as if in emphasis. Looking while another looked on changed them somehow; it made them over completely. Stark, full. She was pretty. His father said so. His look said so. There is a certain kind of woman, etc. But standing there, she was not that kind of woman, she did not want to be that kind of woman. She did not want to be like the dean, like her mother. She did not want the kind of men who wanted the dean, who wanted her mother. She glanced again at her breasts. She wanted the man who wanted these. Fingers dark as slate, Xavier gently gathered her in his palms. The contrast was absolute, hues screaming. He moved his hands, weighing one, then the other. She felt fearless, filled with the need to be touched. She desired his desire; she craved it. A boy who stole for her, a boy who had crossed dangerous seas, a talented boy. He would never wait tables. Yet in his eyes she could see his yearning. She could see her power. His look was worshipful, he stood like an acolyte before the crucifix. This was the kind of woman she wanted to be. Kneading fingers, they were finding her. The watch shuddered.

"And I bet they're not even finished," he whispered.

He touched her, he was touching, his hand slipping lower. He listened as her breathing stumbled, caught on ragged up-takes of air. She hung from his neck as if she were bound to the trunk of a tree, hers the sounds of a woman being flogged, of a woman banished.

April had done it with the captain of the hockey team, Eileen had done it with a freshman at Boston College, Karen had done it last summer with a lifeguard in Provincetown. They were full of tales, of descriptions. It was purple, it was brown, it was pale. It was smooth, it was wrinkled, it was bumpy. It curved like a gaff, it was like a slender shoot, it was swollen like a mallet. It hurt a lot, it didn't hurt, it hurt but only a little. There was blood, there was blood, there was no blood. He cried afterward, he laughed afterward, he seemed embarrassed afterward. In the backseat of his father's Lincoln, in his dorm room, on the beach. The moon was full. He said, I love you, he said, Did I hurt you, he wanted to know if she was finished. He said, It will be better next time, he said, It will be better next time, he said, It will be better next time. And when Laura asked, her voice hushed, "Did you come?" they responded as one, like a Greek chorus: "Of course not."

That time her mother had explained it all to her, that time she talked about the pill, the diaphragm, the importance of condoms, Laura had come home and thrown up. Dungeness crab, sunset melon on the bathroom tile.

"No," she was saying, the word emphatic, incontestable. "No."

She covered herself with her arms, edged away. She stuffed

her bra into her pocket, anxious to button her blouse, to cover herself.

He said, "I'm sorry."

The moment was graceless, uneasy. "Me," she said. "I'm sorry. I am." For the first time, she understood that she could deny him. She could hurt him. The reins had slipped from his hands. Now she indicated the piano. "Play something else."

He played. He played as if the piano were some hated foe, an enemy made of wood and hammer and string. Crazed improvisations, his hands striking hard, the fingers lightly flexed, coming down like daggers, the strings complaining, yielding finally. These fingers, they had touched her. They could touch her.

"You always play like that?

"Like what?"

"You play like you can't help yourself."

Her statement made no sense to him. "Why should I want to help myself?"

He walked her to the T. A light drizzle fell. They kissed standing at the turnstiles. The clerk in the glass booth looked away.

Xavier said, "You're not angry?"

"No." Their breathing was white. The train was coming, the sound of its brakes like metal tearing. "No. It was . . . The meal was wonderful. Your music is wonderful."

Along the stairway just off her parents' bedroom, a step creaked. Andrea called her name.

Laura feared her mother would get one look at her, become filled with eerie knowledge, and scream, "Who? Who?" But her mother was sitting up in bed, the newspaper in her hands. Laura was taken aback by her mother's appearance. Andrea looked like a woman who needed to bathe, to wash her hair. She looked like a woman in an institution. Her nightgown was askew. She had been sleeping poorly, she told Laura. It was probably the flu.

"Where were you?" Andrea's tone was cross. The evening

254

before, she had found herself in the butcher's neighborhood. No: she had gone to the butcher's neighborhood. In spite of everything. Because of everything. But a talk. That was all. It would be innocent. The butcher would understand. Sunsets, etc. She had gone up the three flights of stairs, past the same children playing in the hallway, past the same reek of curry, fashioning her smile, thinking, A talk, a talk. The door opened immediately at her knock, as if he had been standing on the opposite side these past months, waiting for her.

It was not the butcher, but a woman. A smiling woman. She wore a stained bathrobe, gripped a spatula. Heavy, bovine, her hair under a net. She looked like a reader of supermarket tabloids, like a woman who runs up enormous bills on TV shopping channels, bills she cannot pay. The sounds of frying came from inside the room. Smiles fled right, left. Two women, staring.

"I was looking for—"

"He's not here." She regarded Andrea with suspicion. Then she set the spatula on a counter. Her tone assumed a note of resignation. "He's not here yet." She was a woman waiting for a man to come home.

It was like being shocked by a mirror. They seemed sisters in humiliation. In that moment, Andrea realized she would never forgive Frank the glimpse of the soiled bathrobe, the unhealthy pallor. She would never forgive him the curlers, the spatula, the odor of grease.

"I'm very sorry," she had told the woman.

"Where were you?" Andrea demanded again. She rattled the paper for effect. "I was getting worried."

"Eileen. I was with Eileen."

They had not talked in weeks. Andrea thought: soon we will talk. They would sit down and talk like they used to, the kind of talk where everything is said, nothing is left unrevealed. She lowered the newspaper, asked what had happened at school. She wanted to know where she and Eileen had gone. She asked if there were any messages.

But her nightgown had come open. In the thin light of the room, Andrea's breasts looked bloated. They hung like encumbrances. They had taken on a leaden color. An unloved color.

"Laura?"

Laura wanted to run over, cover her mother, scream, Button yourself up, please. Instead: No, nothing happened at school. She and Eileen had gone to the bookstore. Laura stole toward the door, desperate to get away. She could feel the bulge of the bra in her pocket. Nothing, she murmured, nothing had happened at the mall. The chicken, the wine, the fruit. She thought she might be sick. No. No messages. Then, "I'm going to bed." This from down the hallway, the girl was already closing the door to her room.

Andrea turned back to the paper. A gas leak in Chelsea, a rape and abduction in Jamaica Plain. The investigation into the death of Quinto Bernal had been concluded; there was a photo of a grinning McCormick. He had known the outcome all along, he was quoted as saying. His faith in the system was unwavering. A sale at Filene's Basement began that weekend, the doors would open at seven on Saturday morning. There would be the mounds of clothing. There would be the frantic women. They would sweep through the store like routed soldiers, plunder and dropped booty marking the path of their retreat.

Six

The Mexican's double take was broad, exaggerated. A grin jumped to his face, his eyes screamed conclusions: the sale had been approved. The notion transformed his features. He was a magnate of the border suddenly, an international entrepreneur; his name would be whispered in distant centers of world commerce. He would repair the hole in his kitchen wall, he would buy his wife a new set of drinking glasses. Now he came around from behind his desk, hearty with false hopes, and thumped Reed on the back. "Sit, sit," he whispered. He had the bottle out, he was already reaching for the dusty glasses. He paused to turn the photo of his family face down.

"García—"

"Sit."

Reed sat. García poured. He hoisted his glass, intoned, "Salud." The tequila burned. He poured again. "Amor—"

"García, I need your help."

"Anything, anything." The Mexican leaned to pour a third round. Reed stayed the bottle with a wave of his hand, said that it was not about the site. It had nothing to do with Yates. García froze, the bottle poised in the air between them. Like a man who has just learned the world is flat after all. Reed rushed his explanation. There was a friend. A friend in a bind. It wasn't Reed's fault. Not really. So maybe it was. The point, the point: he wanted to help this friend. He wanted García to help him help this friend. She—

García blinked. "A woman?"

Reed nodded. García said, Then you have not been back to Boston. Then you have not yet talked to Yates. You have been in Mexico the whole time. What was it, a week? A week and then some. Reed stared down the throat of his glass, said, Yes, yes. Yes.

"A woman," García repeated. It was no longer a question. He eased back in his chair, regarded Reed for a long moment. He held the bottle as if it were a cudgel. The Mexican's face migrated from one inference to another, a man adding two and two together and ending with zero. No border magnate he, his name would not extend beyond the state of Coahuila. He would repair nothing. He would buy his wife nothing. Reed worried García might stand, scream, "Commission, commission, what about my commission." Reed said, "I'm willing to pay—"

García clicked his tongue. The offer embarrassed him. The gringo embarrassed him. A crude people in the end, if they only knew. The nuances were lost on them. True, the Mexican wanted matching dishware. True, in matters of business, the Mexican was a gouger, a biter, a back-alley brawler. But the look on Reed's face was not the look of a businessman. It lacked the assurance, the casual certainty. It was the look of a man who had embarked on an odyssey. Of a man who had nailed his soul to the door of his house. Let the neighbors stare. There are those who will lose at chess all for the love of a heart-stopping gambit. García leaned forward, rested his elbows on his knees. His look was digging. Reed saw again the destroyed teeth, the lined face, the heavy jowls. García said, "You and this woman . . ."

"Yes."

"Ah." The Mexican nodded slowly. There were many things he did not understand, he would never understand. But this he understood. Bottle still in hand, he steered it toward Reed's glass, poured. He filled his own. The Mexican raised his drink like a battle standard, like a torch. Reed paused, a man on a narrow ledge, waiting to see which way the world will tilt. "Amor," the Mexican said again.

The sound of complicity, a promise of help. Reed grinned, García grinned. They belched in fraternal communion. They were compañeros, men saving a woman. Corny, facile. Yet the heart swells, our acts move us outside ourselves. The impossible is a little less so. Then the Mexican was on the phone. He made a second call, a third. Jabbing vowels, consonants rattling. A man swinging into action. A city official. He had connections, he knew people. A man who could succeed where all others failed. It was how he liked to think of himself. Now a gringo sat in his office, a gringo with desperate eyes, a tremor to his voice. A gringo in need of help. He, Ignacio García Saavedra Hidalgo Obando Montenegro, would help. The phone wedged between his ear and his shoulder, he pulled a sheaf of papers from a drawer. A man with the power to move the world. He wanted to know her name, when she had been arrested. Reed responded softly, in tones of unmistakable woe. The Mexican listened, then blustered into the phone. García pulled a page free, ran his eyes down it. He wanted to know her age, her hometown. What she looked like.

"She's beautiful," Reed whispered. As if the word had been coined with her in mind.

García's eyes rose. Of course she was beautiful. He made another call, still another. He barked into the phone, he pounded the desk. His sounds were cragged, determined. He stood then, hitched up his pants. Water ran foul from his pipes, his father would be forever disappointed in him. But he was a man fired by the romantic, one of the remaining few who adhere stubbornly to the notion that in love we transcend ourselves, we do honor to the species.

"Come."

The sun was gone, the first stars were out. On the drive over, Reed tried to explain. He tried to make sense. A figurine, a convulsive belly. The Rio Grande at night. Much rain, a lone egg. Big, dumb rock. The car kept overheating. A brute in boxers, a brute saying, "I thought we'd have a little chat." Mexico City, the ruins, the mariachis. Then a pair of pants like the cowboy used to wear. Darting tongue, surging ass. Then, "Do this." And now. And now. García stared. Reed talked on, feverish noises, a man desperate to make himself understood. A rambling account, disjointed, fragmented. Yet its meaning was clear: a man enamored. A man bitten by guilt. Potent mixture, it made García sigh in the end.

At the river, Reed followed García into the Mexican aduana. They moved from office to office, each larger than the one before, the furniture more expensive, the air conditioner more powerful. In a hot land, one's station in life is measured in terms of BTUs. Frigid, roaring air, more real than nameplates finally, than titles. García introduced him to Teniente Mondragón, then to Capitán Morales, and then to Colonel Ortega. They were ascending the ranks, García was owed certain favors all along the way. Reed understood the Mexican was using up hoarded capital, calling in his chits. At each introduction, there was a long period of casual conversation, relaxed laughter, men asking about families, about work. Did you see the new barmaid at Cantina Flores? Mondragón, Morales, Ortega—each rolled his eyes. García cackled, made like a man holding soup bowls. Their chortling was maddening, it took forever. Reed sat moodily, listening to the ricochet of Spanish.

260

Finally, finally, Colonel Ortega made a phone call, produced a single sheet of paper. It bore his signature. At the other end of the bridge, García flourished the scrap in the guard's face. Stepping from the car, Reed could see the cinder-block structure, the lit windows. He wanted to rush up, break down the door. But, "Over here," García told him. They talked to a corporal, a sergeant, a Chicano lieutenant. Each office was identical to the previous one. The lieutenant glared at Reed, saw only a man despoiling the purity of La Raza, watering the blood. The lieutenant switched to a strident Spanish. Reed felt like a Paris absconding with Helens, an instigator of wars. The lieutenant shouted, García was shouting. Each gestured wildly, waved fingers in the face of the other. García circled the office, thumping the walls. Red faces, spittle flew. García slapped the desk with his palm, tore at his hair in exasperation. Latin anger, visceral, scalding. Reed worried blows were in the offing. But then both men went quiet, they smiled. The best of amigos suddenly, García saying, "Did you see the new barmaid at Cantina Flores . . ." García and the lieutenant shook hands. Outside, the Mexican said, "Tomorrow."

"Tomorrow? But—"

"Tomorrow." She would be released to Mexican authorities first thing in the morning. He had gotten the lieutenant's word.

Reed took a step toward the cinder-block building. García grabbed his arm, urged him toward the car, gently insisting that Reed spend the evening at his house. Reed said he did not want to impose. He would stay at a hotel, they could meet in the morning. García would not hear of it. Reed was secretly relieved. His sense of dislocation ranged far. Tomorrow seemed geologic ages away. The night would be long, harrowing. A tacky hotel room, a bottle of cheap liquor in the effort to drown all sensation. Reed was no moralizer. He had pirated cable, lied on his 1040 (long form), tinkered with the emission controls of his car. He had a drawer at home filled with a stapler, a pencil sharpener, a hole-puncher, and scores of pens, "Yates Electronics" emblazoned in gold. He owed parking

261

fines in Chicago, Indianapolis, and New York. At ballgames he sneaked to the better seats at halftime. But minor indiscretions, the way of life on earth. Yet twenty-four hours earlier, he had been hurling himself at her, he had been nibbling on her sex. Spare, scant strokes of hair, they seemed unearthly. The injustice of it was acute, indisputable. His dreams would be populated by hobgoblins, bogeymen, all in heated pursuit, while he tried to escape in that maddening slow-motion peculiar to nightmares.

García's wife was delighted to see Reed. She touched his arm, she caressed his cheek, she embraced him. The girl was there, the boy. There was the battered linoleum, the bare bulb. The water was still brown. The large TV was going, a game show in which one won millions of pesos. Dinner was a gray slab of gristly meat—"Goat," García explained happily—and glutinous refried beans. García's wife said they were thrilled that he had returned so soon. It was a pleasant surprise. She had mentioned to her husband several times how much she had enjoyed the company of señor Reed, how she hoped one day they might see each other again. And now here he was. She smiled. As if fate were funny ultimately, as if fate were an old friend. She said that she hoped his trip home had gone smoothly, that he had found his wife and daughter well. García shifted uncomfortably, hefting apologetic looks Reed's way. Reed's stomach stirred uneasily; the meat had the consistency of an old boot. His family must miss him very much, she continued, he was away from home so often. She talked on, but García had ceased translating. On TV, a skinny man in a bad suit won a three-day vacation for two, all expenses paid, to exotic Fort Worth (airfare not included).

After dinner, Reed and García sat on the front porch, nursing glasses of rum. The night was warm. There were the sounds of traffic. The smell was dense, sulfuric. They could hear the scurrying of a rat in the alleyway. García lit a cigarette, the flicker of shadows across his face making his features long. He said, "You and this señorita . . ."

Reed shrugged. A man affecting nonchalance. "She wanted a ride north. She was pretty. So I gave her a ride north." He felt diminished in García's eyes. He felt the full weight of each of his forty-six years. He seemed a foolish man, his head turned by a young face, an expanse of thigh. A man driven to outrageous acts, unthinking acts. Now he made a quick, cutting motion with his hand. "It's nothing."

García took a pensive puff, then paused to consider his cigarette. "And yet you are here."

And yet he was here. This said everything. It said far too much. Sitting in the diner across the river earlier that afternoon, Reed had finally risen, paid for the coffee, made for the car. A sober man, a decided man. A man of imminent sense. Hardheaded, in the throes of a cold logic. A man of the city to the end. Too bad about the girl. But he sorely missed his wife, he missed the sight of his daughter at the end of each day. Guilt over Andrea had come to insinuate itself with increasing frequency. She was his wife after all. He had a daughter to think about. This meant much. It should have meant everything. Too bad about the girl. He had done what he could. She had asked for a ride to her father's. He had given her a ride to her father's. He had given her a ride to Mexico City. He had given her a ride to the border. He had gone to extraordinary lengths. He had risked arrest, public scandal, all when he should have been at home hanging storm windows.

Too bad about the girl.

But life is like that.

Yet at the door of the Toyota, he had spied the figurine squatting in the nook between the seats. A gift for his daughter. He should have bought the serape. Now he would live out the rest of his days within sight of the statue sitting dutifully on the mantel, its eyes following him around the room. The secret locked in its head. Unflagging witness, it would never give him peace. The girl, the girl, but the girl, it would whisper all night long. The voice would find him in his sleep, puncture all dreams. Reed had flopped across the hood of the car then, resting his cheek against the hot metal. Half-sounds had bubbled from him, bits of noise, shreds of nonsense. A man gibbering.

I, it had occurred to him, I am not like that.

Foolish girl, hopeless quest. He should have discouraged her from the first. But give me the leaping salmon. Give me the box turtle crossing eight lanes of traffic. Give me the violinist who plays on, though her A-string broke three measures in. Give me the horse that draws the milkwagon. Give me missionaries to those regions frequented by cannibals, lepers, or the CIA. Give me the dumpy woman who dons a bikini at the beach. Give me faded photos, tattered ribbons, tarnished medals. Give me those pets who traverse continents to find the masters who have abandoned them. Give me all first kisses. Give me failed painters, starving musicians, minor league ballplayers. Give me unrequited love. Give me dogs who go off to die by themselves. Give me the woman with three children who finally throws the bum out. Give me the fox, old buildings, those who fish from downtown piers.

And then he had been driving south, the bridge rising to meet him.

But García was talking now, his expression contemplative. Sympathetic, Reed realized. The Mexican meant to help. He knew of a man, García went on, his name was Eliazar Borges. He fell in love with a gringa across the border. This gringa, she was not rich. She was not even that pretty. She worked as a clerk in the post office. But Eliazar Borges, it seemed he could not get enough of her. Like many a plain woman, sex had become her passion; it was how she made her way in a world that too often ignored her. She had developed a varied and creative repertoire in the bedroom, along with a complement of sexual gizmos and gewgaws mail-ordered from forbidden magazines. Eliazar Borges was a simple man. Prior to meeting this woman, sex for him had always been one part of the day among others, the thing you did between dinner and sleep. He took to calling her two, three times a day, saying, Please,

please, I must see you tonight. I must see you now. This gringa, she would say, Yes, I would like to see you as well. I will be at the restaurant Moderno at nine o'clock. Eliazar Borges, he would tell his wife he had work to do, that he would be out late. He would appear at the restaurant Moderno at eight, he would sit at the bar and drink. He would have another drink, another. He watched women coming and going. If one tried to speak to him, he would wave her away. He was waiting for his gringa. Nine o'clock came, ten o'clock. Go, he would tell other women, I am meeting someone. But the gringa rarely appeared. The next morning, he would call her, say, Please, please, I must see you tonight. I must see you now. This happened again and again. For every three nights that Eliazar Borges sat in the restaurant Moderno and waited for her, she might show once. His wife grew suspicious, of course. She threatened to leave him, she threatened to take the children. She threatened to have her brothers come and break his legs. But still, Eliazar Borges would go to the restaurant Moderno, he would wait. Occasionally, other women would come, sit next to him, say, Buy me a drink. But he did not want other women. He was a fool, he knew. " 'She has stolen my balls, Nacho,' he told me. 'She has stolen my balls and she will not give them back.' 'Leave her, Eliazar,' I told him. 'She is no good.' 'But I cannot, Nacho. I cannot.' "

"He sounds gutless," Reed muttered. The ice tinkled in his glass. García bent to find the bottle, the liquor flashed metallic in the moonlight.

"Gutless," the Mexican repeated as he poured. Reed could see the man turning the word over in his mind, milking its sense.

"A coward," Reed explained.

"In the end, his wife left him. Her brothers, they cornered him one night, gave him a beating. I went to the hospital to visit him. 'Now, Eliazar Borges, now will you please stop this nonsense? Will you please forget about this gringa? Your wife has left you, she has taken your children, men beat you in the street. She has not only stolen your balls; she has destroyed your life.'

" 'I cannot, Nacho,' Eliazar Borges told me. He was weeping. 'I cannot. You see, my balls . . . my balls have never looked finer than when they are in her hands.' "

The Mexican nodded sagely, pausing to top of their drinks. "Gutless?" García shook his head. He turned his thick, heavy face toward Reed, made his voice musing. "I think perhaps Eliazar Borges was very brave."

Reed sighed. He felt far from brave. He felt mired in confusion. It had been too long since the world last bothered to make sense. "What will they do to her?"

García tossed his cigarette into the street. They could see the ember burning from where they sat. "She has not done this before? Then nothing, I think. Oh, the room she sleeps in will be unclean, the bed will be hard. They will give her food that a dog should not have to eat. They will speak unkindly to her. They will try to frighten her. But it is her first time; they will do only enough so that perhaps she hesitates before trying again. It is when they catch you a second time, or a third, or a fourteenth time—I knew one man, in the space of a month he was caught thirty-three times. This is true . . ."

They put Reed in the boy's room. Reed made extravagant objections. Unwell child, it felt all wrong. But they insisted. The boy glared at Reed, then made himself a lumpy bed on the sofa. Reed retired to a room filled with plastic soldiers, a stuffed tiger, a wooden train. A weathered baseball mitt, the pocket shiny as fruit. Outside the window, crickets were going; a truck backfired in the distance. There was the faint whir of helicopter rotors chopping the air. Reed lay on the bed, wishing it were his ball glove, his wooden train. At age ten his evening routine had been unvarying. Dinner, the last of the chores (hay for the cows, oats for the horse; check the latch on the chicken coop), the radio: "The Shadow," a ballgame—the Cubs, or the Tigers—perhaps an address by Ike. Saturday nights he always polished his shoes. Then a bath, three full minutes of brushing his teeth. A final prayer, then bed. His mother had taught him a slew of prayers. Important words, he had understood, possibly decisive. Prayer was like insurance; it covered all liabilities. Without it, your mother might die, your father, the horse; the commies might conquer Kansas. And Ike would point his finger at you.

Reed sat up in bed now, glanced around, then sheepishly slipped from under the covers. He eased awkwardly to his knees. Foolish, he knew. But his was the faith of underwriters. He made a tidy tent with his hands, placed his elbows on the bed. Like drawings of pious virtue in Sunday School pamphlets (ages eight to eleven). He waited for a prayer to come back to him, for some spark of memory. Or else penitent words, beseeching phrases, a single, heartfelt supplication. But his mind was a remote, treeless tundra. There on his knees, he waited for some sign, a signal: burning bushes, booming voices, startling lights, a tremor of the earth. But there was only the growing cramp in his leg. He grimly struggled to his feet, made a show of collapsing into the bed. As if God might be watching, He was as exasperated as he. I'll never fall asleep, Reed told himself miserably. Never. And then he fell asleep.

He woke to a presentiment of urgency, of so much still to be done. The world was incomplete. It was the feeling one gets when discovering the roast is still stone-cold in the center, leaves are falling outside that will have to be raked and bagged. The 7:14 has already left. The roar of the garbage truck; did he set out the trash? Has he mailed the electric bill, the phone bill, the oil bill? Did he deposit the check. Insufficient funds, and his family would freeze to death in the deepest part of December. A pack of wild dogs would scratch at the door. It was not dogs, but García who knocked, announced, "It is time."

The sun was coming up as they arrived at the river. The shadows of the customs booths were long, guards moved about. Change of shift. They parked on the Mexican side of the river and smoked. "She will emerge from that door," García told him.

"When?"

It could be five minutes. It could be several hours. The Mexican didn't know. Now he embarked on a running commentary concerning the women who strolled by, the Mexicans heading north, the gringas heading south, the gringas in their cars. "That one is nice," he said. "Her? No, I do not think so. But this one—" He leered. Reed turned, saw a rangy blonde standing next to a Mercedes, Minnesota plates. She had the legs of a high-jumper. She wore a pair of shorts and a spandex number that advertised her breasts. She looked like a girl in an orange juice commercial, a girl you hope your son marries. She would brighten your door at holidays, smile when you passed her the turkey. You would leave the room when afternoon talk shows featured men who had run off to Aruba with their daughters-in-law. García said, "The man who has that to gaze upon every night, the man who wakes to her each morning— he will be disappointed in heaven."

Reed laughed. García wagged his head. He had a theory: there is a woman against which a man measures all other women. But it is rarely the woman one would think. It is rarely a man's wife, it is rarely a man's mother. In unusual marriages, of course, it might be a man's wife. But this was not often. Perhaps this was sad; yet García was a man speaking from a place beyond sentiment. A man condemned to the truth. In unfortunate men, he went on, it might be a man's mother. This, too—luckily—was rare. For most men, it was a woman he barely knew, a woman say he had met only once. Perhaps he had never met her. He had seen her in the street one day, or boarding a bus, or pausing to straighten the hem of her dress. Perhaps he had never even seen her, he had only dreamed her, or imagined her. Say he saw a woman from the back, a woman at a distance. A woman sweeping the street, or a cook in a restaurant, bent over the stove. When she finally turns, she is not so attractive, she is not as he had imagined. But the myth outstays the reality. It is the thought of her as seen from behind, that first glimpse, in which our mind completes the

268

work, fleshes out the unseen face, the hidden breasts—it is this woman, this creature of the imagination, that we carry with us everywhere. That we imagined we had once seen. That we are certain we have seen. It is this face, these breasts, that are stamped into a man's memory. That he dreams of one day finding. But of course he never will. "She does not exist."

García stabbed his cigarette at the windshield and murmured, "She is very fine also, I think."

Reed turned, expecting to find another pale gringa, or a thick-breasted latina. She was neither. She stood squinting into the sun. A girl lost, a girl abandoned. A girl of myth. There was a deep, shifting sensation to Reed's stomach, a fizz to his thinking. Something inside him came loose, battered at the windows of his brain. Then he was clawing his way out of the car.

Her eyes grew wide when she saw him. Uncomprehending stare, a mirage, her mind insisted, a white lie we tell to the troubled, the despairing. She swayed on her feet, emitted a shallow moan of surprise. Reed made meaningless, inconsequential motions with his hands. García came up behind him. He glanced with new respect at Reed. The three of them formed a loose triangle, an uneasy triangle. She looked up at him, her eyes glinting. Reed hesitated, then eased his arms around her. She slipped into them like a ship moving into safe harbor, an animal coming in out of the rain. A child returning home. Her hair was dirty, stringy, her odors ripe. Yet Reed thought her beauty overwhelming, a beauty that subjugates. She pressed her head into his shoulder, she sagged against him. Reed was like a man leaning into a heavy wind, bracing himself against a force of nature. She put her mouth to his ear, her voice jagged, raspy: "Mi cariño. Mi querido. Tú eres mi vida. Te heché mucho de menos. Te quiero mucho." More muchos followed. Reed understood nothing but the heated rush of her breath. "Tú eres mi río, tú eres mi mar." Meanwhile, García had produced a hankie. His noises were loud, honking, chased by sniffles. The Mexican honked again, his eyes moist. He could not contain himself, he was overcome. A man of sentiment after all. He cried at weddings, at wakes. He cried at the death of the bull in the corrida, at the prone, bleeding rooster in a cockfight. He cried at stories of love on TV. He cried over kittens, at spring rains, at the smells of cooking at the end of a long day. He was the sort of man who woke in the middle of the night in the midst of a boundless joy, as if the stars, the moon, the feel of his wife's fat arms were sacred blessings. "Tú eres mi corazón, tú eres mi cielito." The Mexican wept openly now. A man anxious to share in the moment, to wrap himself in it. García stepped toward them, placed a hand on Reed's shoulder, another on hers. His features were ragged, breaking, tears streamed down his cheeks. He rested his face gently in the cranny between their heads. The guards blinked. García sniffed. Reed grinned. Socorro grinned. They kissed. The sun hovered above. It burned just for them.

They went to a large restaurant where Reed watched the others chow down. Starving Mexicans. Their eating was immense, daunting, as if it had only recently come unyoked; it now ran wild. Huevos rancheros, carne guisada, tacos de machacado, carne asada, chorizo, papas con huevo, a stack of tortillas steaming in a basket. The table shuddered under the weight of the dishes. Rich, steaming coffee, large glasses of papaya juice, beaded with condensation. García reached, ate with hearty motions. Socorro's hands flicked over the table, lean arms hastening food into her mouth. Their appetites intimidated. Reed sipped a cup of coffee, his stomach bilious, jittery. García and Socorro talked between mouthfuls, an effusive, content tribe, they seemed imminently at ease in the world. They switched between Spanish and English like skiers on a slalom course. It seemed García had been to Chiapas. He said, "I knew a woman there . . ." Socorro laughed, she ate, she drank. García talked about the time Eduardo Gutierrez tried to sneak over the border and was discovered by la migra hiding in a large bag of coffee beans; the time Imelda Martí tried to float across in a hollowed-out tree trunk that sunk in midriver; there was Timoteo Torres who hid in the bathroom of an Air Mexicana flight only to find himself in Guatemala City.

"You'll scare her," Reed cautioned.

No, no, that was not the Mexican's intention. Now García talked about how his aunt had once crossed in the belly of a wood stove. She emerged in El Paso, smiling through a face of creosote. He went on about Julio Riojas, a soccer player of local repute. Twice Julio Riojas had tried to run across the bridge, hoping to outrace the guards, and twice he had been caught. The third time he brought along his soccer ball, dribbling it in and out of traffic, evading cars, evading guards, cutting back and forth like the star forward he was. He dribbled across the bridge, through the streets of Eagle Pass, and on beyond. As far as García knew, he might still be dribbling. He talked about how his grandfather had fought with Pancho Villa in the Battle of Torreón—they knew victory was theirs only when they saw the buzzards circling above the camps of the enemy. There was that dogfight where, at the height of the moment, when the matter was on the verge of being decided, both of the dogs had turned on their masters, fled the ring, and raced side by side off into the sunset. Socorro listened eagerly. Stories of struggle, stories of freedom. They filled her with hope.

She got to her feet, muttered, "Discúlpame." Twenty heads turned, watched as she moved toward the restroom. Twenty men thinking what might have been.

García glanced at Reed. His smile was lewd. "Hermano," he whispered.

Reed grinned. A man in the middle of a vast sea of envious faces. The prettiest girl at the dance is his. He had taken Sally Van Neustaadt to the senior prom. Big pale Dutch girl, awkward, gawky, she wore braces. But she was magnificently bosomed, the faintest saddle of freckles adorned her nose. One glimpse of her bare breasts coming unburdened in the closed confines of his father's car would prove sufficient, he had been sure, to better his life forever. Word was she had touched Todd Jenkins, she had touched Kenny Armbruster; Ned Zabinski claimed she had kissed it. The night of the prom, she began pulling at a bottle of sloe gin early. Sally Van Neustaadt. He would get her drunk, wait for her to touch it. Perhaps put her mouth on it. In the weeks leading up to the dance, lurid images had filled his head, made him pant with yearning. But sloe gin. She touched nothing, puked all over the front of his rented tux instead. To his chagrin, she dug tissues from her bodice and dabbed drunkenly at his tux. She snored all the way home. Seven minutes past her curfew, and her father was out on the front porch, a shotgun in his hands. Reed dumped her in the yard and sped off, smelling of vomit and shame.

Socorro returned. Prettier than Sally Van Neustaadt. They quickly settled into a discussion of what to do next. They were intent, earnest: schemers, hatchers of plots. Reed looked from one face to the other, experienced a mushrooming sense of camaraderie. Two days ago, it had all been so simple. He was a man of whimsy, a man gamboling with a beautiful girl before retreating into the familiar shell of his life. Now he felt like a man of principle, a man of conviction. A man to be contended with. Better than all the stock deals, the buyouts, the take-overs, the mergers. There is an excitement that comes with the close of a deal, the sense of having outfoxed life, tricked the world. Yet from where he now sat, such matters seemed mere gimmicks, sleights-of-hand. But a girl going north. No trickery here, no marked decks, no two-headed coins, no rabbits from hats. An honest tussle with life, the moment enjoined head-on. He felt like a spy, a provocateur, a man with a taste for suspense.

García settled back in his seat. He made a production of lighting a cigarette. A man holding court. This of the crossing—it was complicated, he explained. It was very complicated. There were many dangers involved. The river could be dangerous, la migra could be dangerous. She had been caught once, that made it more dangerous. And even if you did get across, there was the matter of what to do next. Then, too, much depended upon the coyote. It was a business like anything else. There were good coyotes, and then there were coyotes who would betray their own mothers. There were coyotes who truly knew the land, who truly understood how the thing was done. And then there were coyotes who knew nothing. They did not know what they were doing, they got lost, they ran at the first sign of trouble. They ran before the first sign of trouble, just after they had received your money. It was a complicated business. One had to be careful. But you wanted a good coyote. You wanted someone who knew what he was doing. This was not the kind of thing one hoped to save dollars on. One could save dollars on buying a new car, or on a new pair of shoes. But not this. García knew one man, he wanted to get across. He could have chosen one coyote and paid a hundred dollars, or another, who wanted three hundred dollars. García made sad eyes now, then crossed himself.

Reed scowled. "How much?'

Socorro said, "I have money—"

Reed held up his hand. "How much?"

García considered. For his friend, very little. Reed rolled his eyes. Almost nothing, the Mexican insisted. The details, the details could be discussed later.

"But you know someone?"

Sí, García knew someone. The question offended him. Of course he knew someone. Was he not García? Had he not invited the gringo to his house, broken bread with him, given him a bed to sleep in? Of course he knew someone.

The Mexican stood. The girl stood. Reed blinked. His stomach rustled with objections. A provocateur, maybe, but he wanted to bask a while longer in recent successes. "Now?"

"Now."

Reed thought he had seen the worst the town of Piedras Negras had to offer. He was wrong. They drove to an area even more ramshackle than the rest. A dead, bloated dog lay in the middle of a dirt road. The odor of sewage was tight, suffocating. At the door of a large warehouse, García got out, spoke with one man, then a second. Back in the car, he drove them to a tiny tar-paper shack standing off from the others. Ignoble structure, lonely and menacing. Reed found himself thirsting for a drink. At the door of the shack, two men looked up. García spoke to the one who was cutting his nails with a blunt knife. His name was Efraín. Efraín gazed at Reed, then at Socorro. The other man seemed bored, uninterested in all things. As if he had given up on the world long ago. The shack smelled of dung. Efraín said something to Socorro, then something else. He was asking her questions, quick, rapid-fire flurries of Spanish. She barely had time to respond when he came up with another. They were like threats, like blows meant to reduce resistance, meant to subdue.

Reed said, "I want to know what he's saying."

Efraín glared at Reed. As if Reed were a nuisance, an intrusion. Efraín had already assessed the situation. A young girl wants to get across, the gringo will pay. The girl is pretty; the gringo will pay much. The gringo will pay whatever is asked. Efraín knew enough to know this. One word from the girl, and the gringo would pay very, very much. It was not the gringo he was dealing with, but the girl. The gringo was like a cow, like a pig. They were bargaining for its milk, for its meat.

Efraín spoke again, ignoring Reed. He made a point of ignoring Reed. Efraín gestured for the girl to sit next to him. The act was demanding. He was a cutthroat, a bully, Reed decided. Socorro hesitated, then sat. The second man showed new interest. As if the world had unexpectedly become a fascinating place. Efraín went back to cutting his nails. A dull knife, it was painful to watch. One slip and a thumb might roll to the ground. But Efraín was unconcerned. There was a girl who wanted across, he was a man who knew how to get her across. There was a gringo present, waiting to pay. It was a fine day.

Reed said to García, "I want to know what he's—"

274

"Cállate, hombre," Efraín snarled. Reed's ears burned. The second man cackled. His toothlessness was shocking, a yawning abyss in the middle of his head. Efraín shifted closer to Socorro, spoke. She listened intently, answered in a small voice.

García whispered, "He says that there is a group going across tomorrow morning. No, no, he refuses to say how. He says there are spies from la migra, there are other coyotes who want his business. He says in this line of work, one must be very careful. It will cost two hundred dollars. If she has the two hundred dollars, she will come with him now. No, he cannot say where. Other coyotes, spies from la migra. No, he refuses to say. She will be placed with the others, and at the appropriate hour, someone will come for her, explain what to do. She must understand that once she is across, she is on her own. If she wants passage to Houston, to San Diego, that can be arranged. But it will cost more. For two hundred dollars, he offers only to help get her across, to get her beyond the interior checkpoints. Even then, if something goes wrong, if la migra appears, if bandits appear, that is not his responsibility. It is a risk that must be undertaken." García's expression tightened. "He wants to be sure she understands: there are no guarantees."

Efraín continued to cut his nails. His demeanor was superior, disdainful. Socorro peered at Reed, said, "What do you think?" She was again the girl in the bus station, a child afraid.

What did he think. He thought it sounded dicey. He thought it sounded horrible. He did not trust this Efraín. He did not trust this land. He did not trust himself. As if his capacity for judgment lay behind him, he had lost it long ago. Yet she trusted him. She was counting on him. The thought frightened him. He was a man who could tell you how to replace a solenoid, he could name all nineteen stops on the Orange Line, he could tell you which securities on the market to avoid, which were sound. He could mix a fabulous martini. But this was a hut with a man wielding a knife. He turned to García.

"What do you think?"

García shrugged. "The man is right: there are no guarantees."

Reed massaged his eyes. "All right."

Efraín looked to Reed for the first time. The moment had come to milk the cow, to slaughter the pig. "Doscientos dólares." He put down his knife now, began patting Socorro's knee. She flinched with his touch, but did not move from her seat. Reed stared, worked his mouth. "Doscientos dólares," Efraín said again. His fingers were kneading, massaging the kneecap, the flesh just above it. The worn skin of his hand spoiling her perfect legs. The other man rolled his eyes, lechery like a shadow falling across his face. Efraín had forgotten about Reed, about García. There was only the matter of the two hundred dollars. There was only the matter of the girl.

Reed was not a brave man. Yet Reed was not himself. He experienced a bone weariness, a piercing impatience at the ways of the world. The truths he lived by, the minor rituals of his life were like some barely remembered dream, the phantasms of a deranged man. He longed for the simplicity of his own bed, the familiarity of his wife's arms. But his bed, his wife were twenty-five hundred miles away. The instant seemed harsh, graphic, the colors too sharply delineated. The excitement he had experienced half an hour earlier had turned to dread. No spy he, but a bean-counter, a purveyor of numbers. A month lived at this pace and he would be dead. Reed swallowed, looked away, then looked again. The battered knuckles of a thug, the burnished thigh. But that thigh, that thigh, it seemed suddenly the only thing in the world. He felt, not courage, but a swelling love for that thigh. It was like watching a vandal slash at a painting by one of the masters, like watching a Renaissance sculpture break apart under the blows of a hammer.

Reed said, "Tell him to move his hand."

Shocking voice, it sounded like another's. Certainly not his own. He was a man who wanted to go home, a civil man, a man habituated to social convention. But this seemed beyond all convention; it seemed the state of nature, black as evil. Pay this Efraín two hundred dollars, dispatch the girl into his care, and he could go home. But, "Tell him," the voice said again. The voice of a stranger, of a man of daring. Reed licked his lips. The shack filled with swift glances, shifting looks. García stared, Socorro stared. Here came the voice again—he could feel it, he was helpless before it. Like a gale gathering far away. He said, "Tell him to move his filthy hand." He took a step toward Efraín. Efraín's fingers froze on her knee. He knew no English, but he heard the tone in Reed's voice. The universal language of anger. Reed took another step and then one more and he was wondering what he was going to do and he realized he had no idea at all. He hoped the man behind the voice knew.

The toothless one lumbered to his feet, crossed his arms over his chest. He was one of those men who looks much bigger standing. Efraín sneered, his hand still on her knee. Warnings set to in Reed's head. On the playgrounds of his youth, he had always hung close to the teachers, fearful of bullies. The moment was rigid, failing. But then García sidled toward Reed, took up position at the gringo's side. Imposing presence, the Mexican seemed to contract, to make of himself a dense post. A short man, a squat man. Compelling power in his girth. A brick of a man. García nodded. Reed nodded, his face a mask. But inside, his affection for García sprung wide. He wanted to hug the Mexican, to shower him with contracts. The toothless man sat down. Efraín looked from Reed to García, then back to Reed.

Efraín moved his hand.

Socorro went to stand between García and Reed. Efraín adopted an amused expression. But when he spoke, he spoke to Reed, his eyes weighing the gringo. García said, "He says—"

"I don't care," Reed said. "I don't care what he says." He

took Socorro's arm. The three of them backed out of the shack. Efraín began to shout, gesturing wildly. He kept shouting. The toothless man spat, mumbled, "Cállate, hombre."

In the car, they were silent. As though they were still listening to the conversation. García turned the key, found the road. They drove for ten minutes. They were each waiting for another to speak, to return the world to perspective.

"Stop the car."

García blinked. "Stop the car?"

"Stop the car," Reed murmured. "Now."

The Mexican stopped the car. Reed flung open the door, thrust his head clear. Bile lurched up from his belly, spewed forth. A man who did not have the stomach for such episodes, a man who belonged elsewhere. A man who should have married Sally Van Neustaadt.

"Sorry," he moaned when he was finished.

Socorro leaned forward from the back seat, stroked the thinning hairs on his head. "I am not." She kissed him. "I am not sorry."

García hooted, drummed his thighs with his fists. This gringo kept surprising him, his motivations a jungle that fell away without warning to reveal safe clearings, sheltered havens for the soul and its wants. It made one think that not all might be tawdry delusion. It made García believe in the power of belief. Now he said, "I have a plan." He indicated himself with a stab of his thumb. A man thick with deliberations, heady with calculations. "No te preocupas," he told the girl. "Worry about nothing," he explained to Reed. "Nada." Naturally, he said, it would take a little time. Now a proper host, he went on—a proper host would invite them to his home. A proper host would invite them to spend the night at his house, to a fine dinner with his family. Yet he was ashamed to say that he could not do so. There was the matter of his wife. She would never understand. She would never, ever understand. Wives, you see, wives . . .

The Mexican coughed. In the morning, he continued after

a moment. He would contact them in the morning, all the details would have been arranged. His face went impish. For now, however, might he recommend the Hotel de Playa, or the Lugar del Sol? García nudged Reed with his elbow. There was always the Cuarto de Amor—

"There." It was Socorro. She was pointing. "I wish to stay there."

It was the garish facade of a chain from the States. Ice machines on each floor, a tiny pool in need of cleaning. It could have been a motel in Des Moines, a motel outside of Cleveland, a motel at the intersection of interstates. "Are you sure?"

She was sure. The door opened onto cheap shag carpeting, the mass-produced painting on the wall, the glasses wrapped in paper, the miniature cakes of soap, the monogrammed towels, the ribbon across the mouth of the toilet: For Your Protection ("It is broken?" "It's not broken."). It could have been Iowa. Yet she explored each item carefully. The resourcefulness of the human race continued to amaze her.

"Frank?"

He was sitting on the bed. His expression was haggard, whipped. She settled next to him, took his hand. Her features deepened. She seemed on the brink of some grand pronouncement. She looked like a judge about to hand down a sentence. Reed felt himself shrink. He had abandoned her, after all. He had behaved disgracefully, a Peter at the third crow of the cock. He prepared himself for blistering words, screams of reproach. He steeled himself for the anger of a woman.

She said, "We will eat pizza, yes?"

Still another experience. Each day was unprecedented; she was only just realizing the extent of the world. Reed picked up the phone. Border town, the voice on the other end spoke a fractured, but understandable, English. Socorro was in the shower. Clouds of steam wafted through the open door. His mind went to her back, to her belly, to the shape of her buttocks. A girl impressed by wrapped bars of soap, by pizza pie. Reed hollered, "What do you want on it?" "What does one have on it?" she yelled. "Anything. You can have anything you want." He meant it suddenly, he wanted to make it true. "I want everything." "Everything?" "Sí." "Even anchovies?"

"Sí. We must have these anchovies."

They sat on the bed and ate. She in his bathrobe, Reed in his jockeys. Fat man eating eight different toppings, extra cheese. An old movie on TV, Jimmy Stewart speaking Spanish. They were like a married couple enjoying an empty Sunday afternoon. Her hair was wet, the robe kept parting. He stiffened below, the anticipation straining. The pizza was mediocre. But she loved it. She folded each slice in half, ate it like a sandwich.

"Tell me: why did you come back?"

Reed paused in his chewing. A good question. Reasons collected in his head, jostled against one another like members of an unruly crowd. None of them was up to the task. They each seemed paltry, too threadbare. There are acts that outstrip our thinking; we explain them to ourselves after the fact. After it no longer matters. "I forgot something."

She smiled, considered her pizza. "And tell me: which are the anchovies?"

She moved over him that evening like an archaeologist combing the ruins of an excavated city, like a child scrambling over the wreck of a junked car. She lowered herself over him gingerly, her breasts teasing his mouth. Reed lay beneath her, a man looking across a vast landscape, an eternal geography. Her breasts, her hips, the thin grin of hair inhaling him. Their lovemaking was languid, lazy. She would not move for minutes at a time. Then she would move. "Not yet," she pleaded. She did not want it to end just yet. Straddling him, the whole night ahead of them, her tone turned conversational. She could have been riding a bicycle. She talked about the time Benito Santiago plunged a knife through the heart of his brother, Domingo, and how Benito's arm then shriveled up until one day it simply fell off. She moved. She told him about the time a student from a large university in the States came to study the town on a grant, but promptly fell in love with Esmeralda Chavez. Unfortunately, there was Emilio Chavez, husband of Esmeralda. Fortunately, the price of the student's life came to exactly his camera, his tape recorder, and his four pairs of blue jeans. She moved, he moved. She told him about Cesar Quintana, who everyone said had the evil eye. One look from Cesar, and your wife would wither up, your crops would cease to grow, your burro would run away. When Cesar died, hundreds came from miles around to attend his funeral. She moved, she moved again. Reed groaned. "Not yet," she whispered. "Todavía no." She picked up Eve's book, read from a long, disconcertingly detailed passage concerning genital mutilation among the Mayans. Unpleasant stuff. Reed felt himself soften. She ground herself against him. He reared achingly. "Not yet," she murmured. Then an excerpt from an Aztec codex. The final assault on Mexico City. Montezuma was dead. The fighting was fierce, hand-to-hand. The canals filled with blood, with the bodies of the slaughtered. The fires had begun throughout the city, the sky darkening with smoke. And still the army of the Spaniards advanced, they plucked warriors from the rooftops of the buildings with their cross-bows and muskets. They took sabers to the women and children. She squirmed without warning, a rider spurring on a stead. "Todavía no," she said. Toward the end of the siege, when the Aztec defeat appeared imminent, one young warrior vowed revenge: " 'The day will come when we will rip your still-beating hearts from your chests, and feed them to the gods. The gods will then slake their thirst on your blood that has drained into the sacred chalices. The warriors among us will feast on your arms and legs; our women will dine on your torsos; children will make sport with your heads.' "

She moved. Reed counterthrusted in response. "Todavía no," she demanded. The speech ended with a roll call of gods: " 'Quauhpopoca, Xipe, Uitzilopochtli.' " A creeping momentum entered her voice, an encroaching, gathering power; it quickened with her movements. " 'Tlaloc, Tezcatlipoca.' " The names took on the flavor of incantations, haunting prayers.

Reed shivered. She mistook it for urging, for lust. Her hips began a slow gyration, tight clockwise revolutions about the axis of her pelvis. She paused then, and began moving in the opposite direction, like a reversible spool reaching the end of its thread. Reed grunted like a caged animal. Her hair raged in his face. " 'Quauhtemoctzin. Tonatiuh. Quetzalcoatl.' " She moved in earnest now. Her smile surrendered to a look of shock, of sudden feeling. Reed made thin, bleating sounds. She tossed the book aside, he heard it slap against the floor. Her actions went quick, jerky; she flung out her hair. Her sounds went guttural. She brought both hands up, gathered her hair into a mound on top of her head. Dusky moss at her armpits. She rode out the last of it, her eyes closed, her back arching. Reed was a man baying, a man begging for mercy, a man whose heart was tearing from his chest.

"Ahora sí!"

Reed felt himself pouring forth, it was singeing.

They lay still, animals stunned by electricity. Her breathing was soblike. Reed wheezed, a man at the top of a long bank of stairs. When the phone rang, neither moved. It rang again. "Let it ring," he mumbled. But no, she said; it would be García. He felt her shift, heard her say, "Bueno." Then she was shaking him, her eyes large, bewildered: it did not sound like García.

Reed gathered the phone to him. Cranky movement, cranky voice. "What?" he barked.

"Frank," he heard. "Frank, now."

Reed fell off the bed. Hard, bruising tumble. Socorro's face materialized above the edge of the bed, features full of concern. Reed scrambled to his feet, like a man coming to attention. "How did you find me?"

"Were you hiding?" the Old Man asked.

He didn't wait for Reed's answer.

"Frank, I can find you whenever I want. I can find anybody. I can find out anything. But you know this." Reed knew this. Yates's powers could only be guessed at, one of the financial

Illuminati. A man not bound by the traditional restraints. It was how he had made his mark, how he ran his business. It was how he lived his life.

Reed began to explain. Simpering, weasel voice. Socorro was watching. He felt himself redden. But: car trouble, intricate negotiations. Difficult finding the appropriate site. Yet he had found it. It was ideal, perfect. "Perfect," he repeated. The word sounded imperfect. It sounded wounded, unconvincing.

Reed could hear Yates's sigh. He could practically see the shake of the Old Man's head. Yates had seen it happen before. Young men, bright men, eager men. In their early years, they are hustlers. Men who can get things done. Men on their way up. Their futures stretch before them, reaching, arching destinies. They could have headed any of a hundred lesser organizations. But then something overtakes them, some mutation of the spirit. Life lies in the intangibles. They are passed over for promotions; the fire begins to wane. And as they age a corrosive bitterness sets in. It eats at them, it reduces them. They are men upon whom one can no longer depend. Yates sighed again. His voice was even, unimpeachable. "Who was that?"

"Who?"

"Who answered?"

"The maid." It was just past eleven o'clock.

The Old Man cleared his throat with a rip of phlegm. Reed felt a pouring panic. "So Frank," Yates went on. "You coming home?"

Of course. As he had said: detailed negotiations, car trouble. He had even been sick. "It's the truth." His tone was cloying, pleading. His color deepened. Socorro was watching. He hated himself suddenly. He hated Yates. But he did not have enough money to hate with impunity. Bills to pay, Holyoke at least. But Yates, Yates could hate with impunity, hate without fear. This was the ultimate and tragic meaning of power finally.

"The truth," the Old Man repeated slowly. Then, "There'll be a ticket waiting for you at the San Antonio airport tomorrow. Your flight leaves at three-thirty. You should be home by dark. You go home, have a nice dinner with Abby, the kid. First thing Friday morning, you be in my office. First thing." There was an ominous pause now. Yates, the master of powerful silences. "This is crucial," he added.

Reed closed his eyes. "It's Andrea."

"What?"

"Andrea. My wife's name is Andrea."

"I see." Yates's tone grew flat, menacing. He had hired a new man that very afternoon. A young kid, bright. Harvard MBA, the London School of Economics, four years with the Fed in New York. A sharp kid, he had a calculating hunger about him. Yates had spent the day showing him around. "And here is your office," he had said.

"Frank," the Old Man continued. "One more thing."

Reed said, "One more thing."

"I believe it was Nietzsche," the Old Man went on, his tone insinuating, oily, crude finally, "who said truth is a woman."

Appalled, Reed dashed the phone to the cradle, as if it might bite off his hand. He stood for a long moment, sickened. But: Boston by dark. Reed looked up to find Socorro studying him. Her gaze was scrutinizing, unsettling. She said, "One is bigger than the other."

"What?" He had forgotten his nudity.

She smiled. A mere girl, her experience was narrow. "One is bigger." She had never noticed before.

Thursday morning early. The final morning. The Old Man had ordained it. Reed's insomnia was genuine. He chain-smoked, paced the floor. He felt two hundred years old. The phone call had unnerved him. Yates would exact galling indignities, dispatch him on minor excursions to Worchester, Utica, New Bedford. Mundane locales, stays at motor lodges: an all-you-can-eat salad bar in the lobby restaurant, traveling salesmen in adjacent rooms, lonely men who watch the all-night porno channel on the in-house cable and faithfully record their odometer readings every morning. The Old Man would look up in the middle of an important business meeting where corporate czars were gathered and say, "Reed, we could use some doughnuts." Meanwhile, Andrea would make like the woman wronged, the woman afflicted; her husband departs on a three-day business outing and returns a week and a half later without a word. On the eve of all future trips, her eyes would glaze over, her face would harden. Yet he knew he would suffer the indignities, he would toil endlessly at placating Andrea. She was his anchor in the end, his mooring.

Early in their marriage, she used to show up at his office for lunch on calm days. Money was short, they were trying to save to buy the house. She would pack a picnic basket with cheese sandwiches, dill pickles, two slices of pie she had baked just that morning, a thermos of apple juice. They would stroll through the Public Garden, sit and eat amid the odors of hyacinth and jonquil. There would be her pale bare arms, the flush of the sun on her cheeks, her moist kisses. They spoke in soft, quick tones; there was so much to say, it seemed there would always be more to say. They had ended the practice around the time they bought the house, or perhaps it was around the time Laura was born. He could no longer remember. But the previous September, the weather warm, she had appeared unexpectedly at the door of his office, picnic basket in hand. The same basket, he realized—he had not seen it for decades. "I can't, I have a meeting," he told her. "You must. You have to." They walked to the Public Garden. There were cheese sandwiches, dill pickles, apple juice. She had baked the pie that morning. Her arms were heavy, but they were bare; her face was creased, but the sun shone on her cheeks. They ate in silence. There seemed nothing to say. She had risen, eyes welling, and fled. He brought the basket home on the train.

The memory made him frown. It made him ashamed. It made him want to do better, to eat cheese sandwiches while talking his head off. Boston by dark. He glanced at Socorro now, asleep on the bed. Andrea would have thought her ugly, his attraction to her inexplicable. His wife would have felt strangely diminished. To Andrea's way of thinking, the woman that would bring down her husband would have gone to a better school than she, come from a better family. Her diction, her makeup would be meticulous. She would be fine-boned, broad-breasted, svelte, her skin the color of pearl. But Socorro's face was blunt, her build low, her breasts small; she was the color of the earth. An urchin finally, an orphan. "She's a mere child," his wife would have ranted. "How could you?"

How could he. Socorro lay spread-eagled on the bed. Lean arms, dark legs; breasts like gentle hillocks. He followed the rise and fall of her breathing. Scant pelt of hair. Her liquor had an oysterish taste to it. It was still on his lips. How could he not. The other woman, it occurred to him. But that seemed a puffed-up notion, it stank of false treachery. She was a girl, untreacherous. Yet spectacular, extraordinary. She owned a lone pair of sandals. Her laugh was unschooled. She was a stranger to lipstick. Her presence was raw, unfiltered, direct. She was bungee-jumping, skydiving, whitewater rafting. Her laugh made him want to ride around in a convertible. He supposed he loved her. The thought made him smile. As if love were a singular quality, an incorrigible idea. But love was bits and pieces, isolated moments. Try to capture it and it slapped you around, then ran away smirking before you could recover. Love was nothing more than what you had when you felt moved to use the word. It was nothing less.

"Socorro?" She stirred. "Choco."

And so the last day. They both knew it. It informed their tones, their looks, it seemed even the hues in the room acknowledged it. They were tender with each other, their voices brief, concerned. She sat before the mirror, running a brush through her hair. Long strokes of her arm, black shocks in the room. She had put on a white sleeveless blouse, dark slacks. The underwear he had bought her. She was like a man girding for battle, a soldier donning armor. In an hour, in two hours, she could be treading across a river, burrowing through a tunnel, hiding in a false compartment. Yet her face betrayed nothing. Olmec features, stark, monolithic. He came up behind her, kissed her gently on the cheek. She turned, smiled. Her face was guileless, trusting. He was terrified for her. If it were he, he would have plopped onto the bed and rolled into a fetal curl. But she was unafraid, eager. One way or another, she was crossing north. Less terrifying than remaining on this side. She feared the smallness of her village more than drowning; she feared a life bent over a hearth more than cave-ins; she feared the unending rains, eternal days of mud more than asphyxiation.

They drove to García's house. The Mexican was waiting on the front porch, smoking a cigarette. A man up early, he looked like a man going fishing. When he got in the car, he shook Reed's hand, gave the girl a formal peck. A man observing the proprieties. He had slept poorly, he announced. This was a good omen.

Reed frowned. "It is?"

García nodded vigorously. He always slept poorly before a day of immense happenings, propitious awakenings. He had slept poorly the night before he married his wife. He had slept poorly the night his daughter was born, before the morning his son came into the world. He had slept not at all when that woman from Guadalajara . . . "It is a good omen."

The Mexican directed Reed to the restaurant where they had breakfasted the day before. Reed, puzzled, asked, "Here?"

"Get out," García said simply.

Reed blinked. "No. I'm going, too." He had to go. He refused not to. García tried to explain. All the arrangements had been made. If Reed appeared—if a gringo appeared—the coyote would conclude that he was la migra. The matter was simple. There was no way around it. García would drop her off, return with the car for Reed. It would take twenty, thirty minutes. No more.

"You could explain," Reed insisted. "Tell him who I am."

García shook his head. It was impossible to explain away the color of Reed's skin. He leaned across Reed now, opened the car door. "Thirty minutes. No more."

Reed looked at the girl. "Socorro—"

She inclined her head. "We will say goodbye over there." And she gestured in that way she had, the jutting of the chin, the puckering of her lips.

Reed walked into the diner, took a seat by the window. He watched the Toyota leave the parking lot. He could see the back of her head, the silhouette of her sculpted features. Then she was gone. Say he never saw her again. The thought was like the sound of shattering glass. Unexpected, potentially dangerous. He tried to calm himself with the idea that it would be for the best. Best for him, best for her. But the idea was slippery, sloppy; it lacked the gravity of the truth. He drank a cup of coffee, smoked four cigarettes, told himself he should be content with the memory. He had a plane to catch, after all, lies to hone. On the flight to Boston, he would cook up a battery of figures, lay them at Yates's feet like alms for a god whose wrath one much fears. He would arrive home with a bouquet of roses in his hand, a smile on his face, creative excuses on his tongue, contrition in his heart. Though say Andrea knew. Yet she would not know, he decided. She could not know. Not really. She would never know. He could tell her, and still she would never know. Words were too clumsy. They would never add up to the truth. Even if she knew, she would never know.

When García reappeared, he placed both palms on the table, put his face in Reed's. The Mexican's features were grim. "Cross the river, then take the old mill road to the west. At Quemado, the road turns north." Five minutes past the checkpoint—it was important to get past the checkpoint, García explained; there were roadblocks along every northern route, this was where the real border lay—there was an unmarked road on the right. "Take this road. You will come to a bait shop on the left. It will be closed. A pay phone hangs by the door. Call my office. I will tell you exactly where to find her."

"I won't see her again, will I?"

"Of course you will," García said. The Mexican's features softened. He had seen this same look on men trapped in mines, on men aboard sinking ships, on men who had fallen in the ring: the bull prepares to gore yet again. He had seen the look on Eliazar Borges. García leaned close. "She likes you."

"She thinks I'm a fool."

"No." The Mexican slid into the booth. "No. You understand nothing." He paused now, choosing his words. A man imparting deep secrets. It was a role he relished. "It is very different between men and women, I think." Consider, he went on: a man is outside of himself in the end. He hangs, he droops. He urinates, he is an arcing stream; little boys write their names in the dust. As if to remember them, to remind themselves of who they are. As if maybe they need this reminder, yes? García spoke loudly, he thumped the table. A man with a theory, a man with new knowledge. But a woman. The Mexican shook his head. She squats. She writes her name on nothing. As if she knows herself completely. She needs no such reminder. What she is, what she is—it lives inside of her. It cannot be mistaken. These differences seem insignificant, but they amount to very much. They say everything. A man looks for a woman, he looks for big breasts, a generous behind. But a woman looks for a man. She does not care so much about how he looks. No: she looks for something else. "For that which is invisible."

"She thinks I'm a fool."

García thrust a finger under Reed's nose. Did Reed know that, among animals, the female is not drawn to the biggest, or the strongest, or the most powerful? This was true, García insisted. It was. No: the female, she prefers a male that has suffered some obvious injury, or is hobbled by some defect. Did he know this? Es cierto. Because it means that this male, he has overcome some great difficulty. He has overcome some difficulty that would kill most others, he has overcome it and now he lives, and he has earned in cunning what he has lost in strength. "The woman knows this. It is this she falls in love with. It is this that she wants."

Reed grinned. Despite himself. Despite everything. "You're full of shit."

The Mexican nodded happily. A man full of theories. Perhaps a man full of shit; yet a man who knew he was full of shit. This self-knowledge made all the difference, it redeemed him finally. Made you want to listen to him. Made you like him in the end.

García repeated the business about the old mill road, Quemado, the abandoned bait shop. The details seemed too many, too rushed. Reed made him repeat it still again. García spoke slowly, like a man explaining the most basic facts to a dullard, a simpleton.

"Tell me now where I'll meet her."

García grunted, shook his head. Not until she had arrived. A gringo rides up in his big car, the coyote will flee. Perhaps pull out a gun.

"How will she get across?"

García sighed. So many questions. He did not know. It was impossible to tell. There were hundreds of ways, countless ways. There were as many ways as there were meters along the border.

"Call my office. Now you should go."

Reed reluctantly slipped out of the booth, thinking old mill road, Quemado, bait. The Mexican cleared his throat. There was still, he reminded Reed, the matter of the coyote's fee.

Reed pulled out his wallet. "How much?"

García wetted his lips. "One hundred dollars?"

Reed cocked his head. "For everything?"

García fiddled with the ashtray. "Por todo."

"But—"

"Por todo."

Reed said, "I'd like to pay you more."

A hundred was enough. Truly. Consider it a gesture of goodwill. Perhaps they would do business in the future; Reed would remember García's act of generosity.

"You're sure?"

The Mexican was sure. But now, the gringo should go. Reed shoved the money into García's hand. Both men stared at their shoes. The moment was awkward. Business partners, but this seemed the least of it. Reed wanted to say thank you, to say how can I ever repay you. What he said was, "About your commission for the site: Yates will pay two, three times as much as you were going to ask. Better: five times, easy. Ask for it. Demand it."

García squinted up at Reed, his eyes tight with gratitude. He was a man already counting his money. He gathered Reed in his arms now, his bear hug unrestrained. García's odors, his bulk, the damaged teeth. They clapped each other on the back, they gripped hard. Two men parting, their affection masculine, uneasy. But Reed had a final thought then, a last worry. "About this checkpoint: what do I say? What do I do?"

García winked, squeezed Reed's shoulder. "Act like a gringo."

Reed drove alone to the border. He crossed the river, the sun glinting off the water. The weeds on the bank opposite, the scorched greens of the golf course. He waited in line on the north bank. The traffic was thick, the cars crowding close as they funneled into the narrow lanes that fed to the customs booths. Hot day, the needle on his temperature gauge quivered. To his right, a young couple. Long hair on the man, his face bearded. The girl had shaved her head. A safety pin through her nose. Her bare feet on the dash, toenails painted black. Bikers, punks, drug-runners; more likely students returning to Madison, to Ann Arbor, to Berkeley, to Cambridge, to Chapel Hill. Socorro's age, though their lives were filled with midterms, frat parties, football games, kegs of beer. To his left, an old couple on vacation. The man gave Reed a snappy salute. White men going home.

Reed remembered to place the figurine in the glove compartment.

The guard waved Reed on through with a perfunctory glance. Reed drove for five minutes, his thoughts indistinct. He turned left at a stoplight, headed for Quemado. The river aped his course. The town of Eagle Pass dwindled behind him. Rolling countryside on his right, the river to his left. Quemado was little more than a hamlet—a flock of frame houses, a filling station, a store, a church. A VFW post. He stopped at the gas station, received elaborate directions from a man who spoke a stilted English. He got back in the car, drove on. The highway rose. The sun blasted down, the heat crashing through the windows. It was as he was mounting a bluff, the whole of the valley beneath him, that his dashboard went red.

Reed pulled over, slapped in irritation at the dash. He raised the hood to a minor rush of steam. He wondered where she was at this moment, what she was doing. His imagination bounded off on a long, loopy vignette rampant with guns, guard dogs, and baton-toting immigration officers. His belly jumped in response. He reached back into the car for his dictionary, just in case. A veteran of these parts, a man who had learned. Looking south now, he could see the near traffic, the snake of the river. He could see Mexico on beyond. Stunning panorama, it seemed a continent lay at his feet. Pastoral scene, though he knew better. Chemicals lurked in the river, begging children wandered the streets, competing with the blind, the lame, the poor. In the end, a tragic land; they sell churches there. Yet the landscape bore a look of eternal peace. The progress of the river was haphazard. A breeze stirred the reeds. There was the faint odor of bilge, ripe and mildly carnal. To the left, on the bank opposite, a man waited on a slip of rock that intruded deeply into the water, cooling his feet in the river. His sandals hung from a tether at his neck.

Bored, Reed huddled with his dictionary, straining to re-member. Tú eres mi mar, etc. He flipped through the pages, muttering to himself. Reed had uttered his share of endear-ments, he had received them in turn. Gushing, cooing sounds, the idiocies of the bedroom. Emotional flotsam. He finally snorted at himself, pocketed the dictionary. He needed to be cool, clearheaded. He was determined to be. He found his cig-arettes, stuck one in his mouth. Tough guy having a smoke. He promptly bit clean through the filter. His throat constricted, his breathing went harsh. His eyes smarted. He was her sea, he was her river, he was her little heaven. He was her mountain, he was her heart, he was her life. Weak, insipid, he knew.

But listen, listen: he was her little heaven.

Nightfall was ten hours away.

Those junctures in life where men in uniform cast cold eyes his way always put him in a molten fear. Air marshals manning metal detectors at airports, security guards in liquor stores, a cop on a horse on Commonwealth Avenue. Upon returning to work after a day out sick, Reed made a great show of cough-ing, of sniffling, of blowing his nose. Yet he had smuggled no knives aboard the plane, he had stolen no liquor, he was care-ful not to jaywalk. He had been sick. But he was certain that guilt screamed wildly from his face, guilt of a deeper stripe; it intimated metaphysical transgressions. Upon leaving a store where he had failed to conclude a purchase, Reed made it a point to smile at the clerk behind the counter, at the guard at the door. Spare smile, sheepish smile: I am sorry I have bought none of your wares. Yet it was a smile that marked him, he sus-pected, surer than a ski mask, than the bulge of a pistol be-neath his jacket—the smile of a degenerate, a miscreant, a man to be watched.

Up ahead, the checkpoint appeared innocuous enough: a beaten mobile home at the side of the road, two unpainted sawhorses bravely trying to bar the way. An immigration officer stepped from the trailer, his gait matter-of-fact. But Reed could not outrun the fear that he had been found out. Say they had captured the girl, seized García, threatened them with clever Yankee tortures, made them confess. Reed thought scandal, he thought hometown papers. There was an unfamiliar, intemperate rhythm to his heart. He thought about Inspector Ross, Ross wagging his finger in Reed's face, Ross saying, "I'll remember you." Reed imagined smashing his foot down onto the gas pedal, the car rocketing madly through the sawhorses. A chase through nine counties, angry sirens at his back. Reed running low on gas, Reed having to pee. Reed with swollen, desperate bladder, hightailing it across the Texas panhandle, posses of vigilantes out in force. Large, bullnecked Texans, ignorant of the Bill of Rights.

Reed braked the car, reminded himself to act like a gringo. Cool, casual, rich. Consumer of staggering quantities of meat. A gringo belonged; a gringo was at home in the world, the envy of all others. Panamanians watch our TV shows, Asiatics covet our science, Russians want our wheat. Given his country of birth, the pallor of his skin, a perch already far along the ladder that fed to wealth, a gringo moves through life with assurances in abundance: the stores will always be stocked, the hospitals will always sport the latest in technological wizardry, the athletes are the finest, the women the prettiest, firemen always arrive in time. Uniformed men will not enter your home late at night in search of proscribed literature.

But Reed was neither cool, casual, nor rich. He was red-faced, sweating, scared. He was running low on dollars. He had given up on the stores, on the doctors, on the women. He had given up on the athletes. The firemen would never arrive; three A.M. could well bring men in suits beating at his door. It seemed he belonged nowhere. The dangerous moments were winning.

The officer approached, his mien bored. He touched the bill of his cap, said, "U.S. citizen?" Reed swallowed, swooned, his voice climbing far too high, and said, "I—"

294

The man mumbled, "Have a nice day."

Reed drove. He watched the checkpoint shrink in his rearview mirror. He permitted himself a narrow smile, an experimental smile; as if God might appear, smite it from his face. But God did not appear. The smile settled in. Flat Texas vista stretched before him, like a hand extended in welcome. A windmill wheeled purposefully to the west. Reed circled wide around a girl on a bicycle. Pigtails and shorts, she waved as he passed. A flock of birds overhead, he could hear their calls. His smile broadened. He found the unmarked road, an unassuming route, little more than a cow path. The car bucked against the ruts. He could see a few cattle in the distance, a grain silo to the north. Some geese coasting on a tiny pond to his left, cat-o'-nine-tails crowding the bank. An owl in a tree. The setting was calming, bucolic. A scene from a hundred years ago. To one side, a disheveled structure of peeling, rotting boards. BAIT, said the door. Then a second sign, written in an unsteady hand: Closed on account of the fishing is good. The pay phone was a battered black knot hanging next to the door.

García's line was busy. Reed smoked a cigarette. García's line was still busy. Reed made a tunnel with his hands, peered through the window of the shack. Racks of candy bars, stacked cases of beer, a low refrigerated unit decades old. A calendar on the wall. Miss November was a tall, buxom woman with amber hair, the lightly brushed mound. Her legs were still good.

Reed closed his eyes, rested his cheek against the window. The day—his life—seemed to have run out of momentum. He took a measured breath, then a second, and dialed.

"Frank," she began, and then she said nothing.

He spoke slowly, cautiously, a man crossing a minefield. He mentioned García, the site; how the car kept overheating. Andrea said nothing. He told her he had tried to call, for days he had been trying. He reminded her of his conversation with Laura. Andrea said nothing. He went on about protracted negotiations, high finance, Mexican trade laws. He told her he

295

was flying in tonight. He gave her the flight number, the time. He asked if she would meet him. Andrea said nothing. He told her about the food he had eaten, the weather he had endured. He told her he had been sick. He told her he missed her. He told her he was sorry.

Andrea said, "Liar."

Her voice was subdued, uncanny. Unequivocal. His heart was a tolling bell. The need to confess settled deep within him. For the first time, he grasped the appeal of Catholicism. He grasped the meaning of purgatory. It seemed he was about to grasp the full meaning of hell. He was a man who had been found out. He was preparing himself now. He was a man who had come to the end.

"Andrea . . ."

"You never talked to Laura."

"I did too." The words were breathless, as if he had been running.

"She would have told me."

Of all the fabrications he had offered, she had managed to fix on the lone truth. He felt wronged, curiously indignant. "But I did."

She hesitated. A bare moment of indecision, he meant to exploit it. He added weight to his tone. "I talked to Laura. I explained everything. You can ask her."

She was unconvinced. He had talked to Laura, he hadn't talked to Laura; this was not the point, they both knew. In the coming weeks, the coming months, she would circle back round to the fact of his prolonged absence again and again, searching for corroboration, keen for any hint of contradiction. But she wanted to believe him. It was this that would save him finally. It would save them.

"I miss you," he tried again.

"I miss you," she said reluctantly. She said it as if it were a sorry admission, a fatal display of weakness.

"I'm flying in tonight," he repeated. Somewhere behind him, geese squabbled. "If you could pick me up, we—"

"The play opens today."

"Miss it."

"I will not."

"All right. All right. I can take a cab—"

"Tell me," she cut him off. "Tell me nothing is wrong."

"Nothing is wrong."

"Everything is the same."

"Exactly the same."

"You'll be home tonight." She spoke like a trial attorney.

"Tonight."

"I want to hear you say it. I want to hear it in your voice. Tell me that nothing, nothing, nothing, nothing is wrong." The sentence swelled with force, detonating on the final *nothing*.

"Nothing is wrong." The pause went on. He whispered, "Andrea?"

The previous evening, she had dreamed the butcher. Vivid, suffocating detail, right down to his lacerating odors. There had been the thick whorls of black hair, the dark, thick genitals. She spread her arms, her legs wide, she was a creature flailing on its back. He fucked her with deft, authoritative strokes, like a man dressing game. Frank had appeared toward the very end, setting himself down at her side, a knife and fork in his hands. Her husband kept asking her to pass the salt.

"Tell me again," she demanded now.

When they finally hung up, Reed slumped against the door of the shack like a man who has been clubbed. He felt neither relief nor guilt. He felt punch-drunk, spent. Lying is a full-time occupation if you want to do it right. It occurred to him that maybe he should simply jump in the car, barrel on into the San Antonio airport, race down the concourse, and position himself at the door to the ramp that would lead to his plane, waiting for a flight attendant to open it. She would be like an angel of deliverance. The temptation was riveting. Odds were, Socorro had made it. And if she hadn't, if something had gone wrong . . . He imagined himself crossing the border yet again, finding García yet again, another Efraín, another hotel room. Time is like a wheel. Indeed. He wanted to hoist time above his head, smash it against rocks. Leave now, and he would set himself free.

A shock of sound then, it scattered his fatigue. The phone rang again. He looked about wildly, as if he expected the geese, the owl to take the call. But the ringing was persistent. He wanted to make it stop.

He reached for the phone. The ringing stopped. He swallowed, unsure, and said, "Bait shop."

Seething Spanish sprang forth. It was like a spike in his ear. It took the Mexican a moment to find his English. "Where have you been?" García shouted. When he hadn't heard from Reed, he had started calling. He had been calling for almost an hour.

"I'm here," Reed said. García's anger seemed unfair. Then, "I made it." Reed felt heartened by the words. He had made it. As if it were he that had been smuggled across, it was his future that hung in the balance. "Where—"

"You are alone?" García jumped in. Yes, he was alone. "There is no one else?" The Mexican was whispering.

"No." Reed looked around. He found himself whispering. "No one."

"Open the trunk."

Reed gripped the phone as if it were the last intact part of his mind. He did not want to lose it. "What?"

"Open the trunk." And then García hung up.

Reed regarded the car with a morbid fascination, of the sort common to those crowds that gather in the aftermath of traffic accidents, plane crashes, and shootouts. He ran to the trunk. The metal was hot to the touch. She might well be dead. The thought made him want to flee. Gringo abducts Mexican waif, forces her to endure unmentionable sexual depravities on bizarre crosscountry spree, then roasts her alive in the trunk of a Japanese subcompact. His voice was tiny, fearful: "Socorro?" He popped the lid, saw a sweaty girl lodged between the spare tire and the jack. She squinted against the sun. He reached in, gingerly eased her to the ground. She weaved on unsteady legs, turned to take in the horizon, the breadth of the landscape. He said, "Are you OK?" "You drive too quickly." She was OK. Yet Reed scowled. He had been hustled. No doubt García's idea, García sure the gringo never would have agreed to it. Though an edifying hustle, Reed saw now. Thoughts of the heavy Mexican made him smile. A hundred bucks, the price of self-knowledge.

True, he never would have agreed to it.

"Where are we?" she wanted to know. "Texas." The States at last. But dry, unspectacular land. The cows chewed contentedly. Not much to look at. He half-expected a show of disappointment, a possible plea: take me back. Instead she clapped her hands. She spun around. She stamped her feet. A child at Christmas. She jerked her head back and forth, hair, breasts pitching. A woman suddenly, a woman having a fit, a woman out of control. Then she dropped to her knees, crossed herself, clasped together her hands. Gracias a Dios, a El Señor Mas Ponderoso, a El Señor Mas Amable. She leapt to her feet, flung her arms around his neck. Her clothes were soaked, her skin greasy, her odor sharp as cedar. Reed clung to her, laughed into her hair. He was a king entering a city, a warrior come home. No: a gunrunner, a rumrunner, a smuggler of beautiful women.

Did I ever tell you about the time I sneaked a girl across the border?

She spied the pond, ran toward it. Reed humped behind her, trying to keep up. "What are you doing?" "A bath," she said. She was dirty, her hair, her clothes were filthy. She was hot. But: "You can't. Not here." He feared landowners, soil conservation experts, Texas cowpokes lurking in the weeds, made moronic and lecherous from generations of inbreeding. Uncouth bait-shop owners, returning with creels full. He feared snakes. But she was already stepping out of her pants, stripping the blouse over her head. "Look: this is the States," he said. She grinned. "I know." Broad pelvis, cantering breasts. Handful of hair. Geese, owl, Reed all stared. She picked her way down the bank. He saw dimpled back, water swirling around her thighs, shadowy cleft of ass, her buttocks like a pair of moons heaved from a primordial earth. He burned to bury his face there. Then she was dog paddling along the surface, a broad smile on her face. As if it were her smile that kept her afloat. "Come in, come in," she called. A pond on a farm. Memories of youth. Memories of home. His heart caught. But: "Come in." Nude girl beckoning. She stood in water up to her waist, tilted her head, wrung out her hair. The droplets on her breasts captured the sun, splintered it into tiny rainbows. Reed peered around again. Fence, distant silo, cat-o'-nine-tails. Closed on account of the fishing is good. The geese had fled, much raucous protest on the far bank. Then he was pitching down toward the pond, shedding clothes. Bare-assed, pale paunch quivering; a breeze lapped at his balls. The ludicrous, flapping kielbasa of him. Big splash of water then, the belly flop of a fat man. Shocking cold, he whooped as he hit. He was a college boy, he was a Swede tearing from the sauna. Blatant nakedness on a bright day. The sensation was illicit, naughty. Mud squished between his toes, some kelplike substance caressed his ankles. Her breasts were buoyant. Reed was rigid. She waded out of the water, turned to face him, the sun blasting at her back. Standing that way, she seemed the only woman alive, a singular creation, never to be duplicated. She reached for him. Their screwing was lunatic, helpless. They scattered the last of the geese, chased away the owl. Bugs bit his ass.

By the time they returned to the car, storm clouds had begun to gather in the east. Gray, billowing thunderheads marching their way. Yet they had nothing to do with Reed. His mood was an unassailable fortress.

"Where is he?" she demanded. She pulled it from the glove compartment, lodged it between them. It seemed even the figurine was smiling in unbridled trinity. The first billboards

300

announcing the bounties of San Antonio rose up ahead. "Slow down," she begged. She was against the window, eyes drinking. The Spurs, the Alamo. The old missions. A room for $29.95.

Reed grinned. He smoked, he drank, he fucked amid the weeds. He drove too fast. "I'm excited, that's all. I'm happy." Simple admission, but it had been ten, maybe twenty years since he had last had the thought. Its truth seemed heavily textured now, unprecedented. He wanted to prolong it, to pack it thick with time.

His flight would not leave for another few hours. In the meantime, he needed a drink. He deserved a drink. "You hungry?" But she was always hungry. A leisurely meal, then. A feast to consecrate these last days. Afterward, he would drop her off at the San Antonio bus station—no, the train station. A train bound for San Diego. A sleeping car. She had never been in a sleeping car. She had never been on a train. This was the perfect ending, he understood now, the exact coda. He imagined them on the platform, train sounds loud all around them. He rehearsed the words they would say. He had never seen her cry, he realized. He decided she would cry. It would be a scene from the early years of the cinema. He had become the director of the movie he called his life.

They stopped. A tacky bar, a man hunkered at one end, drinking with conviction. The bartender needed a shave. A young cowboy was loading quarters into the jukebox. True Americana, it seemed apt. They sat at the counter. "Your biggest burger for her." A milk shake, fries. A scotch for himself. "Your very best." The bartender asked what she wanted on her hamburger. "Everything," she said.

The man smiled. "Everything?"

"Even anchovies."

"Lettuce and tomato," Reed told him.

She ate in that determined way she had, head heavy to the table, face working, thick, sucking sounds through a straw. He drained his drink, signaled for another. Her beauty filled the bar, reached into the dark corners, along the dirty floor. The bartender, the cowboy, the drunk down the way all seemed to bask in her glow. The presence of a young woman rights the world, if only for a moment. She had mustard on her lip. The cowboy approached shyly, tipped his hat. His drawl was long and roaming. He was about Socorro's age. If Reed didn't mind, he added. "Go ahead," Reed told her. She blushed. He was sure? "Go on." There was the slide of the barstool, a moment of awkwardness. Then the cowboy took her in his arms, moved with corny steps around the floor, punctuated by exaggerated dips. Socorro tilted back her head, allowed herself to be twirled around.

"She's a pretty one," the bartender said. He said it without malice, his tone genuine. The world seemed a place of fundamentals finally, a place shorn of the inessential. A drink in his hand, moaning words about loss and hurt on the radio. The stain of the wood walls, the glasses lined up behind the bar, the whiskers of the bartender—even they seemed friendly—were like kept promises. They were like debts that had been made good.

"Yes," Reed said. "She is."

There was an instant when he might have taken the cowboy aside, said, Tell me: you have a job? You have a house? Of course the boy did. He was big, slightly homely, in the way of the responsible. Then listen, listen, this is the girl for you. Be kind to her, be gentle, marry her, give her kids. Grow gray together. This is the girl for all of us. Reed would rise then, slip out the back door of the bar, blubber all the way to the airport. The poetry of it would be precise, fitting.

But the bartender was pouring Reed another drink, and one for himself. "On the house." A talkative man, he had been through two wars—and that wasn't counting his divorces. He had once owned three hundred head of cattle, a ranch house, a bunkhouse filled with rowdy farmhands. His gut had burned all the time, he would get these headaches. He would wake up feeling like nothing could do him better than a bracing fistfight. But now, but now. He had a dog named Jasper, weekends he spent trying to catch catfish. Quail season and he was up before dawn, cleaning his shotgun. There was the taste of good bourbon, biscuits, and chicken-fried steak. The bartender shook his head. It was as if maybe something had passed him by, something that he should have wanted. Something that he should have missed. But let the others figure it. He was all worn out. You do what you can and maybe it's not enough in the end. He hadn't been in a fistfight in years. It was a good morning when the coffee was hot and his bowels complied. He said it again: "Let the others figure it out."

Reed bought the next round. They sat like prospectors long after the vein has run dry, like old-timers, watching youth moving around and around on the dance floor. The bartender said, "Remember when it was like that?" He spoke from a place of melancholy—it seemed a good place to be:

"Remember when the world was an empty afternoon with nothing but a tune on the radio and a pretty girl standing close?"

Reed felt sapped suddenly, all used up. He sagged against the bar for support. He would go home now, he would sit at his desk, he would fight with his wife. He would yell at his daughter. It seemed the business with Socorro had made no difference. Not really. In the end, he was destined for such a life. As if the world were a stage in which he had finally been written out of the script. Reed looked up now, watched the rhythmic working of her hips, listened to her laughter. Like the aspiring diva, the rising star. All the good parts go to her. But wait, wait, she grants us the honor of a balcony seat. For a performance anyway, maybe two. We take it with reluctance; we complain to our neighbor about the lumpy cushions, the obstructed view. But then the performance begins, and we are lost in it, enthralled by the tale. For a moment it is we who are on the stage, it is our drama that lives. At the end, we stand, eyes teary, we clap louder than anyone else, our shouts are choking. And then we go home.

And then we go home. To what? To what? One sells off the ranch, the three hundred head of cattle. One divorces the wives. One spends the day watching young people dance early in the afternoon. To the sparest of times, where joy lies at the edges, meaning is walleyed. You despair of ever making sense. Yet there are brief, isolated episodes, they contain too much of life. You have experienced such moments. You know them. And when you get off the subway at Harvard Square, you are met by the clank of machinery, the smell of diesel oil. The world is composed of grease and pistons. But then you hear the strands of a string quartet playing Bach in the lobby of the station. The cello case holds six dollars and twenty-seven cents. The Bach, the cello case atone for the sounds of the great machines, the sickly smell of diesel. You want to empty your wallet, fill the cello case. You want to pour your soul into it. Mornings when you wake up and peer out the window and are shocked by the covering of fresh snow. There are children upstairs searching for snowman attire. And you go out and shovel the walk, and all up and down the street, other fathers are out, shoveling their walks. It makes you happy to say hi. A fall drive out to the Berkshires, the explosion of colors like a used palette. God still trying to finish the picture. An afternoon at the beach, an afternoon in which every woman seems comely, all the men appear hale, all the sharks are far out to sea. And a day of sledding on Foster's Hill. The police have thought to block off the cross street at the bottom so all you have to worry about is breaking your neck against the large oak on the left. There are old books and aged liquor and sometimes a corned beef sandwich on pumpernickel. There is a bit of German potato salad left in the bottom of the bowl. There are roses pressed between the pages of an album, yellowing packets of letters bound with green twine, a faded garter belt in an attic trunk. An old man in the park, he stares at the run in a woman's stocking. Trite, maudlin, clichés finally, Reed knew. Yet the thing about clichés is that they are still true. Spare moments, distinct, crystalline moments. As if the whole has lost

304

its refrain, you are left only with disparate notes. Yet each takes a lifetime to hear.

"I remember," Reed whispered.

The jukebox went silent. The cowboy bowed deeply to Socorro, then tipped his hat in Reed's direction. "I thank you," he said. The hour was late. A light rain had begun to fall. Reed rose then, beet-colored, thick with feelings. They convened in his face. The bartender said, "Five dollars." Reed shook his head. It was more than that. It had to be more than that. The bartender shrugged. Reed left a twenty.

They drove with the windows down, felt the spare sprinkle. There was the smell of wet asphalt, hints of cut hay. They were entering a final calm. Neither spoke. The silence was bittersweet. Talk would squander it. The rain picked up, heavy, moist drops, rich percussions against the windshield. They seemed to herald their arrival. She reached now, took his chin in her short fingers. Her kiss was open, wet, her tongue warm. Thunder then, like God applauding. Reed grinned. The road grinned back, a curve like a sickle. But he saw only her. There was a weightless shifting, unmistakable sensation, the car fishtailing. Slick pavement, dinning rain. The moment broke over them. Reed, reflexes dimmed by alcohol, by the thickening of the blood that comes from fucking, wrestled the wheel. But the wheel fought back. The wheel winning. The car spun. The windshield spoke. It said flat mesa, it said sheer rise, it said pecan grove on beyond. A distant farmhouse, a light on in the upstairs room, set hard against the grove. The figurine rattled in its nook, complaining. The windshield shouted mesa again, then the wheels hit the shoulder and bounded on past and the rise came up and at them and there was the groan of the shocks and the sickening surge of the tires as they left the pavement and then the car was rumbling down a narrow arroyo, and a tree, the rugged face of the bark, rushed toward them and Reed thought pecan death pecan death, and then the world lurched and everything went still.

Reed swore. He was a decrepit man ultimately, a besotted

man, blinded by kisses. He glanced at her, shook his head in apology. Welcome to the States. Tomorrow we'll arrange for a mugging, a house fire, a possible IRS audit. Her look was compact, frightened. "You OK?" "And you?" They stepped out into the rain. He kicked a tire, the gesture futile. She looked at him, then kicked the tire opposite. He circled the car. Everything appeared intact. A temporary mishap, he told himself; they had weathered far worse. He got back in the car, threw it into reverse, rocking it roughly. The wheels spun helplessly. He emerged again from the car. The rain matted the hair to his head, soaked her blouse. He peered through the haze. The embankment rose sharply before them, deep grooves detailed their trajectory. A runoff ditch to the right. Water coursed down it. Behind them, the grove. Confused branches, the trees crowding close. Pecans littered the ground.

"Stay here."

He struggled up the ditch. Sloppy footing, he fell twice. He puffed heavily. When he finally made the highway, a truck roared past him, mudguards flapping. A car, a second. Reed stood, waving wildly. A muddy man, but he owned his own home, he had a job, a family. A man of the city. A van holding a frightened, defeated woman, children fighting in the back seat. A geezer in a pickup truck, burrowing digit far up his nose. I am you, I am you, Reed wanted to scream at each passing face. Two teenage girls, blonde smiles. The passenger gave him the finger. The next car slowed, eased reluctantly to the shoulder. Reed ran happily toward it. A Samaritan, a man of conscience. But a policeman got out. His cap wrapped in plastic, a yellow slicker on his back. Reed's eyebrows rose. An unmarked car, lights no doubt secreted in the grill. Reed indicated the arroyo. "I'm stuck." The cop frowned. He was a large man, heavy, chinless. His face as featureless as pudding. The kind of man you could see a hundred times and still not remember. "But I just got off duty," the cop said. "I just got off duty. Today's my wife's birthday. Thirty-two. I got the cake in the car right now." He shook his head. "My wife, the kids are waiting. Understand, it's her birthday. Me and the kids, we always light the candles, sing the song. Then we go out to Deke's Ribhouse for dinner."

"Please," Reed implored.

"But you don't understand." The cop sighed. Reed didn't understand. "We go to Deke's, come home, put the kids to bed. Then it's just me and my wife. Lucille's thirty-two today. On her birthday, she lets me have it special. Once a year."

"I think a push will do it," Reed said.

The policeman relented. A man of basic preferences, mundane appetites. But a man who believed in this thing called duty. He had taken an oath after all, now there was a traveler in distress. He turned toward the ridge. He whistled. "Really buried that puppy, didn't you?" Reed nodded grimly. A killer of dogs. The cop was already wending his way along the ditch. Reed staggered after him.

Socorro's gaze went tight. Her eyes darted to Reed. The cop looked at her, muttered, "I was just going off duty. It's my wife's birthday. Thirty-two. I got the cake in the car." Then he bent to inspect the tires. Reed was ready to defer to his expertise. A man no doubt specially trained in exotic rescue techniques. He got in the car, started it, rocked it as Reed had done. The tires sprayed mud. The cop took his foot off the gas, said, "Your dingy is done broke." He held up the figurine. "Your dingy. Your whatchamacallit here. It's done broke." But the piece was intact; save for the already missing arm, it was as solid as stone. "It's a fake," Reed assured him. Though this seemed to confuse the man. "A gift for my daughter," Reed added. As if talk of a daughter might convince one of his good citizenship, his membership in the community of responsible humans. The cop beamed now, returned the figurine to the nook between the seats. A man convinced. "I got a daughter. A daughter and a son. They're waiting for me right now." The thought cheered him. Then, "Push," the cop ordered. Reed trotted back around behind the car and pushed. The wheels spun, wheels going nowhere. Reed slipped, sprawled flat.

Muck on his belly, his knees. He heard the slam of the door. The rain came down. "Tow truck," he heard the cop call. Reed nodded into the mud. The policeman is our friend. The man came around to the rear of the car, bent close to offer Reed a hand. "You hurt?" Before Reed could answer, the man shrank back. His nose wrinkled, filled with sniffing noises. Unfriendly noises. Sniff sniff. "You're not hurt." Reed blinked. "I'm not?" The cop shook his head. Authority in the bill, the yellow slicker. The color of caution. "You're drunk." The man spoke without rancor, as if it were an unfortunate fact of existence. Socorro stood unmoving.

Reed scrambled to his feet, eyes jumping. The cop groaned, "And I was just going off duty. My wife's birthday. You don't turn thirty-two every day." Reed saw this man, saw his life. Split-level house, crabgrass taking over his lawn. Modest home, modest neighborhood. But they were his. A bowler, a beer-drinker, an eater of ribs. Saturday afternoons, he rooted for the Longhorns. He had a hitch on his car for the boat he would one day buy. A man free of ambition, he wanted only to live out his life, to be left alone. Reed felt a sense of kinship, a strong fellow-feeling. "Sorry," Reed tried. The cop sighed, said, License, registration papers. He said, How many? Reed said, None. The cop rolled his eyes, said, "I'm going to ask you one more time: how many?" "Two," Reed admitted. "Hours ago." The cop gazed at the girl, the points of her breasts distinct beneath the wet cloth. Reed wanted to say, They're not that big. The cop studied Reed's license closely, said, "Boston." The sound was distasteful in his mouth. A town of failing morals, unfriendly Yankees, cruel weather.

He made Reed close his eyes, touch his nose. He said, "I got to get home. I don't want to take you in. But say I let you go when I know better, and you run over some kid a mile down the road. I got two kids myself." He made Reed walk toe-to-toe. Then, "Look: you can do this. You're not trying. You can do this, buddy." The cop was rooting for him. Once a year, his wife let him have it special. He wanted to go home. But a man who believed in the rule of law. He made Reed count backwards. Demeaning acts, humiliating trials. Socorro watching. She stood off to one side, breasts pert, maddening beauty. Reed kept hefting glances at her, his eyes apologies. Meanwhile, a flood of biblical proportions. When the cop made him stand on one foot, Reed stumbled, landing squarely in a puddle. The cop massaged his brow. Another year before his wife would let him have it special.

"I'll get on the radio, line up a tow truck. You," he said, finger in Reed's face, "ain't driving. She can follow in the car." He turned to her. "You got a license?" Socorro trembled, unable to speak. "You ain't got a license, we'll have to tow your car all the way in." When she failed to answer, his frown deepened. He seemed more vexed than angry. Yankees, he would never understand them. "Don't move," he ordered now. "Until we straighten this thing out." They watched as the man began slogging back up the rise. The rain came down in thick sheets, sheets waving in a heavy wind. They could see the man standing at the door of the squad car, microphone in his hand. They could hear the screech of his radio.

Socorro's head came around now, agonizing motion, it seemed the very orbit of the earth. Her eyes found Reed's. Her look was long, scared, sad. "Get up," she whispered. The sight of him on his knees in two inches of water pained her. "But he said not to move." "Please, get up." Good citizen Reed, he said, "I don't think I should." A man sensitive to the repercussions. It would be a while before they stuck a Breathalyzer in his face. With any luck, they would charge him for the tow, send him on his way. Send them on their way. The cop wanted to avoid the detailed report he would have to fill out—his family waited. Reed was counting on this last. It seemed a piece of good fortune. Say the cop and his wife normally made mute, quick love in the dark; they set aside one night out of the year for unfettered carnal lunacy. Reed imagined a doughy woman, pancake breasts and tummy of loose girth rioting above a

G-string of startling hue, performing handstands before a mirror. But: "Get up. Please."

When he still refused to move, she grew vehement. "We should leave. Now." He gaped at her, incredulous. "You don't understand—" "You," she said, "it is you who do not understand." Men in uniform, Reed realized, men with guns. Men who wanted to see her license. They were all the same in the end. Men who could detain you. Men who could deport you.

The second time was always worse, García had told him.

Reed heard himself say, "You go. Run."

Her eyes widened. They swarmed with unchecked emotions. She looked from Reed up to the cop, fussing with his radio, then back to Reed. A tremor seized her cheeks. "And you?"

"Socorro . . ." The realization fell down upon him. He had nowhere to run. "Socorro: I'm home."

Her expression crumbled. Racking sobs, her shoulders heaved. Her face clenched like a fist. And then she was running, tearing toward the grove. A man kneeling in a puddle, Reed's heart roared. Lightning cracked, burned her pumping legs, wheeling arms, the fling of her hair indelibly into his memory. The dense line of trees, thick gnarly branches. Pecans everywhere. Reed felt as if his eyes might bounce from his head. Her running was unbeautiful, determined. But beauty was a luxury. She had no time for beauty. The effort showed in her face, communicated itself clearly. She looked like a woman concentrating, a woman trying to add up a long sum of figures. But the answer lay with her churning legs, jerking arms. Jagged rip of lightning, the instant was bald, unadorned. She was a woman storming heaven. Reed experienced a bursting pride. When had he last run like that? He had never run like that. He had lost his last race decades back. He no longer believed in heaven. Even angels grow bored. His was a complacent stock, a fat, contented breed; its members worked out on stationary bicycles, rowed machines going nowhere. A breed going nowhere finally because it was already at the very place

310

you went. A people that lacked the one thing possessed by all others: the dream of itself as a vortex of hopes.

Behind him, Reed heard a large, rending bellow. An unholy bellow. As if the world had wrenched open. Reed turned, saw the cop standing at the top of the rise, mouth working. The man's face jerked from surprise to anger, like boxcars coming uncoupled. Reed wanted to stop time. But time was a crazed waiter falling away over the hills.

To Reed's horror, the cop crouched, a man poised to run. Fleeing girl, he seemed to take it personally. A threat to his beloved Longhorns, the boat he would one day buy. Yet the man's anger seemed atavistic. It seemed too late. Five seconds, ten, and she would be gone forever. But then the cop was barreling down the ditch. Reed cowered, a Buddha of inactivity at the edge of the path. Yet the cop was not interested in Reed; his eyes were searching out the girl, quick girl, calves of proportion, dense thicket of pecan trunks the perfect cover. Meanwhile, pummeling rain, mud everywhere. Fleeing girl, man in pursuit. As old as the species. Yet Reed on his knees, Reed in between, while the grand spectacle raged all about him. More brutal than metaphor. Reed imagined shooting to his feet, a heavy, bruising collision, precious seconds gained. Reed imagined scandal, hometown papers, he imagined pistol-whipping, the stock beating him about the head. Reed imagined cravenly slithering off into the mud while the cop chased the girl. Verities descended then, beat him about the head. There would be tomorrow to contend with, his face in the mirror, his eyes looking out at him. Tomorrow, the next day, the day after that. Tomorrow, the next day, and the day after that.

Then he moved to stand.

The cop drew up short, face big, face heated, face shoved in Reed's. The man's features bulged. Reed closed his eyes. The moment was sustained, dismal. He could hear the cop's breathing, raw and labored. Reed opened his eyes. The cop was bent over, hands on his knees, gulping air, glaring up at Reed.

"I take it," he wheezed, "she ain't from Boston."

Reed shook his head. The cop eased upright, nudged the bill of his cap higher along his forehead, placed his hands on his hips.

Reed said, "She was—"

But his voice was all wrong. The cop blinked as Reed's composure faltered, then broke open. The rain turned salty. The cop looked away in embarrassment. When he looked again, something new had entered his eyes. He was like a man who solves a jigsaw puzzle only to discover that the result is far more beautiful than the picture on the box. He was a simple man with a simple job. He wrote traffic tickets, he stickered cars abandoned at the side of the highway. A man who wanted only to eat ribs, to make love to his wife. Yet his features now softened with awareness. Years ago, there had been that woman from Reynosa. When the cop spoke again, his tone was restrained, almost fraternal: "You figure on going after her?"

Reed turned, saw only the pecan grove made misty in the downpour.

"I was just giving her a ride."

Thursday morning, early. Frigid morning. The odor of snow everywhere. Commuters huddled on subway platforms. On the Mass Pike, cars rolled through the gates, the steel barriers trembling upright. In the harbor, boats rocked in their slips. The lines formed outside the soup kitchens. In Beacon Hill, nannies woke children, dressed them for school. Young Irish nationals, they had no papers. Forklifts rumbled through the warehouses. The archbishop was rousing, the mayor, the governor. The chief of police. The fishmongers were laying out the salmon, the perch; the mounds of mussels were heaped on the wharves.

"Tell me again," she had demanded.

Following her husband's call, Andrea sat for a long while. The house felt immense, hushed. She was at the crest of a decision, and then she was over the top. All that was left was to learn how to live with it. She went to the closet, chose her clothes with care. Midmorning, and the chapel was nearly empty. There was a teary woman in a cloth coat, an elderly couple, and a man in need of a shave. He smelled of bourbon. Andrea genuflected, lit a votive candle. In the rear offices, she found a janitor, asked to speak to a priest. His name was Father Morphy. He had arrived at the parish only the month before. He was young, inexperienced, plump. He stuttered. A mama's boy. If she preferred to talk to one of the other priests, he told her, Father Nucci was usually around at this hour, or—

"I'll talk to you, if that's all right."

Father Morphy gestured for her to sit. Her beauty made him uneasy. Sunny hair, moist eyes, long legs. Faint lines in her neck. His experience was limited to a woman in the neighborhood in Minneapolis where he had grown up. He used to mow her lawn. She was married to a construction worker. She always paid him in the kitchen, making out a check while standing next to the sink. She liked to watch him touch himself. He joined the order the following year.

"How can I help you?"

"It's my husband."

Father Morphy shifted uncomfortably. "Your husband?"

"He thinks he's married to a fool."

She stayed to attend the midday Mass. The older priests conducted the Sunday Masses, the Holy Day celebrations. They left the less important services to Father Morphy. The previous week he had spilled the wine. Now he stumbled through the Our Father. But there was still the scepter, the chalice, the crucifix on the wall. There were the reaching gables, the ornate pendent posts, the finely feathered vault. A sense of calm overtook her now. Ancient symbols, she suddenly loved them all. Andrea loved the musty odor of the kneeling pads, the cracked spines of the hymnals. The pews of burnished walnut, the Madonna etched in glass. The Eucharist, and she savored the cheap wine, the feel of the wafer on her tongue. The Benediction, and there were the bells rendered sacred. Each was like an unexpected bequest. It was as if she and the universe had reached some sort of accommodation. The fact that there was something rather than nothing at all seemed a gift of extravagant munificence.

Outside, the day was rising. The streets were clogged with cabs, pedestrians thronged down the walkways. Bankers, attorneys crowded the elevators. In an apartment overlooking the Charles River, a man chased forty-two Seconals with a pint of brandy. The mercury kept diving. The cabbies shivered while waiting in line at the airport. In the emergency room of New England Medical, a woman sat with four children. Her husband had broken two of her teeth, split her lip. In the pharmacy, the cursors blinked on their green screens. The Metroliner screamed toward New York, Philadelphia, Washington. In the yeshivas, the eyes moved from right to left. The frozen body of a man in the shadow of an underpass off Mission Hill. The whores rapped on the windows of passing cars. In Cambridge, professors of philosophy were opening the doors to their cramped offices. In a dorm across campus, a couple stared in disbelief at the broken condom. In front of the larger hotels, the limousines waited, their engines idling. In Dorchester, orange eviction notices fluttered on doors. Out on the Cape, the sea battered the shore. Inland, the lakes were freezing over, the rivers floated sheets of ice. A city on the portal of winter. At the steam grates just off the entrance to the public library, the police rousted the drunks. One rose, swore, muttered, "Quinto Bernal vive."

Andrea was the first to arrive at work. The theater was hollow and black. She turned on the lights, the heater, she started the coffee. Deep in the building, the old furnace rallied. She was counting the advance gate when the carpenter appeared. He said, "But you look so tired." His concern touched her. His wife had died three years earlier. Andrea knew the extent of his loss by the fact that he never talked about it. "A touch of the flu," she explained. "But I'm over it."

314

The rest of the company filed in, stripped off their coats, set to work. Opening night. The theater filled with the sounds of the show taking shape, the nervous actors, the rushing stage-hands. There is a certain sensibility that belongs to the theater, to art. It is ruinous in everyday life. Here, they found happiness. There were still the last-minute wardrobe changes, adjustments to the scenery. One of the platforms was too low. The countless preparations, there was never enough time. But there is a line that is crossed, a moment when you realize it is happening, a moment when you begin to believe. A moment when you forget the overdrawn checking account, the uninspiring spouse. A moment when the whole of life seems to occur within the confines of the darkened theater, it lives in the agitation of the actors, in row after row of the empty seats, waiting to be filled.

On TV, the weathermen pointed to their maps. An immense snow, they predicted, a city coming under siege. In Braintree, a woman leaped in front of a train. Two hundred people heard her cries. The lottery machines were pumping out their tickets; a record would be set. German shepherds sniffed along the row of lockers at an elementary school. Downtown, brokers roared across the bourses. The trading was high, frenzied, millions changing hands. Eye surgeons worked the smallest of lasers, their fees for each procedure in five figures. One bragged he could perform ten a day. For three dollars in the Combat Zone you could watch a pendulous woman writhing on a revolving platform.

It was a city divided. The social covenant is an act of high faith. The trains will run, provisions will be plentiful, the massive generators will churn out their power. Cars will heed traffic signals. One's home is sovereign ground, one's work is satisfying. One's family is safe. But in the older tenements, in the ethnic ghettos, the homes were falling down, there was no work, one's brother lay in a hospital ward, dying of gunshot wounds. There is a threshold beyond which the violence ceases to be random, the crime is no longer occasional. An accretion

315

of circumstances, they overreach themselves suddenly, they hint at a unique and implacable logic.

A domestic dispute in a neighborhood where parked cars had once held debutantes who fondled boys from Choate, Exeter, Andover. They always had handkerchiefs ready. Now a squad car was dispatched. A crowd gathered. Dark crowd, they stamped their feet against the cold. The cops were young, on edge. A harsh word, a shove. A punch was thrown. A Louisville Slugger came up, the windshield went caving. Backup units arrived, three people were arrested. The roving reporter from Channel Thirteen appeared. She had only a few minutes, she was covering a horticultural show on the other side of town at noon. But, "Quinto Bernal vive," a bystander thought to tell the camera.

Andrea was stacking programs. Each carried a brief history of the theater collective, a listing of the meager awards it had won over the years, an appeal for contributions. She had written it herself. Up in the mezzanine, the lighting man was setting the angles. The makeup crew was laying out the rouge, the powder, the lipstick, the wigs. A janitor swept the stage one last time. Outside, a college student stood on a ladder, changing the marquee. One of the actors gargled with eucalyptus honey and lemon, a splash of whiskey; a secret, he had once read, favored by Olivier. The story was untrue.

The snow started in. It fell lightly at first, a mere dusting. As it grew heavier, the salt trucks came out, the snowplows. Real estate developers were making their pitches to municipal leaders, corporate heads, robed sheiks from countries of sand and oil. The occasional report of a robbery, a knifing that came over the radio was like news from a distant country, from a war zone on the other side of the globe. Computer executives lunched as they always did at McDougal's, at the Oyster Club, at Luigi's. You had to try the pasta e fagioli, everyone said, they made it like no one else. The immaculate waiters stood at one end of the brass bar, they were an army unto their own. A single-malt scotch went for six dollars a shot. Plans were being

316

finalized for the weekend. A ski pass in Sugarloaf, or perhaps a drive down to New York, a good dinner, a show. Men were seducing the wives of other men. A table of homosexuals watched, guffawing at the antics of heteros. Marinara sauce blotted the tablecloth. Wealth was everywhere, even the ashtrays spoke its name.

Out in the streets, the graffiti had begun to appear: Quinto Bernal vive. The name was being repeated among schoolchildren, among men in bars, men whose unemployment checks had long since run out. It was the early minutes of rush hour, the air still pale; yet headlights came on, flashing in acknowledgement. The name was inscribed on the wall above the urinal of a fast-food outlet, it was whispered in the grimy cafeteria of a box-making factory. It seemed a martyr had been born, the battlecry was being taken up.

The older cops—the ones who had walked the beats for years, who had driven the narrow alleyways, men close to retirement, they had flunked the test for sergeant three times, now their asses were big from sitting, their bellies hung over their belts, they suffered from ulcers, hiatal hernias, piles, their eyes were going—had begun to sense the smallest of differences, the fomenting signs. None could have explained, not really. Not yet. They were like animals standing downwind.

Inside the theater, the lights went down, the curtain rose. The audience was still. Andrea stood in the wings. She was trying to calm the lead. A slight girl, a frightened girl. She had never really acted before. But she had no idea, no grasp of the dimension of her talent. She was a natural. Her voice was booming, authorial, hypnotic. It came readily to her. "You'll do fine," Andrea assured her. She spoke softly to the girl, she was stroking her cheek. "Now go; go. Your audience waits for you."

In the outlying neighborhoods, crowds had started to congregate. Their eyes shifted with the peculiar intelligence of the streets. A crowd outside a Black Baptist church, a crowd in the lobby of a bank, a crowd in the parking lot of a supermarket.

An unruly crowd at the door of a liquor store. A mob. There was the tinkle of breaking glass, the amber bottles being lifted off the shelves, the running teens, the excited eyes of men in the act of plunder. There was a fire out near the wharf, the shrill cry of the firetrucks. A fire near the airport, another in the southern districts. The alarms clamored. Three, four flash points, they rose as if on cue. The chief of police quietly canceled all leaves. The hospitals began stockpiling reserves of blood, the staffs were doubled in the trauma units. In Revere, roving packs of vigilantes appeared, they were stopping cars along the roads that led to their neighborhoods. The police were out in number. A supermarket was sacked, the glossy produce rolling to the floor, the display cases of cigarettes coming down. The checkers, the manager, the deli man all fled. A tank filled with live lobsters burst open, the mottled crustaceans crashing to the linoleum.

The moment rose then, a town poised on the precipice.

Brecht loved women. He was the playwright of heroines: Johanna, Vlassova, Mother Courage, Señora Carrar, Grusha. Shen-Te. On stage, his tropes fell like artillery, they reached into the farthest rafters of the theater, they reached on beyond. They penetrate bones:

> What sort of a town is that, what sort of humans are you?
> When an injustice takes place in a town there must be an
>   uproar
> And where there is no uproar it is better the town
>   disappears
> In flames before the night falls.

A summer day, and the city might well have been torn apart, the fires raging, leaping from block to block, the populace tearing at the cobblestoned streets. The simplest of missiles. Barricades would have appeared. But now there was the snow. It fell richly, unendingly. Without fanfare, unnoticed, the moment was ebbing. The gales drove through the alleyways; they clawed at street signs, lashed garbage cans down the avenues, forced people indoors. The storm ripped shouts from the mouths of the angry. The crowds gradually retreated, the city was battening down. There was flooding along the North Shore. Desk sergeants made it a point to overlook the bottles of beer that appeared in the locker rooms, the pints of liquor. There was relieved laughter in the substations. The following morning, the newspaper would report a curious spate of incidents. The story would appear beneath an article detailing the governor's attempt to raise sin taxes yet again. In the suburbs, the wealthy came out in their snowmobiles; hot rum toddies waited inside. In the projects, people clustered in tiny rooms, trying for warmth. The needle goes in. The drifts mounted, covered the graffiti.

In the theater, the curtain fell. The audience surged to its feet. The world had telescoped down to the stage. It was all the crowd knew of the night, it was all they knew of existence. The applause rocked the small chamber, shouts of "Bravo!" rang out. The audience was sparse, but it consisted of the most dedicated partisans. They believed in art, they believed in greatness, in the most authentic kind, in the only kind finally: it requires but one lone believer, a single adherent.

Out at the airport, no cabbie would agree to drive to his neighborhood. On the subway, he sat across from an ancient couple, their faces cratered, toothless, veins in their hands. The man smiled at Reed. Reed smiled back. The old woman leaned forward, said, "He's blind." At his stop, Reed climbed to the sidewalk, stood for a moment and considered the snow, the rabid wind. Down past the boarded-up bank, past the trashed autos, past the abandoned buildings. Past REDEMPTION. From the street, he could see the light through the kitchen window, the light from the hallway, the light up in his daughter's room. He paused in the foyer. There were the high ceilings, the long windows. The floors shone. He could see the fireplace in the living room. The timeless stones, the eternal wood of the mantel. As if nothing had changed, not a moment had passed.

Reed turned at the creak of the stairs. "Andrea?" His bag hung from his shoulder. He held a bouquet of roses in one hand, a clay figurine in the other. A man bearing gifts. "Laura?"

The boy froze on the landing, his dark skin lost in the shadows. His hair was wild, his shirt was open. He carried his shoes.

Seven

Spring. Warm days, crisp evenings. Andrea was in the kitchen. The light streamed into the room. She wore shorts, a cotton T-shirt. A pot of homemade stock simmered on the stove. She was giving a dinner party that evening, a sumptuous buffet. She had been going to the Y, swimming laps every morning. Her legs were firm. Her arms, her thighs were tanned. Her hair was tied back. She was thinking about cutting it short for the summer. She had been reading Sartre on Genet. The theater company was planning to do Beckett in the fall: *Endgame.* A jug of tea steeped in the window. Her rings sat on the counter. She grated the parmesan, sliced the shallots. Her breasts shifted beneath the cloth. Flour dusted the cutting board. Soft-shell crabs and a mushroom risotto. You had to keep stirring, she told her friends.

She talked about taking a trip to Ireland, perhaps in the coming year. A trip by herself. A stack of travel brochures sat on the nightstand in the bedroom. She liked to leaf through them before falling asleep. She could see herself in a thick sweater of combed wool, wool the color of old pewter, driving through the countryside in a rented car. To see the house where her grandfather had grown up, the school he had attended. She would recognize distant relatives in the street, relatives she had never met, she had never known existed. She would stop at inns along the coast, small dank rooms smelling of pipe tobacco. Hard beds in sturdy wood frames. Breakfasts of strong tea, a film of orange marmalade on the knife. Dinners taken alone, she would be the woman seated at a corner table, a plate of mutton and boiled potatoes.

Outside, Reed was high up a ladder, taking down the storm windows. Wasps hovered among the eaves. Laura was in the driveway with friends. April and Eileen. They were washing the car. Their talk drifted up to him.

"You know what I'd like to do?" It was April. She wore bikini briefs, a halter top. A few dark hairs streaked toward her navel. "I want to get dressed up. I mean really nice. A long silk outfit, the clingy kind that shows everything. And high heels, maybe diamonds around my neck. Like that. And I go into some place downtown—"

"Which place?" Laura asked.

"It doesn't matter which place. A nice place. A dark bar with a piano in it. Tablecloths and candlelight, and up high so you can see the whole city through the windows. The waiters are in jackets and ties, and there's a dance floor. That kind of place. Everybody looks at me when I come in. I'm alone, but I look like I shouldn't be alone. I'm alone because I choose to be alone, and everybody understands this. Men send drinks to my table, I don't have to buy a drink the whole night long. They're all dying to come up to me, dying to ask do I want to

322

dance. But they're afraid, you know? I might say no. Everybody would see them walk to my table. They would see me shaking my head. The guy would have to walk away." April paused, straining for details. She had let those three brothers that time, in the back of a pickup. One after the other. Everyone at school knew the story. "Finally, this one guy comes up and sits at my table. He's an old guy, maybe forty. But goodlooking. Big, expensive watch, a diamond tie clasp. Everybody is watching us. Will she dance with the guy? If I dance with him, forty men will slit their wrists. He doesn't say anything for a while, he wants to be cool. It's like the whole room is waiting. Then he takes my hand and leans toward me and asks do I want to dance. And you know what I say?"

"What?"

"I say, 'Fuck off.' Just like that." April snapped her fingers. "I say, 'Fuck off, man.' Everybody sees him walking away. Everybody thinks: what an asshole."

Reed climbed down from the ladder. He could feel the pack of cigarettes in his breast pocket; he was trying not to smoke. After his last physical, the doctor had slotted the shadowy film into place and pointed. It was his lungs, the doctor said, they were coated with tar. Impending emphysema, unless a tumor got him first. Or he could quit. Reed had stared at the film, seen only rich nebulae. On good days he was down to half a pack.

"What else do you need done?" He was in the kitchen, washing his hands.

"You trimmed the hedges?"

"I trimmed the hedges."

He looked a little older, a little heavier. His eyes were narrowing to slits in the folds of his face. The tonsure at the back of his head was growing. When he stood in the bathroom brushing his teeth, his testicles hung like a steer's. He was going out of town next week for a series of meetings. "It's just New Haven," he'd said when she told him she might come along.

"And the drive—"

"I weeded the drive."

This family took their meals in silence, they ate like strangers in a crowded restaurant, forced to share a table. In recent months, Laura had rediscovered her appetite. The girl was filling out, her features broadening. There was a hint of insolence to her mouth, though she had her mother's eyes, the same rich blue pools. Andrea worried she was putting on too much weight. "At fifty," she'd said to him, "she'll look like a cow." Reed thought his daughter stunning. Her curfew was strict: nine o'clock on weekdays, ten on weekends. That time they wouldn't let her drive with some friends down to Newport, she'd heaved herself away from the table: "You know, I'm not a goddamn nun."

The thin light of early evening. Andrea set out the crabs in covered dishes, the rice, she lit cans of sterno. Platters of canapés, crackers, cheeses, pâté. A bowl of stuffed olives, an artichoke dip. A makeshift bar at one end of the living room. Ice in an insulated bucket, the bottles arrayed like sentinels along the table. She wore a long gown, a border of pearls at her neck, opal studs at her ears. She let down her hair. It fell richly about her shoulders, far down her back. Laura was up in her bedroom; she might, she had informed her mother, come down later.

Company began arriving at eight. Their new friends that spring were the Gormans, Carl and Leslie. The Wilheits were there, the Hallorans. In the living room, Leonard Halloran was talking. He was a high-strung man, nervous hands. He worked as a chemist for a large pharmaceutical company. Weekends he participated in reenactments of medieval life. In his basement was a suit of armor, a mace. They had decided, he announced, to sell their house. "I come home, it's like driving through a gauntlet."

"In this market? You'll take a beating."

"Probably." But his wife was terrified. There were evenings when she refused to step outside. They were looking at a

324

neighborhood in Watertown. The commute would take almost an hour. But there were large yards, apple trees, quaint Armenian bakeries. Dotty Halloran wanted to know: "Haven't you thought about—"

"We're staying," Andrea said.

Carl Gorman had appeared with a bottle of champagne, good cigars. The Gormans always brought wine, cut flowers, loaves of sourdough whenever they visited. They believed in tradition, in the classic amenities. You couldn't find this champagne in the stores, he was telling them. You had to know someone. It was like looking for a high-stakes poker game, an after-hours club, a Black Mass. But there was this vintner who owed him a favor. Now he held the bottle by the throat, worked his other hand. "You know what civilization sounds like?" The cork popped. "It sounds like that."

Andrea had a reputation for her parties. She knew how to prepare foods, which guests to invite. She knew how to gauge the air in a room full of people. She would seat obstetricians next to lesbian performance artists, state legislators next to boxing promoters, she would urge sculptors to talk to housing subcontractors. At a single dinner party a few years back, a guest received a phone call telling him he had won a Pulitzer; a woman—a socialite known for her philanthropy—revealed that she had once worked as a stripper under the stage name Mango; a man was served with a subpoena.

Now they congregated in groups of twos and threes, plates resting on their knees. They had all traveled abroad, they were homeowners, they looked to the book reviews, to the restaurant critics for guidance. The women talked about politics, the men talked about food. The news that season dealt with high fecal counts along coastal waterways, a third day of rioting in a city to the south. Scientists had discovered a new supernova. Its light had taken a thousand years to reach the earth. Reed had built a fire, they could hear the soughing of the air as it was drawn up the flue. A small stack of split logs lay next to the irons. Andrea had taken off her shoes, she sat with her feet tucked under her. She was watching the evening unfold, it was like a finely executed plan. She took such gatherings seriously. It was the highest order of intimacy left to her.

Leslie Gorman was telling a story. She worked as an attorney for one of the larger firms. The wife of a senior partner had discovered a pair of lace panties in the glove compartment of her husband's car. "Tiny panties, you know. A strap here, another there, a bit of fringe, and that's it. Purple, for God's sake. The panties of a whore." Someone asked what the husband had said. "That's the thing," Leslie Gorman went on. "She never tells him. Her voice would have been weak, pitiable, you know? So she doesn't say anything. Instead, one evening, when they're getting ready to turn in, she comes out of the bathroom wearing nothing but these panties. Her husband's in bed, understand, reading or whatever, and she comes out of the bathroom and walks across the room and climbs into bed wearing these panties. He doesn't say anything, she doesn't say anything. What can he say? So then, she starts touching him. He says he's tired; he says he doesn't want to, not tonight. Nobody has said anything about the panties, understand? She tells him he has to. Just like that. He's always complaining that they don't do it enough, that she's never in the mood. And now, she's touching him. She's wearing these panties and telling him he has to. She makes him fuck her. She makes him take his whore's panties off his wife and fuck her. They go to sleep without saying anything, the panties lying on the floor at the foot of the bed. The next day, she throws them out. They don't ever mention it. It's like they did this thing now, they did this thing where everything is made clear, and so they don't have to ever talk about it. It never comes up. They both know they know, so now they don't have to know anymore, you know? They're still together."

Leslie Gorman sipped her drink. "They'll be together forever."

Mid-evening, Laura appeared at the top of the living room stairs. The effect was dramatic. The men looked up. She was a little shorter than her mother. She had a tiny waist, a heavy ass. Whereas Andrea looked like a woman one might have once seen walking down the runway of a fashion show, her daughter looked like the kind of woman one sees on the arm of a bohemian poet, or seated at the roulette table. There was something willful about her looks, almost wanton. She wore a sleeveless dress cut low, a touch of paint on her mouth. She was dark from the sun. Her only jewelry: a Zuni fetish suspended in the hollow of her throat. The women moved to kiss her cheek; the men held her hand a moment too long. They wanted to be near her, to touch her, to draw from her a kind of strength. She took up position behind the bar. She poured the wine, she was freshening their drinks.

The box of cigars went around the room, the men exclaiming. Even Andrea took one. Dark, slender Hondurans. The cigar accented the long line of her neck, it set off her pale features. She drew heavily, the smoke wreathing her face. The men looked on approvingly. Exquisite cigars. Someone repeated the line about having been rolled between the thighs of Indian maidens.

Reed stood. "I see we need more liquor."

He was gone for a quarter of an hour. Andrea found him in the pantry, facing the row of bottles. Quarts of Stoli, Maker's Mark, Bombay gin. A half-gallon of Glenlivet. He seemed locked in place. He became aware of her only gradually.

"Frank, what's wrong?"

"Mice," he said. He was pointing to the pellets, to a hole where the baseboards had separated.

"Our guests—"

"I'll run to the hardware store tomorrow."

"Frank, what is it?"

"It shouldn't take much to patch it." Then, "I won't be going to New Haven next week." He looked at her.

"I won't be going to New Haven, ever."

Eiger had appeared outside his office one morning. With the closing of the Quincy plant, he began. The man's voice was subdued. He spoke like a pallbearer. Reed had rocked up out of his chair, demanded to speak to the Old Man. But Yates was on his way to the airport. A meeting in Detroit. "He asked me to take care of it," Eiger had said.

They stood in the narrow space of the pantry now, the walls pressing down on them. The moment felt suspended, in abeyance. She saw the cobwebs along the ceiling, the water stain in the corner, the fissure in the drywall. She was taking it all in, nothing escaped her. A bulb had burned out. The old house appeared shabby, its furnishings abject.

"You should have told me," she said now.

"You've been planning this party for months."

"Should I send people home?"

He shook his head. "It's a wonderful party."

After an evening of drinks, or on a morning early when they were still drugged from sleep, or in the middle of the night, when they both woke in a fit of need, they still sometimes came together. The sex was desperate, joyless. They gritted teeth and flung themselves at each other, as if they were in a Sumo ring. It was an act of physical release. She came with no sound, only jerking spasms. It was like tending to an epileptic. Afterward she seemed embarrassed, silent, like a woman who finds herself waking next to a man she would never agree to meet for lunch. Yet there were still moments of tenderness. They occurred outside the bedroom. An aimless Sunday morning, the two of them sitting at the breakfast table in their pajamas, the salty taste of lox, their fingers dark from newsprint; or a Saturday evening, driving back in from a party, side by side in the car, Reed impersonating the hostess, making fun of the music; that time he discovered her sitting on the toilet, her face covered with cold cream, trimming her toenails ("Do you mind if I watch?" "I don't mind.")—and it seemed life was twenty years ago, that they still had it all to do again. They were helpless in the face of such moments, they had no control over them. They came from afar, like the weather, the change of seasons.

Reed continued to peer at her. But his gaze was unseeing, it registered nothing. She had rehearsed this instant so many times: the things she would say, the sounds of reassurance. Yet there was something more to his expression than the fear of bankruptcy, of social ruin. He looked like a man who has been beaten, a boxer down on one knee.

What she said was, "You know, we haven't been unhappy."

He blinked at her. It was not a question, it was not a statement. She was letting him know. It was the barest of offerings. Yet the moment felt abundant, human. Who was this woman, what was this place? His wife, his home. It begins, and then it is over.

"I was thinking," he said now. He started lifting bottles off the shelf. "I was thinking: you shouldn't cut your hair."

"No?" She was smiling.

"No."

These spring nights. Soft jazz on the stereo. The store of liquor was running low. The talk was easy, unstudied, like moves in a casual game of chess. Everyone had agreed in advance to call it a draw. They were among friends, people like themselves. They were the offspring of farmers, small shopowners, civil servants. They had come up through the ranks, staked out a place for themselves. Five hundred years earlier, they would have been minor noblemen living on estates in vast northern kingdoms, on lands where poachers were hung; the great royal families above, the mass of serfs below. Now they had thirty-year mortgages, certificates of deposit, children who would soon go off to college. These were the new emblems of rank, the crests of class. They had colonized, not geography, but time. Yet the millennium was at hand. History had spent itself. They were like the last of the Boers, like British officers who cling to the old ways in the shadow of a new India.

"Is this authentic?"

Teresa Wilheit stood next to the mantel. She was a slender woman, high cheekbones, linear. "I'm like a boy up there," she often said. But Reed thought her beauty severe, exotic. He could not help being a little in love with her. He had been drinking since four o'clock. He approached her on slow, deliberate feet.

"Authentic?"

"I mean," she smiled, taking it in her hands, "it's so ugly, it ought to be."

There were more drinks, more music. Two of the men began to shadowbox. Playful slaps, but their wives were watching. Leonard Halloran was being backed into a corner. A glass fell, shattered. Andrea knelt, the broom in one hand, a dustpan in the other. A siren sounded out in the street. Everyone pretended not to notice. The candles were burning down, the wax congealing at their bases. Empty liquor bottles lay on their sides. The last of the ice floated like marbles in water. The buffet table looked like an overrun village. The dismembered crabs, the flesh sucked clean; the oozing artichoke dip, the discolored cheese. A smear of pâté on the floor.

Laura could hear her father from across the room. He was drunken, animated, gleeful. She was married three years later, on a Sunday in autumn. The leaves were underfoot, the sky gray. Reed wept at the rehearsal, he wept during the ceremony, he wept at the reception. He stuffed the groom's pockets with money. The bills smelled of cheap aftershave, they smelled of gin. She had met the boy at the University of Massachusetts. The son of a welder, he was a film student. She had the breasts, he said, of an island concubine in a South Seas epic.

About the Author

Marissa Landrau-Pirazzi

A native of Louisville, Kentucky, T. L. Toma has taught in many contexts: in English courses for migrant workers in North Carolina, in literacy programs in inner-city Philadelphia, and in a school for mentally handicapped adults in Boston. He received his M.A. and Ph.D. degrees in philosophy from Northwestern University, where he wrote his dissertation on Marx. In the mid-1980s, he engaged in solidarity work in Nicaragua. His stories have appeared in *Black Warrior Review, Cimarron Review, Fiction International,* and *The Quarterly,* among other publications. He and his wife, Leticia Saucedo, recently moved from Boston to Austin, Texas.